MW01488033

The Purpose of Nuorg

Jahnise sat at Oliviia's side as she cried the way any young lady would cry over the tragic loss of her parents. Her body heaved as she cried torrents of tears. The knowledge that the evolving situation was dire led to even more uncontrollable sobs, as Bongi and Stewig moved in closer to comfort her. Occasionally, she would make eye contact with one of them just long enough to send her back into loud, mournful wails. Oliviia was emotionally and physically spent. There was nothing any of the onlookers could do but try to console her.

Hardcover ISBN: 978-1-62141-685-2
Paperback ISBN: 978-1-62141-686-9

Printed in the United States of America.

MessyHouse Publishing
Franklin, TN
2012

The Purpose of Nuorg

Chris McCollum

This book is dedicated to

**My two brothers, my sister,
my nieces and nephews…
more pieces of my puzzle.**

1

"What kind of creature is that?" Mystic stood mystified, gazing slack-jawed at Bubba's latest find.

The Wolf, the Cheetah and their two-legger friend, Frederick, were searching an enormous room for clues. They initially feared the spacious chamber was, at one time, used as a morbid game room. Now, after diligent research and reflection, they discovered it was a solemn memorial room, chasing the history of this mountain fortress back long before these leggers were born.

At Mystic's side, Frederick stared with the same amazed look at his four-legged friends. "I can't say that I have ever seen a legger exactly like that anywhere in my travels."

Bubba stayed quiet, sitting and staring. After a short pause he asked, "Neither of you have any idea? I can truthfully state there has never, ever been talk of a creature such as this anywhere on the Great Plains."

Frederick crossed his arms across his chest, let out a long sigh and toggled his head around. "These creatures are not supposed to exist. It must be some kind of trick, but after all we have been through recently, I guess this really doesn't surprise me either. What do you say, do we keep staring at this or do we continue searching for some answers?"

"I say we keep searching for answers, Frederick. This fellow isn't going anywhere." Bubba cut his eyes to Mystic. "What say you, Wolf?"

"I agree with both of you. Let's continue with our search of this place. There are a lot more rooms to check out and these creatures in here, as you say, are going nowhere."

Just as Bubba turned to follow, he could not be absolutely sure if it was so, but out of the corner of his eye he thought he saw the slightest twitch along the upper eyebrow of the very tall and stationary creature. He shook it off, later giving credit for the illusion to the room's strange shadowing effects.

Frederick led the way out of the expansive memorial room. "If it is alright with the both of you, I think I would like to lay Sig to rest with those who have preceded him in service to this mountain fortress. Bubba, did you find a cloth to cover him?"

"Yes I did and we need to examine that as well. I've noticed there are several of them here."

"Very well, go get one. We will lay Sig to rest and get on with our business. Mystic, a marker?"

"Sorry, Frederick, I found nothing proper."

"That's okay. I don't think Sig would mind if we come back to that."

"Me neither." Mystic looked longingly down the corridor, hoping Sig might happen to fly down it once more.

Bubba returned soon after, dragging a very thin but heavy cloth with him. The cloth was woven with a tight, solid weave. A colorful crest of the fortress was embroidered in the center of it. He set it at Frederick's feet. "Here you go. It is very heavy. There must be a hundred of them down at the far end of this corridor."

Frederick reached down to pick the cloth up. He felt the smooth, silky texture and immediately realized the value of the piece. "Bubba, you are correct, this cloth is very heavy. I should also tell you that I believe it is spun from pure gold thread. Look at the exquisite detail in this insignia. Again, the mysteries continue to bombard us. Sig had so mush more to tell us."

Mystic nodded his head. "It is up to us now, Frederick. Let's give him his moment then get moving."

"As you wish, Prince."

Frederick draped the cloth over his shoulder as he walked over to retrieve Sig's body. With no fanfare, they laid him to rest beside so many other creatures who had given everything before him. Sig was placed next to the feet of a large four-legger whose eyes were locked into a permanent downward stare and covered with the golden cloth.

"I think that should do nicely," Bubba noted.

Frederick turned to his fellow leggers, "If you two would follow me?"

***

Jahnise reverently removed the book from Ian's chest. He held the book where he could read the complete title. "M, y, s, t, e, ah Mr. Ian, you were pointing to the letter "e". Now, what kind of hint will we find that to be? 'Mysterious Encounters', what is this book? On another day we may find out." He focused his attention on the young girl at his side.

Oliviia knelt down beside her parents, Ian and Colleen Mecanelly. She wept openly. "We are too late. Why did I not run faster? Why did we not return faster?"

Jahnise knelt to the ground with her. He placed his arms around her shoulders and let her cry. They sat together as Donkhorse and Stewig sadly looked on. Bongi took a few steps back with Rakki.

"Rakki, you need to find Hugoth immediately, wherever he is. This is a very bad development. Tell him we need him here at once. Everything is going downhill very quickly."

"Yes, Bongi, except I have no idea where Hugoth is at this very moment."

"I'm sorry, Rakki, but you must leave with hopes that you find him soon. When you do find him, you must bring him back, understand? There can be no discussion otherwise. He must come." Bongi turned his gaze to Oliviia and Jahnise and then back once again to Rakki. "Please Rakki, go now."

"As you ask, Bongi. May I ask one question before I leave?"

"Certainly, you may."

"Exactly how bad is this?"

"Hugoth sent Ian to seal the cracks, and he failed. Not by his own faults, but he failed nevertheless. The cracks are not sealed. If there are more cracks out there - and more likely than not, there are - Nuorg is more vulnerable now than ever, especially since Mr. Ian is...gone."

"I see." Rakki also stole a glance at Oliviia, "I will find him, Bongi. I will."

"Rakki, also tell him that Colleen is gone as well and two of the children are missing."

"I will tell him." Rakki pondered the circumstances for a brief moment, "Wait... Bongi, how do I get out of here? The entrance sealed behind us."

***

Madaliene's eyes locked with Hemoth's and Lightning's for one clarifying instant. "These people are why the ax-pike brought us here? What are we supposed to do with them?"

The bedraggled crowd was feasting on the ample food stored within Frederick's bag. After she tossed enough food their way, she stepped through the crowd to Hemoth's side. The Grizzly Bear studied how the famished two-leggers ate, as though they were afraid their next meal would never come. Lightning, the irregular Badger, watched with the same concern on his face.

"These poor leggers must be eating for the first time in several days. Where do you think they came from? A town? A village? Where is it?" Lightning had never witnessed a scene like this before in the Great Forest and was not at all happy about what he was witnessing. He asked the questions to Madaliene and Hemoth, not really expecting an answer.

Hemoth stood on his hind legs. "I am looking back down the trail from where they came and I see nothing. Perrie, did you see anything when you flew over?"

A lovely young Falcon sat perched on his shoulder. "I didn't see anything that I would consider a village, sir. There may be something farther out. Shall I fly scout?"

"Perrie, I am not sure what that means, but if it means that you will fly over the surrounding areas, being very wary of other wingers who may want to see you captured, search for any type of gathering place these leggers may have come from and return here safely, then yes, I want you to fly scout. But, I want you back here safely more than anything else. Is that understood?"

"Yes, Hemoth, I understand. I will fly low like Sig taught me. It will be difficult for anything to attack me if I fly low and fast. I will return, I promise you."

"Very well." The Grizzly Bear stepped closer to Madaliene with Perrie on his shoulder. "Princess, Perrie is going to fly scout for us. Is that okay by you?"

Madaliene was standing with Lightning, watching the two-leggers as they continued to devour the food she had given them. She raised her eyes to Hemoth's sturdy shoulder and looked her Falcon squarely in the face. "If you do not return to me safely, Perrie, I will not be happy. You must return to us safely even if it means cutting your flight short and exposing our position. If the latter happens, we will handle it together. Do as Hemoth asks of you."

Perrie politely curtsied as best she could. "I will be back, Princess. I have been taught well. I am young, but I am beginning to understand the dire reasons for our mission. I will not fail Nuorg or any of you." She was off with no further conversation.

Madaliene, Hemoth and Lightning watched as Perrie flew out of sight, "Fly safe, Falcon."

2

"My word, what is your problem now? You have to be the whiniest creature I have ever met in my short life! Am I to expect this mood from you all day?"

The well-dressed young two-legger was stopped in the dead center of the intersection where four of the very busiest roads led to eight of the very busiest towns in the whole entire area of his world. He was arguing with, what seemed to be, every two-legger and contraption within hearing distance. Leggers of all numbers were yelling at him, asking if he needed assistance and trying to push their way around him. They were getting nowhere fast. He was stoically unmoved by the two-leggers' inconveniences. At the center of the traffic disaster sat the reason for this hold-up. The young two-legger looked to be simultaneously angrily yelling and desperately pleading with a large red and black four-legger that decided to quit traveling at the worst possible moment. The slumped four-legger was akin to a Horse at first glance, but was not nearly as handsome. His proportions were skewed slightly from what one normally thinks of a Horse. It was hard to tell if the beast was worthy of a second look as he sat stubbornly plopped in the middle of the dusty crossing. The passers-by that were not yelling for them to move could not help but stare or laugh at the humorous situation.

"Do you think this is working?" murmured the embarrassed four-legger, quietly to his companion. "It had better, 'cause when I get up from here, I will draw even with you. I promise. I have never stooped this low for any reason. This road is filthy! Not to mention the bugs I have crawling all over my haunches."

To the observers, it actually looked like the two-legger was attempting to carry on a conversation with the four-legger, which caused even more loud laughter. Sure, folks yelled at their animals, but they never expected them to yell back. That would be quite a story, at least in this part of the world.

The two-legger, somewhat annoyed, sternly answered, "Would you please be quiet and act like a normal draft animal? Do you think you could do that for me please?" That did not go over well...the four-legger seethed.

The four-leggers that did circumvent the disturbance could not help but chuckle. Most of them knew what was going on and could not help but take mental notes of the grounded four-legger's face. Lots of mocking whinnies, barks and snickers were heard that day by those tall ears. "Oh yes, dear young one, oh yes. Your day will surely come when our positions are reversed."

"Did I not ask you to hush?" Again, it looked to all like the two-legger was actually conversing with the four-legger. All of the passers-by knew that could not happen. Again, the four-legger seethed.

***

From her position among the small trees to the south of the intersection, a very protective four-legger suspiciously eyed the movement of every two and four-legger that overtly avoided the show going on in the intersection. She was looking for a particular pair of creatures, one four-legged and one two-legged that may be in too much of a hurry as they passed this way. It had come down the signal chain that they would be passing, although no one knew for sure who they were. She was big, loveable and patient. As long as her two companions kept most of the traffic at bay, she would scrutinize every passer by as if she had a magnifying lens. Her large brown eyes, full of life and obedience, portrayed a loving personality, but hid a very defensive and aggressive interior should anyone mess with her loved ones.

Something about that pair did not look comforting. While all creatures from this area dress immaculately, even in their worst fits, this two-legger looked too ragged and the four-legger with him looked worn out. She immediately tagged them as suspicious. With eye-contact and a nod from her short, compact snout attached to a large square head, she glanced to her left and sent the first sky-traveler on a parallel course to trail these two leggers closely. As she turned her attention back to the intersection fiasco, she could not help but notice the absence of her other medium sized, sky-traveling companion to her right. She noticed, in his place, a rather small, even for a sky-traveler, chubby little winger with bright eyes. An extremely aggressive attitude hidden beneath the innocent, outward appearance would lead one to initially misjudge this brand of winger. She did. "And just who might you be? And what have you done with my companion?"

"I ate him. I was very hungry," it stated as alert and focused eyes never stopped surveying the steady flow of traffic. "I have had a very trying trip, so I ate him."

Obviously stunned, she turned and faced the creature. She completely took in this little fellow's stature, blinked her eyes incredulously, and then dead-panned, "You ate a Falcon? You are not large enough to be noticed by a Falcon, but you ate a Falcon?"

"Absolutely, my dear. I didn't care for his looks. Looked to me to be quite the slacker. Feather tone. That is what gave it away. That is why I ate him. He had poor feather tone. You can always trust feather tone." The small winger was not giving anything away with this conversation, nor did he turn his stare to her or anywhere away from the continuing stream of leggers. "I suggest you take a look at that pair of leggers coming round the outskirts of that mess in the middle there," he said nodding toward the melee.

"Which pair?"

"The smart looking pair there, nicely attired, shiny buckles and overalls, an acceptable coordination of mismatched fittings," came the reply.

"I think you are mistaken, little one. I have sent the first Falcon after the leggers that I tagged as suspicious and in need of following."

"Well my dear, you are wrong."

"And why am I wrong in your opinion?" she asked in a very politely perturbed tone of voice.

"You are not wrong in my opinion. You are wrong because you are wrong. The pair of leggers you have sent the Falcon in pursuit of cannot be the pair you are looking for. May I ask what pair are you looking for? Do you have any idea or is it just guessing on your part?"

"Excuse me? Then I assume you must know the ones I am looking for since you are so adamant that the pair I chose to trail is the wrong pair."

"Yes I do. I am so elated that you were able to so quickly discern that I do know who you are after. Thank you ever so much for crediting me with that."

She was beginning to tire of the little winger's condescending banter. A low growl oozed out, "Who are you, where did you come from and what do you know about my being here?"

"My dear, don't fret. It is so obvious that you are in on the play there in the intersection. So obvious. It is good for you that the two-leggers overlook us as they do or they too would have figured it out," chirped the not so charming little observer.

"You are a very curt little thing are you not?" she asked.

"If by curt, you mean very sure of my intentions, confident to a fault, smart as any Owl or so on, then yes I am a very curt little thing. However, though little I may be, I can assure you my mind is more than capable of overpowering any short comings having to do with my small stature and, if pushed, I can travel the skies as fast as your Falcon cohorts," he returned.

"I must ask you who you are, why you are here and how do you know me. If you do not impress me with your answers then I will be eating you!"

"How dare you speak to me that way? You really have no idea who I am even though I know everything about you? No creature has advised you of my mission? Is there anything at all within the confines of that thick square head of yours?" he spat.

"There was no answer to any question I asked within that little speech. For your sake, you better start giving me some answers," she growled as she inched closer to the winger.

"Why for this tree's sake do you growl and threaten me? Can you not distinguish that I am up in this tree and not on the ground where I would be at your mercy? You can't climb a tree. Why should I not just fly off and leave you to your own canine ramblings? Several creatures warned me there would be times like these. I should have stayed in the conifer with my mate and her squabs!" This last detail was a complete lie. "I have no business leaving them at a time like this. The Eagle. It was all his fault. Why oh why did I lend him an ear that day? O folly, folly, folly." The little trickster spun the web of his story even more.

He began to pace sideways and back on his perch. He was not all that high off the ground. If she wanted to dispatch the little nuisance, she certainly could. When he mentioned the Eagle, she dropped her guard. Very interested in hearing his story now, she softened her tone. "What Eagle? What was his name?"

At that very instant, a voice called to her from the intersection. "Belle, come quickly."

Now she was at odds of what to do. Tofur was calling her. This little, now bothered, gray sky-traveler had just piqued her interest and the second Falcon had returned. "Where have you been?" she demanded.

"I am sorry, Belle. I felt a strong urge to follow that pair of leggers myself for a few beats, to act as a diversion. Soon, I felt no urgency to diverge if I may say, and headed directly back. What have we here?" the Falcon inquired as his eyes intently followed the side-to-side pacing of the smaller winger. "Lunch?"

"No, no. Don't eat him. He is not lunch. But do not let him out of your sight until I get back. No, wait. Do not let him off of that branch. I want you to find out who he is and how he knew where to find me. If he is not here, alive and kicking, when I get back, you will be my lunch. Understand?" She immediately turned and ran off toward the two-legger who was still arguing with the bigger four-legger.

***

"I'm going to have her take a bite out of your hind quarters if you don't keep cooperating! I promise you I will. Let's see what she knows and maybe we can stop this charade." Tofur promised.

"I will never stoop to this again. Of that you can be positive," grumbled the very agitated creature.

"Would you please stop complaining? Do you have any idea of what cooperation means? You are so stubborn!" Again the passers-by were laughing as the two-legger continued to try and converse with the animal.

Out of the taller grass to the side of the road came a large bounding four-legger. Handsome to behold--rather beautiful to behold, she was an amazing creature. Jet black with touches of deep mahogany, muscles rippling with every powerful stride, onlookers of both two and four legs admired her as she passed. Noticeably missing a normal length canine tail, she maintained complete direction and stability with her sinewy legs and large firm paws. Barrel-chested, with no noticeable defining mark between her head and shoulders, her neck was an extension from both to both. She gracefully leaped over a stalled cart much to the owner's dismay. She landed just as gracefully as she leaped, which was a sight to see given her box-like proportions. Smiling, she dashed to the two-legger's side, wagging the stump of her tail. "You called, Tofur?" She glanced at and couldn't help snickering at her four-legged companion. "You look hilariously striking, Jak!"

"Oh not you too," the four-legger moaned.

Tofur bent down to look the Rottweiler in the eyes. "Well, can we stop this little game yet? Jak is about ready to revolt. I don't think he can take much more of this humiliation. You know how tightly wound he is." Then he laughed.

Belle answered, "I think we have what we came for. Get him on his hooves and let us reconvene over at my lookout. But first, clean him up!" She laughed and immediately retraced her path to further question the little sky-traveler. There was much more to him than met the eye.

Tofur reached down and made an attempt to repair Jak's harness. Since there was nothing wrong with it, his attempt to repair something that was not broken appeared clumsy at best. "I hope you are happy now," he mumbled into the large ears. "If you had messed this plan up, I would have rode you hard and put you up wet."

"Yes, I'm sure you would have. Don't try me or I will sit here for good."

Tofur laughed hard, "I'll wager you would not. Come now, get on your hooves and let these fine two-leggers get on with their business."

Jak had to get the last word in. "Fine two-leggers, are you serious?"

***

Whistler was not the best Falcon for a "see, but don't be seen" caper. His tail feathers were shaped in a way that allowed wind to sneak between them and produce a noticeable, yet not unpleasant sound whenever he flew. The faster he flew, the more pronounced the whistling sound. It was best for him to fly as slowly as he could when tailing as he was now. He had no problem following the pair of leggers as they crept along the main road. His sight was keen enough to give him an advantage of distance and the limited whistling blended in well with the breeze. Something was bothering him about the leggers. The pair was slowing down far too often to make adjustments to the four-legger's load. He had to get closer yet remain cautious.

***

Belle quickly returned to the two wingers. When she returned, the smaller one was still pacing non-stop back and forth and back and forth. "Belle, my dear, this gray little thing is making me nervous. He has not ceased this incessant pacing since you left. Not only that, he keeps muttering on and on about an Eagle. What Eagle? I don't know. He won't say. He has been told of something that has put quite a dent in his realm of comfort. What did he tell you earlier?"

"Really, Taytay, he has revealed nothing to me. I'm at a loss just as you. It looks like we are about to lose him though."

"Maybe we can shock him back to reality? Would it not, at least, be worth a try?"

"What do you suggest?"

The Falcon abruptly jerked his handsome head upward and moved a bit higher in the tree.

Without warning, Belle thrust herself upward and let loose a menacing, ferocious bark that shook the leaves of the tree. She also brought her bared teeth within the tiniest distance imaginable from the little winger. The shock of the moment slapped the small fellow back to a coherent state.

He stopped pacing. "What? Why would you perform such a violent act towards me you big canine ogre!"

"Welcome back to our time, little fellow." Taytay said with hint of caring in his voice. I thought you were gone silly."

"Excuse me? I would never have gone silly. I may have tried going silly, but not gone silly. Never mind that, as I was saying an Eagle came to visit me several day-rounds ago." The Dove's story began to meander between straight-out lies and faint tidbits of truth. He would leave it up to his new companions to sort out the facts. "He was very concerned about the future of all of our lands. Why did he pick me? I can't begin to tell you."

"How did he know about you?"

He looked straight at Belle, "I can't tell you that answer because I don't know it. There are far too many things I don't know about this for me to be very comfortable with any of it." He continued, "The Eagle, I believe his name was Vincen, came into my glen seeking volunteers of the wisest and noblest sort, spouting some nonsense regarding the return of the terrible years. Nobody could fathom what he was saying. I had a hard time myself until we were able to speak alone. Those in my area respect me much more that either of you seem to. Anyway, he was directed to me by just about every creature in my area, for obvious reasons, and I took it upon myself to get to the bottom of his meddling."

"Wait. Please back-up a click. The return of the Terrible Years? Are you serious? Was he serious?" asked the shocked Falcon.

***

Whistler was going to have to push his luck. Should he make a bold move on the pair or just swoop in and see what he could and quickly retreat? He opted for the latter. A quick swoop should be just the right move. It wasn't. Just as he was lining up the direction of his attack, the two-legger pulled hard on the cord binding the left saddle bag on the four-legger's back. The contents of the pack exploded beneath the outer covering, sending a medium sized catch net directly in to the path of Whistler. The Falcon could not avoid it. He was snared instantly with no ideas for escape remotely entering his mind. He fell hard from the sky and landed bruised, but alive a short walk from the four-legger.

The two-legger was too surprised to talk. After checking the wide-eyed look of amazement in the eyes of the four-legger, he ran to where his captive lay dazed in the net. He hurriedly kneeled to the ground and began gathering the net. By gently pulling the net together from the corners, he bundled it together and lifted it from his prey. "Are you alright Falcon?"

"Well what do you think? You nearly killed me! What is that contraption you just used on me? Wait, did you just talk to me? Are you a Talker or am I dead or nearly dead?" The Falcon was shocked for the second time.

The two-legger quickly put the net back down over the Falcon's beak to shut him up. "Quit talking back to me. Do you want to expose me? You have no idea who may be in this area."

"Blah, blah, mumble...," the net loosened, "You started talking to me first!"

"Well stop talking back," the two-legger whispered loudly before pushing the net to Whistler's beak once again.

"No, okay, okay. I'll stop talking for now, but you have some explaining to do."

"Who are you with and why were you following me?" the two-legger asked.

"You knew I was following you?" Whistler whispered in return.

"Of course I knew. That noise you make is quite noticeable to people like me because we can communicate with our four-leggers and she is the one that heard you. She noticed you right after we made it through the intersection...around what we perceived to be a deliberate distraction, which we did not need at all. We, too, are following somebody, only now he or she is behind us and we snared you as a diversion of our own in hope that our prey would happen upon us. But, we had to use the net on you instead of them because we thought you were spying on us for them. Which you were not because she never heard the whistling noise until just after you were sent after us. Plus, we wanted to know who you were anyway..."

"Would you please take a breath? I am lost. I thought one was supposed to put one thought in one sentence? You just rambled me almost to crazy." Whistler was worn out. "Let me go and I will lead you back to my group. Then, after you settle down, we can all discuss our plans. Then, we will see who is after whom. Will that work for you?"

"Yes, yes, I suppose it will. But how will I be able to keep tracking the one I have been sent to track if I go back with you to meet who sent you to track me and will that put us too far behind our prey to track them as we should, knowing what the reason is for us to be tracking them to begin with."

"Whoa, whoa." Whistler could only shake his head, "Oh my. Is this a habit with you? Is this how you normally carry on conversations? Please, let me up and everything will be fine. I will introduce my group to you and then we will formulate a plan for you to continue your task."

"Okay, I will release you...Just hold still and don't panic." The two-legger did exactly as he said. He released the Falcon and loaded the net back into the exploding saddle bag.

The draft four-legger ambled over to the Falcon, "So," she motioned to the two-legger and with a very deep feminine voice asked, "Can you tell he hasn't talked to creatures like us in a while?"

"Wow," replied Whistler.

3

er hand quivered as she raised the quill from the ink well and set it to the diary parchment.

Day 27. I am still not sure of the role I am playing in this vilely concocted plot. But, in order to quell the uprising of my folk, I will go along with the visitors--even though the heartache suffered at their hands seems to be increasingly insurmountable. The rider returned today on that evil black steed of his. I often think that horse is more involved with whatever plan is being hatched here than the rider or any of the others in his group. How one animal can reek so fervently of bad tidings is hard to comprehend, but reek that animal does. You can see it in the beast's eyes. They glare--no, they boil with badness. My horse and those of her group want nothing more than to stay as far away from the black monster as possible. A friend told me earlier the foam that bubbles from its snout sizzles like aig on the frypan when it lands on the ground. I have no idea how long they will stay. I wish they would leave immediately. Almost a month has passed since they came. My folk have been uprooted from their comfortable homes and have been forced to work in every available mien to accommodate the visitors. I have been spared from the uprooting, I think in part to preserve the look that all is well, but the messages I have written under duress, the words I have been forced to utter...needless to say, it makes bile rise in my throat. I am sickened by my actions. The rider is coming for me again...I pray that this diary survives if I don't. I don't know how much longer I can go along with this act before my temper forces me to unleash the power of the heirloom. I have so misused it before. Father, comfort my heart...Ev.

Not to raise the suspicions of the Rider, she quietly secured the diary with a knotted string, wrapped it in an old worn dress, tied it snugly with a ribbon made of long curly brown hair and placed the large collection of writings back into the wall. The fiery red, curly tresses that fell to her waist exactly portrayed the personality within the young maiden, while the fair skin did little to diminish the staunch conviction within her to do good. Her eyes, blue as the sky, saw good in lots of things and lots of people but saw none in those she now called the visitors. Daily, although her smile began to dwindle, she carried on the rituals of leadership instilled in her by generations before, but still, she was frightened. The Rider claimed ownership of the one living thing that she had left from her family, her messenger. Sure, she still had her favorite horses and her livestock, but he took her messenger. The only connection she had with her sister half way across the world was now precariously in the hands of the visitors and she could not be more apprehensive about her future. Her folk called her "Princess". The visitors called her "key number two". Her only sister called her Evaliene. Like her brown-haired sister, she was also called a "Talker".

The knock on the solid door had a metallic sound to it. Why the Rider felt compelled to wear battle armor where ever he went did little to quell the mystery behind his arrival two days after the original group of visitors invaded this quiet little town just west of the Green Glen. Again the agitated knock resounded loudly through the front room of Evaliene's chambers. She heard it loud and clear, just as she had heard it the first time. Knock. Knock. Knock! Again, much louder than the previous times. The Lady of the house had just finished hiding her diary. She came into the front room, brushing her hands off on her plaid wool skirt. A skirt of this type was never meant to be worn by a person of her means; however, it was just one of many precautions she used to blend in with the folk of her adopted town. Not many knew her secret and up until now no one else needed to know. She had moved to town rather uneventfully, but so had a lot of other two-leggers about the same time. The ones that came after her acted differently toward her with good reason. She remained humble and kept to herself, but occasionally one or two of the new town folk would slip and call her Princess or some other type of royal moniker. Usually this type of talk wouldn't raise an eyebrow, but with the new visitors in town, she made it known to all, in no uncertain terms, that calling her Princess or anything of the like would not be permitted for any reason.

"I'm coming, can't I have some time to prepare for my guest before he should barge into the room!" She yelled not too politely to the strange man on the other side of the door.

"I suggest you learn to act more quickly when I knock from now on!" the gruff Rider shouted in return.

After hearing his outburst, Evaliene walked toward the door even slower than before, mumbling something to herself about what her father would do to a common thug like this thing beating down her door, while she double checked her heavy sash buckle. She quickly glanced over the door at the door frame to make sure the board concealing another hidden storage compartment was secure. Nodding to herself, she smiled a short smile before putting on the face of a worn down prisoner. She lightly slapped her cheeks to redden them up a bit to camouflage her calm demeanor. She stopped just short of the door, poised herself, turned the large knob and greeted her antagonist.

"Good day sir. I saw you and your handsome steed barrel into town this morning. What is the evil nature of your visit with me today? Do you have more lies you would like me to address with my folk here? More false messages to send out for you? Just what exactly do you need from me today?" she asked with the politeness of a Jackal.

He cautiously glanced around to witness the usual small group of nosey town folk who made a nuisance of themselves whenever he approached this dwelling. He growled at her through a strong, set, clenched jaw, "I need for you not to make a scene, be quiet and let me in." He grinned. "You know what is at stake here if you make a spectacle with me or any of my friends while we are in your ridiculously stupid little town, if indeed it is a town at all. More like a trash yard if you ask me. We have Pigs where I come from that wouldn't lie in this mud hole if they were dead."

She curtly replied through a wonderfully fake smile, "I asked you once, now what do you want this time?"

Anger rose in his bones with every condescending word she spoke. He continued, "I'm telling you, you need to speak to me with respect, you spiteful wench. Remember what I have of yours? I could easily bring it back to you in pieces if you wish. There was a little incident earlier this morning during the ride in that nearly sealed its fate." He laughed, "As if it had not been already sealed. Listen closely to me now," his voice dropping to a raspy whisper, "Whether you cause me to or not, if that creature claws me one more time, I will chop its feet off."

He held up his right arm, and then shoved it in her face so she could get a good view of his blood stained sleeve with long diagonal slits ripped into the mail that protected his flesh. "This mail cost me plenty of coin and I don't intend for that creature of yours to rip it from my living flesh!"

Evaliene could not help but smile a tight-lipped, wry smile. She briefly glanced over the door and thought to herself what she alone could do him without the help of her messenger whether he wore the mail, full armor or not. Feigning weakness, she sobbed, "I am sorry. Please, you promised you would not hurt her! You said you only need to borrow her and I obliged. Do not threaten her again or you can consider someone else your puppet in whatever game you are playing." She pleaded with the Rider with as much theatre as she could muster.

"Do not disrespect me again, verbally or otherwise, because, if you do, your messenger will take the punishment in your stead. I promise you that!" he spat.

The town folk gathering near the dwelling were getting restless and began a covert movement that was quickly detected by the Rider. He hurriedly bullied his way into the room and demanded warm mead to drink and hard bread with dried fruit to eat. The two-legger had grown fond of the mead from this house. It had become habitual for him to demand it any time he was near. He found himself longing for it. Before his travels, he would demand that she supply him with at least two weeks' ration. It never had quite the same effect on him as it did when he drank it at her table. The bread was nothing special, the dried fruit was dried fruit, sweet and chewy, but the mead was more than ample to wash the rest down. The Rider stormed to the table, yanked a chair out and sat down hard. As he banged his good forearm down on the table, he yelled again. "We have spared your town and all of you in it because we could, not because we wanted to or needed to. If you or any of the pitiful others here decide not to cooperate with any of us, we will destroy the town and everything in it! Do you understand me? I am leaving this miserable waste dump tomorrow to take the latest bit of good news to my governor. When I return, if anything here has changed or if I even think it has changed out of our favor, I will personally set fire to every dwelling within my sight. Is that clear?"

Evaliene had to change her demeanor fast. The Rider's fuse was burning very short. She returned to the quiet, unassuming maiden. "I am sorry, Sir, please calm down. Here is your drink. I will fetch your food for you. You say you are leaving tomorrow? For how long? I apologize for upsetting you."

The Rider's stay proceeded with no further outbursts. She kept his mug topped off with mead. She had noticed early on that when he got angry, he often said things he was not supposed to say to her. She found she could use this method to gain information she would not get otherwise. The more mead he drank, the easier he was to control. So far, today had been a good day. The governor? Which governor and why? Are they really going to spare the town after they are through with it? Burn down the dwellings? She had lots to do once he left. After eating and drinking his fill, the Rider abruptly left. She saw him out and bolted the door behind him. Evaliene walked to the table, picked up a chair and carried it back to the door. She stood on the chair and pried the trim piece from the top of the wooden door frame off to reveal the hidden compartment. She took a heavy object from the space, replaced the frame board and returned to the table. After laying the object on the table, she said to no one in particular, "So you're going to bring her back in pieces?" She lightly tapped the object then removed a heavy cloth bag that covered one end. When she did, it was, as she suspected, glowing.

***

Evaliene's hand was not shaking today as she opened her diary.

Day 47. I can hardly believe the change the Visitors have made on this town. I am not sure this can last much longer. The Visitors seem content to occupy our town forever. Why are they here? I have no more answers to that question today than I had on Day one. I haven't been made to write false letters under duress in a few days now. I hope that period has ended. I am so tempted to smash the entire lot of them, but I fear we would be back to square one trying to find out the reason behind these people. The Rider is growing more condescending and vile with each passing day. The accident on the mountain has made him merciless, not that he had much sense of mercy to begin with. His right arm is all but useless to him which some of us know will work to our favor should a fight break out. My Protectors are begging to dispatch them all. I cannot let that happen yet. The poor townspeople are at a loss. They have yet to pass any blame towards me for the invasion; still I think it may come before this is over. The food is gone and the harvest has been in for some time now. The Visitors brought nothing with them. They have pillaged our stock of nearly everything. They have not taken to violating the townspeople. If or when they do, that will be their end. My Protectors will not sit idly by and condone that type of action. I certainly will not. I will order them all dispatched and it will be immediately taken care of. There shan't be one left breathing. I hope Mad got my letter and the real message I intended. Surely she can unlock the code. There seems to be some commotion outside my window. I have stayed in all day, not wishing to bring anymore attention forwarded my way. I wish this would all go away.

Evaliene wrapped the diary and packed it away in its hiding place. The ado outside was becoming increasingly disruptive. She closed her curtains and stepped outside. In the street, the Rider had a man tied to his saddle. He kept spurring his black Horse to run. The Horse refused. "Now that is odd," she thought. "Why doesn't that monster do the Rider's bidding?"

"I demand to know what is going on out here." She quickly walked out of her door and into the center of the melee. She glared at the Rider. "Why do you have that man tied to your saddle horn?"

"What concern is it of yours, lady?" asked a Visitor, holding the Rider's Horse. "I'd say it's a good day for a bit of discipline, I would."

"How dare you even think such a thing, you imbecile?" Evaliene did not back down. "Unbind him immediately or else!"

This exchange got the Rider's full attention. He returned the glare. "Or else what? This is the man who so kindly loaned me the Horse that very nearly killed me! I will not unbind him, nor will anyone here or I personally will be responsible for their last breath. Do I make myself clear? He knocked one of my men unconscious, stoled him of his overcoat, then, as if that wasn't enough to get drug behind a Horse, he sent his puny little Horse on a mission to do me in!" He was literally fighting with the black Horse to move. He spurred him repeatedly. With blood running freely from the wounds opened by the spurs, the Horse remained absolutely resolute, it was not going anywhere. "Now, my lovely, if this stupid Horse of mine would do as he was told...we could get on with this."

"You will not continue this, you despicable and vile man," Evaliene promised. "And, might I add, the more you bark like this in public, the more these locals realize how stupid you actually are. Your mastery of your own language is reprehensible."

"Go shut her up," the Rider exclaimed to his crowd. "I don't care how you do it. Just don't let me hear that voice again today or ever!"

"I'll get right on it, sir," one of his followers shouted over the commotion. He did not make it to Evaliene's side. He never took another step. He was lost in the crowd and his body was never found or asked about.

"Did any of you stupid people hear me? I said shut her up!" The Rider was dismayed at the lack of obedience by his men. Again he shouted into the crowd. "Someone shut her up!"

Another lone voice answered back, "Fine, I will take her. I rather think I'm gonna enjoy it too!" Exactly what happened with the first to answer the Rider happened with the second and again, his body was never found.

Evaliene had enough of this. Furious, she raced back into her dwelling and quickly bolted the door behind her. In haste, she forgot to draw the curtain near the dining table. As she madly grabbed the chair and threw it beneath the door, she checked her sash. Good, the buckle was in place. She recklessly climbed the chair, reaching up haphazardly to pry off the frame board. She snatched the heirloom out of the hiding place then yanked off the heavy cloth cover. It was glowing so brightly that it radiated through the window curtain before reflecting off of the shiny silver pendant on the Horse's bridle. The Horse accidentally caught sight of the glow as the livid Rider nearly pulled the bit through the animal's throat causing him to rear up.

"It can't be!" the Horse yelled to no one in particular. "She can't, not now, not yet!"

The Horse violently reared up again, high enough to intentionally cause himself to topple over. The action caused the Rider to lose all hope of maintaining his balance. He tumbled off his crazed steed causing the Horse to fall on top of him, crushing his leg with the full brunt of the four-legger's weight. The fall sent his head crashing down on the hard-packed dirt path immediately leaving him unconscious. The Horse, on a mission, wildly struggled back to his hooves, but the Rider stayed down, knocked out and partially crippled for the rest of his life.

The Horse staged a raging fit before barreling head long through the dazed onlookers, the front garden and into the front door, boldly freeing it from its hinges and bolts. As the Horse crashed through the entrance, the door took a short flight across the foyer, hitting Evaliene full in the side and knocking her ungracefully to the ground. The heirloom, thrown from her hand, sailed under the heavy couch near the mantle and landed with short slide, followed by a thud as it became tightly wedged under the sturdy oak frame. An eerie glow escaped from the slit between the dust ruffle and the hard wooden floor. Evaliene, instantly realizing she was under attack, painfully scrambled on all fours toward the nearest wall she could see with her groggy eyes. She fought dizziness for her senses and grasped with both hands haphazardly at her waist while positioning her body with her back to the wall. She glanced up menacingly at her attacker, ripped the buckle from her sash and took a second to scan the room for the heirloom. She then set her sights on the mad Horse. She was on her feet in an instant, wielding the flexible blade of a finely crafted dagger in her left hand. She screamed for the animal to stop, "You! How dare you burst through my door! I might not kill you with this, but you will feel pain! You have overstayed your welcome here! I should have never trusted you!"

The four-legger backed himself into the doorless opening enough to block out the charging horde of visitors and special town folk who were soon to follow. Fortunately, he was large enough to do this. The Horse did not have much time with the dagger-wielding, outraged lady of the house coming at him from the front and the over-protective town folk nearing his unprotected backside. He knew her people would be coming for her rather than taking advantage of the pandemonium-induced distraction outside to whittle down the ranks of the visitors. The Horse shouted back at Evaliene, "What do you think you are doing? In one self-centered blink of your eye, you may have ruined everything with your out-of-control, red-headed temper tantrum! It is not time for that! Do you not know what I am doing? What we are doing?"

Evaliene was speechless.

"Speak up, Princess! Has no one briefed you on what is going on here?"

"How do you know I am a princess? Nobody is supposed to know that!"

"Yes, of course I know who you are. I'm sure every four-legger in this country knows who you are. I had a good idea who you were the night I first met you and your white Horse. Sadly, we have dispatched several of our own in order to protect your identity from the two-leggers outside of your Protectors. Your Protectors know. Have they not told you? We have no failsafe way of knowing if you are the only Talker remaining here or not. We certainly hope you are. The whereabouts of your younger sister are closely guarded."

"You know of her too?" Evaliene was beginning to feel pain, her head was reeling.

"I know much more than you think! Rhiannon is below your rear window. Grab your diary, your escape bag and the heirloom! Don't forget anything! Go out your back window, climb down the ladder. Rhiannon is saddled up and she knows where you are going. I can't tell you and neither can she! Do you understand? We have no more time. What is the signal for your people to take arms against the visitors? The time is not right but, thanks to you, the time is now. Well, what is it?"

"What signal? Rhiannon? She won't get near you. She despises your existence! You burned that bridge with your despicable behavior. You, the black Rider's steed, she will never speak to you again!"

"Why are you two-leggers so inept? Forget that for one moment will you? You must have a signal to give your protectors when you are in danger. What is it? As for Rhiannon, she is my mate. We were born for each other. It's a long story and you have to go! Again, what is the signal?

Evaliene was struggling for balance. She scooted over and lifted the couch off of the heirloom. She stuck the dagger back into her sash buckle, managed to stand and dashed to her bedroom. She grabbed the escape bag from behind the door and her diary from its hiding place. Folded over in pain from where the door blasted into her side, she hastily crammed the diary into an inner pocket in the bag. Still slumped over, she raised her skirt high enough to slide the heirloom into the holster in the top of her riding boot. It was uncomfortable, but necessary. She straightened up as much as she could before running back into the front room. "The signal, the signal," she muttered to herself. "What have I done?" She remembered.

"Hurry, Princess, I am being bombarded. They are throwing objects at my hind quarters to get my attention. Soon I know I will feel the stabbing sensations from weapons of every sort. Set the signal and flee!"

"The signal," she exclaimed. "Yes, I remember." She struggled to the front window, threw open one shutter, ripped down a curtain and hung it over the window sill.

Immediately and without so much as one verbal order given, her people retreated from removing the black Horse from the door and turned on the Visitors that had ravaged the town for the past several weeks. They were relentless. Spurred on by the townspeople, the Protectors were making quick work of the rag-tag Visitor army. Two of them retrieved the crippled rider and stole him away before any of his underlings could make a fight to save him. They did not kill him; he was too valuable breathing. The rest of the Visitors were fair game. If they tried to fight, they were dispatched. If they surrendered, they were taken prisoner. Within the ways of the Protectors, being taken prisoner was much often worse that being quickly dispatched.

The black Horse began kicking and snorting as a ruse to fool those Visitors still capable of being fooled. Most were not in any condition to care what the Rider's Horse did. He put on enough of a show to allow Evaliene time to get out the rear window, down the ladder and onto Rhiannon's back. No sooner had her full weight settled into the saddle, the graceful white Horse took off at a feverish pace with only two wingers in pursuit. With a tip of a wing, the second winger signaled the remaining Horses and assorted four-leggers to stampede in circles around the town to further draw the attention away from Evaliene and Rhiannon's escape. The path had been scouted and the guardian Horse knew exactly where she was heading. Evaliene, still doubled over in pain, did not.

4

Perrie scanned to the horizon for clues. The assembly of two-leggers had to come from somewhere. She attentively searched for a vestige of a marauded village or signs of a lengthy encampment. With one eye always open for an impending attack, the other eye focused on an origination point for the hapless travelers. As she flew, she worried. She knew it was taking too long. There was no place to find.

How he knew she was there was not for her to know. Still, he saw her and still he watched over her. He too, was keeping one eye open for an attack on her. Truth be known, he was keeping both eyes open for her benefit.

***

"Perrie has been gone for a very long time, Hemoth. This bag has a lot of supplies left in it, but there is not much food. This group has eaten nearly all of it. What should we do now?" Madaliene looked up to her protector as he stood on his hind legs thinking Perrie would soon appear with news, good or bad.

"Princess, Perrie has been gone too long for my liking. We can't make any plans without some information from her. We need to ask more questions of these leggers. Surely one of them has answers." The Grizzly spoke to Madaliene without taking his eyes from the surroundings. "I really can't see anything."

Lightning sat slumped on the ground, eyeing the two-leggers as they filled their empty stomachs. "Princess, is there any food left for us or have you given it all to these two-leggers?"

Madaliene reached far into the bag and pulled out the last of the fruits. "Here you go, Lightning. There is just enough left for one meal each for the three of us and a few bits left for Perrie, if she will hurry back." She tossed him a few fruits.

"Thank you. So you say this needs to last?"

"Yes, Lightning, it certainly does."

Lightning lifted his tired, hungry mass and stood beside Hemoth. “What do you think we should do now?”

Hemoth continued to search for an unknown quarry. “If Madaliene is running out of food, we are going to have to find some other way to feed these leggers. As far as our next Nuorg-related mission, well…I’m not sure.”

Lightning nodded in agreement. “Hemoth, do you feel a need for a long nap?”

“Yes, I do. We have to put those kind of thoughts out of our mind, Lightning. There is no time for that now. Princess, have you heard any of these leggers talking about anything?”

“No, Hemoth, I have not. I think it’s time we question them again.”

“One of them must know something, Princess. See if the older one will start talking again.”

Madaliene stepped over to the older man’s side. He was slowly munching his way through the last bit of food she had tossed him earlier. “Sir, what more can you tell me about where all of you came from? Why are you here?”

The older legger slowly chewed his final bite and looked at her with eyes nearly void of emotion. “Little girl, we have no where else to be. None of us has a home to go back to. We have no idea if we are free from those that left us alive or merely awaiting their return to complete what they started. Why are you here? Where did your group come from?”

Madaliene paused, “To be honest with you sir, we are from all over. The Falcon that came in with us is from the far northwest, the largest Grizzly is from the far north, the other Bear is from the Great Forest, which I assume is somewhere in the middle and I am from, well…I don’t really know where I am from. Are you sure you can’t tell me more about your group?”

“Miss, that sounds very interesting and could very well be a rouse to get some of my folk talking to you about things you don’t need to know about. Might that be your reasoning for the questions?”

Madaliene could not figure out the older legger. “Why would I offer all of our food to you, if I wanted to do away with you? I am here to help you, but if you feel you don’t need it, just tell me and we will again be on our way.”

"If that is the way you want it then fine. Leave us be. We don't need help from your group. We have eaten our fill of your food. We will survive one way or another, if it is meant to be."

Madaliene stood up shaking her head and walked back to Hemoth. "Hemoth, we should go. These people do not want us here. Why did Lightning's ax-pike bring us here to begin with? Maybe these leggers are not the reason for us being here after all."

Hemoth smiled at his charge. "Princess, could there be another reason? And if so, what is it? I would love to know."

Perrie came in flying low as she was instructed. She was not showing any sign of tiring, "Princess, Hemoth, I am sorry it took so long. I found a lot of nothing out there, too much nothing to be legitimate. Someone has changed the landscape beneath our feet. There is not one iota of anything for miles. There is no sign of another winger or legger of any kind except for these we have here, however, a large winger is watching from on high."

Madaliene and Hemoth immediately jerked their heads skyward; they scanned the blue sky with eyes that could never see as high as the watching winger was drifting. "We will have to take your word for that, Perrie. I know I can't see any movement up there at all." Madaliene continued to scan for what she could never see.

"Believe me Princess, it is definitely up there."

"You say you saw nothing of note anywhere. Is that correct Perrie?" Hemoth was not looking skyward any longer. He stared into the young Falcon's eyes. "Absolutely, positively correct? You saw nothing?"

Perrie met Hemoth's stare. "Without a doubt, Hemoth. There is nothing out there."

Hemoth once again looked to the sky. "Then where did they come from?"

Perrie joined Hemoth staring skyward. "Hemoth, we have to find out. They could not have just appeared."

Hemoth laughed, "Why not, Perrie? We did."

Madaliene moved in closer to Hemoth's side. Lightning soon joined them. Shortly, all eyes were focused high into the sky searching for something none of them could hope to see. For a moment each was lost in their thoughts, rehashing the last few days. Lightning noticed the absence first.

"Where did they go?" Lightning asked, flustered. "They were just here."

"What are you talking about Lightning?" Madaliene turned to see what was missing.

"The two-leggers, Princess, where did they go?" Lightning walked around trying to spot the group.

"Hemoth, Hemoth, look—they are all gone!" Madaliene was frightened.

The Grizzly Bear and the Falcon were greeted by the same sight as Lightning and the Princess. "First, they come from nowhere and now they disappear to nowhere. Everyone, gather in. Lightning, get us out of here!"

"Wait Lightning! Don't do anything yet. Take a look over there. Look at where they sat." Madaliene pointed with a wide sweeping gesture. "What do you see?"

"The food," answered Perrie. "They did not eat the food you gave them, they…they increased it."

"Yes, they did eat it," Lightning added. I saw them chomping on all of it."

Scattered about lay the food Madaliene had tossed from Frederick's bag to the two-leggers and more. She walked over and picked several pieces of it up. She held it for the others to see. "Can someone explain this to me? There has not been a bite taken from any of this, yet we watched them eat it all. Now…now there is more here than I gave them. What is going on?"

Hemoth hurried to her side. "Let me see that Mad!" The Grizzly took a few fruits from her hands and plopped them into his mouth. As he chewed, he spoke, "This tastes normal to me. There is not even the slightest tooth mark on it. Princess, gather this up and place it back in the bag. We may need it yet."

Madaliene collected all of the food. "Hemoth, how strange is this?"

Lightning began to collect what he could from the ground. "Mind if I eat some of this? I'm a bit hungry."

"Sure Lightning, go ahead. I don't see what it can hurt now."

Madaliene ate a few fruits herself. The food tasted even better than it had before. Was it because they were hungry or was it because of something else? None of them seemed to care. Again, high above them all, he smiled as he soared.

5

Tofur lightly lifted the thick ropes that made up the reins of Jak's bridle. They were necessary only to give the look of normalcy when the group intermingled with non-talkers. Under any other circumstance the reins would not be tolerated by Jak or his kind for they reasoned since they could talk to the two-leggers they would either do what was asked of them or not. It was really very simple. Should a four-legger not want to do as a two-legger asked and a very good reason could not be given for doing so, then the four-legger would not partake of the activity and no amount of two-leggers could change the determined four-legger's mind. A two-legger had to be very sure of himself to even attempt to put such a contraption as a bridle on a four-legger such as Jak. Two-leggers had been seriously hurt when they fell into the path of a well placed kick by one of Jak's ilk.

"So Belle, what have you been able to figure out for us? Have you seen any sign of who we are supposed to be after? I'm sure you have watched several leggers pass by this little diversion of ours." Tofur asked as he attempted to maneuver the three of them through the slow moving throng of leggers. He led Jak at an angle which brought them to the side of the roadway where they made a sharp turn and headed back to the rendezvous spot.

Belle was walking close to Tofur's right side as obediently as she could. She was trying not to be too excited or look unlike other two-legger's Dogs as she perfectly kept pace with Tofur. "We have discovered two interesting pairs that we want to follow. But, you two will love the new winger that has decided to join our litter," she said with a smile.

"Another winger?" asked Tofur. "From where has he come and how is he now a part of our litter?"

"He says an Eagle sent him to us. Does that mean we keep him or eat him?"

"I guess that depends on what he has to say," Jak added.

Belle laughed again. "Oh I think you and he are going to get along quite well Jak. You both have a lot in common."

"Oh my, that did not sound very convincing, Belle. Can you at least warn us? What is he like?" Tofur was amused at Belle's tone of voice and knew there was more to it than just a new addition to their, as she called it, litter.

"I'll just say...talkative. No, he is also very sure of himself. Very determined little fellow he is. I'm afraid I will have to leave it at that. You two can make your own minds up shortly."

"Great. He sounds truly like a new best friend for me, Belle." Jak was nothing if not intrinsically sarcastic. "Wonderful. You don't have to introduce me if you don't mind. Go ahead and eat him." Jak knew Belle very well. He also knew the new winger must have perturbed her somewhat.

"No legger is going to eat any winger, not yet anyway." Tofur was smiling and could not wait to meet this new creature. He must be something very special.

***

Belle and the others needed to return soon or one of the wingers she left may soon explode. Neither of them had moved a feather since the stand off had begun. Taytay had begun to ask questions but the little fellow would have nothing to do with it. Instead, the two positioned themselves slightly apart from each other on the same branch. The larger Falcon stared down the sides of his beak directly into the head feathers of the smaller winger. The small winger stared right back up at the Falcon and did not give in one little bit.

Taytay was watching the smallish grey winger as if it would make a scrumptious mid-day meal. The little winger was peering back through black glaring eyes as if he were the one pulling sentinel duty. Their stares were locked in a standoff. The first one that flinched or blinked would lose this battle. The smaller of the two could not hold his words any longer. From his tiny beak he relented to his immense ego. "You are one lucky Hawk. I hope you know that had I had the right mind to, I might have eaten you already and I still might if you move one feather on your little crest there."

The Falcon was not at all amused. "Just how do you think you would accomplish that impossible feat you miniscule little puff ball? And I am not a Hawk."

"Wouldn't you like to know how I would do just that? I'll bet you would. I eat wingers like you for snacks or when I just get bored of staring at them."

"Is that so? If Belle had not threatened to eat me if you escaped, then I would have certainly eaten you already."

"So her name is Belle is it? See you have already given me more information than I have given you. You still don't know my name, but I know yours and the big black Dog's. Yes, my method is breaking you down. You will soon lose this contest and I will ravenously dine on your flesh, you overgrown Sparrow."

"Sparrow? Did you call me a Sparrow? You, you can't be much larger than a Sparrow yourself, you, you... what are you? Let me answer that, you are lunch!" Taytay unfolded his wings. He stretched them wide and back. He moved his head down, his powerful beak open to within the thickness of a feather from the tiny beak and unblinking eyes of the determined grey creature. His eyes flared, his chest expanded...

The new winger had not moved even the smallest feather on his head. His eyes were dark as a cave and staring holes through the Falcon's crested head. He growled in the lowest voice a creature his size could, "Go ahead, I am very hungry, make me happy. All I need is one good excuse to rip you apart. I know Sparrows and you dear Hawk could not knock a small Sparrow out of its nest."

Taytay was very deliberate now with his voice inflection. He flatly said, "I am not a Hawk. Are you out of your head? Are you crazy? I am very hungry too and you are so small you would only be a few bites worth but I am more that willing to give you a try."

"You are the very lucky one here. I can see your friends are back now so I may let you live a little while longer, but beware, I will keep my eyes on you!"

"Tofur!" Taytay called out without breaking his stare, "Can I eat this little nuisance?"

Belle laughed then looked up at Tofur, "See that little grey winger? That is who I was telling you about. Cute little thing isn't he? Taytay, Is he causing you any trouble?"

"His pesky attitude just about gave me an excuse to have a bite to eat and I mean a small bite to eat!" He remained close enough to see the wingers gizzard through his throat, his glare had not let up.

"Ah, let the little Pigeon have a go at it will you?" Tofur was tickled. They had witnessed the stand-off for the last few threats. "I'm sure he is of a good nature."

"Pigeon!" That did it. The grey winger whirled around and locked his eyes on Tofur now. "How dare you, you adolescent two-legger! How dare you call me a Pigeon! I am not a Pigeon! Pigeons don't have the knowledge I contain in one of the smallest feathers on my entire body! Pigeons are clumsy foolish wingers. I, boy, am a mourning Dove and I am more intelligent than any of us gathered here! Never call me a Pigeon again or I will very likely eat you too!"

"Whoa, I think I do like this tiny thing, Belle." Jak was nodding his large head at Belle. "Pretty feisty winger, I'd say."

"Excuse me?" The Dove was now glaring at Jak. "Feisty winger? You, you jack a...."

"Calm down!" Belle bellowed this loud enough for all those close to completely understand. Down at the intersection, it was heard as a vicious bark from a vicious Dog. "You, Dove, don't say another word. You, Taytay, perch on Tofur's shoulder immediately! I'm going to do the talking now. Is that understood?"

The Dove looked up at the surprised Falcon. "I won...Hawk."

Taytay grimaced and swooped down to Tofur's right shoulder. "Please."

Tofur laughed.

Jak just continued nodding his head.

Belle asked, "Where is Whistler?"

***

"Good, the trap went back in almost as fast as it came out. That is good news if we find we need it for repeated uses. Do you think we will need it for future uses? I think we will and if we do then it will be ready. What is your name, Sir Falcon? Why do you whistle when you fly? I'm sure I can fix whatever is making that confounded noise. Come here. Let me have a look. I think it is will be a quick fix, I really do. I should hope to keep the procedure completely painless..." He continued fiddling with about every loose strap, string or cord binding all of the assorted bags, sacks, and other conveniences loaded on the back of the four-leggers tall and broad flanks.

"Good gracious sir, would you mind terribly if I ask you to speak one question at a time? The way you are assembling your quips is first annoying and second, quite confusing." Whistler figured this two-legger may have just discovered his unique ability to converse with those kinds other than his or he was rapidly losing his sanity. "How long have you been a Talker anyway?"

"Let me interrupt here." The well muscled four-legger shook her head. "I will answer that. First, what shall I call you, winger?"

"Call me Whistler. That's what I have been called for as long as I can remember. At least, since I could fly. My given name is quite complicated, maybe later on that."

"Fine, Whistler. I am Porcene."

"Unique name."

"It is an old family moniker I was bestowed. This two-legger is Mariel Fraunchesca. He travels from a very large township down a ways from here. Two-leggers run rampant there. Four-leggers are scarce. He stumbled into me one evening not too long ago. Actually he was pushed into my path by a group of two-leggers as I was briskly traveling a stone walkway within the confines of his large town."

"You mean he was shoved into your path on purpose?" asked Whistler.

"Yes. From what I could gather from him - he has been rambling since we, uh, met - he was intentionally thrown in my way. He rambles so much I haven't fully figured his story out."

"Are you two discussing me? I guess you are since you are talking about a two-legger and I am the only one like that around here. What about you Falcon, are you going to let me have a look at that problem of yours? I mean, after all, if you are to join us on our quest you can't be flying around all over the place with that constant whistling sound following on your tail. Tail, maybe I need to fix your tail. Does it bother you at all? I mean that whistling. Does it bother you in the least? It didn't bother me but like I say, it is quite noticeable. Well it is to four-leggers. Me, not so much...?" Mariel did have a bit of a rambling tendency.

Whistler was dumbfounded. This legger was not all there. Couldn't be. "Did you step on his head when he fell in front of you?" he asked.

"Not that I remember. It was almost as dark as pitch out that evening."

"What has he told you?" Whistler asked.

"Oh yes. I'm sorry. Let me get back to that. I gather that he was having an argument of monumental proportions when these thugs had enough. He says they were all laughing at him and threatening all sorts of damage to him. I can't determine that to be absolutely true, but that's what I have so far. I was pulling an empty cart. I was able to avoid him but the cart knocked him senseless momentarily. He has been this way ever since. I feel awful."

"But why are you together? Why are you out here following the creatures I am following?" Whistler was getting more curious with every word Porcene added.

"Falcon, er, Whistler, I am waiting. Come here. I will make quick work of my inspection of your feathers. I'm sure that is the problem. Oh me, what were we doing, Porcene, before he got here? We were going somewhere. Oh, what was it? Well, Falcon. Come on. Let's get to it. Did I pack the net again? Oh me, it did work well didn't it? Porcene, who is this winger? Oh, oh I remember now." Mariel was rambling.

Porcene exhibited a little shudder, "See? I couldn't just leave him behind. Somehow he became engaged with the cart and I drug him all the way down the road. The leggers did not follow us so I believe they think they succeeded in getting rid of him for whatever reasons."

"But, all of this stuff on your back, what is it? Where did it come from?"

"Good question. It all belongs to Mariel."

***

"Are we being watched? I don't like this at all. What was all of that commotion about?" The first well dressed two-legger stated to the other. "I don't like this. I don't like this at all."

"You are over reacting. What did they tell us? You may be watched? There may be birds or animals tracking your moves? Animals? Birds? We are men! I know I don't fear animals or certainly no bird for that matter!" The second two-legger was very sure of himself. What harm could animals or birds do to them? They were properly armed and animals could not reason. Right? Animals could not communicate. What was there to fear? The two-leggers needed to do their job and report back. That was simple enough.

"Where were we to meet the rest of our group? This is the most unorganized plan I have ever been a part of. They said just walk west. Well we are walking west, for ten days now. Who are we supposed to meet? Who are "they" anyway? Who gave you the first message?" The first two-legger was furious with whoever had hatched this plan. "We have no money, we have run out of food, our clothes are becoming badly worn, my shoes are soaking wet and have so many holes in them that I should throw them away, if I had another pair."

"Why do you complain so? We will be paid very well for this simple task. If we have to walk for 30 days, what should it matter? You left no one behind? You are carrying your pay as if you want it known to everyone we pass. You enjoy yourself at every stop we make. Why do you care at all how long this takes?"

"Where is the money now? You failed to mention that I am the smarter of the two of us here. I'd expect you to listen a little closer to me when I speak of situations I feel ominous. I have heard several murmurings during our short stops since we have set out that would not make a lesser man wary, but me, oh yes I can tell something is afoot. Something is keeping tabs of our every step."

The second two-legger was tired of hearing these kinds of derogatory statements from the first. Why did he insist on dressing so formally? This choice of attire was not functional to this job and did little to help them blend in with the populous. As far as being the smart one, well, that was arguable. "We should meet up with one or more of the Rider's men soon enough. They know we are seeking them. We will give them the message as we were told. Once they have received that message from us, we will deliver the reply back to our contact. That is simple enough. Stop your complaining!"

***

Taytay answered Belle, "I don't know. Where did you send him?"

"I sent him to tag along behind a pair of leggers that I thought looked suspicious," Belle responded a little agitated.

A voice came from the smallest of group, "And I can assure you it was the wrong pair!"

"Really?" inquired Tofur. "How would you know which pair we should follow? You seem awfully sure that we are tailing the wrong ones."

"Because you are tailing the pair that I came with!"

"The pair you came with?" If Belle wasn't confused yet, she was getting there. "Well how do we know that you aren't the enemy here?"

"Because young lady, I haven't destroyed any of you yet. Had I the mind I could have easily taken care of you and the Hawk long ago." This Dove was a little hard to like.

"I am not a Hawk, you tiny speck of molt! I am a Falcon! Understand?" Taytay did not like this small grey know-it-all.

"Sweet barley!" Jak had heard about all of this he wanted to hear. "All right, that is it! Belle, if you don't do something about this bravado-induced verbal jousting; I am going to squash both of them!" Jak eyed both of the wingers with growing frustration.

Belle added, "Jak is correct. I am tired of the ridiculous talk between you two." She looked directly at the Dove, the instigator. "Who are you and where are you from and what do you know?"

"I don't have to share any of that information with you." With that he turned his ahead and stared off into the distance.

"Okay. Fine." She got his attention. "Now let me tell you something. I am very hungry. I am a voracious eater and when I get very hungry I will eat anything. Now you are a small little crumb at best and would hardly be worth the effort, but in your case, I would waste my energy to eat you just to shut you up!" She started with a mild growl and ended with a ferocious bark.

The Dove was taken aback. "How dare you?" He looked at the others, "Is she completely serious?" Every creature nodded in agreement. "I guess that means that she is. Okay, to save you the trouble I will tell you. I am called Tine. I am from across the great lake to the east. I came here with two companions. We are trailing a worrisome pair that your group completely missed while your little show was going on earlier. We have every intention of capturing them for answers. There is trouble brewing in my homeland over what some are calling a return of the Terrible Years. It is a complicated matter and I volunteered for the mission. My companions are very serious creatures in their own right. You don't want to mess with them. They have brought all kinds of traps and weapons along. Is that sufficient enough of an answer for you?"

Belle was trying to remember the pair that Tine said passed through their diversion. "Yes, I guess that will do for now. Listen to me. I want you to drop the attitude. Do you understand?"

"Yes, I understand, but I will eat this Hawk if he doesn't back off."

Taytay looked off, shaking his head in dismay.

"Yes well, we will cross that bridge later. If you are so sure we missed the pair we were supposed to catch, well then tell me, where are they? Tofur what do you think? Did we miss them after all?"

"I don't know Belle. I was very careful. I thought I saw every legger that came by us. I'm not sure. We may have to take his word this time. If Whistler would get back we could ask if he saw anyone strange."

Tine chirped in, "That's just it. They don't look strange. They look completely normal. They are not wearing signs on their back warning that they are evil!"

"I know, I know. They could be anybody out there." Tofur sounded dejected.

***

"We have to meet with my group. It will be a big group. Maybe we can share information to come up with a new plan." Whistler was thinking ahead.

"That should work. We must catch the two leggers we are after as soon as we can. We must drain them of information so that our new plan will be viable." Porcene was an intelligent creature.

"Okay, you keep up with Mariel. I will return to my group. I will come notify you where the meeting will take place. You can spot the ones we are after without any trouble, can't you?"

"Oh yes, no trouble at all. Go. Fly quickly. We are wasting precious time."

Whistler was off. He was a noisy but swift flyer. He flew into the middle of his group just as Tofur finished speaking.

Jak noticed him first. "Well good to see you again Whistler. Heard you coming for some time now. Do you have any news?"

"Oh I have good news that we need to act on very soon or we will risk losing our quarry."

"Such as?" Belle was ready to move. The bickering bored her. She wanted to get on with the chase.

"I met up with the pair you sent me after. Turns out they were pursuing the same leggers we are pursuing."

"Really?" asked Tofur. "So the little Dove may be telling us the truth after all. Not in a believable way of course, true nevertheless."

"Who? Him?" Whistler cut his eyes and nodded in the direction of Tine. "If you say so. Yes, we need to get going. Taytay track me. I'll find a place to hold them up after a few leisure beats. Please hurry." Whistler flew back to Mariel and Porcene without hesitation.

Tofur turned his attention back to Jak's harness. To stage the breakdown he had easily unbuckled several key buckles allowing the harness to fall far enough down to entangle the four-legger's legs. Tofur's job now was to re-buckle the buckles and adjust the straps once again. "Now, this should get you back in traveling mode. This goes here, this one goes here. There you are, now we are good to go."

"I'll be good to go after you get this embarrassing strappage off of me. I am not a draft animal. I thought I made that very clear to you when you were much younger." Jak never really felt comfortable doing all that much work. He wasn't really lazy. He would rather use his mind in ways that would have other creatures doing his work. If all was to be truthfully told, he was a draft animal and a very good one at that.

"You don't have to go through this again, Jak. Pretend you are not an obnoxiously arrogant creature again, won't you? It would sure make our journey more pleasant." Belle and Jak had been in Tofur's family since the little two-legger could walk. They were aging, but aging quite well. Tofur's energy had its own way of keeping them young.

"Belle, you know I try, but you also know that deep down inside I am an obnoxiously arrogant creature. You cannot expect that to change right away can you?"

"Right away? How long has it been Jak 13, 14 years now?"

"Alright you two, enough with the reminiscing, let's get on with this." Tofur adored these two four-leggers and they felt the same way about him. Whistler and Taytay both joined in the admiration circle. Whistler was the fastest, Taytay the smartest, at least that's what they said. It was actually the exact opposite of that. It didn't matter to most observers and certainly not to them. "Taytay, would you mind too terribly if I sent you to locate your cousin?"

"Tofur, I would be glad to. What about the little Pigeon?"

"I assume that decision would be up to him. He is welcome to stay with us. I'd like to chat with him a bit if it is fine by him. What do you say, Tine? You riding or flying?" Tofur was hoping the Dove would travel with himself, Jak and Belle.

"I'll stay with you, thank you."

"Fine. Taytay, we will be back on the road in a quarter click. You will find us quickly I presume?"

"That will not be a problem, master."

"Then be off."

As Taytay was disappearing through the trees, Tine shouted out, "Once again, I am not a blooming Pigeon!"

***

Rhiannon ran a course carefully planned in advance for this exact time. Why she was running it now was only due to one thing; that was the fiery temper that this beautiful red-headed princess could not control. The timing of the plans was sketchy at best. The strong white Horse, guardian of Evaliene, wondered just how bad things could get from this point on. She had only one objective on her mind at the moment and that was to run to the rendezvous point where, hopefully, her aides would meet up with her. Leaving Broanick behind was not what she had in mind either. His role had taken a terrible turn after the Rider forced him into the Visitor's service.

***

The hero of the four-leggers of their area, Broanick caused a stir wherever he traveled. A more handsome Horse had never been seen since his birth. Capable of speed known only too much smaller four-leggers, he could race the wind and win on most occasions. His heart for others was too big to break. He captured Rhiannon from the first day they met. An arranged pairing is how the two-leggers described it. Rhiannon called it fate. She missed her hero. She was too strong to be heart-broken, but she would miss him deeply until they were reunited. He had warned the Horses and small four-leggers on many occasions that the Rider may be pushing Evaliene too hard. They could only hope that he did not upset her too much or she could unleash a power on him that he would not survive. A dispatching of the Rider too soon could spell disaster for the Cause. Ever since the Rider first fitted him with that ridiculously heavy battle attire, Broanick had learned much of the Rider's plan, but the Rider never gave away who was really in charge. The Rider was a mentally weak two-legger that could have never master-minded the plans that were being carried out around this world.

The frequent trips the Rider made over the mountains were long, hard journeys. Immediately after arriving at a destination, the Rider would dismount, converse quickly with a cloaked specter, re-mount, dig his spurs deep into Broanick's side, rip the bridle bit almost clear of its fastenings and slap muscled, sweaty shoulders repeatedly with the sharpened, metal tips of the reins. Each time the black Horse would burst forward with incredible speed that very nearly threw the Rider off and down the mountainside. Broanick never got a chance to study the specters, nor did he let anger get the best of him. If the anger had risen much higher in the Horse on any of those days, the Rider would now lie motionless at the bottom of a forgotten, rocky landscape; thusly the mastermind of these plans would have one less henchmen. Broanick willed himself to the Rider's purpose although it absolutely sickened him.

***

Rhiannon continued a prolonged, full-speed gallop. Running as fast as she could was not her mission. Her mission was to run faster than she possibly could and run much farther than she ever had before giving in to exhaustion. Evaliene remained slumped over her guardian's graceful neck with both hands tightly clutching the hand carved saddle horn. The pain from the accidental bash from the door was her own fault. Had she not lost her temper and un-wrapped the heirloom, the Rider's black Horse would have never crashed through the door in the first place. Yes, it was her fault and the pain was staggering. She did not loosen her grip on the saddle horn for the entire ride that she remembered. With her feet secured in her stirrups, she drifted in and out of a pain induced sleep. She tried to speak to her guardian on several occasions only to be drowned out by the wind rushing by as Rhiannon kept to her full gallop, kept by her mission.

***

The black Horse kicked wildly at the two-leggers behind him. Wedged in the door he could not distinguish between good two-legger and bad. He was positive that his hooves had made contact with smaller breathing bodies because of the many crunching sounds coming from behind him in tandem with loud gasps and cries of pain. He only hoped that the unwelcome visitors were the only two-leggers on the receiving end of those vicious blows. He managed to stuff himself completely through what was left of the door frame. The remnants thereof came crashing down behind him. He immediately turned to burst back through the door when a tall muscular man with a strong jaw, black hair and bright dark eyes holding a very large weapon of some kind stepped in the doorway to block his path. This legger was not a Visitor. This legger was not a local either, he was a Protector of some high rank and he did not seem pleased at all with the actions of the black Horse or the condition of Evaliene's dwelling.

"Hold it right there you beast!" The legger demanded. “I know you can understand me, but I can’t understand you. You need to find some way to be tellin’ me all you know about the lovely lady that used to be here.” The Protector cocked his head to the side, his eyes demanded answers...fast.

This was not going as planned. It was obvious to Broanick that this Protector was not a Talker. Of course he wasn't a Talker. He was a Protector. These folk came from completely different lineages. Loyal to the death they say. The Horse looked about the room for something to communicate with. "Oh this is going to be difficult," he said out loud.

All the Protector heard was a few neighs and a short whinny. He stomped heavily to the rear of the dwelling. Broanick turned his large head to the legger and did his best to motion him to the window. The legger picked up on the gesture and quickly made his way to the Horse's side. Broanick repeatedly stretched his nose out the window huffing and neighing continuously. Actually, he was saying, "She is safe with her Guardian. She has started on the next step of the journey." It would have made for a very humorous sight had the situation been completely different.

Miraculously, the Protector asked, "Can you take me to her?"

Broanick couldn't believe the good fortune. He adamantly nodded his head up and down. "Yes I can take you!" He began pulling at what was left of the heavy armor he was wearing, fortunately most of it was pulled off by the dismantling of the door jamb. "Get this costume off of me!"

The legger understood. He quickly began unbuckling buckles and untying straps to free the Horse of his shackling. "Do you know where she is goin'? I have to make contact with her quickly."

Broanick could only shake his head. "Do you not understand that I cannot answer your questions!?" To the Protector, more neighs and whinnies.

The last piece of the heavy, armored costume fell to the floor. The legger snatched up the reins before he led Broanick out the door. He casually jumped onto the Horse's back like he was jumping a short fence then settled into the saddle. The saddle was a little snug for the new rider but it would have to suffice. He called two of his men over to Broanick's side. "Find every Visitor. Do not let any escape. Send the wingers after them if you must. Have the locals keep watch over them. They have as much at stake as we do. I'm sure they can deal with them in a decent manner. If the Visitors fight, dispatch them. I do not want one of those filthy leggers leaving this township breathing, is that understood? Imprison those who don't fight and the wounded. Do not give them any special care. Treat their wounds and leave their healing to time. I am going to the Princess. I will return, brothers."

The older of the two spoke, "As you say Sean. What of the Rider? How do we treat him?"

"Yes Kelly, I almost forgot about that one."

"Really?"

"No! Of course not! Watch him closely. He won't remember too much of that going on now. For now, let him squirm in his pain. Let him think all is as close to normal as it can be after losing your dignity as he did. When the time is right, I want the two of you to take him to the special little room we built beneath the blacksmith's shop. When or if he wakes up, in the end, make sure he goes back to sleep. Follow him to his home. If the word is given, capture him there. We need to question him for information and I want to do that personally. Do not let him escape or enjoy his stay. I want him broken when I return. If he is worse for the wear...so be it. Give me your bag, Paddy. Are there provisions in it?"

"Yes little brother. There are provisions for a few days. We will take care here. It will be as you say."

"Fine, this four-legger and I are off." Sean grabbed the strap of the bag and tossed it over his back. "If he takes me to the wrong place, I promise you I will be back even if he won't!"

That last comment ignited an explosion deep inside Broanick. His nostrils flared, foamy saliva spurted from around the bit in his mouth. The Horse excitedly bounced around on his front hooves. "This is going to be fun!" he snorted. Before Sean ever tapped the first boot heel to the black Horse's flanks, Broanick reared up while Sean smiled. He expertly leaned far into the Horse's thick mane for balance. Once the powerful front legs touched the ground, the Horse and Protector were violently propelled forward by the massive, muscular hind quarters of the four-legger. Yes, this was going to be fun.

***

The absolutely flawless white mare raced through the country-side with her charge holding on with a weakening grip. Rhiannon had paid a dear price for this mission as they had called it. It took her away from her mate, she was told to avoid him completely and talk only of him in hateful terms. She was requested to act as she loathed the very pebbles under his gait wherever it may take him. This was difficult for her. They were born to be a pair. He fared no better with his role. He was forced to be the Rider's steed. The original Horse chosen for the Rider was as despicable as the Rider. The four-leggers of the land could not imagine his beginnings. During one failed attempt to dispatch the Rider before he and his kind took over the town, the nasty steed was killed leaving the Rider angrier, more adamantly evil to all of those creatures around him.

The expected accident occurred as the despised pair returned from a scouting attempt earlier in the year. Word spread the Rider or something was coming to hunt down the Princess. How the information of her whereabouts got to his leaders is not known. As predicted, nearing night fall the pair came thundering down a steep trail out of the mountains. A cleverly devised and concealed rock wall, of the Protectors design, fully blocked the path diverting anything and everything coming down the path directly off the mountain side. Cruel? Probably. No, it was absolutely cruel. It was meant to dispatch the Rider and his steed. The Protectors of the Princess were not a group to take any threat to her lightly. They had dispatched lesser threats than this. They did what they had to do.

That night the Rider was tired, his Horse exhausted. The Rider beat the flanks of the Horse pushing him. He pushed too hard. Coming down the path at the speed which they were traveling, the Horse could not stop, for it was hard to slow for an obstacle not seen. The pair barreled into the rock wall. The Horse was fatally broken on impact. The Rider was tossed over the wall to miraculously land in a pile of brush left after the concealment of the wall was finished. No one even tried to explain this fate. He laid there without thinking the rest of the night. The impact into the wall broke the steed's neck. The subsequent rebound sent the steed off the mountain. It was his last journey. The Rider awoke the next morning in a furious rage.

Three Protectors watched the entire event as it unfolded. They were none too happy with the outcome. Had the Rider been on his Horse when it fell over the edge of the mountain then the Protectors would have had a successful plan, as it stood now the Rider was still alive and still very capable of wreaking more havoc in their adopted town, if he made it to town. Those assigned to the project silently watched the Rider all night. Was it too much too ask for him to not awake at day break? They had time now to throw the man off the mountain's edge, but maybe that was not the way things were meant to be. A single sentinel left the others to take the unfortunate news back to the Captain. He was sure there would be some finger pointing and was man enough to take it. He stayed away from the main path. He did not want to deal with any of the Visitors, should they come searching for the Rider. The Protectors would deal with the entire lot of them when the proper time came.

***

"What is going on with my blasted head?" the man dressed in all shades and types of dark grey clothing asked himself. "And where is my mount?" He painfully raised his head to take a look at his unfamiliar and uncomfortable surroundings. His head was pounding, his eyes blurry, and his brain barely functioning. Battered and bruised by his impact with the ground, his exposed face and neck showed bloody signs of a battle he was fortunate to have survived. The sizable pile of branches had cushioned his landing enough to let him live another day, but they had taken a toll on the tender flesh. Gouges and slices wove an oozing, crimson webbing from his hairline to the stiff collar of his riding jacket. He felt a thudding pain in his back that ran from behind his legs all the way to the top of his head. His lungs, pounded from behind by his landing, were hardly able to retrieve a breath of any kind. "What happened to me?" he asked himself.

The Rider managed to get to his feet, spurred on by a morning shot of adrenaline racing through his entire body. Though wracked with pain, he was so irate with his current situation that nothing would stop him now from taking his frustrations out on the town folk. Every muscle in his body was begging for mercy but on he went. He cursed loudly as he made his way down the path onto the flat ground before the town. His shrieking and loud cursings were noticed by his watchman on the flats. The watchman raced to his side, afraid for his own life but more afraid for a sentence dealt on him had he not come to the Rider's aid.

The Rider milked energy from his anger. After attempting to walk for what seemed to him to be a complete day, an able-bodied thief finally caught up to him and offered him aid.

"Get off your pitiful mount," he spat. No greeting, no thank you for meeting me, no nothing. "Give me your reins and find your own miserable way back to town. You better be sure to make your way there quickly because I'm about to call a meeting of you worthless beings. If you are not there when I start the meeting you will have a painful and short remainder of your life! Help me on this nag." The Rider was not used to unsightly steeds, if this particular ride could even be called a steed.

The stunned accomplice desperately tried to comfort the Rider as he helped him onto the worn-out saddle. "Be easy with her, Sir, she is old. I have no idea if she will make it back to town if you don't go easy with her."

"Do not dare try to tell me my business, you blithering fool! I will ride this creature till she dies under me if I see fit. I may ride her hard enough to leave her gasping for her last breath at the edge of the town. I don't care if you ever saddle her up again. Right now my only concern is me! This poor excuse for an animal may well be the next problem of mine. You should well know how I deal with problems! Get on your way." He kicked the small Horse in the side, nearly killing it on the spot or so he thought.

The Horse was small in stature, sure, but a poor excuse for an animal? That statement was untrue. The Morgan wanted badly to throw its rider, stomp on the tiny battered head and drag the thing all the way back to town. Oh, this was not going well. What had she been told? "Do whatever you have to do to get to our version of the end." What did that mean anyway?

"If this two-legger kicks me one more time, his dispatching will come at the bottom of my hooves." Acting cowed, the wise, speckled Morgan Horse began the trip back to town. The way in which the Rider survived the accident was going to have to be explained and she was going to have a seat close by the narrator to hear it all if that was possible.

The Rider tried to spur the animal on. He quickly realized that the sharp spurs he normally wore were no longer attached to his boots. Instead, he slapped the reins over and over against the Morgan's neck as hard as possible. This tactic did nothing to amuse or hasten the Horse. It did, however, make her very irritable. "My skies, what is this two-legger's problem?" she asked herself. "I will hurry but it is for the sake of the end, not out of my concern for his wants."

Satisfied with the creature's speedy gait, the Rider withheld beating her with the reins. He assumed he had made his point to the dumb animal. "I do hope you can keep up this pace, you miserable little pony. If you don't, I will gladly do away with you myself when we arrive." Of course the Rider had no idea that the miserable little pony understood his every word.

"Well that went better than I expected," the Protector or able-bodied thief said out loud as he watched from a short distance away. "I hope one particular Visitor doesn't wake up until long after this unscheduled meeting takes place, if so, explanations may be hard to come by." As the Morgan and her mount headed back, the Protector added one last thought. "And Rider, I hope my little Horse can put up with your callousness long enough to get you to town. If not, I may be loading you into a pyre wagon."

***

The small Horse was making very good time. It seemed senseless to the Rider to use the reins again to whip the animal. It was doubtful any more speed could be forced out of the creature. During the ride, he had time to collect his thoughts. He was determined to rethink the entire previous night again and again and again. What had happened? The trek back from the mountain after he had witnessed the return of those mangy animals and the lone man had been uneventful. He had not needed to force the hand of his captive. Everything had developed in plain sight. It was there near the end of the final trail down the mountain when everything went black. The dark night, the steep trail, the great speed which his mount was able to maintain down the steep path...that was it! It was coming back to him. Where had the wall come from? Why did they hit it dead on? How did he survive? Where was his steed? Where were his belongings? Where was the prisoner? He jerked the Morgan to a violent halt. She jerked her neck back, pulling the reins out of his hand. She reared. He held on.

"The bag!" he screamed. He was irate. He was insane with rage. It wasn't this Horse's fault; still, he had to take his anger out on something. She was the only living thing around him. He never enjoyed raging against objects that could not feel pain. This Horse lived, breathed and bled. Beating this poor creature senseless might satisfy his hostility. With savage intensity, he began pummeling the Horse's thick neck with the reins. He was disappointed that the reins lacked the sharp, heavy pieces of metal that he always fitted on the loose strap ends. He was further enraged by his missing spurs. No matter how hard he kicked the sides of this beast, he could not bring blood with the smooth heels of his riding boots. He kicked the Horse's flanks to no end. He slapped the reins on the neck over and over again. He grabbed clumps of coarse mane hair and jerked them repeatedly to no avail. He screamed curses at the creature's lineage while ramming a fist into its saucer-like jaws.

The sturdy little Horse stopped abruptly again, but not because the Rider wished it so. The Horse had had enough. This was the end of the road for the Rider. With a wild streak second to none, the Morgan reared up so high that she almost toppled over. As the Rider leaned forward to counteract the vertical positioning of his body in the saddle, the angry Horse, bent on inflicting serious damage, slung her head backward into the Rider's head as it came forward. With a crushing sound, the two-legger's head was bashed by the total strength contained within the Horse's powerful neck. The rider was immediately unconscious. He fell from the saddle and landed with a thud on the hard ground. The Horse spun around. She reared again bringing her hooves down, aimed directly at the Rider's head and chest. At the last minute she adjusted her body allowing only one hoof to land on the downed two-legger. That hoof crushed the Rider's favored arm at the elbow, maiming him for the rest of his miserable life. Blowing hot, violent breaths toward her smaller opponent, she flipped him over like a small doll with another swift kick of her front leg.

The Rider rolled over onto his broken arm. The stabbing pain brought him back to his senses. He yelled out in pain as the Horse reared again for the final blow. But at the last minute, something inside her begged her to stop. She did. She turned and ran for the mountains as fast as her short legs could carry her. Remorse consumed her. She felt that she had failed her mission. Little did she know that she would not have survived the Rider's show of hatred had she carried him all the way back to the village. He had planned to dispatch her as soon as he had climbed onto her back. She lived to fight another day. The Rider had escaped death also, but he would bear the painful scars of this day until his departure from the living. In the minds of most creatures of good heart, that day could not come soon enough.

The Rider groaned in agony. The damaged arm splayed unnaturally at his side. His mouth and eyes were filled with the gritty dirt from the road. His chest hurt badly, leaving him unable to take breaths deep enough to expel the grime from his throat. His thick riding glove on his good arm only managed to rub the grit further into his eyes causing more pain. Finding no strength to stand, he rolled over on his stomach to keep the sun from burning his face to a crisp. He weakly searched beside him for the soft shoulder of the road. Spying it not very far to his left, he painfully managed to crawl to it with one good arm and two very battered legs. He laid his face down in a soft spot of thick grass and seethed. "Revenge, I will have my revenge." Pain trumped anger. He slept lightly, haunted by nightmares to come.

***

She glimpsed freedom for the blink of an eye. How much longer could this last? This filthy bag was now her home. From the instant she was snatched, the Rider imprisoned her within it. A heavy cord wrapped tightly around both of her feet allowed for no movement outside of the bag. With both feet bound inside the bag, it was misery, claustrophobic hysteria. Inside the lightless bag, day-round after day-round on end, she was suffering from dementia on every degree. The Rider was not a Talker. Who was questioning her? The voice was familiar. It was feminine, but weak, so very weak, barely distinguishable as a Talker's voice at all. Was the Talker disguising her voice? Why did it sound so pathetic? Why was she never allowed to see the Talker? She was always trapped in the bag while the Talker spoke from across the room, or at least that is how it sounded. The bag must be thick. That would cause the voice to sound so masked. The Rider had let her out of the bag on rare occasions, but even this had ceased recently. She was sure it had something to do with her relentless attempts to maul him. She had left her marks on him more than once. What was the reason for the preposterously tiny chains he had woven into a shirt? Her razor sharp talons had torn through that flimsy adornment with ease. The questions were ridiculous in their lack of consistency. She heard the Rider demand a question be asked of her and once she answered the question, the Talker gave a completely different answer to the Rider. Who was the Talker protecting? Enough of this, she was going to escape soon or exhaust her last breath trying. Even if they dispatched her, what would that matter anymore? In this bag, her life was over. What caused the ruckus that almost allowed her to escape? Was it an accident? Did the Rider escape? Why had she not heard his vile voice since then? Who has her now? Questions, too many questions. She had to get out. She had to get back to her life.

6

Jahnise sat at Oliviia's side as she cried the way any young lady would cry over the tragic loss of her parents. Her body heaved as she cried torrents of tears. The knowledge that the evolving situation was dire led to even more uncontrollable sobs, as Bongi and Stewig moved in closer to comfort her. Occasionally, she would make eye contact with one of them just long enough to send her back into loud, mournful wails. Oliviia was emotionally and physically spent. There was nothing any of the onlookers could do but try to console her.

"Oliviia, we need to get you out of here. Will you let Stewig take you back to the Keeper's dwelling? Jahnise and I will escort your parents back for you. I know you are hurting, dear, but your father was trying to tell us all something and we will need you at your best to help us figure that out."

A frail, shaken voice answered as best it could. "Yes Bongi, I, I...I just feel so guilty. It was my fault. It was all my fault. I should have sealed this crack like I was told. I just didn't want to be by myself. I made them come with me, all of them. Now...now it's just me. I am all by myself because of myself. Bongi, do you understand?"

Bongi shifted his weight slightly, "No, Oliviia, I don't."

Jahnise still held her tight in his arms. His grip on her had never wavered through the sobbing. "Oliviia, it's time for you to go. Let me help you up. You have cried enough. We must get you to a different place. Please let Stewig take you from here." Slowly and carefully, Jahnise raised the shaken young lady to her feet.

She gripped his side tightly as her strength returned. "I hear what both of you are saying. I can go with Stewig now, but I will need my time to grieve at some point. You will allow me that, won't you? When the time is right?"

"Of course we will Oliviia. You must never think otherwise." Bongi was very concerned with her mental well-being, but now there were other, more important things to take care of and she was all they had left of the Mecanelly clan.

Oliviia took a final look at her parents, straightened her lovely frame, wiped the remaining tears from her eyes and walked up to Stewig. “Sir, do you mind giving me a ride?”

Stewig stood at attention. “I would call it an honor, Livvy.”

Jahnise held her steady as she climbed on the back of the White Rhinoceros. “Stewig, take her to the Keeper’s dwelling. Stay with her should she need anything.”

“My pleasure, King.” He turned and they were off.

“That is one strong young lady there, King,” Bongi whispered as Oliviia rode Stewig down the long tunnel, his three-toed feet marking their travels with solid clumps echoing between the rock walls.

“I will agree with you whole-heartedly, Bongi. Now, we must get these two to their resting place. First, I must ask you, is there anything odd about the way they are positioned?”

“I don’t see what you may be implying, King. Should I see something?”

“No, you shouldn’t. But, you knew these two better than I did. If they were trying to tell us anything, I would hate to destroy any symbolism by moving them too quickly. Mr. Ian was adamantly pointing to the fifth letter of this book’s title when he passed. That, I must think, is significant, is it not?”

“What book is that, King?”

“Bongi, it seems to be a journal of some kind. I can’t see it that well in here, but the title reads ‘Mysteries Encounters’? Why would that be a title? It makes me very curious.”

“That even sounds odd to me. Ian was quite the eccentric legger. At which letter was he pointing?”

“The fifth letter, M, y, s, t, e…yes, he was definitely pointing to the e.”

“This gets even more interesting. Do you think it has to do with who or what pried their way in here?”

Jahnise rubbed his chin, “I am not sure my Okapi friend. I do not know enough about this place to make any judgment of any kind. This is a question for Hugoth. Tell me, Bongi, should we transport Ian and his wife now, or shall we wait until a place is prepared to receive them?”

“The latter question I will answer first, King, the reason being odd indeed for our land.”

“Why do you say that?”

"In Nuorg, no creature has to die, King. Our river runs with water that can restore their condition."

"You mean it can give life to those who have passed?"

"Yes, I mean exactly that. Why did Ian or Colleen not use it? There is a water sac on his belt and on her bag. This is a question even Hugoth will not have the answer for."

"That poses an interesting scenario indeed, Bongi."

***

Perrie flew to Madaliene's shoulder. "Princess, I saw those two-leggers. I know they were here. I can't see them now, no matter how far away I look. Where are they?"

"I know, Perrie, we all saw them. My thinking is that they were never here at all. Maybe we imagined seeing them to validate our being here. Maybe the ax thingy made a mistake."

"I guess maybe it did or could have."

Lightning handed a piece of parchment to Madaliene. It had scribblings on both sides. "Does this shed any light on our predicament, Princess?"

"Where did you find this, Lightning?"

"It was lying over near where the old two-legger was sitting or where we think he was sitting."

"Really? This is well-written in tiny script. I should be able to read it." Madaliene dropped to the ground where she stood. She sat cross-legged with the parchment laid across her ankles, her elbows on her knees. "I can read this well enough, but none of this can be true. There is no way..."

"Princess, what is so impossible?" Perrie still perched on Madaliene's shoulder, trying to read the parchment for herself.

"Hemoth, Lightning, both of you come closer please. I want to read this to you all."

Lightning walked up behind her, Hemoth stood to her front. "Go ahead, Madaliene. What does it say?"

I can only guess bad luck finds us in this position. We have been wandering for days on end to retell the story of what has befallen us. There are 23 of us left now, mainly children and a few of us too old to do away with. The Talker is gone, his son distraught as one might imagine. I wish we had all been spared of this drudgery. They came on us in the night like cowards, completely dressed in black with cloaks and hoods to match. They immediately began taking the lives of the healthy, strong ones and called out for any Talkers to show themselves. Well, Karl's father let it be known that he was the only Talker remaining among us. He was captured instantly and beaten, for reasons unknown. The remaining 23 of us were passed over for various reasons, I assume. I never saw one face of our attackers. Those dark hoods covered the faces of every last one. The eyes were hidden as well. I was helpless to fight them off. Oh, to be 50 years younger! I am writing the ramblings of an old man and I believe I hear someone coming again.

I must write quickly, they have returned and they are sparing no one this time. I am the last of five and we will not last long. If you find this letter, you are reading the last words written by me, Zachary Clermoneau on le quinze mars, 1…. A tip of my hat to my mother country. This wi…

"What date did he say, Princess?" Perrie was on the edge of her perch.

"He wrote the date in French, Perrie. The group must have been from that area, or at least he was. I translate that to be March 15th, but the year? The year is blurred. Something made the ink smear. Part of the last line has been wiped away. The style of handwriting seems to be very old, ancient really. This must be a trick of some kind. How did they leave and the letter stay? How old can this letter be? Hemoth, answers please!"

"I am sorry, Princess. I have no light to shed on this at all. It is way over my head. Four-leggers don't keep up with dates like you two-leggers. When are we now? Were they even here?"

"Now that you mention it, Hemoth, I don't know when we are. We could be any 'when', as you say. Lightning, does that ax thingy of yours take us into different times? I mean is this the same year we left in Nuorg?"

"Princess, to be honest, I have no idea."

"Perrie, do the wingers keep up with time where you are from?"

"Yes we do, Madaliene, but I am not sure it is kept the same way. We need to find you another two-legger to ask. What year was it in your mountain?"

"I was last in the mountain during the year of our Lord...wait a minute, I have no recollection of the year at all! It's as if something erased it from my memory!"

Perrie nodded, "So you are saying that those leggers we just fed, but really didn't feed, were here, where we are, over...what? Fifty years ago?"

Madaliene shook her head, "I don't know. From the writing style it could have easily been 100 years ago."

Lightning shook cobwebs from his head, "Wait a click here. You are trying to tell me that those two-leggers that were sitting right here," he pointed at the ground, "and are now gone," he waved his paw, "were actually here 100 years ago, whatever that is? No, I'm sorry, that sounds preposterous. Even if it was 100 day-rounds ago, I would still think that a ridiculous statement. They were right here!"

Perrie looked into the distance. "Princess, what if the time changes only from Nuorg? That means that every time we use Lightning's ax, we must pass through Nuorg first in order to return to our proper time. Is that correct as you see it?"

"I have no idea, Perrie. That sounds very impossible to me. But, the idea of Nuorg existing sounds pretty impossible as well and we know it does. Where is all of this going? Hemoth?"

The Grizzly Bear started walking around in circles, ideas bouncing around inside his large skull. "You will get no answer from me on this one, Princess. I once knew someone who could answer this for us. I haven't seen him since I left his side to become a Bear again."

"Hemoth, who are you talking about?" Madaliene's attention piqued.

"I am talking about the only father I knew, Princess. Bellon, the Fallow Stag."

"Fallow?" Lightning asked, "I have never heard of a Fallow before."

"Actually, Lightning, Bellon and my second family were Fallow Deer."

"I have never heard you speak of them before, Hemoth. Why haven't you told me about this?" Madaliene was short of demanding an answer.

"If I had to guess, Princess, it would be because I miss them so much. I knew them longer than I knew Hugoth. Bellon and his mate took me in. They raised me after Hugoth and I got separated. They were part of a magnificent herd. They would know, but Bellon lost his life protecting his love one day while I was out playing with the fawns. I should have been there to save him. I wasn't and it bothers me to this day. He and the other elders were very wise."

"Hemoth, you can't be saddened by something that happened so long ago. You have had time for that wound to heal. More on that later, let's get back to the here and now, whenever this is." Perrie was raised in a completely different way than either of the others, different values, different life lessons. She was able to shut herself off emotionally from past horrors or problems. She focused on the present and the future. She was determined to know if they were currently in one or the other.

"Why are these things happening?" Madaliene asked the question with no intention of getting a real answer. She folded the parchment up and stuck it in the bag with everything else. Maybe, at some point, Frederick could make some sense out of it. "Lightning, bring your ax thingy over here. We are leaving this place."

Lightning hurried to her side. "Yes, Princess. Everyone get close now." He once again held the ax-pike in front of him and asked a variation of the now familiar question, "Take us where we need to be."

Without pomp or circumstance, the four creatures were once again whisked away by the workings of the ax-pike. When they were able to get their bearings, they were both shocked and disappointed.

7

The Morgan carefully slowed her gait after faking her fear solely for the Rider's enjoyment. She hammed it up as she ran wildly off toward the mountain in no particular direction to make her fear of him seem more believable. If it had been up to her, she would have stomped him until he could breathe no more, then she would have stood over him to watch him take in his last breath. This Horse had no love lost on the Rider and his gang of thieves. She couldn't call them Visitors as they requested because she knew they were not. They were sadistic and vile two-leggers whose only true goal was to destroy everything in their way to wherever they were going. She had a good idea where that was going to be, but she did not use that type of language. When she felt clear of the Rider's deadly gaze, she accelerated to a comfortable gait that should take her near the same end of the mountain trail where she and her accomplice had been told to pick up the Rider. She heard a loud long whistle in the crisp air followed by two shorter ones. That was her cue. Her two-legger had seen her. She ran quickly to where he was scouting the trail for stragglers. She found him beneath a large conifer tree. "I want you to know that I almost killed that fool. If his boots had spurs, he would be dead right now. That's all I'm saying."

"That is quite understandable, Justine. Now let me saddle up and let's be on our way. We have nothing else here to do." After her rider saddled up, they were off with no regrets.

***

The thundering sound violently echoed in the fallen Rider's head. A massive knot on the back of his head pulsed in pain with every beat of his joyless heart. His mangled arm was not responding to any command from his brain. He rolled on to his back, using his left arm he grabbed his injured arm and held it above his chest. The Rider slightly lifted his head to view the disaster that was once his right arm.

"Someone will pay for this. Maybe everyone that ever crosses my path again will pay for this. I will find the owner of that Horse, and if I don't, I'll find someone that reminds me of him. Yes, there will be payback of my own choosing whenever and wherever I want to get it." He laid his head back on the ground, as a piercing pain shot through it. "Ahhhh! Everyone will pay for this. Everyone!" He rolled his body to the left and again laid his head down. The pain on the side wasn't quite as bad as the pain at the back of his head.

The thundering roar grew louder as a pack of Visitors headed toward the Rider. He shook with angry, erratic convulsions as he realized what was happening. His men were soon to arrive to see their leader in a weakened state. This was exactly what had happened to the original leader of the Visitors a few months earlier. He had been thrown from his Horse in much the same manner as the Rider. The fall resulted in a severe head wound that destroyed most of his thought process. He had also sustained several deep cuts and broken bones. One moonless night on another mountain trail, the Rider stopped to talk over scouting locations with the original leader. After helping him off his Horse, the Rider guided him over to the edge of the mountain. Word spread quickly through the Visitors that the original leader had slipped on a wet piece of bark and plummeted off the mountain side. Oddly enough, there was no wet bark at the edge of the mountain. There was nothing but bone-dry, solid rock. The closest tree branch was 30 steps away. The Rider was never happier to be the leader of a legion of men – stupid men but his men. In his mind, he was smart enough for them all.

After a valiant effort, he stood waiting for the looming detachment of riders. It wasn't long before they arrived. Before the first one was off his Horse, he was yelling at the top of his lungs. He pointed at the closest man to him, "You, take two men with you. Find what is left of my steed. Retrieve the mount's armor and the bag. Do not return without that bag. If the bag is not moving – that is, if the content of the bag is not breathing, you are doing yourself a disservice by returning. I will personally remove you from the living if that thing, that creature in that bag, is dead or dying! My mount fell from the cliff. What are you waiting for? Go!"

The lead rider asked, "Where do we expect to find your steed? Is he still running?"

"No, of course it's not still running! If it were still running, I'd still be riding it, you fool! Where will you find it? I don't know, don't care! Just find it now!"

Again he pointed at the closest man with the biggest Horse. “You. Off your mount."

"Excuse me?" He asked.

"Give me your mount."

"Nah, I ain't gonna do it, sir. Who do you think you are?"

He looked at the man with blurry eyes, "You heard me. Off the mount!"

"Sorry, sir, it ain't gonna happen." He walked his Horse right up the Rider and looked down at him. He leaned down to the Rider's face and repeated himself, "It ain't gonna happen, sir."

The Rider was being threatened because of his weak condition. This man was not planning on taking over leadership, but he was determined not to give up his Horse to anyone. The Rider sneered into the man's face. He thrust his good left arm at the man's throat, grabbed him and threw him to the ground where he kicked him for good measure. "Now, I'll have your mount. Tie this man up. I know exactly what I want to do with him."

The defiant man did not look like the owner of the puny Horse that nearly killed the Rider, but he did have a Horse and it was the same color. That was enough justification. He took hold of the saddle horn with his left hand. With an enormous amount of adrenalin pumping through him he tossed his pain wracked body into the saddle. He stared into the eyes of every man left in a saddle, "Anymore questions, doubts, mutinies? Well isn't this nice, back to camp!" He kicked his new mount with a vengeance meant for the puny Horse and the defiant rider. He snickered.

***

At the bottom of the cliff that fell treacherously from the side of the mountain, the despised black Horse lay lifeless and broken. The heavy body armor had done little to protect the animal from the violent throes against the rocky outcroppings along the fall. The animal had never felt them. However, amid all of the pieces of dark grey and black plating placed on the animal by the Rider to protect his mount during travel or skirmishes, there was slight movement. The bag! The bag contained movement of some kind. The bag had been lashed to the saddle horn for the past several months every time the Rider saddled up. There was either a treasured or despised article in the bag and it was still moving. Miraculously, it was still moving. A sharp rock had gashed the thick, heavy bag during the tumble just enough to allow a slight glimmer of hope for the occupant. She wanted out. She desperately wanted out. She was barely breathing; but the light seeping through the rip in the bag was, just maybe, enough of a stimulus to pull her through. She struggled to maneuver an eye close enough to the opening to see daylight again. Instead, she heard loud, clumsy footfalls as the recovery team came near. Sent after the Rider's gear and the bag, the members of the team were relieved to find the lifeless mount in the middle of the scattered pieces of what, the Rider thought, was necessary adornment for any steed he rode. Within their ranks, the Visitors secretly had their doubts as to the importance of such regalia, but since the leader demanded it, the decoration was accepted. Each member of the team was thrilled with the discovery of the bag and, if possible, even more elated to see that the bag still contained movement, albeit weak movement.

"I've got it," one shouted, quickly grabbing the bag. "Clean up this mess. Bring as much of this ridiculous mount armor back with you as you can. I have what matters most. I must get this back." He surveyed the rough side of the mountain. The sharp rocks, jagged trees and huge boulders could not have been kind to the bag's occupant, but that really did not matter much to him. What was important was that inside the bag, the prisoner still had life, fleeting though it may be. From studying the path of the fall, even he could surmise the amount of damage inflicted on the creature. "It may not be with us much longer and we need to see if there is anything else it knows." He held the bag up high and shook it for show.

Inside the bag, the dim glimmer of hope was extinguished.

***

As the blood pumped through her veins, ignited by the cold sharp air she breathed, Evaliene could feel the pain ebbing within her mid-section. She forced herself to sit up to enjoy Rhiannon's race into the night's wind. She remembered the days prior to this mess she was currently in when she and Rhiannon would spend every night galloping along newly blazed trails with nowhere else to go and nowhere else to be. Those times would be back after she found a way to rid her town of the hideous Visitors. She leaned in toward Rhiannon's ear. "Rhiannon, do you have any idea where we are heading? Is there a rendezvous spot ahead or are you just running to run?"

"Yes, Princess, there is a rendezvous set up for us ahead. Why?"

"I need to place something in the saddle bag."

"No, I cannot allow you to do that. The diary and the heirloom must stay on your person. If we get split up the heirloom and the diary are of no use to anyone else. I know you must be uncomfortable, but you have to believe me." Rhiannon never broke stride. She was truly amazing.

Evaliene agreed with her, "I trust you, Rhiannon, just tell me what I need to do."

"Please, Princess, just hold on. I will take care of the rest. We must put a great distance between you and the town. The Visitors will come for you."

"I have to admit, I was fooled by your act. The loathing toward Broanick was excellently performed."

"Yes, Princess, thank-you, but please do not talk about him right now. I can't break my concentration. You are my only concern at the moment."

The wind Evaliene was facing was not caused by a natural occurrence; it was completely caused by the speed at which the white Horse was running. Evaliene smiled as she huddled close to the Horse's neck. She made herself as comfortable as possible in the custom saddle that had been handmade just for her and Rhiannon.

***

Broanick ran the same path as Rhiannon. They had gone over it a multitude of times. Each knew it as if they had ridden it every day. Sean had not ridden a Horse with as much determination as the one now beneath the saddle. What was it about this Horse? He was running with a purpose which Sean could not fathom. Tirelessly, Broanick ran. Sean wished he could communicate with the beast, knowing that any attempt at that would be futile. He wasn't a Talker. The brief stab at communication they had back at Evaliene's abode was enough to tell him that. He let loose of the reins and rested in the saddle. This Horse knew what was going on.

Broanick had two scenarios in his mind. The first was to find and secure Evaliene, the second was to find and protect Rhiannon. Hopefully, he would satisfy both at once. The night's darkness was relentless. The journey started before sundown but now they had run well past midnight. The moon was doing no favors relating to navigating, the sliver that was noticeable through the building clouds was as much a nuisance as it was an aide. From a few beats off, the black horse was invisible as he beat the trail into the thickening forest. Sean's heavy cape mostly concealed any light colored clothing beneath it. They appeared, to any casual observer, a swift moving, ghostly shadow, not even a cognizant thought or full apparition. The path did not completely aid Broanick's progress either. Branches and brambles galore took swipes at both Horse and rider. Small rivulets of blood intermingled with sweat from the muscular Horse's flanks and foam from his mouth, forming damp, sticky goo which nearly covered Broanick's fore quarters. The Horse could not think of his unfortunate state of being – his only thought was to reach Rhiannon. Once he rejoined his mate, he could think ahead toward the coming events but not now. His muscles ached, the sides of his belly chaffed from a small piece of bark wedged between him and the saddle, his eyes watered constantly from insects and debris, and yet he galloped on. Sean clung to the reins with pale knuckles, hunched down over Broanick's bulging neck to avoid the same inanimate objects that attacked the Horse continuously. Suddenly a gap in the trees broke around them. They rode on.

Sean could take no more, he yanked the reins, pulling Broanick's head up and around to his shoulder. Broanick violently snorted his displeasure. He struggled begrudgingly to a stop. Sean loosed the reins then immediately dismounted. Falling to his knees, the two-legger gagged loudly and coughed to the ground in an attempt to clear wretched bile from his throat. Broanick stomped around the rider, neighing loudly to raise the man again. After what seemed to Broanick an eternity, Sean slowly regained his composure. He feebly grabbed the reins that dragged on the ground to hoist himself to his feet. Not an avid equestrian, Sean used common sense to check the tack. Fortunately for Broanick, Sean pulled the bark from beneath the saddle's lip. "I suppose that should make you feel a bit better now, shouldn't it? I'm not a horseman there, you black beast, but I tell you, I'm doin' the best I can to stay atop you. I'm a wee bit better now. In all of my 27 years I have never encountered a creature more determined than you. Let me remount and you can be on your way once again." Sean grabbed the saddle horn with both hands. He threw himself up on Broanick's back and held on tight. "Off with you there, Horse."

Broanick took a few haughty steps before accelerating to a full gallop once again. He figured they would make the rendezvous point a little after sun up.

***

Evaliene was exhausted. She had no reason to believe Rhiannon could run another step. She was hopelessly tired. Barely coherent, she whispered in the white Horse's ear, "Rhiannon, how much further must we go? I feel that my side is about to be the death of me."

Rhiannon never missed a beat. She answered, "How dare you even mention pain at a time such as this? I will not hear of it until we arrive at our stopping point! For all that is good, Princess, toughen up."

She was too weak to argue. She would not say another word in complaint or question. She muttered, "Yes, Rhiannon."

"Through this stand of trees, across a shallow river, then our last leg up into the hills. It shouldn't be more than a few hundred clicks or so. Wrap the reins around your waist and the saddle horn. If you fall, you won't hit the ground." Rhiannon said nothing more. As day broke, she increased her speed as she emerged from the trees into the open space before the river.

As she was told, Evaliene secured herself to the saddle with the reins. She laid her head down and wrapped her arms round Rhiannon's neck. For the remainder of the ride, she lapsed in and out of consciousness.

Rhiannon approached the oncoming body of water with single-minded determination. She splashed through mild current, water drenching Evaliene's back as splashes cascaded over her. She stumbled slightly as her hooves flailed to find the bottom as she crossed over a deep pool in middle of the cold, revitalizing liquid. Dirt and dust poured off her rounded sides, her brilliant white coat once again dazzling in the morning sun. She ducked her head completely under the surface as she climbed from the deeper water. Shaking her snow white mane victoriously, her hooves clawed into the grassy bank, pulling her and her cargo free of the river. Up ahead, the end of the trek was thankfully in her sight. She trotted up the hill. Behind a tall rock face, she finally rested. It was up to Broanick to meet her here and protect both she and the princess. The white Horse quivered uncontrollably as the gravity of the situation bore down on her. Too tired to pace, too afraid to make her presence known to the world, she remained hidden, pressed tightly against the back side of the large slab of grey granite. Her companion stayed tied in the saddle, blind to current developments.

***

The pace Broanick kept was borne from love of the beautiful white Horse and the call of atonement for deeds whose days had long since passed. He was of a line directly descended from the cursed Horses that carried the lamented villagers on the deadly rampage all those years ago which decimated the great Wolves of the Great Forest. If there was one thing he was destined to do, it was to amend the ways of his ancestors and their weak-minded brethren. This order of duty would be carried out regardless. Death, despite its best efforts, would not take him before duty was satisfied. If a creature could be called immortal, Broanick was that creature. He had searched for his true calling for years. Not one content with status quo, he pursued false lead after false lead until the night he came face to face with Rhiannon and her young keep resting a few days' travel from the village they would eventually call their own. It was at that moment when destiny's loud peal sounded in his ears. A strange sense of relief pounced upon him when he made eye contact with the young two-legger sitting gracefully astride her flawless white mount. The waist length, fiery red hair flowing down the back of her riding jacket. The bright blue eyes with the stern, determined look peering down on him. This was his reason for being. He studied the young two-legger before he became aware of the white Horse studying him.

"I'm sorry for staring, Ma'am. What mission are you on?"

The young rider did not answer. Her Horse slowly turned to face him as Evaliene laid the reins into her grip. As the pair rotated, their eyes burned holes into Broanick. Whatever these two were up to, Broanick decided, they were as determined as he was to stop at nothing in order to succeed. The white Horse spoke first, "Who might you be and why is our undertaking any concern of yours?"

"I am on a journey to find answers. That is all. There may possibly be hintings of revenge, purgement, justification, righting the wrong and so forth, but primarily, I am searching for answers." Broanick could hardly turn his eyes from the penetrating glare the radiant white Horse aimed his way. Her keep in the saddle stared at him as sternly.

"I suggest you be on your way then, fellow. We have our own agenda to keep and you are not a part of it. Once you are clear of my eyes, we will continue our course. We are not to be followed. Is that clear? Should you be caught trailing us, her Protectors will make quick work of seeing you take your last breath. Is that also clear?" Rhiannon stated each of these rude comments with a take-no-prisoner approach for she knew the Protectors would do just as she warned. She also secretly knew she had no idea where they were.

8

Mariel could ramble without ceasing for long stretches of time. Fortunately for Porcene this was one of those times. She wasn't listening and as long as he rambled she didn't have to keep him out of trouble. Mariel had rambled from the time Whistler left them until now. Porcene's ears perked up as she caught the faint whistling sound emanating from Whistler's tail feathers. What was Mariel speaking about? She didn't seem to care. She was, however, elated that the Falcon was headed back to them so soon. The conversation must have taken place quickly. In her mind, a few extra bodies would not be a bad thing. The sooner the prey could be overwhelmed and captured, the sooner they would have more information to share with her secret-sharers. It seemed all creatures had groups of secret-sharers. She had no problem with this as long as they shared secrets for the good of all. Maybe this new group was a collection of secret-sharers. She could, at least, hope for that. What to do about Mariel's ramblings was another story. He would have to be a brilliant thinker in order to assemble all of the gadgetry he loaded on to her. There were all sorts of pockets and pouches, bags and small boxes, cylinders and gizmos to spare. He had taken some time loading his goodies on her, taking so much time that she had run out of patience with him before he ran out of trinkets. They had left 12 moon times ago after receiving word on their targets. As a favor she had allowed a feisty little winger to join the two of them at an old friend's request. So far the little fellow had done nothing but brag about himself. Porcene could tell he was no braver than Mariel. He used mouth loads of bravado to hide his short comings. Whatever the case, she took a liking to him even if it was for his tentative lack of bravery. He could put on quite a show if needed.

Whistler flew rapidly once he left his group. After a 100 or so pursuit beats, he zeroed in on Porcene and her amiable two-legger. He noticed the draft four-legger turn his way well before he angled for landing. He thought maybe he would have Mariel make an attempt at repairing his feathers. If this operation was to take place covertly, then a preceding announcement did not need to be made on his behalf every time he took wing. "Ah, there they are and I am, as usual, expected." Whistler dove in and gently lit on Porcene's strong back.

"Good to see you back so soon, winger." Porcene remembered names as well as any creature, still on some occasions she would rather just use slang.

"And it's good to see you again as well my fine, large draft creature." If Porcene wanted to use slang, then Whistler thought he might use it as well. "So, I see Mariel is rambling still?"

"Oh my, yes he is. He's nearly driven me crazy. I don't know what your appearance triggered in him, but I tell you, he has not stopped since you left. I am glad to see you back so soon. Mariel." No response. "Mariel." Still no response. "Excuse me, Whistler." Porcene moved in behind the talkative two-legger and not-to-gently nudged him to attention. "Mariel, the Falcon is back. We should listen to him then get moving."

Whistler laughed.

"Why yes, yes of course. Falcon? What Falcon? Oh yes, the winger we caught in my flying trap. Of course. Of course." Mariel turned around glancing at the sky for the winger. "Porcene, where could he be? He should be back by now."

Whistler watched the loony two-legger with amazement. "Is he serious?"

"See what I mean? I am afraid so." Porcene again nudged Mariel. She placed her broadside directly in front of Mariel. "Mariel, down here. Look on my back."

"Oh yes, oh yes. There you are. How are you, sir? Have we met?" Mariel offered his hand to Whistler.

Whistler's eyes could get no bigger. The bottom half of his beak hung open in a stupor. He shook his head.

"Yes, Mariel. Of course you have met. Remember, the trapped winger?" Porcene was concerned. Mariel's mind was getting worse. Was it playing games on him now? She turned her head as far as she could to Whistler. "I am sorry, winger. We have to meet up with your group soon. We have to figure out what is wrong with him. Please help me keep him in check until we meet them. He is beginning to worry me. We don't need that right now!"

"I'll do what I can, Porcene. I promise. I will help you."

"Thank you. Where do we meet?"

"I will hold you two up about four or five leisure beats from here."

"And by that you mean...?"

"I'm sorry. I said four or five leisure beats. That's the distance from here to the meeting spot."

"And that is...how far in four-legger speak?"

"Really? You don't know distances in beats? Peculiar."

"We are from different parts of the world, you know." Porcene had never heard of any distance measurement allocated in beats. "I presume a beat to be a flap of your wings?"

"I thought it was a universal measurement.. It's not? Well I'll tell you but it is a long story."

"Give me the highlights then." Porcene was interested in hearing the complete story, just not right now.

"Okay, there are three distinctly different beats; pursuit, leisure and training. They are measured with Eagle wings, not to be confused with wings of smaller sky-travelers, like Falcon or Hawk or other beats. One pursuit beat is as far as ten ancient oak trees are tall. Are you following this?"

"Yes, so far I have understood what you are saying. So say that an ancient oak tree is approximately 35 spans high or 245 hands high then we will be meeting up with your group about, I don't know, the end of that field there?" Porcene needed to think about this some more.

"Yes, I think that about sums it up." Whistler now had questions of his own.

"I hear you discussing numbers, Porcene. Is it true? Are you discussing numbers? I love numbers. 35 spans equal 245 hands, hmm that means an ancient oak tree is about 143 feet high in two-legger measure. And a pursuit beat must be equal to that as well so if we are to meet them in four or five pursuit beats then we must be on our way since they will be waiting for us in a short measure, well not really short measure, but somewhere in between in 572 feet and 715 feet. My, that is not that far at all. Why, they might as well be right out in the open. Will they be out in the open, I mean your group? If they are out in the open won't everyone see them? Well I guess it's really okay if everyone sees them. They have all seen them already. I don't know if it will be a good idea for two and four-leggers alike to be carrying on conversations with each other. That might be weird to two-leggers that aren't Talkers or two-leggers that don't believe Talkers can talk to four-leggers. My, that's a lot of answers to formulate." Mariel needed help. Porcene and Whistler were hoping the others might offer it.

Porcene reached her big head out to grab hold of his coat tail. If she needed to drag him with them, then she had no problem with that. The three of them set off for the short walk to the end of the nearby field.

At the far corner of the field, Belle sat awaiting Whistler's trio. The sun was setting fast. Her coloring allowed her to blend in with the ragged growth behind her where the others were lying in wait. They had traveled through the trees in case someone was watching for them. The apprehension was not merited. No creature was watching or waiting for them. In this part of the world, no two-legger cared about much of anything. The Terrible Years meant nothing to them. What mattered to these two-leggers was the here and now. The past was the past. Study it and learn from it but it can't be dwelled on. They looked after today and forward to tomorrow, not much past that. She saw them coming. Whistler saw her.

"Porcene, look over there. See the big black and tan Dog? That is my contact. Follow her."

Porcene stepped off the main road, Mariel in tow, and followed Belle as she led them along the tree line to a small opening in the scraggly trees. There Tofur, Jak, Taytay and Tine were expecting them.

Tofur met them on their way in. "That was easy, Belle. You found them fast." He glanced at Mariel. "Hello sir, the name's Tofur Polinetti, what shall I call you?"

Whistler interrupted Tofur, "Uh Tofur, before you get too deep in a conversation with uh, Mariel here, let me warn you. He tends to ramble a bit."

"Thanks for that advice, Whistler." He returned to Mariel. "You sir, your name is Mariel, right?"

Mariel's eyes widened, "You, you are a human? Why, you sure are. I thought I'd be talking to animals for the rest of my days. I am so happy to make your acquaintance. Where are you from? Have you seen my Horse? She is truly a splendid animal. Porcene, where are you? I know I had her a minute ago. Have you seen her? About this tall, no actually much taller, more like this tall." Mariel raised his hands to many different levels without paying much attention to it. "Boy, come check my bags, I have all sorts of gadgets that may interest a young lad like you. Please come have a look. Where is my Horse? Have you seen her? Oh, I guess not. You probably don't know what she looks like. A lovely Belgian draft Horse. A remarkable creature. A coat like soft gold with white socks on her feet, a proportionately correct white blaze running down the middle of her face. Truly majestic she is. Have you seen my gadgets?"

Tofur was flabbergasted. Whistler had not been lying. Mariel did nothing but ramble. On and on and on. "Mister, Mariel, hello! Could you please stop talking for a moment?"

"Oh I'm sorry, was I rambling again? I hate when that happens. It seems to so much of late. I think it started when my Horse ran over my head with her cart. Oh not to worry, it wasn't her fault."

"Please Mariel, stop talking...just for a minute. Let me comprehend what you have said so far. Please, just stand here...no talking."

"Bu.."

"No. No talking. Promise me?"

"I promise, but just in case..."

"Please, Mariel. Stop talking. I will be right back. Here is your Horse. Just relax. I will be right back." Tofur rolled his eyes at Whistler, “Geesh! You weren't kidding. That is unbelievable."

Whistler laughed. "I told you so."

"Whew." Tofur walked over to Jak and Belle. "What do we do now? Do we swap information? We are burning good time here."

"I have never in my life seen another creature as gorgeous as that Horse of his. How do I look? Should I go talk to her? Do you think she will notice me? Look at her! I wish Mariel would take all of those bags and boxes off of her. My, my."

Belle turned up to Jak, "Excuse me?"

Tofur could not help but laugh out loud. "We needed this. We really did."

Belle walked over to Porcene. The Horse was beautiful. There was no debating that. "Porcene, who is the leader of your group?"

"Well I want to say me, but I better not. I would love for Mariel to take over that role, but we have to get his head straightened out. Strangest thing I've ever seen. I guess the one you need to talk to is over there." She nodded toward Tine.

Belle shook her head and winced, "You are kidding right?"

"No, I'm afraid not. Tiny is our leader. He recruited us for this expedition. He seems to know his stuff."

"You have to be kidding. You have to be kidding." Belle said it under her breath again. She looked up at the lovely Horse's head once again, "Really?"

Porcene nodded. "Believe it. But as soon as Mariel comes around, I think he can take over."

"Oh my." Belle walked over to Tine, who was sitting on Jak's back. Porcene followed, pulling Mariel who had his hand stuck down one of the many bags tied to Porcene's harness. Jak became nervous as Porcene approached. His long ears started twitching and his knees, all four of them, nearly buckled.

"Tine, Porcene tells me that you are the leader of their group."

Porcene interrupted, "Tine? His name is Tiny. Who called him Tine?"

"Why, he did." Taytay chimed in. Now he was chuckling too.

"Tiny? Now it all becomes clear." Whistler was laughing so hard his chest was heaving.

"Well, Jak, do you have anything you would like to add?" Belle was now quietly laughing also.

Jak continued to ogle Porcene. His eyes glazed over. He was having serious trouble standing. His face looked like one big swoon. "Noooo. Noooo, I don't."

***

A pair of well-to-do two-leggers should not, as a rule, attract so much attention and they weren't...from the other two-leggers. However, several wingers and four-leggers were recording the pair's every step via the many channels of communication afforded them. With the majority of four-leggers deciding the skills to converse with the two-leggers were too labor-intensive to pass to their offspring, a few pockets of devoted four-leggers continued the practice. There existed in many lands a complete absence of Talkers. In those lands, not only did the animals not talk with the two-leggers, they did not talk with the wingers either. To compound matters, these non-talking four-leggers, to date, had nearly ceased all methods of talking with each other outside of their own kind or species as the two-leggers phrased it. The world was becoming a less than hospitable place to travel freely. The disturbing part to all of the Talkers was that none of the now talkless creatures seemed to care.

"I tell you, Barth, we are being watched. I promise you that draft Horse we passed, remember the one loaded with, I don't know, maybe every possession the owner ever had, that Horse was listening to every word we said."

"Sure she was, Ligon and I was listening to her as well. She was quite a talker, I'd say. Yes, I'm sure she understood every word we said. My word man, you are talking about a Horse, a ridiculously large, draft animal. If she was listening at all, I'm sure she was only interested in hearing if we had a hand full of oats to offer her. Oh, yes you are most definitely the wiser of the two us, absolutely." "You don't have to believe me, but I'm telling you, again, that animal knows something."

"I'll tell you what I'll do. I'll go back, find her, and put a blade through her...will that make you feel better?"

"You know we have no time for that. But yes, it would."

"If that Horse comes chasing after us, then I will do just that. Can we get back to the plan now?"

"Mark my words, Barth, she knows."

***

"Porcene, who are all of these creatures? How long have they been in our company? Where is Tine?" Mariel suddenly noticed the crowd around him. "How will we go about our business if all of these creatures tag along behind us? What are we doing here? Did you see how well my capture net worked? Splendid wasn't it? Have I used it yet?"

Tofur was dumbfounded at Mariel's completely haphazard way of rambling. He stepped nearer to Porcene, "What is Mariel's problem? Has he always been this way? Is he ever quiet?"

"Lad, I'm afraid I've known him no other way. He's been rambling ever since he was hit in the head by my run-away cart. It can drive one mad at times. Tiny said we must bring him against my wishes. He heard he was a very brilliantly minded two-legger." She looked back at him, "But, so far...I just don't see it."

"I see. Does he have any books or papers with him that I might study to diagnose his problem?"

"I'm sure he does. I hope he does. If you can read, be my guest." She swung her head to her right side. "There should be some books on this side. Good luck." She swung her back to the group. She caught Jak's stare and gave him a wink. Jak crumbled to the ground in a heap. She did her best to contain her giddiness.

Belle bore witness to Jak's tumble and grimaced. "Oh my." She turned to the Dove. "Well Tine, looks like we need a plan. What have you got in mind?" Belle was ready to get moving. "If those two-leggers passed us, we need to catch them before they lose us. Wait, Taytay, Whistler."

"Yes, Belle."

"As soon as Tine gives us a description of our prey, go find them. That shouldn't be hard for you two." Belle then turned to Tine, "What do the two-leggers look like? Please describe them to us."

"Very well. They are both average height for two-leggers. Stop, I can't call them two-leggers anymore. Such a dumbed-down term. They are called men. The two men we are after are of normal height, almost as tall as Porcene's shoulders there. One is wearing or was wearing a long black riding coat, no hat. The other is wearing or was wearing a tattered overcoat with a matching hat. Both have dark hair and reek of watered-down mead. Every stop they have made has been to quench their hunger and mainly their thirst in some roadside tavern. If I'm using too many two-legger words, please stop me. You creatures from the back-woods, mountains and what have you are so, so uneducated. There is a new language out there, learn it! One is called Barth, the other Ligon. Porcene has overheard them talking about meeting a rider or one of the rider's men at some junction along the way. On the way to where? I don't know. That is why we cannot fall too far behind."

Belle and the others were slightly put off by the condescending manner in which the tiny Tine spoke to them. "Okay, rather a rude way of addressing us, but you got your point across. Taytay, Whistler... go find them."

"Excuse me, Belle." Tine was not finished yet. "I'm sorry. Taytay can go, but Whistler cannot join him."

"I beg your pardon?" Belle huffed.

"Whistler cannot go. I forbid it."

"You forbid it?" Belle huffed again.

"Yes, you heard me correctly. I forbid it!"

"Why is that?" Whistler asked.

"Because, those "two-leggers" have ears! They can hear you coming. We can't keep our mission secret if they can hear you coming after them."

"Why you little..!" Whistler was angry now.

Mariel stumbled into the verbal jousting. He sidled up next to Whistler. "Aha there it is!" With one quick motion, he ran one hand down Whistler's sleek body and with his other hidden hand yanked a lone malformed feather out of the Falcon's tail. "Tine, I think both Falcons can fly together now."

"Owww!" Whistler hopped up and down. He jumped from his temporary perch on Porcene's baggage and flew off in pain.

Out of concern for his fellow Falcon, Taytay took his defense. "Mariel! What have you done?"

Mariel held up a very deformed feather. "I don't know for sure, but he might want to change his name now." Mariel smiled a triumphant smile. "Who are all of you? Have you seen my capture net? Where is Tine? Porcene, have you met Whistler? Are we camping here? Why are we camping? Should we not be chasing our quarry?"

Most of the creatures were still marveling at Mariel's quick movements and subsequent plucking of Whistler's tail. "I can't believe you did that." Taytay felt co-violated. "Can't believe it!"

Belle growled fiercely at Mariel, "Could you not have warned him?"

"If I had warned him, he would not have let me do it. What is your name, Dog? Are you a Rottweiler? I hear Rottweilers are very protective. Have you met Porcene? She is protective too. Where are we?"

Unknown to the arguing crowd, Whistler had flown back into the fray. He returned to his perch on Porcene's back next to Taytay who was shocked at his arrival. "Where did you come from? I never heard you land!" His entire body showed surprise. "You mean it worked? Mariel fixed your tail?"

Whistler nodded, "It worked!"

"Now," Tine concluded, "If you please, will you two Falcons hunt down our prey?"

Taytay looked at Whistler in mock surprise, "Whistler, he called us Falcons! The little tiny ball of grey molt called us Falcons! I am so happy. So, so very happy. Do you see any tears on my face?"

"No, Taytay, I don't, but I feel like I could cry. Am I crying?"

"Enough with you!" Belle had to regain control. "Off with you both. Track them, find them, report back to me. We will make your direction through the woods. When we hear back from you, and if it is safe, we will once again travel the road."

"Upon your orders, Belle." Taytay and Whistler both lifted a wing as if saluting. They took wing immediately.

Tofur was not distracted by the spectacle of the tail feather plucking. He found a treasure in a few saddle bags roped to Porcene's flank. He was a well read student. He delighted in reading new books. He pulled a few from the bag and stepped from under the trees to scan their titles. One book intrigued him more than the others. *The Modern Sciences; Inner Workings of the Human Brain, Parts 1 and 2.* He considered this book a fantastic find. He continued reading the book's cover. *Written and illustrated by Dr. T. Mariel Fraunchesca, Physician to the Royal House of...*the rest of the lettering was scraped away. "I must be seeing things." He read it again. It said the same thing the second time. The second book was titled *"Gadgets, Inventions and Other Things" written and illustrated by Dr. T. Mariel Fraunchesca, Physician to the Royal House of...*again the lettering scraped off the book's cover. The third book was titled *"Curing Dimentia and Boredom Without Really Trying" by Dr. T. Mariel Fraunchesca, Physician to the Royal House of...*"What? This really has to be a joke." He was giddy with excitement. "Wait, that is not how I was taught to spell dementia." He put the first two books back in the bag for safe keeping. He rushed around to the front of Porcene and held the book cover to her face. "Porcene, do you know anything about this? It seems Mariel is quite the literate man. Has he said nothing to you?"

Porcene reared her head back a little, "Tofur, you can't hold anything that close to me and expect me to see it clearly. Take a step back please."

"Oh sorry, my mistake." He stepped back and held the book up to her again. "Is this a bit better?"

"Yes, thank you. Now what do you want me to see?"

"The book and who it was written by. Can't you see it?"

"Sure I can see it, but I can't read it."

"You can't what?"

"I'm sorry, Tofur, I can't read."

"Really, we must correct that right away." He turned to Belle, "Belle, can you read?"

"Read? Read what, Tofur?"

"This book. Can you read this book?"

"I'm afraid I can't read any scribblings in a book or anything else. I can read trails. I can read danger."

"No, you're kidding me. We have a book here and none of you creatures can read it? Only me?"

"Tofur, I can read it." Tofur looked at Jak who was standing again now.

"Hmmm," Porcene said out loud, "And he's smart too."

Jak heard what she said and crumbled to the ground again.

"Oh please, Jak, would you get up? We have no time for this now."

"Porcene, would you please stop flirting with him long enough for me to speak to all of you?"

"Hey, I couldn't help it. I'm smitten."

Tofur turned back again to Jak, "Don't you dare crumble to the ground again, you stubborn a..."

"Hold on, hold on. Tofur, what have you got to tell us?" Belle was very interested in whatever he had found.

"It's a book. Lots of them. All of them, at least the ones I've seen, were written by Mariel. This book right here," he held it up, "is entitled *"Curing Dimentia and Boredom Without Really Trying" by Dr. T. Mariel Fraunchesca.* It is spelled a bit peculiar, but it says dementia never the less." The creatures wore blank expressions. "Don't you understand? Mariel wrote this book and he is experiencing some form of dementia right now. I can read the book he wrote and hopefully find a way to bring him back to normal! Don't you get it now? He is indeed a very brilliant man."

Jak had moved closer to Porcene, "Read it then Tofur. Read it now. I believe it is obvious to all of us, the man is behaving abnormally."

"Oooh, big words," Porcene was having some fun with Jak.

Tofur spun back to Jak, "Do not even attempt to crumble again. If you do, I'll put blinders on you so tightly that you will never see this Belgian again. Am I making myself clear? Belle, please, you and Tine make a plan or something. I have to find a way to cure Mariel. Tine, can you read?" Tine swayed from side to side trying to buy a little time. "Well, can you?"

"Um, no I can't." Tine dropped his head a little. "I'm sorry."

"Geesh! Belle, make your plans. Let me know when they are complete."

***

"You know, Whistler, I never knew how annoying that sound you used to make was until now. Something used to grate on my nerves every time we flew together. Now, I'm not annoyed at all. Mariel performed a great service to us all."

"As much as I could take what you have just said the wrong way, I must admit, you are correct. No wonder I was called Whistler. Now what will I be called?"

Taytay continued stalking the road, "Whistler."

"Fine, do you think we are following the right road. It seems deserted."

"How would I know? These roads are nothing like the paths where we come from. I have never seen as many two-leggers in my lifetime as we have seen in the past few day-rounds. These paths are immense and wide enough to allow travel in both ways without the inconvenience of stepping aside to let others by."

"Do you think these two-leggers will notice us flying over them if we spy them at all?

Taytay swept both lanes of traffic beneath him. "From what I hear, they can't see that well. I find it hard to believe they could see us as high as we fly." The cousins continued flying over the road hopefully taken by their prey. "At the next crossing of these roads, I want to turn back and head the way we came. They may have stepped into one of those dwellings we passed."

"That's a good idea. Here comes one now." The Falcons made a wide arc before making their way back down the road, their keen eyesight getting a workout. "We should pay close attention to those crowded dwellings down there."

Far down below, seated on hard wooden chairs beneath a densely thatched roof, Barth and Ligon pored over a roughly drawn map given them at the start of their journey. It was stored in a deep pocket on the side of Ligon's overcoat. His coat had pockets for many surprises. "I find it hard to believe this map was drawn by any man with a shred of learned penmanship. Look at the markings, wide unintelligible scribblings for the most part. How are we to follow this?"

"You seem to have named yourself as the smart one Ligon. Put your brain to work and tell me where we go from here. Are we even taking the right road?"

"If what his contact told us is correct, then yes. If I was given this map and asked, from the information I could find legible, if we were following the correct road, I would say no. But again, I can't read anything here, save for a few scraggly lines I suppose to be mountains and the worn one here that may or may not be a body of water, maybe a lake, a river, an ocean? I don't know."

"Ligon, we have been gone ten days. Did the contact mention to you how long this trip would take?"

"No Barth, he did not. He told me we would know when we got there. We would be paid for our delivery of this map and we would be on our way."

"I guess we are wasting valuable time resting our feet in this flea trap, drinking this watered-down ale and attempting to eat these stale buns." Barth rose from the table and left a few coins beside a pewter mug. "Let's get out of here. I'm beginning to think we are being watched. I don't have a good feeling about any of this anymore."

Ligon pushed back from the table, took a distrustful glance around the room and followed Barth out the door. The night air was cool and refreshing. He was never so happy to be out of a place in his life. A stray four-legger, curled up by the eating-room fire, watched the two-leggers as they exited the door. He casually stretched his legs, wagged his tail, ate a few scraps of food dropped by the two-leggers off of the floor and made his way out the back door of the dwelling's kitchen. Once outside, he ran to the patch of forest where the moonlight stopped. He had instructions to meet the sentinel there.

***

Tofur opened the book. The first few pages offered previous book titles by Mariel, the publishing company, "Hewitt and Sons" and a biography of the author Dr. T. Mariel Fraunchesca. Tofur walked around in circles searching for enough moonlight to read the first few pages. He was getting more frustrated as time went on. His youth was glowing with impatience. "Why couldn't I come upon this earlier? There is not enough light to read even the first page completely. My eyes hurt. My head is beginning to ache." Clouds were moving in overhead. The dim moonlight was being replaced by increasing darkness. "If I have to wait 'til morning then so be it!"

Belle easily noticed the frustration settling over Tofur. She watched as he valiantly searched for reading light. She stepped closer to him when she heard him talking to himself. "Tofur, you must rest now. When we hear back from the Falcons, we will have to move fast. You must be prepared when the time comes. Please, come and rest with the others. I know you are bound and determined to read that book, but wait until you can actually see it, please."

Tofur glanced down at Belle. He knew she always had his best interest in mind ever since she was a puppy. "You are right, Belle." He exhaled loudly, hoping to relieve a little of his pent-up frustration. "I am knocking on the door of maybe bringing Mariel back to our world again. I want to help him so badly. I know there is a much bigger goal here, but it has been so long since I was able to do anything but walk alongside you and Jak. I have something to offer here. I have a lot to offer. I just want to help."

"Stop it. You've said enough. Get some rest. We will continue this soon enough." That was it. Belle tugged on his pant leg until Tofur relented. He followed her over to a broad tree trunk, sat down with Mariel's book in his lap and fell asleep instantly. Belle lay down at Tofur's side. Before closing her eyes, she took another look around. Things had settled down nicely. Mariel finally wound down and was seated comfortably next to Porcene, dozing without a care in the world. Jak leaned against a tree. She could see grey feathers just above his withers, his thick mane keeping any wind off the winger. She made eye contact with Porcene who was still alert. "Will you keep the first watch?"

Porcene whispered, "Of course I will."

9

Frederick stared at the corridor ahead of him and all of the doors lining both sides. Nearly every one had been rigged to trigger an explosion of some magnitude upon opening. The doors that stood open signaled safe rooms, the closed doors were still armed.

"Where do we start? Either of you have an idea? I am open for suggestions."

Mystic glanced at Bubba, "How about you, Cheetah? You normally have a way of cutting through the complexities of a situation. What have you got to say now?"

Bubba yawned, "I have not gotten over what we have witnessed in the last few clicks here, Mystic. I don't know where to start. Frederick, why did they rig every door? How were they going to enter the rooms? Had they already found out everything they needed?"

The questions were numerous, the answers unaccounted for. This was only one level in the mountain. Had every room on every other level been set as a trap? The answer was less than obvious.

"What I wouldn't give for Lightning's ax-pike about now." Frederick stuck his hands in his pocket and blew out a long breath. "What is the question we need to answer first?"

"Should we go back to the first library for clues? Sig must have had a reason for leading us there in the first place. He knew we would find some answers there or, at least, a good line of questioning." Bubba looked up to Frederick for an answer.

"That's a good point, Bubba. Let's go back and see if we can start this over again."

Mystic had another idea. "Frederick, you go back to the library. I think Bubba and I need to do some more research on these remaining safe rooms. You have more business being in a library than we do. We can use our four-legger abilities in other ways."

"Very well, Mystic. You two go ahead. Find out everything you can. I am very interested in what changes the posers may have made to the original state of this place. Try to deduce what was left by the builders and what was changed, desecrated or modified by the fake Gann and Gamma."

"Do you think the changes will be obvious?" asked Bubba.

"Yes, I do, but the changes would only be obvious to a creature who knew what this place looked like before any changes were made. Wait... That makes no sense at all."

"Yes, it does. I know what you are trying to say. The changes will be clearly noticeable if we look upon them as the builders would. I mean, we look at this place as we are looking toward the future, not as we would be looking toward the past."

Mystic anxiously tapped the hard stone floor with his front paw, "Come on, Bubba, there are a lot of rooms here."

Frederick studied Bubba's idea. "Wait a minute, Mystic. What he said actually made a lot of sense. When you enter a room, try not to notice anything until you get to the far side, opposite of the door. From there, look back. If there is something in the room that does not flow, make a mental note of it. After you have thoroughly scanned the room in that way, only then should you check out the irregularities. Wow, that sounds complicated."

"Frederick," Mystic answered, "No, actually, it doesn't. It sounds like it might work. The posers had too much to do in their time here to be that careful. That's why they set so many traps. Any changes they may have made should be fairly obvious to us. But, we won't know if we don't get started. Come on, Bubba."

Frederick agreed, "Be careful...both of you!"

"We certainly will try, sir." Mystic led Bubba as they began their trek down the long rock corridor.

Frederick felt a shiver throughout his entire body. He shook it off and returned to the library, the scene of Sig's demise. "Sig, I wish you could have stuck around a bit longer."

***

Jahnise knelt at the side of Ian and Colleen Mecanelly. He studied every wrinkle and every stain on their clothing. He tried to read everything and nothing into their final positioning. He came up empty. "Bongi, there is nothing here except the clue Mr. Ian left with his finger. He cleary pointed out the "E" in his book's title and that is all. If the Nuorg water can heal him, why did they not use it? Why did they choose to die? Did they not have more to live for? What about their children? All I can ask is... why?"

Bongi stood close-by with little to say. He simply shook his head. "I can't answer any of those questions, King."

"We must move them out of here. They deserve a proper burial. Oliviia may know some of the answers that evade us now. We must get back to her. May they take their last ride on your back?"

"Yes, of course. Can you find something to secure them with?"

"I think so, Bongi. I will cover them as reverently as I can and lay them over your back, Mrs. Mecanelly first." Jahnise lifted Ian's head off of Colleen's lap and delicately laid him back down on the floor. He used a cloth from Ian's front pocket and water from his water sac to clean the man's face. "Ah, Bongi, Mr. Ian was a handsome man. Such a shame he had to experience the end of his life like this."

Bongi watched and appreciated the gentleness of Jahnise's actions as he carefully respected the empty shells of each two-legger. Waves of emotions rolled though his four-legged body as feelings of denial, senselessness, outrage, helplessness and many more flooded his thoughts. He stood silently at attention as Jahnise loaded each of the two-leggers on his strong back.

Jahnise inspected the area around where the Mecanellys fell for some clue to the attackers. He found nothing of interest. Embedded in the wall was the handle of a sword or blade of some type. The handle was plain except for an embossed "M" where the wielder's palm would rest. "Bongi, this sight puzzles me. Why is this handle protruding from this rock wall?"

"The crack must have opened there along a line stretching from the floor to the ceiling. The blade must have become stuck when the crack closed. I don't know much about that phenomenon, I'm sorry."

"You mean to tell me that when the attackers came into Nuorg, there was an opening in this wall? How can that be? It is solid rock." Jahnise pulled hard on the handle, it wasn't coming out of the wall. "This just can't be, Bongi." He studied the "M" on the handle. "Which one of our friends commanded this weapon?" He stepped over to Bongi and inspected the palms of both Ian and Colleen. Ian's hands were soft and free of any markings. Colleen's right hand was clear, but her left palm clearly displayed the imprint of the handle's "M". "Mrs. Mecanelly, there is more to you than I initially surmised."

"What are you saying King?" Bongi was very interested in where Jahnise was headed with this conversation.

"From what I can gather here, Colleen was protecting Ian. She wielded the weapon with her left hand." Jahnise was physically acting out and narrating what he thought were the last actions of the Mecanellys. "With her left hand, she lunged through this crack, leading with this blade. He stepped back to examine Colleen's left side. He quickly found what he was looking for. Stepping back to the wall he continued, "She was struck in the side by another blade from beyond this wall..." Jahnise looked to the ground, inspecting it with meticulous detail. "As I suspected Bongi."

Jahnise bent closer to the ground, beyond where the dim lighting cast its faint glow. He took his stick in his hand and slammed it against the ground. A bright light was instantly emitted from the stick's bottom. About a hand's width from the floor, the majority of a dull metal blade stuck awkwardly into the room. Jahnise took his stick and slammed it against the blade, once, twice, three, four times. Nothing budged. He looked at Bongi, "That is a well-made blade, my Okapi friend." Jahnise's eyes widened. He took a deep breath. Clasping his stick with both hands he slammed it violently against the rock wall. "If there are any answers beyond this rock face, expose them to me!" He demanded. A cracking sound emanated from the wall.

"King, did you break your stick?" Bongi asked nervously.

Jahnise was not sure. He held up his stick and examined it. "No, Bongi, my stick is not damaged."

The cracking sound continued. Suddenly the bottom of the wall opened up slightly. Jahnise and Bongi looked on expectantly. A soft clanging sound interrupted the cracking noise. The blade, complete and intact with hilt and handle, fell to the floor. The room went silent. A cool breeze blew through the opening. Jahnise was once again on the floor. He peeked through the opening as the breeze cooled his face.

"Is there anyone there? Can you hear me?" He looked up at Bongi for clues, then back to the crack. "Is there anyone there? Can you hear me?"

A quiet rustling sound reverberated through from the other side, then a voice, a girl's voice, "Who is there? Father, is that you?"

Jahnise was stunned. He, nor Bongi, had ever experienced anything like this before. He looked at Bongi, completely speechless. He held his hands open. Turning back to the crack he said, "No child. Your father is not here right now. Are you okay?"

The faceless voice asked, "Who are you and where are my parents?"

"I am a friend, child. Are you alright? Are you safe?"

Another young voice answered, "Tell him we are okay, Emiliia, but we won't be safe for long if they come back. We have to hide!"

Jahnise did not know what to say. "Emiliia, is that Patrick? Is he with you?"

"Yes sir, Patrick is with me. Where are our parents and where is Livvy?"

"Livvy is fine. Your parents were hurt. Who did this? Who tried to take you? Who came through this crack?"

"Emiliia, I think they are coming back. We have to go now!"

"Sir, tell my parents we will be fine. I must get Patrick to safety. They are not very fond of him right now. I don't know where that will be. I will take care of him. I don't know where we are, but for now we are safe. If you can find out who this belongs to, you will know who broke in and where to find us. Oh, and tell Bongi they also have Ev."

Jahnise was amazed with the young Mecanellys. He raised his head just as something came sliding out of the crack. No sooner had he backed away from the opening and what came out of it, the crack closed with a powerful snap. The light from his stick was waning, but it was still bright enough to illuminate what Emiliia had passed to him. He eyed it with concern. "Bongi, these children...who taught them how to survive?"

"That would be their mother, King."

"What did Mr. Ian give them?"

"Mr. Ian gave them the gift of superior intelligence to know how and when to use the skills their mother taught them."

"You don't say?"

"They are quite a family, King."

"I'll say they are, Bongi." He picked up the clue and placed it in a pocket of Ian's coat. He stuck the blade in his belt and carried the journal. "We need to get out of here. We must tell Oliviia and the others what we now know--very soon."

"I agree, King. Are we ready to go now?"

"Yes we are." Jahnise poked his stick on the floor and it lit up again. He carried it as a torch to lead Bongi and escort the Mecanellys from the tunnel.

***

Stewig left the entrance to the tunnel open as he and Oliviia headed toward the Keeper's dwelling. Rakki remained with them. He had not yet flown off to find Hugoth. "Rakki," Stewig asked. "Please wait here for Jahnise and Bongi. Tell them how to close this entrance then you go find Hugoth. I want this place guarded continuously, no one in and definitely no one out. Who do we have that can do that for us?"

Rakki paused for a moment, "Is the Golden back? He flew scout earlier, did he not?"

"He was told to fly the gap earlier. He should be back by now. I will send him to you when we get to the Keeper's dwelling. Only then will you leave for Hugoth."

"Yes, Stewig, I will do as you say. What about Karri?"

"It may take both of you to find Hugoth. You two need to stay together until you receive orders from Hugoth to the contrary. I will send the Golden back as soon as I can."

"Sounds good to me, Stewig. You need to get this young lady back so she can rest. She has a lot on her mind right now."

"I am aware of that Rakki, but we also have other pressing needs. I must take care of one thing at a time. Oliviia, I am sorry for the delay."

"Think nothing of it Stewig. I will have my time. We need to get organized. We need to seal the cracks now more than ever. I can't let my parents give their lives for naught."

Rakki spoke directly to Oliviia, "Young lady, you are wise beyond your years. Please accept my condolences for your loss." He bowed before her.

"I sincerely appreciate that from you, Hawk. Now, the greatest thing I can do in their memory is succeed where they could not. It will be my only goal to do so. Thank you." She leaned closer to Stewig's ears.

"How fast can you get me back, Sir Rhino?"

Stewig wasted no more time. "We shall leave immediately, Livvy."

They took off at a steady pace. Rakki stayed and waited patiently for Bongi and Jahnise to emerge from the tunnel.

***

Madaliene, Hemoth, Lightning and Perrie could only stand bewildered where they had just landed. Madaliene quizzed the Badger, "Lightning, did you do everything as you normally do?"

Lightning had not noticed their new surroundings...obviously. "Why yes, Princess, why would you ask me that?"

"Take a look around us. Does anything here strike you as, I don't know...familiar?"

Hemoth agreed, "We are exactly where we were when we left here an instant ago."

"That can't be so, can it?" Lightning began to doubt what he was seeing.

"There must be something different here."

Perrie looked down the road. "There is something different. Look down there. Our visitors are coming back, only earlier than last the last time."

"What did you say?" Madaliene was certain she didn't hear correctly.

"Are you saying those people are coming back to see us again?"

"Yes, Princess, that is exactly what I am saying. They should be within your eyesight very shortly."

Madaliene strained her eyes to see the on comers. Hemoth stretched his neck upward. "I can definitely smell the lot already."

Lightning did the same. "I can too, Hemoth, and they smell the worse for wear."

"What should I say this time?" Madaliene was at a loss for words.

"I suggest you don't get angry with them right off, Princess. That got you nowhere last time." Perrie did not take her eyes off of the nearing crowd of two-leggers.

"Right. I guess it's too late for all of you to hide. Just stand beside me, if you will. Maybe we can head this thing off."

Hemoth and Lightning flanked Madaliene, Perrie perched on her shoulder. The 23 two-leggers came closer and closer with no fear of the large Grizzlies. Soon they were silently looking into Madaliene's eyes. Each group stood their ground unflinching. The bedraggled bunch of two-leggers looked just as hungry this time as they had the last.

Madaliene took one step forward to address the crowd. "Please excuse me, kind people, but we are lost. Can you tell us where we are? I will trade you food for information if you are interested. We have plenty."

The two-leggers stared at her without answering one of her questions. Madaliene recalled the last visit with the group and called one of them by name. She walked closer to the group.

"Monsieur Clermoneau." Madaliene tried a totally different approach.

She whispered to Perrie, "Do you, by chance, know the language he grew up with?"

"Yes, Princess, I am learned in his land's language, I can't carry on a conversation with him, but I can get you started."

Madaliene continued looking through the faces as if searching one individual out. "How do I say, 'My name is Madaliene' and 'Are you hungry?'"

Perrie cocked her head toward Madaliene's ear. "Thank goodness you are asking easy questions. Say this: 'Je m'appelle Madaliene. Avez-vous faim?"

"That's it?"

"Yes, Princess, say it just as I did."

Madaliene walked into the crowd as they stared, mystified at her. "Je m'appelle Madaliene. Avez-vous faim?"

Immediately the crowd's silence broke. From each person, questions began pelting her. She was overwhelmed. "Perrie, I can't answer all of these questions. Pick out the easiest ones for me!"

"Oui, mademoiselle!"

Perrie laughed. "Princess, the youngster there in the ragged coat is hungry." The affirmations came from everywhere. "And that one with the hat, and that one, and that one, and that one..."

Madaliene reached into Frederick's bag and began tossing food to them all.

"Merci, mademoiselle, merci." The chorus resonated throughout the group.

Madaliene repeated her first question. She found exactly who she was looking for and moved toward him. "Monsieur Clermoneau, je m'appelle Madaliene." The old man looked surprised. She changed back to her language, "Sir, I think you can understand me even if I don't talk in your language. Am I correct?"

The man looked at her, both confused and frightened. "How do you know that, mademoiselle?"

"I…I…I...um, I was hoping you did. I am not very fluent in your language. I apologize for that. My group is lost. Can you tell me where we are?"

"Are you a Talker?" The man glanced past her to Hemoth and Lightning.

"Yes, I am. These are friends of mine. We are on a journey and we were brought here for reasons that are not clear to us. We are hoping you can help us. Is that possible?"

He looked back to her. "Yes, but it must be fast. We are trying to escape the marauders that attacked our village several weeks ago. They came in the night and captured or killed all of our able-bodied. They left us, the old, the weak and the children, at least some of us. We all know they will return."

This did not sound like the description written on the parchment. She handed her bag to Hemoth. "Please pass out this food to these leggers, Hemoth." She turned back to the old man. She studied every detail of his dress. His pockets were torn, his buttons, for the most part, were missing and he had a sack tied to his waist. Protruding from a hole in its side was the corner of a piece of parchment. Madaliene gasped. "Excuse me Monsieur, is that letter falling out of your sack there?"

He looked embarrassed, "Why, yes it is, mademoiselle. I am not within my wits presently and my dress, well, it has seen better days." He opened his sack and handed the parchment to Madaliene. "Here, mademoiselle, please bear this for me. We are not long for this world and I need to give this to someone who might survive all that is coming."

His last statement did not thrill Madaliene or those of her group that overheard him. She questioned him further, "What does it contain? Is there a message I must get to someone?"

"It tells of the attack on us. Yes, you must get it."

"I must get it to whom?"

"You must get it to you!"

Madeliene was taken aback by the response.

"Do you know who I am?"

"Oui, Mademoiselle Madaliene, I know who you are. We spoke earlier today. I have prepared this letter for you. It expounds upon the first one I left for you. I am very glad you returned to us. In the coming days, the world will be grateful as well."

Perrie, Hemoth and Lightning all heard the same thing. They blankly stared at Monsieur Clermoneau as he and the 22 others in his group vanished into nothing.

"Whoa!" Hemoth exclaimed.

Perrie stood astonished on Madaliene's shoulder. Lightning's mouth hung open.

Madaliene unfolded the letter then lifted her head to stare at nothing.

"This day is becoming unnerving." She began to read the second letter aloud.

Princess Madaliene,

You are the one we were told would appear. When you returned to us, all doubt was erased. We are, as you probably surmised, no longer with the living. We have been gone since the second wave of attacks. I owed it to the children to hold out for you and yours before we passed over. I had to take the children to the other side with some vision of hope. Their short lives were full of misery and heartache. You, Princess, have eased them into their eternal destiny. We will be forever grateful to you. The last thing they will remember from this land of the dying is your unselfishness and beauty. As we each pass over, we will ask a blessing for you. The remainder of this letter has details about so many things. Keep it with you. There will be one among your group who can decipher the code.

Avec l'amour et l'espoir,

Monsieur Zachary Clermoneau

Madaliene continued to stare at the letter. "This is crazy."

Hemoth stepped closer and put a huge paw on Madaliene's shoulder. "Princess, this is bigger than all of us. Do not put all of this weight upon you right now. We will guard you, the letter and all you have with our lives."

Lightning nudged her in the side. "What Hemoth says is true Princess. I will sacrifice my life for you as need be."

Perrie agreed. She lightly tapped Madaliene on the head with her beak. "Princess, you are truly blessed. Remember, it is not solely your fight."

Madaliene sunk to the ground. As she slumped on her knees, she began to cry.

***

Rakki perched at attention near the entrance to the tunnel. He hoped the wait would not be long. He thought of no reason any fellow Nuorgian would want to enter the tunnel. How many others even knew about it? How many more were there? These questions and others were front and center in his mind. His wait was longer than he had hoped for. He heard the soft clip-clop of Bongi's hooves echoing through the hard walls and the quiet footfalls of Jahnise. A light radiated through the entrance first. It was followed immediately by Jahnise as he walked out into the open.

Jahnise spotted Rakki, "Good to see you my friend. Are they sending anyone to escort us back to the Keeper's dwelling? I do think the Mecanellys deserve some reverence and privacy as they are transported through the Burg. Is there a cart available?"

"I am not from this Burg, King. Would you like for me to acquire one?"

"Yes, dear Hawk. Please see if you can locate one for them. You do not need to take much time, but I would feel so much better if we can properly cover them."

"I will return as quickly as I can."

Rakki flew a straight line to the center of the Burg. He spotted a few small carts, but none big enough for two bodies. Seeing nothing of use, he turned back. Soon, he arrived at Jahnise's side. "I found nothing, King. There is a shortage of large wagons in this Burg. I would guess the only large one is bringing the intruders back from the mountain. What do you want me to do?"

Jahnise placed his chin on his stick, "Yes, Rakki, Bongi tells me this kind of thing is a rarity here in Nuorg. Has any creature ever died in your Burg?"

Rakki shook his head, "No, King, it never happens anywhere in Nuorg. This is more than a rarity. It is the only time it has ever happened. The water here normally prevents that from happening. Of course, we have never been invaded before...ever. I guess times are changing in more ways than one."

"You see, friend, that is the dilemma on my mind right now. Why did Ian not use the water? Why did Colleen not use the water? Is there ever a reason to pass rather than stay? I am sorry, Rakki, I am wasting your time. I know you have other things to do. Please be on your way to find Karri and Hugoth. We don't need him off defending Nuorg on his own. We need him here. We need to get our plan together. I see this getting worse, not better."

"You will take care of everything here then?"

"Yes, Rakki, I will take care of everything. Go find Hugoth."

"As you ask, King."

Rakki flew toward the mountains and Burg One. First, he would find Karri. Then, they would find Hugoth and Mystic, the Eagle. Things were becoming increasingly complicated.

Jahnise returned to Bongi's side in the tunnel. "New friend, we have no cart in which to carry Mr. Ian and his wife. Since this kind of thing, and I mean death, does not happen in Nuorg, do you think it is necessary to take them back before we issue them a proper burial? How will your fellow Nuorgians handle this? Can we not have a private ceremony for them, at least a temporary one?"

Bongi thought quietly to himself. "I believe this may be a pre-cursor of things to come King. We should expose this to my fellow Nuorgians, so they may begin preparations should it become common. We have never dealt with this here. We never before had to. But, remember this too, King; we are all from the upper lands. We have all experienced death before, just not here. "

"I think you are correct, Bongi. You must tell me more about the water. Let us now proceed to the Keeper's dwelling. We must, at least, ask Oliviia's opinion."

"Very well, will you please lead the way?"

Jahnise put his long arm around Bongi's neck, "I will be honored to do so, Bongi."

As Jahnise and Bongi stepped from the dark tunnel into the land lit by the yellow ball in the Nuorg sky, a very unique phenomenon occurred. Bongi's load became lighter. It not only became lighter, it went away altogether.

"Jahnise, what just happened?"

Jahnise was looking ahead. He did not notice when the Mecanellys disappeared. "What did you say, Bongi?" When he glanced back at the Okapi, he instantly noticed the reason behind the sudden question.

"Where did they go?"

"I don't know! When we stepped out of the tunnel, I had no load on my back. That has never happened before."

"Quickly, Bongi, move back inside. This would be an awful admittance on our part to lose the Mecanellys." He led Bongi back inside the tunnel. Again, he was at a loss for words. He stood at Bongi's side without a thought in his head.

Bongi was startled. He looked at Jahnise for an explanation. "King, they are back, aren't they?"

"Yes, they are."

"What is happening?"

"I can't explain it."

"Try."

"I am at a loss."

"Try anyway."

Jahnise was witnessing for the first time another mystery of Nuorg. He lightly patted each Mecanelly. "They are still here, Bongi. Let's try this again." He again led Bongi out of the tunnel. Again Bongi had the same reaction.

"King, they are gone again."

Jahnise nodded his head, "Yes, they are gone again." He patted Bongi's bare back from his neck to his tail. "Please step back into the tunnel."

Bongi did as he was told. Again, the load burdened him. "They are back?"

"Yes they are back. What is the explanation for this? You know this place better than I, how can this happen?"

"Like I said, it has never happened before."

Jahnise removed his hat and rubbed his head. "Step back outside again please."

Bongi, again, did as he was told. Once again, same as before, the Mecanellys disappeared. "Jahnise, they are gone."

"Yes they are, Bongi. I am completely baffled. We could keep this up all day." He raised his eyes to the yellow ball in the sky. "Bongi, what is that?"

***

Rakki pressed on to find Karri. With her head start, she could be anywhere. More than enough time had elapsed for her to fly past the mountain and on to Burg One. Where should he look first? What path would Hugoth take to stay out of plain sight? The answer, to him, was obvious, The Path to Where I Was. It led past an entrance where Hugoth could enter under the mountain. Eventually, the many twists and turns would lead Hugoth to the cavern under the Forever Trees. He would then use the same conveyance to gain entry to Burg One that they had used after Charlie's demise, but that could take a long time. He and Karri flew those tunnels together. He hoped he would find one of them there. He tilted his wings and dove for the path.

Mystic the Eagle perched north of the hidden entrance. He saw Rakki coming and rose to meet him. "Rakki, what is the latest development?"

They spoke as they flew. "Greetings, Sir. I am afraid things are not well here."

"That much is certain, Rakki. I need details."

"Where is Karri, Sir? I need to know she has found Hugoth before I say anymore. He is needed back in Burg Four immediately."

"She is with Hugoth under the mountain. She is leading him to the cavern beneath the Forever Trees. Why have you come for Hugoth? Why is he needed so suddenly?"

Rakki scanned the ground below them, "Mystic, Ian and Colleen were attacked while sealing a crack. Neither of them survived. Emiliia and Patrick were taken. Oliviia escaped, she ran to find help. She found us, we returned with her, but we were all too late. She is not doing well. She is with Stewig at the moment. Bongi and Jahnise stayed with her parents. You need to get back also. It is imperative that we start a plan for Nuorg's defense. Oliviia is very upset. Do you know about all of the tunnels? Do you know where the cracks are appearing?" Rakki flew on, dazed.

Mystic listened to Rakki although he was sure he had not heard him correctly. "What did you say about Ian and Coleen?"

"Sir, did you not hear what I said? Did you not listen to me? I may regret saying this, but are you hearing only what you want to hear? I know you are the oldest creature in Nuorg, but are you too set in your ways to realize what is going on? Did Vincen's visit not wake you up? We are in trouble here, Sir! Things are not idyllic as they used to be. We are under attack. We must have a plan...and we don't! No one ever really planned for this!"

"Rakki, I am struggling with the current state of things, yes, as everyone is. Ian and Colleen are both...gone?"

"If you mean gone as dead, then yes, they are both gone. Quit trying to sugar-coat everything. Ian and Colleen were killed by a group of invaders that squeezed through a crack. Ian knew where the cracks were and he did not get them sealed in time. How many cracks are there? Do you know?"

Mystic was silent.

Rakki was in no mood for silence. "Well? Do you?"

The old Eagle cut his eyes to Rakki, "No, Rakki, I don't. You have every right to question me as you have. I have been in a state of artificial happiness since Princess Madaliene proved her worth here. I was mistaken. Her appearance and actions here should have proved to me that Nuorg and the land above, all the good that we hold dear, is in trouble. I have acted with so much stupidity. My years should prove me wiser than this. We have mountains of trouble on our wings, son. Follow me." The Hawk followed the old Eagle as he made a violent turn in the direction of Burg One. "We will need to head Hugoth off."

10

"Look there," Taytay spied a pair of two-leggers walking off the porch of a dwelling. "That certainly looks like our pair to me. How about you?"

"They fit the description Tine gave us exactly. What is that behind the dwelling? A four-legger ran out from behind the dwelling and is making a swift go of it, heading for the edge of the forest to the back."

"Yes, I see it is. It seems to be in quite the hurry. What you say I go check out the four-legger and you watch these two-leggers. I can't see how either of them can get anywhere faster than we can. Now that you are flying quietly you can hang up here and keep tabs on them. When you get a bearing on where they're headed find me. We will return to let the others know. I want to find out what spooked that four-legger." Taytay slightly nudged the air with his tail sending him on a direct route tailing the four-legger. Whistler stayed high above the two-leggers watching their every move.

The four-legger made his way through the tall grass to the edge of the trees. He was told much earlier to snoop around the crowded dwellings for anyone suspicious, whether it be of the two-legged, four-legged or winged variety. Nothing had caused a single hair to stand on end until now. The two-leggers he overheard complaining at the table got his full attention. A map, a contact, scribblings, delivery? Lots of these words were key phrases he was told to listen for. As they made their way out the front, he made his out the back to meet a sentinel. The sentinel would relay the information down the line to whatever asked for it in the first place. He felt important doing this kind of trailing. It beat a normal Dog's life! He was to wait for the sentinel beneath the fourth tree past the twisted elm on the wooded edge. He made this short trek many times in preparation for this very moment. He knew every step by heart. He impressed himself with how fast he made it to the elm tree. Without looking back, he stepped lightly into the woods being very careful not to make any strange noises that might alert something watching for him other than the sentinel. He found the fourth tree and waited. From deeper into the woods and from high over head, something else was watching him and listening.

The time passed too slowly. The four-legger spoke to himself, "The sentinel should have been here much sooner. I can't wait here forever. I have to get back to put another ear to the ground." He waited just a little longer before deciding to call it a night. He stood up to make his way back to the two-legger dwellings. About the same time he stepped out of the woods, a large shadow silently approached him from behind. As soon as his head cleared the last tree, he felt a stinging pain above each hind leg. He yelped loudly, giving his position away to anything listening. He stumbled out into the open while the attacker continued. He turned his head around trying to get a glimpse of the creature on his back. He saw broad wings with feathers flying everywhere. The winger on his back was stabbing talons into his back as it moved from his hind-quarters forward. The four-legger continued yelping from the pain the attacker was inflicting on his back. The attacker was now digging talons into the soft neck flesh of his victim for grip and desperately fighting to rip at the legger's eyes with his beak. The four-legger could not deter the winger and no amount of head-shaking would dislodge it.

Taytay heard the clamor from his vantage point way above the melee. He could not believe what he was seeing. He dove down for a better view. The winged attacker was viciously working to bring down the four-legger while the legger was fighting to shake it loose. This kind of scene never before played in the Falcon's eyes. The winged attacker was ruthlessly trying to bring down the legger. Taytay was shocked with the winger's ferocity. The winger was beginning to best the legger. Right or wrong, he decided to join the fray. At the least, maybe he could discover the problem between the two. It might end up being none of his business, but this was a reprehensible display of behavior more suited to stories he'd heard of two-leggers during the "Terrible Years". Without a further thought concerning his well-being, he clinched his wings tighter to his body and continued his dive even faster. He was aiming for the winger on the four-legger's back as the attacker continued to claw and peck at the legger's eyes and snout. Taytay was diving faster than ever before. From the corner of his eye, he saw another winger join him in a parallel dive, both headed for the attacker. The pair of Falcons dove with four claws equipped with razor sharp talons at the ready. Taytay gave Whistler a look, and instantly all four claws, talons extended, hit both of the attacker's raised wings dislocating them from their sockets. The attacker was instantly in severe pain while being jerked unwillingly clear of the wounded four-legger. The pair of Falcons unceremoniously dropped the attacking winger in a clump where he fell. Taytay rose to the left, Whistler to the right, making two tight turns leading them back to the legger. They arrived in an instant to the legger's side. Badly cut and bleeding, he was struggling to stand.

"Please legger, get down. We can get you some help." Whistler felt terrible. "What caused that winger to attack you?"

The wounded legger slumped to the ground per Whistler's pleading. He breathed heavy, gasping for each breath. "I was to meet...a sentinel in the woods...I was waiting for him...waited too long...wanted to get back to the dwellings...listen...more news...confused day he was...returning...didn't show...leaving the woods...it attacked me."

Taytay, for another reason unknown to him, asked, "What news did you have for the sentinel?" The four-legger was a mess. There was nothing they could do for him except get help.

The legger coughed then answered, "Pair of two-leggers...have a map...deliver to contact...collect money...think they are being watched...I hope you two are on our side...thank..." The two-legger passed out.

Whistler met the glance of Taytay, "This fellow is in bad shape. What do we do?"

"He is still breathing. Let us hope for the best. What kind of winger was that? Did you get a good look at it?"

"No. It was attacking this fellow so ferociously, it never lifted its head enough for me to get a good look. When we hit it, it was still attacking. Did you?"

"No, I didn't. Same reasons. I never saw anything like that before. It certainly didn't come from our home."

"You are right about that. Where is it?" Taytay scanned the ground between them and the woods. "We dropped him right over there." Curious, he hopped over where the grass was patted down by the falling winger's weight. There were feathers and a few stalks of grass stained with the creature's blood, but no body. "Whistler, could he have flown off?"

"There is no way he could have done that. We hit him so hard I heard his wings, both wings separate. He did not fly away."

"Then? Where is he?"

The legger was stirring again at Whistler's feet. "Where did you come from? What attacked me? I have to get back to the dwelling...My master will miss me soon..."

"Brave legger, we are on a mission of our own. We, I think, are tracking the movements of those two-leggers you overheard. The information you relayed to us will help us plan what to do next. Will you be alright?"

"Yes, I think I will. I have a kind master. He will take care of me. I need to go." The four-legger courageously got to his feet and began making his way down his trail to the dwellings. He turned back, "Please come back. I want to know if my information helps you." The four-legger headed back once again, stumbling and limping badly.

Taytay watched with sadness in his eyes, "Whistler, is he going to make it?"

"I don't know. That is one tough hound there."

"His poor ears were almost ripped off his head! What possessed that winger to do that to him?"

"I would like to know where that winger went!"

Taytay agreed. He added, "I'd like to know what sent him, where he was sent from and what happened to the sentinel. Not in any order, mind you, but I'd like to have an answer to each of those questions."

"We will find out, Taytay. I promise you that. I need to get back to those two-leggers. Now I want to catch them sooner that ever before. When we sight them again, one of us needs to report to Belle."

Taytay, once again, stared at the empty spot in the grass. "Don't you mean Tine?"

"No, I mean Belle. Follow me."

***

"Let's follow this road a couple more hours then rest for the night. It's a good night to sleep under the stars. Maybe we don't have far too go."

"Sounds good to me, Ligon. Maybe we don't." Barth was tiring of the journey. So far they had not heard one word from their contact. He told them he would meet them during the course of their journey at a spot yet to be chosen. Their job was to keep walking until he told them to stop. Neither of them could figure why so much secrecy was involved with the map. They were not sure if anybody could even read it to begin with, they certainly couldn't. "Ligon, you were saying back there you couldn't read the map. Do you think anyone can? I admit...I tried. Can our contact read it?"

"I'd say he would have to. If not him, then who? Is he taking it to someone else? Again, our only job is to deliver it. If I remember correctly, we were not supposed to look at it, were we?"

"Hmmph, how were we not going to look at it? The stupid creature it was attached to had already unrolled it for us. Again, how were we not going to look at it? Do you still have the storage sleeve it came with?" Barth was concerned. For some reason he was not convinced the trip was progressing as it should.

"Sleeve? What sleeve?"

"The sleeve that was covering the eyes of the courier, I thought you picked it up with the map. I told you it was important and to pick it up! You mean you left it?"

Ligon for once was unsure. "No, I didn't retrieve it. The animal was dead. I wasn't uncovering its eyes. That is a sure sign of bad luck where I come from. You never look into the eyes of the dead."

"Okay genius, if the man paying us to deliver this map wants the sleeve also, what do we tell him? Oh we're sorry. We don't have that. It was concealing the eyes of the dead! Who cares? It was a dead animal!"

Ligon's calm exterior began to show signs of stress. "How far back was that, Barth?"

***

Tine wasn't sleeping. He wasn't nestled into Jak's mane anymore. He had flown off as the others grew weary. Tofur's frustration with them created the diversion he needed to slip off and scout on his own. The Falcons were doing as instructed from on high. He decided that a much closer vantage spot would allow him to hear the conversations of the two-leggers. He tailed them from the moment they stepped off the porch. Silently flitting from fence post to tree to bush, he stayed within earshot of every word spoken between them. This latest conversation was stunning. He saw the Falcons' return and headed immediately back to the group.

Whistler spotted the two-leggers not too far from where he left them when he rushed to Taytay's side. "These leggers move so slowly. How do they ever get anywhere?"

I can't see another path or trail off of this main path. I say we report back to Belle, see what she wants to do, then take up the chase?"

"Answer me something here cousin, what exactly are we to do with these two when we catch them?"

"I haven't the slightest idea, Whistler, I haven't the slightest."

***

Tine's burst interrupted the lazy night, awakening everyone from a somewhat sound sleep. "Porcene, we must back track. It's urgent. We must leave the newcomers to the trailing and we must go back. Where did we first sight the two men?"

Startled, the Belgian opened her eyes wide. She tried to focus on the small bouncing winger. "What are you saying, Tiny? Who has to go back? Go back where?"

"We must go back, you, me, Mariel. The less than moronic men we are following only have half the package. It seems they left the map's case where they picked up the map. The key to reading the map is hidden on the case. Those dolts neglected to bring the case. We must go find it. We must!"

Porcene nodded her head in agreement then told Tine, "True, we need the map case, but we are not going back for it. You and me, Mariel? Uh, uh forget it. It will take speed to re-track our path and we don't have that. I suggest you send the Falcons back. They have more speed that all of us combined."

Tine listened attentively to Porcene's assessment. "Wonderful idea Porcene, I should have thought of it. You are, of course, correct. When they arrive, will you instruct them? You have more of an idea where we met up with the men than I. I must return. I was trailing them close enough to hear every word they said. They have no reason to talk softly. I can hear everything. I'll catch up with you. Formulate a plan to trail us." Tine flew off as quickly as he flew in.

"That was interesting." Belle tuned her floppy ears to the conversation as soon as Tine flew in. After the Dove left again, she asked, "Porcene, what do you think should happen now?"

"Belle, at some point I need to fill you in on what we know. Things are happening so fast now, I'm afraid I don't have time. Can you call the Falcons in?"

"I can't but Tofur can. He has a trinket he uses just for that."

Tofur was slow to wake. He overheard the end of Belle's statement. He removed Mariel's book from his lap and clutched it snugly at his side. "I have a what?"

Belle turned to him, "Call the Falcons back. We have another task for them. From what I have heard, they are the only creatures in our group capable of what we need."

"No problem, Belle. Cover your ears." Tofur reached inside his vest. He pulled out a short whistle on a fine silver chain. He gave five short blows. The piercing shrill of the whistle shot through the early morning, disturbing perceived serenity. "They should be arriving shortly."

Belle lifted a paw from each ear. She learned early to cover her ears tightly when Tofur got his whistle out. "Porcene, what is your plan?"

***

Without a second thought, Taytay and Whistler responded to the five short bursts. They wheeled about immediately, fixated in the direction of Tofur's call. Taytay eyed Whistler, "I hope there's no problem. That was the emergency blast, was it not?"

"Indeed it was, cousin." Whistler could not comprehend how silently he flew since Mariel adjusted his tail. "Do you hear that, Taytay?"

"I hear nothing."

"Nothing at all." Whistler accelerated past Taytay. "You hear nothing at all."

***

Tofur let the whistle drop to his chest. His attention was, once again, consumed with Mariel's book. He sat down to begin reading when Mariel meandered over to him. "So, my boy, what do you have there?"

"I found one of your books, Mariel. I hope to read it here shortly."

"One of my books, you say? I don't have any books." He showed his empty hands to Tofur, making it clear to himself at the same time.

"No sir, I have one of your books from Porcene's saddle bags. There are quite a few in there. Close to a small library's worth."

"Yes, I think I like books. Did I put them in there? I need to read one of them. Are they any good? What are they about?

"Uh, I guess you put them in her bags, you brought them with you."

"Did I? Who wrote them? Never mind, matters not. I always wanted to write books. Do you read?"

Tofur could not believe it. It started again. The rambling. "Of course you wanted to write books and you did! You wrote at least three of the books in the bags. The one I'm holding right here, see?" Tofur held it in front of Mariel. "You wrote it! It says right here, "Curing Dimentia and Boredom Without Really Trying" by Dr. T. Mariel Fraunchesca. That is you, sir. You wrote this book. Can you not remember it at all? You even misspelled dementia."

"You must clearly be in error, boy. Have you seen my Horse? Quite a large one she is." Mariel stiffly twisted his body searching for Porcene. "Seems I have quite a crick in my neck this morning. Why, there she is. A handsome one is she not?" Mariel made his way to Porcene. "Good morning, Horse. Good morning, Dog." He nodded to each. “Where are we? Dog, who are you?"

Tofur stood watching Mariel in dazed stupor. He searched frantically for a place he could sit and read. He noticed Jak sleeping by a tree. "You there, Mule, wake up you lazy swine! There is a morning upon us you might just miss." Tofur laid the book on Jak's broad back. He readjusted a few harness buckles and relocated a couple of packs. He fashioned a slant back chair on Jak's back. "This will do me well. Jak, keep up with whatever is said. Take me wherever they go. Stay interested in the conversation, but do not disturb me unless it is absolutely unavoidable. Oh, and Jak?"

"Yes your highness?"

"If that lovely beast of a draft animal makes eyes at you again, don't crumble beneath me. Have a little back bone, would you?"

"Yes, your highness." This was Jak's intended term of endearment when addressing Tofur. In reality, it was a polite way of saying ‘whatever’. "Did you forget that you called in the Falcons?"

"Jak, I told you I was not to be disturbed."

"Have you actually started what you were not to be disturbed doing?"

"No, you can't find it within yourself to stop talking to me. How can I start?"

"Just thinking here, you called both Falcons back, do you think you should call them down as well? They will be looking for the gauntlet, no?"

"Oh my word! How come you're so proper all of a sudden? Yes, they will be seeking the gauntlet." Tofur sat up straight. He untied the flap and reached his hand into the pack. He withdrew a long, left-handed glove with thick padding completely around the forearm. He tied the pack closed before putting on the glove. "Gauntlet secured. When you see them coming, I'll hold it to them." He blew the whistle once again. "Why is it they must land on the gauntlet after I call them in?"

"It's customary. It's what legends are made of. You know that better than any two-legger I know. You are the most accomplished Falconer in our land for your age Tofur."

"In any land Jak, for any age, I am the best Falconer, bar none." Tofur, again, began reading the first page of Mariel's book.

"Yes, your highness." Jak moved closer to Belle, not Porcene. He did not want to be too forward with the mare.

***

Taytay and Whistler were waiting. High enough to view the landscape, low enough to beckon at Tofur's call-in. "Do you think he forgot to call us in, Taytay?"

"He could have. I know there is a lot going on down there." Taytay nodded, "Let's make our way down."

Four short bursts interrupted the conversation.

"There it is. Shall we land the gauntlet?"

"Absolutely. Let us show ourselves proud. I am not sure our cohorts are aware of the presence which they keep. You think he should put on his cape? His feathered hat maybe?"

"Hmm, maybe not. Let us seek the gauntlet!"

With a slight rush of wing, the cast stooped. Both Falcons in a well rehearsed routine raced from the sky as a pair of falling lightning bolts.

Jak luckily noticed the incoming wingers. "Ahem, ahem, ahem! Tofur they are almost on us. The gauntlet, please!"

"Oh sorry." Tofur slammed the book closed. He put it behind him and with one fluid movement, slid off Jak's back. He stood at parade rest, offering the gauntlet to the Falcons. Mirror images, each Falcon in perfect unison, pulled up pompously to perch. They lit on Tofur's arm with hardly a feather ruffling. They nodded humbly at Tofur as he smiled, remembering their days in competition when the trio would routinely lay waste to the competition. He leaned over whispering, "Very well done."

Mariel and Porcene watched the spectacle with much admiration. Belle stood proudly by. Mariel exclaimed, "Such an exemplary fashion of Falconry, young man. Do you know these two? Have you met my Horse?"

Tofur smiled and nodded, "Yes I do, Sir. I know them very well. And, I have met your Horse. Have you met my Mule?" He elbowed Jak on his front shoulder, laughed and then smiled at Belle.

"Good, good. I suggest we get a move on then. I'm sure wherever we are going is awaiting us as we sit here gawking at this lovely cast of Falcons." Mariel glanced knowingly at the book laying across Jak's back. "Well, I see you are a reader. How do you like my book so far?"

Every living eye stared in amazement, every ear not sure of what it was hearing. "Excuse me Sir?" asked Tofur politely, "Do you recognize this book?"

"Absolutely, dear boy, I wrote it. Why? Should I not recognize it? Have I lost my mind or something?" Mariel was behaving differently, no one knew why. He turned to the Belgian, "Why, Porcene, are you making eyes at that Mule? Oh, I can see now, he seems to be a very handsome specimen. Is that your Mule, boy?"

"Uh, yes, Sir, it is my Mule." Tofur turned hesitantly to Jak and whispered, "Is this a little odd or what?"

Jak whispered back, "I believe it's 'or what'."

"Yes, it is definitely 'or what'." Tofur returned his attention to Mariel. "Doctor, no less that a moment ago you were not behaving the way you are now. Could you explain your sudden change in personality to those of us here?"

"Well... yes and no. Since I was much younger than even you, I have had, oh I don't know, shall we simply say...moments. Yes, moments in my life where for some reason or deciding circumstance, unknown or controlled by me or my actions, I switch personalities like one might put on a new outer coat. Which one was I? I don't mean for you to recognize that particular one from another or have a name for it, but, oh...how was I acting?"

Belle, Jak, Porcene and the Falcons were confused to say the least. Four-leggers have never witnessed a creature with more than one personality. They were each at a loss for words. Eye contact was being made between the four-leggers that would have made one dizzy had anyone tried to keep up with it. All eyes eventually fell on Tofur. Hopefully, he could make some sense of this. Tofur felt every eye as they landed on him two by two.

"Well Doctor, if I had to describe the man you were a few moments ago...I would have to say capricious, maybe disoriented, repetitive, not completely sure of where you were or what was going on. Does that help at all?"

"Well yes and no. Can you be more specific?"

Jak blurted out without taking any time to measure the consequences, "Maybe you were acting like a nut?"

"Very well, Mule, I will add that comparison to this boy's list of descriptions. Now, any of you other animals have anything to say? How about you Porcene? What say you?"

"I don't really know. Ever since we met, you have been acting the same way; kind of scattered? After all, you were thrown under my path as I was barreling down the road. I thought maybe you had been hit too hard in the head. What do I know?"

"Oh don't de-value yourself there, girl. The blows to my head could have very well triggered the personality change you all witnessed. How about you, Dog? I believe you are a Rottweiler, are you not? Your name is Belle? You see I can hear everything no matter what personality I assume, but I can't comprehend it all unless I am living within this personality that you are witnessing here and now. Oh dear, I believe I am confusing myself."

Belle waited for the doctor to stop speaking before answering the questions. "Yes Doctor, you were acting with no direction; a purpose maybe, but no direction. Yes, I am a Rottweiler and yes, my name is Belle." A perplexed look came about her face. She skewed her neck a little then kept staring at Mariel.

Mariel gestured to the onlookers with his arms, grouping them closer together before he continued speaking. "Come now, all of you I would rather speak to you collectively as a group than as individuals. Please gather together, Porcene, not too close to Jak...we don't need him collapsing again now." He winked at the Belgian, "Do we? I imagine this must be rather odd to you animals, witnessing a phenomenon like me. I have several personalities, one you have witnessed already, one that you are witnessing now, one who invented and built all of the contraptions stacked on Porcene's sturdy back and at least one more. I hope you don't have to witness him. He, uh, uh, shall I say is not all too pleasant."

Tofur was intently reading the end of chapter one when he heard the last thing Mariel said. "Excuse me Doctor, what do you mean by 'he's not all too pleasant'?"

The others were very curious with the statement as well.

"My dear boy, that one is a violent person. Very violent, very mean. Not the kind of person any of you would want to make angry. I don't know where he comes from. I can't make him go away, but I do have to witness the aftermaths of his actions. That may be the reason those men threw me in front of Porcene as she ran past me. If I had been him, they would not have gotten the opportunity to do that. Oh no, it would not have boded well for any of them, not at all."

Belle got Tofur's attention. She whispered, "You need to read all of that book, and quickly! I do not like what I am hearing here."

Tofur agreed, "It does make one tend to wonder a bit, doesn't it? I will do my best." He raised his eyes back to Mariel. "Doctor, do you have any idea what triggers the changes in your personalities? Where I come from, my family has several physicians on call. Two of them deal with the sciences of the brain, as they say. There have been many competitions when I sat in on their conversations during rest periods. Could be that I over heard something we might be able to put to test with your ways. What do you say?"

The two-legger's conversation soon became boring for the four-leggers and wingers. Belle begged, "Tofur, we have to structure a plan to move forward. Will you and Mariel please move your conversation to a more private place?"

Tofur looked annoyed with the question. "Excuse me? Are you not interested in what we can find out from him?"

Belle answered, "You find out and let us know. We are very interested in what you find out, not how you get there. We must move on and to move on we must have a plan. The day is burning beneath us. We have two leggers to track and capture in one direction, a map sheath to recover in another, a reason to an end to find for our journey and I think you can handle Mariel's situations alone just fine. You go with him, ask your questions, formulate an answer between you or a way of dealing with his changes and return. We will make plans for everything else. Now go, hurry."

"Okay Belle, I will do just that." Tofur's tone of voice was not particularly cordial. He walked over to Mariel, took his arm and led him a short distance away.

The four-leggers gathered around Belle with the wingers on the ample backs of Jak and Porcene. "Good suggestion, Belle. I'm not sure I want Mariel knowing all the details of our plan. Porcene, how well do you know him?" Jak was transforming into a much wiser four-legger than the others had seen before.

Porcene shook a few leaves from her mane, "Not more than a few weeks. I just did as I was told."

"Wait, who told you what?" Belle was stupefied as more surprises manifested themselves before her. "Are these new bits of information ever to end?"

Taytay and Whistler cocked their heads in unison toward Belle. "What do you want us to do? We need to fly or something. We are not getting any closer to that!"

"Fine, fine, Taytay what do you know about the case?" Belle responded.

"Why, Belle, we know nothing. We just got back, remember?"

Porcene spoke, "Falcons, it was me that Tiny chatted with when he returned. He mentioned something about the case the map was carried in. For some reason the leggers we are following left it behind. According to Tiny, the leader of the two leggers reminded the second of the importance of the maps protective case. You two are to go retrieve it from wherever it was left. How will you know that? I can't say. If these leggers are as reckless as I believe them to be, they will have caused damage of some kind to man or beast, whatever stood in their way. I suggest you back track our entire journey and inquire as if anyone or anything noticed anything unusual when those two passed through. We know it has to be before the intersection where our Mule here practiced his acting. Is that enough to go on?"

Belle was now pacing, "It has to be enough, Porcene. Taytay, Whistler, you two need to get moving. Leave it to your own inclinations regarding your methods. Do as Porcene described. Inquire, ask around, get nosey, get belligerent, just get going. As soon as you retrieve the case, find us as quickly as possible. Hopefully we will have the map by then. Now go, the both of you!"

"As you wish, Belle. Come on, Taytay, we'll improvise something. Please give our goodbyes to Tofur and Mariel." With no further delay, the Falcons were winging it back. Back to where they did not know, but they were flying there at full speed.

***

"So Doctor, you say these changes in your personalities come without warning. That sounds odd. They must be triggered by some kind of stimulus. Just as you became your batty self after the collision with Porcene, you became who you are now right after I called in my Falcons. What do those two moments have in common?"

"My, you are quite a learned young man, Tofur. The stimulus factor may be right on the money. I never got to that chapter in my book. Do you think it could be as easy as a bump on the head or a loud noise of some kind that may change me?"

"I don't know for sure, you are the doctor after all, among other things. But back to the personalities; do they come to you in any specific order? I mean are you the good doctor always after you are the aimless one, or, does the inventor come immediately before that? When are you the violent one? We really need to know where that certain one lies in the order of things. We will need to provide some kind of protection from you if that scenario unfolds against us."

"What? No, no, no, I am not violent towards friends and sometimes not at all, it is just that I can get, shall we say, out of hand if someone tries to harass those I am with. I am still a good person, just not very civil…uh, at least that is what I am told. I have stirred from that person in some very awkward situations."

"Okay, do you think we might be able to control that version of you to our advantage? I mean, should we need protection, could we evoke that personality on demand?"

"Oh my, that is a very ingenious thought to ponder. We must experiment. What could the stimulus be? Is it mental or physical?"

"From what I can determine, it must be physical, maybe not an action as much as a sound. You changed last, as I said before, when I called in my Falcons. You think it may be as easy as a call from my whistle? Could we experiment with that option while we are away from the others, just in case?"

"Splendid idea, my boy, splendid idea. Let's see, give it a try. See if anything changes."

Belle stood watching as the two Falcons sped out of sight, her strong head held proudly skyward, her triangular ears alert. "They should be fine, don't you think?" She really spoke to no individual legger. "Now, let's get a plan developed of our own, shall we?"

With all three wingers away and the two two-leggers working out the kinks in Mariel's personality quirks, that only left the Belgian, the Mule and the Rottweiler to determine their next move. Jak moved slowly to Porcene's side. "Well, Porcene, any ideas?" Belle turned her head, nodding in agreement.

A sharp shrill sound came piercing through the silence hitting Belle's sensitive ears like a hammer. She hit the ground and threw both paws over her ears. Tofur blew a second blast and a third in quick succession. Only after the third whistle and a long pause did Belle uncover her ears. "Tofur has got to warn me before he does that!" Slightly miffed, she got to her feet slowly.

"Well, doctor, did anything change? Are you the last you or someone else?" Tofur eagerly waited the answer.

"Dear lad, let me see that whistle and whatever do you mean?" Mariel stretched his hand open, expecting Tofur to immediately lay the whistle within it. "You know, I think I can make that a lot more efficient. Let me see it please?"

Tofur didn't know what he should do. Not having any other thought in his mind at the time, he placed the whistle in Mariel's outstretched hand. He looked on inquisitively and cautiously as Mariel inspected the whistle to the nth degree.

"Yes. I think I can tune this opening just a finite bit, then maybe reshape the air entry slot, yes I think I can do much for this sloppy design. Lad, shall we return to my Horse. I have packed some tools that will allow me to refine this instrument of yours." Mariel peered slightly behind Tofur, "Yes, there is Porcene. Shall we make our way back?"

"Certainly, Doctor, certainly." Tofur made eye contact with Mariel hoping to see some kind of change in his appearance.

"Doctor? I am certainly no doctor. I am a scientist, mainly, I guess some folks would consider that a qualification of a doctor, but I practice the science of invention and I am normally called Professor." Mariel passed Tofur and made his way back to Porcene's side.

Tofur watched as Mariel rummaged though the pack sacks. When he arrived back with the four-leggers he mused, "I believe we have three personalities down and one to go."

"Really?" asked Jak. "Who is he now?"

"The persona you see now is the man who invented all of those gadgets and gizmos fastened all over Porcene's back."

Porcene did not look amused. "I'm of a mind that I have never seen this peculiar legger in my life. Where did he come from?"

Tofur couldn't help but laugh out loud. "The legger at your side, lovely Belgian, is no other than Professor T. Mariel Fraunchesca. He intends to improve upon my whistle, seems to think it rather mundane."

"Here they are! I knew my tools would be in one of theses packs. I know the man who packed them for me. Very close, very close." Belle watched as the professor sat on the ground, tossing tool after tool to his side. "If he can tone that thing down at all, I will be his friend for life. Tofur, I want you to know you nearly cooked my brain when you let loose on it just a while ago. I told you to warn me whenever you were ready to blow the blasted thing. I'm surprised the Falcons have not returned yet." Fortunately they were too far away to make the sudden return.

***

11

The ride back into town was not pleasant. The Rider cussed and fussed the entire ride when he was not coughing or spitting up blood. If it had not been for his wicked heart, he would not have lived. Something inside him steeled him to weakness of any kind. He was meant for evil. It would take an equal or greater amount of good to defeat him. In his mind that quantity of good did not exist. Some fraction of it failed miserably on the mountain side. He would remember that mistake. Whoever was responsible for it would pay for that stupidity with their lives.

Storming back into town, the Rider wasted little time with formalities. Yelling and screaming as he passed small groups of his men, he demanded them all to follow him to the intersection of the only two roads that led in or out of the village. He hastily assembled his crowd by painfully climbing on the back of a flat wagon. Using it as a stage, he continued ranting at his underlings. "Who knows what happened to me back there on the mountain? Where is the bag? Who brought it back? If there is any man here who knows something and is not telling me, he will die by my own hand before this day is over!"

A crowd gathered to hear the now livid leader of the visitors. The crowd included not only his followers, but original villagers as well as a few well placed spies. On and on, the Rider swore curses at whoever planned his accident. Threats were aimed then fired off at any creature unfortunate enough to fall within his sight. The clamoring went on until dusk began to set in on the village. The Rider ranted non-stop. Even his most loyal underlings tired of the show. Finding any excuse to resume a normal day, most of them faded away, except the spies. The spies were volunteers from the Protectors. They were eager to hear every detail the Rider spouted, knowing that the madder he got, the looser his tongue became. He could very well divulge secrets no one else knew. They were so hoping that would happen. It did. Near the end of the tirade against everything good in the world, the Rider made one comment he never should have made. He made it unknowingly to more spies than underlings. The underlings were normally under the spell of too much mead to pay real attention anyway, but the spies were sharply coherent; they heard and noted every word.

The Rider scanned the crowd for his main thugs. He could not find a single one of them. They had succumbed long ago to the special mead poured into their steins earlier that day, just as the crowd assembled. Angry with their absence, he climbed off the trailer. Powered by sheer hatred, he limped back to his quarters. He promised himself it would be a long night for those not in attendance. If he had to choose one thing he loved in his miserable life, it would be his well-crafted art of inflicting pain on those much weaker than he. His fun would not take place on this night. Once he closed his dwelling's door behind him, he fell to the floor in agony. The injuries of the day were no longer hiding. From his feet to his head, his body was wracked with mind-numbing pain. Outside his window, more notes were taken. He would not awake until late the next day.

***

"Did he actually say the Governor? Which Governor? Did anyone understand which one he was talking about?" The questions were coming in rapid succession. The spies were meeting with the Protectors committee in charge. One of them stated, "I was as close to the maniac as I could stomach, all I heard him say was Governor."

An average looking gentleman sat without speaking at the end of the long wooden table. Dressed in relative finery, he transcribed every word spoken. With skilled swoops of a quill pen, he compiled page after page of notes. In the margins of these pages, he wrote his own thoughts as they came to mind, regarding each version of each spy's story. "Is this the last of you to speak?"

The door creaked open allowing the last spy to enter. "I have just come from his place. The barbarian is in tormenting pain. Our planned accident did not have the desired outcome, but he is in a seriously bad way. He took no more that two steps beyond his threshold when he fell to the floor, moaning like an injured tormented soul."

"Well, we aren't positive he has a soul yet, are we? No creature that despicable can harbor a soul in my opinion. I have seen evil creatures in my day that can't compare with that spineless slug." The note taker looked up at the crowd. "Why he is still breathing is, well…obviously he is still here for a purpose, someone more powerful than all of us wants him to live another day…for what reason? I don't have the imagination to fathom. How is Evaliene? She hasn't lost her temper lately, has she?" The scribe assembled his writing tools. Flicking the remaining ink from his quill, he proceeded to wipe it down with the hem of his long thin jacket before placing it in his deep side pocket. After stacking the sheets of now dry notations, he placed them in a binder, tied it tightly with a brown cord, tucked it under his arm and bid a good evening to those gathered before anyone gave him the word that Sean, their leader, was missing. "One last item to handle tonight men…recover the Rider. He is vulnerable in his present condition. When the time is right, take him with force."

Word quickly spread. When told of the scribe's directive, Kelly and Paddy wasted no time removing the nearly comatose Rider from his prone position on his own floor. They secreted him off to the special room Sean mentioned for questioning.

12

Hemoth watched as Madaliene cried. There was nothing he knew to do that would comfort her. She had been through enough to bring an older two-legger to their knees and there she sat, only 16 years old. Instead, he called to the Badger. "Lightning, please come with me. Let us leave the Princess to Perrie's watchful eyes while we devise a plan to continue on. Perrie, we can count on you to protect her for the next short while. Can we not?"

"Of course you can, Hemoth. Why shouldn't you be able to count on me?" Perrie scowled.

"I did not mean to insult you, miss, I'm sorry, I was out of line. I certainly meant better." He looked to Lightning. "Lightning, you and I have to get started."

"Yes we do, Hemoth. What will you ask of me?" Lightning stared at Madaliene with big, cloudy eyes. He was also feeling very down at the moment.

Perrie nodded them on. "Off with you two. Come back with a plan, right or wrong, we need to do something soon!" She looked back to Madaliene. "I will watch her. She is going nowhere."

Madaliene was kneeling on the ground with her legs tucked under her, sitting on her heels. Her head and shoulders slumped to her chest, her lungs continuing to heave. "Perrie, what have I done? Why is this all coming down on me right now? I can't stay strong all of the time. I need a break from this."

"Princess, that is why we are with you. You have two of the strongest creatures on this earth at your sides. You have me and the others fighting this unknown enemy with you. There is no need for you to feel like you must take all of this weight on your own."

"I know you are here with me. I know they are all here with me, but, I just took the lives of eight men without batting an eye, without giving them an option. A short time ago, I was of the mind to break the arm of a starving boy for bullying a smaller boy. Why did I do that? The ghosts and Lightning's ax thingy, how are we supposed to deal with those... oddities?"

"Those are questions that certainly need answering, Princess, but I can't begin to do that for you." Perrie looked off.

"Perrie, who can?" Madaliene wiped the remaining tears from her eyes. She slowly got to her feet and crossed her arms tightly across her. She looked to the sky, squinting her eyes. "Who can, Perrie?"

"Princess, I can understand your remorse for what has happened, but what would someone else have done? How would anybody else handle it? It was not a choice you had a lot of time to consider. If those invaders had succeeded in killing us first, where would the new future be headed? We are all on a pre-destined course here. How else would or could you explain it?"

"Perrie, I don't know. I really don't know." Madaliene was coming around. Her body language began to change as the guilty feelings dissipated. She was becoming the strong Princess again. "And, what we don't know, Perrie, will make me even more determined to find all of the answers." Madaliene uncrossed her arms and defiantly clenched her fists and placed them squarely on her hips. With her eyes still glistening with the teary moisture, she called to the Bears, "Hemoth, Lightning, it's time we do something. Let's get back to Nuorg as soon as possible. Lightning, tell your ax thingy that is where I want to go because it is where we need to be!"

Lightning heard Madaliene's resounding confidence and came to her at once. "Yes, Princess, I will let you tell my ax-pike what you just told me, if you don't mind." Lightning was inspired by her confidence, but he was not completely sure about telling the ax-pike what to do.

Hemoth stepped to Madaliene's side, "I am at your service, Princess. I see that you already have a plan to follow. I would have guessed as much."

"Hemoth, I most certainly do. Lightning, if you please?" She took the ax-pike from Lightning's grasp. "Wow, this thing is really heavy! That shouldn't matter, gather close to me." She lifted the ax-pike off the ground. "Really heavy." She sat it back to the ground. "Anyway, ax thingy, take us back to Nuorg, Burg One if you please, or thereabouts...really...close maybe? Oh, just get us out of here!"

Lightning and Hemoth looked at each other with lots of skepticism. They had no idea where they would end up now. Perrie dug in tight to the shoulder of Madaliene's jacket. "Oh mercy." Lightning got in the last word.

***

Frederick passed through the burnt door and back into the history library. He paused for a moment to collect his thoughts. There was no one in the room with him, so he began talking with himself. "What are you planning to do now, Frederick? Where do you suggest we start?" He shook his head. "Honestly, I don't know. Let's see what other titles we can find in here. Surely, there is a lot of information that survived the fire. Yes, I hope so and I need to find it." He made his way back to the farthest corner of the room and began reading title after title. Row after row of books, all sizes, begged for Frederick to pluck them from the shelves. Once again, Frederick spoke to himself. "There is no way I can begin to digest all of this information. There must be thousands of books in this room alone."

He pulled a large tome from a middle shelf. As he brushed off the front cover, he sighed. "What title do we have here?" He read out loud, "*'Metamorphosis as an Early Defense Mechanism'*. "Is that history? I have no idea." He placed it back on the shelf. He pulled another, slightly smaller book from a higher shelf. "*'Whatever You Need to Know is in This Book'*. Really?" He thumbed a few of the pages. "It certainly doesn't look that way." He replaced the book and selected another. *"Everything You Need to Know is in The Other Book'*. Huh?" He tried another book. "What is this one about?" He read the cover, "*'Trust Us, It is in the Other Book'*. What?" Frederick placed the book back where he found it. He stood motionless as his thoughts collected themselves. He scanned the room to see if any creature was in there with him. "Mystic, Bubba, either of you in here?" No answer came.

***

Mystic and Bubba trotted through the seemingly endless corridors searching for clues to the changes the posers may have made to the many facets of the fortress. "Bubba, I'm not sure anything looks different in here. Everything looks to be in its natural state to me. This place is so extensive, how could they have time to change anything other than rigging the doors to kill us?"

"I agree, Mystic, I can see nothing out of the ordinary in the least. What would they have wanted to do?"

"You are asking the wrong question to the wrong creature, Bubba. We could inspect these corridors for years and find nothing. I say we go back and help Frederick with whatever he is doing. This is crazy."

"I agree, Mystic. Let's go back."

***

Frederick heard no answer to his question. He pulled another book from a lower shelf. He read this title aloud also. "*'So, Are You Not Paying Attention?'* I'm losing my mind!" Frederick placed the book back. He hurried to the next row over and pulled down another, smaller book. "*Everything is in the First Book.*" He opened the dusty cover. On page after page were written the same words:

"We know you are here and we know what you are looking for. You need more information to move forward and that information is in the first book you picked up. You may think yourself crazy, but you are not. Go back to the first book.

Frederick shut the book and stuck it in his pocket. He retraced his steps and located the large tome. He took it from the shelf before quickly making his way to the soot covered table near the door. After placing the book on a cleared spot, he paced around the table fiddling with things in his pockets. "Even after all we have been through, it is still hard for me to believe that someone in the past has already solved or addressed the problems we are facing." He cupped his hands over his mouth. He blew a deep breath into them before rubbing them together. "There is no time like the present, I guess." He sat down at the table. "Here we go." Frederick opened the book.

The days that lie ahead will be challenging at the very least. This book contains a complete knowledge of everything our association has been able to discover during the construction of "An Chead Slibh de Dhia". This is the 7th and final volume. Volumes 1 – 6 will be located in the other libraries. There is no need to collect them all. We have not assembled them in the same library for the very reason you have just witnessed. Should all of them be destroyed, as in the recent fire, things may become even more difficult for you and your friends.

If you read from page one of this book, you will only be revisiting the paths your group has taken from the day the "well" located the Prince in the outer lands of the Great Forest. None of the events leading up to that moment should you concern yourself with at this time. You may want to skip to Chapter four. You will find the history picks up approximately where you are...

Frederick didn't know what to think. Of all of the experiences, so far, this was definitely one he wanted to remember. He jotted down some notes. He quickly perused the pages as he made his way to page one, chapter four. Occasionally, he slightly wetted his forefinger to get a better grip on the page corners, allowing him more speed with the process. He desperately wanted to stop and read a few paragraphs to explore the actual details of what had taken place unbeknownst to him, but he passed on the opportunities. "Ah, here we are page one, chapter four."

Sitting alone at one of several reading tables to survive the inferno, Frederick contemplated their next move. From the corridor the Prince called to him...

"Frederick, we are back." Mystic and Bubba entered the room. "There is far too much to explore here with any chance of noticing anything different. All we were able to do was appreciate the broader scope of this place."

"He's correct, sir, the corridors extend far beneath this mountain and, I'd venture to guess, all of this mountain's neighbors in all directions. This fortress is not merely contained inside one mountain." Bubba hopped up onto the table in front of Frederick. "So, what about this book has interested you so?"

Frederick smiled at the two four-leggers. "This book, friends, tells the world of our adventures, those we have been on and those we are about to experience."

Mystic rose off the floor, put his front paws on the table at Frederick's side and looked down at the pages. "You can't be serious, Frederick!"

"I am very serious, Prince."

Bubba stared directly at Frederick. "Close the book, Frederick. Close it now!"

"But..." Frederick placed his left forearm across the open pages and ran his hand under the back cover of the book as it lay on the table, lifting it slightly. "Bubba, are you sure?"

"Yes."

"Very well, then." Frederick closed the book.

"Now why did you do that?" Mystic had no idea what the other two were thinking. "What were we about to do?"

"We were about to change everything." Bubba looked away, perplexed.

"How?" Mystic's face was blank, seeking answers or an emotion he could wear.

Frederick clasped his hands together then placed them under his chin. He stared at the table, "What now, Cheetah?" He raised his eyes. "What now?"

A disturbance beyond the door got their attention. Cautiously, Frederick led Bubba and Mystic to the opening.

***

Hemoth recognized their surroundings immediately. "Princess, we are not in Nuorg."

"Where then are we? Wait..." Then she couldn't help but notice the detailed craftsmanship surrounding her coming into focus. "Why are we here?"

A familiar voice asked, "Where are the letters, Madaliene?"

"Uh...they are right in here." Madaliene took his bag from her shoulder and handed it to him. "There are two of them in there, side pocket."

"Yes, we know."

***

Lightning looked up at the canopy separating the cavern floor from the base of the Forever Trees. He had been here before. "Madaliene, we are where you wanted to be. Welcome back to Nuorg and Burg One!" He was taken back by the silence. "Hello? You are here, Madal..." The Badger slowly turned around to see that no one was accompanying him. "Hello? Is anyone else here with me?"

From atop his shoulder came one reply. “I am here, Lightning. Where are the other two?”

“Oh, mercy.”

13

Rhiannon eyed the dawn expectantly. Soon, she hoped, Broanick would be galloping to her side with comfort and duty in his words. Evaliene was resting in her saddle, the discomfort in her side temporarily blocked out by a deep sleep. Never one to admit to snoring, Evaliene snored audibly, not too loudly to be a threat, but enough to let Rhiannon know she was still alive. Rhiannon's hooves nervously patted the ground, sending sprinkles of dew covered, early morning dust into the air. As she waited, she tried to keep the events of the preceding days to a minimum. This was no time to reminisce over the past. "Leave it there," she told herself. "Leave it there."

And as he ran, Broanick's mind also drifted.

***

The two-legger, Broanick noticed, did not use the normal side saddle, as did the majority of female two-leggers. There was something special with this one. She sat in an immaculately made, very well-worn saddle which looked to be customized just for her. There was no gaudy ornamentation of any kind on the saddle. There were no jewels, no studding, no fancy stitching. It was simply an impeccable, hand-crafted saddle for riding. Judging by the keep's light, relaxed feel for the reins he immediately surmised she was quite capable of handling herself when riding under any circumstances. He noticed no nervous ticks or irregular breathing, no eye twitches, no beads of sweat on her exposed skin. She was cool and very much in charge. He could imagine the response from the white Horse would be explosive if even the slightest hint of command was given. He heard a very faint whisper within the two-legger's breath. The white Horse began confidently walking toward him, circling, keeping the rider barely out of his reach. He was impressed by the beauty of the two and the air of superiority that emitted from them. Broanick never flinched as the Horse and rider silently circled about him, nor did he bother following them with his eyes. He stood at ease, letting them study him as they pleased. He had nothing to hide. It was the rider who spoke next.

"Horse of black, the night will hide you, let you loose to wander.
Horse of white, the day be for you, the black one's dream to ponder.
Rider for you, two blessed for comp'ny, a gift you shall not squander."

"Excuse me?" Broanick heard the words as if they were spoken directly to him. Could she be a Talker?

"Excuse you? Why should I excuse you? Am I correct to assume you know no other Talkers? Shall I also assume you refused to believe there were any of us that remained?"

Broanick tried not to show any surprise. "You are correct. I know no other Talkers and I also believed the last of the Talkers died out many years before your time."

"You can't know how many years I have been living. You know nothing of me Horse. How can you even conceive of what you don't know to be? There are more Talkers. We are still around. I despise the fact that you even suggest such a ludicrous notion."

Rhiannon moved closer to Broanick to allow her keep to look down more directly at him. The black Horse did not move.

"Since you can understand me two-legger, my name is Broanick. You can address me by what I am called, not what I am."

Rhiannon tensed noticeably, "Do not speak to my keep without permission." Her delivery was even and deliberate, emotionless. "Should she wish to be spoken to by you, she will tell you so. Again, we are being watched. Should she give the wrong signal, an arrow will slice through your chest, lodge in your heart and you will fall to the ground dead. I would be very careful if I were you."

Broanick was impressed. His eyes, once again, looked upon the exquisite beauty of the white Horse. "You have quite the imagination. You suggest me to believe that somewhere above or below us you have protectors watching our every move? What else should I be led to believe?"

A slight adjustment of the rider's head in conjunction with an imperceptible tap of her foot at Rhiannon's side was all it took. The white Horse swayed to her right as an arrow passed neatly at her side, landing between the front hooves of Broanick. Again, the black Horse did not flinch. “Very well, we are being watched. How do you know that I have no followers as well?”

The two-legger answered, “If you did, Broanick, I would know by now, and if you did, they may all also be dead by now or under a threat of their lives given their disposition. My Protectors do not take their job lightly. They are very good at what they do.” She barely raised her hand that was free from the reins. The trees came alive with nearly a full 100 imposing figures, stepping out from everywhere. None of them said a word. “Do you have any other questions or doubts, Horse?”

Broanick’s eyes swept the area surrounding them. “No, no, I do not. Not at this time.” He was impressed. “If I may, who are you?”

Rhiannon answered, “No, you may not.” She felt the knee movement. “We will be leaving now. You will be staying. Do you understand?”

“No, I do not understand. What was the significance of the poem? You have to answer me that.”

Rhiannon began to prance in place, rearing up slightly, ready to explode.

The two-legger answered, “When we are safely away, one of my Protectors will answer some of your questions. He will explain to you the poem. I will not, not now.”

Rhiannon, powered by her muscular legs, exploded into the moonless night. Before Broanick could utter another word, the Horse and rider had vanished. The white Horse was spectacular. He would find her again. If it took his life, he would find her again. He had no sooner watched the pair vanish when he felt the loops of three ropes lightly land around his neck.

Rhiannon galloped into the darkness, hooves pounding in rhythm with the beating of her heart. Evaliene held effortlessly in saddle. Rhiannon broke into a clearing then quickly headed for the tree line on her left side. Feeling the distance traveled from the black Horse’s position was sufficient, she slowed to a brisk walking gait before stopping beneath a large oak tree canopy. “That went perfectly, Evaliene. How did you know he would be there?”

“I don’t believe I did, really.”

***

Broanick ran tirelessly through the night. For every step traveled by his steed, Sean steadfastly held tight to the reins. Broanick was impressed with his rider's tenacity. "Finally," he thought, "A two-legger worthy of his weight." They had to be nearing the rendezvous point. The night had not revealed the distance traveled. Soon, the morning's sunrise would reacquaint him with his whereabouts.

"You brave Horse; I can't fathom where you could be taking me. I do hope it is toward the princess." Sean spoke to himself. It was of no use to try and converse with the swift, muscular four-legged animal beneath him. He was not a Talker now and he would never be in his future. The Talkers were of more royal blood than even the royals as a general rule. As a Protector, he had one mission in life; protect Princess Evaliene - to the death, to the end, to whatever or whenever – that was his only purpose. Not his only purpose for living; simply his only purpose while living. Having no time to prepare for this excursion, his store of arms was noticeably absent. The knife he carried at his waist and his keen wits would have to suffice should an altercation arise once he was reunited with his charge. Just as Broanick did, Sean hoped the meeting place was soon to come upon them.

The horse and rider continued in full gallop. The sun was breaking on the horizon. The mountains began to separate themselves from the low clouds. A small river ran directly ahead, then the foothills awaited where Rhiannon would be standing watch with her keep. Broanick measured the distance – a short run easily, he didn't see the trouble. He ran with mental blinders, the route, so carefully ingrained in his head, could have been run with eyes tightly closed. Past the river, Sean spied a moving line beneath the break where the foothills began. Distance blurred the details, slowly coming into view, but what did he see? Should he call Broanick off? Should they slow the pace? Skirt the direct path or plow directly into whatever awaited them? Each of them, without uttering a sound, decided on the latter. Nothing, they thought, would stop them now, not this late in the chase.

From their haven higher in the foothills, Rhiannon and Evaliene watched as the swarm of wingers gathered below them. "Should that bother us, Rhiannon?" Evaliene asked.

"Those particular wingers are not bothering me, Princess. Should they keep amassing, I might see a problem. Who are they waiting for? Is this a meeting of some kind?"

"Lovely Horse, I cannot begin to say. I have never been in this region before, remember? My location has solely been your responsibility. Who laid this plan we now follow?"

"Of that, I am not sure, Princess."

"Rhiannon, we need to find something...a place to hide if need be."

"Princess, that place has already been located. I know where it is and we can get there if necessary."

"Can we get there without being followed, if we are spotted by any of those below?"

"We can if they mean us harm."

"Then you intend for me to use the heirloom? Is that correct?"

"Yes, Princess, it is. If need be, you will unleash that thing on whoever or whatever poses a threat to us. There will be no question. Is that clear?"

"Yes, it is."

"Get it in your hands then."

"But, what if they mean us no harm?"

"We will concern ourselves with that, if that happens."

"Very well." Evaliene removed the heirloom from its holster in her riding boot. "I have it, Rhi."

"Good. If I give you the word, use it." They continued to watch the gathering of the wingers, fascinated by the vast number accumulating. "Princess, do you notice anything strange down there?"

"Obviously, I do. Why do you ask that question?"

"Because, to me, they look anxious for some reason I can't fathom. They seem more scared than nervous. Normally, you see wingers flitting around in a group. Those are standing still as stones. From here it is difficult to discern, but, I think they are terrified of something."

"I will take your word for that, Rhiannon." Evaliene noticed movement beyond the gathered wingers. "Look there, Rhiannon, can you see that?"

"Where?"

"East, at the break of the horizon. Is that..."

Rhiannon stared past the gathering. "How can you see anything out there? Are you using the...?"

"Of course I am!"

"Well that explains a lot. I can see nothing out that far." Rhiannon turned her focus back to the wingers.

"It's a Horse and rider."

"Is it Broanick, Princess? Who is in saddle?"

"It is hard for me to believe his involvement, but yes, it does look like him with none of that ridiculous armor. The rider is one of my Protectors. I believe they call him Sean. Again, when am I to know all of this?"

Rhiannon began to stamp her feet nervously. "You will never know it all, Princess. Too much information would surely mean your demise. You will learn more than enough as our journey continues."

"What do you know of the letters I have written? Why have there been so many?"

"Once again, Princess, there are those things that you will not know for now. I am sorry to keep you in the dark, but I must."

"Very well, they are getting closer. The wingers seem to have noticed them as well."

"This could be interesting or disastrous. Keep a close watch on the wingers. If they attack Broanick and Sean, hang on. We will rush to their aid and you will use the heirloom. Any questions?"

"No. I hear what you are saying very clearly."

On the other side of the wingers, Broanick continued his torrid pace. The wingers watched as they neared. Each winger froze as the Horse and rider neared. Those still flying in dropped out of the sky immediately.

Broanick, finally coming out of his goal-induced stupor, noticed the wingers ahead. "Not here! Not now!" He continued his charge, Sean merely along for the ride.

High above even the highest flying winger, she soared.

***

There were only five of them now. Five left to fly the world. Five true Messengers--that was it. No more to come. No more to train. They had grown old and weary. They were more than ready to pass along their responsibilities to a new age, but, the new age never came. None like her had been born since her youngest sister. Two brothers, two sisters, they were all that was left of their family, their clan, their kind. Why had they been chosen? The answer, for lack of a better explanation, was why not?

***

Broanick galloped full speed into the throng of wingers, avoiding those not quick enough to part in his path with adept hoof movements. As he reached the mass' center, he slowed to a stop. The wingers gathered closely to him, every eye glued to him. He surveyed those gathered. Almost every type of winger imaginable was represented. He did not hide his disappointment well. Sean had no idea of what was going on around him. He sat attentively and watched.

Broanick studied the wingers with interest. "Where is Cahmun?"

A large winger approached Broanick. He wore brownish, gray wings with a white chest and belly. His head was roundish with short, spikey feathers and a grey stripe on each side. Close to an Eagle in size, his feet were white. "Cahmun did not make it. Are you Broanick?"

"I am Broanick. Who are you and what do you mean he did not make it? He did not make what?"

"Cahmun is dead. He was killed when they attacked our coastline. I am Pandion, an Osprey and Cahmun's father. He shared with me all of the details. It was my duty to carry out his wishes. His mother, Ossifragus, awaits my return with our instructions."

Broanick became distraught. "The coastline was attacked also? Where are the rest of you?" He spoke to the entire group. "Who do we have from the south, the west?" No winger spoke up.

She was low enough to hear whispers of the conversations. It was against her specific plan to get involved, but, she did have the option to use her own judgment in situations such as this. She circled down to the gathering.

An immense, ominous shadow drifted low over the assembly. Sean saw the enormous creature as it flapped its huge wings to land. Broanick shuddered as she set down in front of him. The smaller wingers scattered in silence.

Evaliene and Rhiannon watched the events unfold. "This is invoking a slight change in plans, Princess. Hold on." Rhiannon hurried down the path with Evaliene holding tight in the saddle. She held a steady gait until the ground leveled out beneath her, she then galloped to Broanick's side.

She saw the white Horse and the princess heading her way. She nodded to Broanick before turning her entire body in the direction of the incoming white Horse. She patiently waited their arrival before uttering a single word. As Rhiannon and Evaliene approached the outermost wingers, she spread her vast wings wide, hiding Broanick, Sean and a host of smaller wingers behind them. She bowed low, making a splendid sight to behold.

"It seems the crowd is expecting us, Rhiannon. Why is that so?"

"It does seem that way, doesn't it, Princess." Rhiannon paused as they neared the edge of group. The wingers parted, each one curtsied or bowed as the magnificent white Horse carried her charge to greet the giant winger.

"Do all of these wingers know who I really am, Rhiannon? Who told them?"

"Princess, those of us in duty to you know and the others are expectantly assuming." Rhiannon continued directly toward the largest winger she had ever encountered. Broanick beamed with pride behind the curtain of wings.

At long last, the newest and largest addition to the flocks bowed deeply to Evaliene, then, she spoke, "Princess O'shay, meeting you face to face is both an honor and my curse. White Horse," she swept her wings back. "Please step closer to me and the other leggers. I want to say this one time." She folded her wings to her side, patiently waiting on Rhiannon to position herself beside Broanick.

Broanick beamed, "I am relieved to see you two in good health, Rhiannon." The two Horses nuzzled, as expected.

"Was everything in order back at the village before you left? Is the Rider in the grasp of the Protectors?"

"Yes. Everything is secure. There will be questions surrounding our hasty departures though. My rider set the next phase in action before we left. I can only wish he was a Talker."

"He isn't?"

"Unfortunately, he is not." Broanick stared at Rhiannon as if he were, again, trying to capture her beauty in his mind.

Evaliene turned her attention to the gigantic winger. "May I ask who you are, great winger?"

"No, Princess, you may not. I will not answer any questions yet. Please listen and remember what I have to say. It will be in all of the gathered creatures' best interest to get as close to me as they can. I will only say what I have to say once. Then, I will be back to my duty."

Evaliene glanced to her hand, observing that she was still holding the non-glowing heirloom. "Very well then winger, you have the floor."

She did not thank Evaliene for the opportunity to speak. She spoke eloquently and precisely. "What I have to say is this; beware of the intelligents. There are four others like me who report back on your progress toward driving out the intruding dooms. We are spies for the good. Look around you all. You wingers are all that are left in this side of your world. There remain about the same number in the other parts. Do not let your guard down. The ones responsible for the decline in your numbers will be back. They want to cut all methods of communication off. By eliminating your kind, they will succeed. They are ruthless and evil. They will win if you fail." She looked for the Osprey, "You there, Pandion, you must seek out Vincen, the Great Eagle from the Great Forest. He holds the same esteem in his territory as do you in yours, with one exception. He has been to Nuorg."

Pandion stepped in closer. "Are you telling me that Nuorg actually exists?"

"Yes I am, Osprey." She adjusted her head to make eye contact with Evaliene. "Princess, your sister is looking for you. If she doesn't find you first, you must find her."

Evaliene straightened in her saddle. "Is she? Did she get the letter? How? My messenger is captive. Which letter did she get?"

The huge winger answered, "The one she was meant to get. You two must find each other." That was the end of the conversation. The giant winger spread her wings, flapped them a few times and disappeared into the morning sky. On her way up, she once again warned the gathered, "Beware of the intelligents."

***

In the village, the Protectors were having little trouble subduing the visitors who remained. When word got around that the Rider was imprisoned, his minions gave little fight. It wasn't their fight. Several broke under questioning and those that didn't initially give up answers were quickly forthcoming with any details they knew or could make up when shown the Rider. His condition was not suitable for recording in the journals. Let it be known that certain methods were used to retrieve information from him. The methods were not entirely civil, but, the Protectors were not always civil people.

Paddy left the blacksmith's shop at dawn. He first noticed the bag hanging on a tall bush in front of the princess' dwelling as he stepped past her fence and onto her grassy yard. He searched everywhere in the cottage, hoping the princess had not left anything of importance behind. The sun rose. He was relieved when he found nothing. As he stepped past the tall bush, again he eyed the ragged bag. This time it moved. "It can't be!" he shouted. He reached high, but could not touch the bag. He frantically searched the grounds for a long stick of some kind to rescue the cloth sack from its snag. He found a long-handled rake someone had tossed aside during the melee. With it, he lifted the bag off the branch and brought it down. The content of the bag was still moving, but very weakly. Paddy took his side knife from his belt and cut off the knotted draw cord. He carefully placed the bag on the stone walkway, opened it up and delicately removed the breathing creature from within. He became ecstatic, "You are hurt badly, brave one. I will guarantee to you, you will fly again soon." He raced to his dwelling. With everything already happening, there was now even one more very important thing to do.

***

Sean sat waiting for any command from Evaliene. "Princess, what was all of that about? Not being a Talker, I can only guess."

"Sean, I wish you were a Talker. The winger just warned us to beware of the intelligence."

"What did it mean by that?" Sean shook his head.

"I wish I was more sure, Sean. I do." Evaliene leaned over to question Rhiannon. "Rhi, do you or the black Horse understand that message?"

"Princess, his name is Broanick and you know that. Please call him by his name and no, we do not. Do we, Broanick?"

"I am not sure Rhiannon. It will take some studying on all of our part. That must begin now."

Evaliene interrupted, "First, we must find my sister."

Sean twitched. "There is no way we can do that now, Princess! We will need a small army to find her. Where do you suppose we get one?"

"Sean, I have a plan for that. We will have to use those creatures you see here - not all of them, just as many as they think necessary." Quickly, her focus turned to Pandion, "Osprey, perch up on my Horse's neck, would you? Our visitor thought highly of you, I assume I should also."

Pandion did as instructed. "Yes, Princess? What will you have me do?"

"I am not sure yet, Pandion. You shall be in on our planning. You must petition the group of wingers here and find out what they know. Select a few with leadership and knowledge. If I am correct, each of you knows more about this than either of us two-leggers."

"You may be correct, Princess. I will do as you say. Give me a little while to gather what they know. I will get back to you as I can."

Lost in the proceedings were the majority of the wingers. The large group settled into three or four smaller groups, each with an impromptu leader. Pandion noticed this, immediately calling those now in charge to his side.

Evaliene watched with confidence as the Osprey played his role. "Rhiannon, what now? Do you or Broanick have a plan? What about you, Sean? Should you ride back or stay with us?"

"Princess, my first plan was to take you back with me."

"I'm sorry, Sean, that will not be happening. You will stay with us. We will send some of the wingers back to the village. What of the Protectors? How many can you spare from there?"

***

Set in his ways and settled in to his new community as well as could be expected, the oldest of the three sons, Paddy, was the most qualified for the current emergency. He gingerly carried the bag's traumatized prisoner as carefully as possible through the village. He must get to his dwelling quickly and, at the same time, transport the badly hurt creature with care. Time passed much too slowly, in his mind, as he made his way down the narrow alleys and roads. He stepped to his door without wasting any time. Met at the door by his loving wife, he placed the creature in her capable hands. "We must have her flying again soon, Jeenay. There isn't another option. Do what you can, for all of our sakes."

His wife looked down at the creature in her arms. “She is hurt terribly, Paddy, but I will do everything I can.”

“Thank you. I know you will. I must get back to my brother. We have so much to do with Sean searching for the princess.”

“I understand, Paddy.” Jeenay spoke with a captivating accent, her personality gave everything she said a nice lilt. “Oh, Paddy, this can’t be…?”

“Yes, love, I’m afraid it is.”

A tear rolled down Jeenay’s beautifully sculpted cheek. She turned her attention to her ailing patient.

***

“Princess, when can we send a winger back? Kelly and Paddy need to know what to do.” Sean was not happy about the new turn of events. He thought he would simply locate Evaliene and return her to the safety of the village. That was not an option now.

“We shall wait, Sean, until the Osprey informs us as to what they are capable of. Without that information, we can’t make any plans.” Evaliene watched closely as the Osprey carried out her instructions. “He seems very capable of handling the situation.”

Sean watched as well. “It amazes me how much intelligence these creatures have…”

Evaliene cut his sentence short, “What did you just say about intelligence?”

Sean answered combined with a quick sideways glance, “I said it amazes me how much intelligence these creatures have. Why?”

“That huge winger just warned us to beware of the intelligence. Why would she say the intelligence? I realize the different dialects and so forth of the animals’ way of speaking, but, normally the usage of proper grammatical devices is a constant.”

“I’m sorry, Princess, you lost me. What are you saying?”

“That winger, Sean, she warned us of the intelligence. She did not say beware of intelligence, she clearly said beware of the intelligence! I don’t think she was speaking about intelligence as an entirely mental aptitude.”

"I am sorry, Princess. I am not an educated person beyond what I have been taught to protect you. You are not making a lot of sense to me. What are you saying?"

She chastised her Protector, "Sean, never in my presence again will you speak of yourself as being uneducated. Is that clear? Of course you are educated! Because you are educated in many ways that I am not is, by no means, a liability. Enough on that already, I am inclined to think the winger was warning us of a creature or creatures with a high degree of intelligence. That makes the warning even more perplexing." She scanned the groups of wingers. "Sean, does anything about this hodge-podge of wingers strike you as odd?"

"Princess, I can't answer that. Truthfully, everything about this is odd to me."

"No, look carefully at these bunches. What is missing? There is nearly every type of winger represented here but one particular kind. Am I wrong?"

Sean studied each group. With his eyes, he intently surveyed each individual species of winger assembled around them. Something clicked in his head. "That is odd, isn't it, Princess."

"So you see it the way I do? There is one type that is not represented here at all. Not in any shape, size or color."

"Do you think that really has anything to do with what is going on around us?"

"I am not sure yet. It is scrumptious food for thought though, is it not?"

"Yes, Princess, it is worth thinking about."

"Yes it is, indeed."

***

Pandion was very comfortable with the leadership role thrust upon him by Evaliene. A lot of time had passed under the bridge and everywhere else since he was last summoned to a role similar to this. Those now beneath him in rank, more or less, did not feel slighted in the least after meeting him. His eyes comforted each one of them and, too, he had felt the sting of death from the seemingly perpetual onslaught of evil. That alone made him one of their own.

"Alright," he began. "Tell me what each of you brings to the table. From the looks of it here, I can see we have swift flyers and fast flyers of all sizes. Tell you what; I want each of you to pair up accordingly. Once you find your running mate, find three more wingers here to make up your particular group. It will be up to the princess to give you further directives. Those that remain will make up our supporting staff. Come back when you have your company complete. Remember, you must be able to get along with those you select to fly with you. No excuses. Better not to make a mistake from the get go. I will let the princess know our intentions." Pandion flew to the princess. He lit on the saddle horn.

"That was rather a quick meeting, wouldn't you say, Pandion? What have you to tell me?" Evaliene was impressed, so far.

Pandion advised Evaliene, Sean and the Horses of his plan. If acceptable to all, he would report back to his groups and get them on their way.

"What say you, Princess?" Pandion bowed his head.

"Under these dire circumstances, I say do as you have planned. I would much rather learn something about each of your chosen, but time will not allow that. I will trust you explicitly, Pandion and, by the same token, hold you solely responsible for their actions. Do as you must, Osprey."

Pandion never blinked an eye. "As you instruct, Princess. I, too, will hold myself solely responsible. I will leave on your command and I do promise, Princess, I will return to you, but first I must meet with my squadrons."

***

Rhiannon and Broanick stood happily side-by-side. This tolerated mingling had been looked forward to by each Horse. Finally, Broanick felt he could be a non-despised four-legger again. The ruse was beginning to take a toll on him.

Evaliene bent over Rhiannon's mane. She whispered to her. "Rhiannon, dear Horse, would you wish me to dismount so that you and Broanick might spend some private time together? I'm not sure how much free time we will have in the coming days."

"Thank-you, Princess, we can wait for that time. Though we greatly appreciate your offer, we will not leave you for any reason right now. Rest assured, we are happy to once again be a pair."

"Very well," Evaliene sat up in the saddle. "Sean, it's time you tell me what you know about all of this."

"I was afraid you would get around to asking me that, Princess."

***

"So this really is all that is left?" Pandion looked over the crowd of wingers now gathered in front of him. "They have actually done it. Have any of you actually seen the perpetrators with your own eyes? Who are they? Who is leading them? This is murder! I was sadly hoping the attack on my coastline was a rogue group of attackers, but, what I am hearing is that they have been making these attacks wherever we are. That is brilliantly evil. They have efficiently cut all lines of communication off. We must defy the odds and survive!" The Osprey was visibly demonstrative. His anger flared from every feather. "We will stop this! We will!"

***

Evaliene asked Rhiannon to take her over near where Pandion was storming about. "You must get me closer. We need to hear what has him so worked up."

"Yes, Princess, something has set him off."

"Sean, you and Broanick stay back and keep your eyes open."

Sean objected, "Princess, we need to get you to a safer location. Right out in the open like this, well...I don't think it wise."

"You are correct, Sean. Give me one moment with the wingers."

As the two left his side, Sean shook his head helplessly. He sat silently, but agitated.

Rhiannon trotted hurriedly to Pandion's group. Evaliene's attention focused once again on the Osprey. "Excuse me, Pandion, I can't help but notice you are becoming very agitated. What is causing it?"

"I apologize, Princess. It seems the collectors have been cleaning up after situations that are both unknown and appalling to me. It is not what they have done, it is what or who caused the situation to occur in the first place that upsets me. Do you know, Princess, throughout every region of the world represented here today, there have been literally hundreds of attacks on wingers? I am not talking about running them out of a particular area. I am talking about mass annihilation of the highest degree. I can only speculate, but I believe the intent is to cut off every line of communication known to us all. The poor Pigeons have nearly lost their will to fly and they are the best communicators we have!"

"I was afraid something like that was taking place. Not too many wingers left in the skies where I was either. Pandion, quickly tell me who is missing from this group. Don't scan the group again, just tell me. I find it odd there are none of that certain group represented here."

Pandion closed his eyes. He visualized the groups about him. Without opening an eye he answered, "Yes, Princess, why do you suppose there are no representatives of that species?"

"I was hoping you could tell me."

"Princess, we must leave here immediately." Sean was speeding in her direction, Broanick's nostrils flared. He yelled loudly, "Pandion, divide your groups. It is not safe here any longer. We have been spotted."

A panicked cry escaped from the assembly. Wingers flew off in every direction. High in the azure blue sky, the reason was clear. Hundreds of wingers dotted the blueness off the horizon. They were heading directly at the meeting area. Each of the incoming wingers flew lazily on as Pandion's groups scattered for safety. Broad, black wings with finger-like feathers on the ends attached to muscular thick bodies slowly materialized in a zigzagged line that stretched forever to the naked eye. Evaliene stood her ground, holding tight to the reins while Rhiannon pulled hard in the other direction.

"Princess," she said through her bridled teeth, "Let me run. You have to get out of here!"

"No, Rhiannon, these wingers are not attacking us."

Pandion sided with Evaliene, "Princess, is this a wise move not to fly? If you wish to die, I will stay at your side."

Sean moved Broanick tightly beside Rhiannon. "Princess, if one of those wingers dives on you, fall behind me. I will deal with the threat."

"That won't be necessary, Sean. Look."

The lead coal black winger lit a short distance in front of Evaliene. Those flying behind him did the same. Hundreds of them lined up side by side, row by row until every last dot in the sky landed. It was a quite a sight to see.

In a raspy-edged voice, the first winger to land addressed Evaliene. "Princess, I am Corvus. We are Crows. Our numbers are still strong. We have not been decimated yet as the others have been. I will attribute part of that to our smarts and the rest to pure luck. We were summoned to your aide by your messenger. Where is she, might I ask?"

"Come to me, Corvus. Perch on this saddle horn."

Corvus did as he was told. "What have you to say?"

"Corvus, my messenger was taken from me long ago by some thieves. Much more than common thieves they are too. I have not seen her in...I can't remember how long. She must have taken it on herself to send for you. I take it you are a friend of hers?"

"Yes I am. A relative of mine was raised in the same forest."

"That must be the Great Forest?"

"One in the same."

"Are these all of you left?"

"No, no it is not. The majority of us are in hiding. We have our ways. Being this color has its merits."

14

The Falcons made good time flying at their pursuit beat. Normally when Tofur's whistle blew they would turn instantly to his side. They would have done the same on this occasion, except they were too far down range. Nearing the familiar intersection now, Whistler asked as he continuously scanned the ground far below. "How far are we to fly before we start investigating?"

"That seems to be the most broad ranging question I have ever been asked. I can't say that I know how far. Here is the intersection where so much happened earlier, I presume we should start asking our own questions now. Do you remember anything odd in the actions of the leggers before we arrived here?"

"I think all of them act pretty oddly. You do mean the leggers not in our company, correct?"

"Why, of course I do. I know what each of them have been doing...the same as us. I'm asking if you recall anything in passing. Did you see or hear anything we could follow up on?"

"That is what I thought you meant. My answer to that would be no."

"I understand. We have all been too caught up in our own mission to notice there may be others out on missions or assignments of their own. I think we should drop down and start nosing around. Follow me."

Whistler agreed, "Lead the way. Let's get on with this. The sooner we have clues and retrieve the map case, the sooner we can get back to the others."

The Falcons descended to tree level, continuing to scan for any gathering of leggers or commotions. Actually, if they could find any creature to communicate with, they were willing to give it a try. Whistler was the first to see breathing activity below. He gracefully swooped over toward a medium-sized four-legger grazing beside a clump of trees. The legger hardly missed a blade of grass as the two wingers appeared beside him. Not wanting to be intrusive, the pair silently stood by, waiting on acknowledgement from their host. They watched in unison as one blade after another was clipped off close to the ground before being noisily ground into a green paste between the legger's flat teeth. The legger eyed the Falcons warily and kept chewing. After what seemed to be a short eternity, it spoke. "Can I help you?" The legger seemed hospitable enough; still, there was an edge of annoyment not completely hidden in his tone of voice.

"Thank you so much for asking, sir, we certainly hope so," Whistler answered. "We are searching for any signs or information that may lead us to the end of a mystery, if you will."

"What he is trying to say," added Taytay, "is this; have you been privy to any talk of a pair of two-leggers coming through this area and stealing a map from some poor creature? From what we hear, the creature got the bad end of the deal. We heard he was killed."

"Maybe I have heard of something similar to that. Why is it any concern of yours?" A slight wrinkle above the eyes gave away any hope of the legger denying the information. Regardless, he kept eating.

"Simply put, we must know what you know. It is imperative that we return to the spot of that unfortunate deed and recover an item that was overlooked by the attackers. They are not a very smart pair, nor are their hearts in what they are doing." Whistler was taking the lead in the conversation. "There was no need in killing the messenger as they did. We are here because we are the ones who should have taken delivery of the package. We are part of a bigger group and will not take lightly what has happened."

"What he is saying is the truth, should you have any doubts." Taytay hoped he added credence to Whistler's statement. He didn't.

"And who are you and why should I believe you have better intentions than those who took whatever it is they took?" The legger didn't really care, but he was hungry and these wingers were interrupting a very good meal.

"We are Falcons from the South. We are accompanying our falconer, his Dog and his Mule on a journey for the greater good. The details are many and our time is limited. Do you have any information you can share with us? I will plead with you if I must." Whistler took a step closer to the legger.

"No, you won't have to beg, but the news was not well received around here when it happened. I suggest you talk with the collector. He knows all when it comes to killings around here. You will find him circling high above us. He is always on the prowl for those kinds of events, be it natural or un-natural occurrences of the like. He and his kind are very capable with what they do."

Taytay asked, “Is he called the collector by all?

“He is called that by everyone around here. We could call him by a viler name, but the collector works well for us. I’ll warn you, if he is on the ground, the smell will be as ripe as his breath. It won’t bode well for you if you two cannot tolerate his practices. He and his kind are very particular. They do us a service, and in doing so, we respect them for it. Please try to ignore as much as you can if your stomachs are weak.”

“Very well, sir, where might he be?” Whistler was not sure about the validity of legger’s comments.

“Like I said before, he will be up in the sky circling if he is not busy collecting. You will have to find him yourself, but I doubt that he is very far away. Now, if you don’t mind, I will get back to minding my own business.”

“Thank you for your help, sir. We won’t hinder you any longer.” Taytay said the goodbyes while Whistler took wing. He caught up with him shortly after. “It sounded to me as the legger was forthcoming about what he knew.”

“Yes, Taytay, I think he was. I have a weird feeling about the collector. I think I know what he collects. Keep your nose open, we need to head for the worst smell we can imagine or a horde of high-circling dark wingers.”

“I was afraid of that.”

The pair searched the sky and the ground for most of the next few clicks. They spotted what they were looking for off to the west. They flew there quickly. A group of oily feathered, medium-sized black wingers circled a smaller group directly below them. Taytay’s ill feelings towards the collector’s duties were well-founded, for not far below them lay a dead four-legger surrounded by a few of the dark wingers. Off to the side, a second four-legger was conversing with, what looked to be, the leader of the flock. Taytay flew in beside one of the circlers. “Where can I find the collector?”

The winger answered, “He’s down there with the livin’. You got a dead ‘un on your hands? Eh, talons? We are kinda busy right now. It may take a few days on this one.”

“No, no, we need to talk with him about an event...might have happened a bit ago, don’t really know exactly when it happened.”

“Sure, be my guest. Try to wait ‘til he quits with the livin’ there, they tend to be pretty upset when this happens. Can’t say that I blame them much.”

"Thank you. We will." Taytay led Whistler to the ground. They waited reverently as the conversation continued.

"So, what do we do from here?" The livin' asked.

"You keep on doin what you were doin. Nothing should change far as that goes now. We will be respectful of your dead 'un. You need to move along now. Can't be too pleasant from your perspective now."

"It is hard to let go of that life."

"If I might say so, that life is gone now. Nothing left but flesh and bones. That over there is not what you knew. What you knew has moved on to that other place, a better place and you should be too. Compassion is a difficult emotion for me to command, so if you will, please move on now. Don't look back. You don't want to remember like that."

"Very well, do as you do. I will remember in another place." The four-legger turned and walked away with not even one glance back. Life here had an efficient way of separating the living and the dead.

The dark winger looped his bald head to the Falcons. "You got a dead 'un I need to collect, do you?"

"No, we have nothing for you to collect, we have questions." Whistler cringed. He was waiting for a blast of rancid breath that never passed his way.

"Hah, I see you been talking with the Goat! I see by your actions he told you that the smell of my breath was a bad and terrible thing. Funny thing, that Goat, his breath has got to be the worst-smelling thing around these parts... Well, not the worst, but it is close. Call me Motrey or you can call me the collector, makes no difference to me. Can't get caught up with that kind of thing."

"Motrey it is." Taytay liked this winger, not much in the appearance department, but the creature did have a way about him.

"You had some questions?"

"Yes we do. Our questions refer to what you call a dead 'un. We don't know when it happened, but an odd pair of two-leggers robbed a messenger who was bringing something to us. Before they took what they wanted from him, they killed him. It seems, from what we have heard, the robbers left a case or wrapping of some kind over the creature's dead eyes because the eyes kept looking at them. Do you remember anything like that recently?" Whistler relaxed his posture when he left the question hanging.

"Oh yes, I do. I remember it vividly. It was eerie alright. I never saw a pair of dead 'un's eyes like that before. We collected it as we do, and left whatever it was hanging in a tree over where the brave creature died. Quite a specimen it was too. I would never have guessed a pair of two-leggers could make a dead 'un out of that creature as easily as they did. The strange thing about that is we collected two more leggers that looked just like the first one. Something must have gotten to them earlier, maybe poisoned their foods or something. All three of them looked like they could easily take care of themselves. Big, strong black Dogs with patches of brown on them, mighty fine looking."

Whistler and Taytay grimaced at the details. "There were three of them and they were all dead?"

"Yes, there were three. If there were more, we never found them. Did you know them?"

"Yes we did, we knew them very well." Whistler couldn't look Taytay in the eye.

Taytay's eyes fell to the ground, his feathers wilted. "Belle is going to be heart broken."

Whistler added, "She will be devastated."

The collector noticed the body language. "So you did know them?"

"Yes, we were always afraid they wouldn't stay put. They were supposed to wait for word from us before following. It sounds like they did their own bit of investigating and intercepted the messenger. Those three... never thinking of themselves."

"You know how they were, Whistler." Taytay continued, "Too young to be afraid and old enough to think they could succeed. Motrey, could we ask you to take us to where you found the first one? We need to retrieve what the two-leggers left."

"Yes, I will take you. Let me get my folks started over here first."

The Falcons watched as the collector joined the other wingers. After a short conversation, a second one came to his side and they both headed back. Those remaining quickly got to the work at hand. With sickening sounds, one after another began to tear the dead 'un apart with powerful, cutting thrusts of their sharp beaks. Whistler and Taytay turned their heads away from the carnage. The collector made his way back, he couldn't help but notice the misty eyes watching him. "Sorry about that, what you saw there can be quite disturbing. What is more disturbing is that it doesn't bother us at all, never has. This world is strange you know that? This world is strange." Motrey nodded solemnly, "Follow me."

***

The professor busily found the tools he needed among several that were scattered between him and the tool bag. Carefully, he selected the perfect tool for his intended purposes. Tofur watched closely as his whistle was delicately refined and adjusted before his unsure eyes. Again and again, Mariel would make a slight adjustment with a tool then admire his work beneath a large magnifying glass. Over and over again, Mariel meticulously made almost the exact movement with his tool, honing the whistle as only he knew it should be.

As Tofur watched the craftsman's process, Belle, Jak and Porcene proceeded to make the plans to catch their prey. Time was flying by and progress had to be made sooner than later. Belle was leading the meeting.

"I have no idea, Porcene, where you and the professor come in to play here. Why are you following the two-leggers anyway? Who set you two in motion? We have been attempting to trail those two since they left our country. Tofur's family is well-connected. We were told of one mission, and that was to tail those leggers and report back any information. Now it seems to me that we are the ones in charge and if we ever get any information back to his family, it will be a sheer stroke of luck! Is this making any sense to you, Jak? And, by the way, you can cease with the "mildly dumb" act for the time being. We need to you be on your game from here on. Porcene, what do you bring to the table?"

"Yes," Jak agreed. "What do you bring to the table besides your good looks and ample load carrying ability?"

"Wait, Jak...you were acting dumb? All this time?" Porcene was impressed. "It must take a lot of smarts to act like a complete dolt."

"Excuse me?" Jak admonished her.

"Hold it, that isn't going to get us anywhere. Again Porcene, what can you do to improve our talents?" Belle took the conversation over again.

Porcene seemed slightly troubled, "Belle, I can't tell you why I am even here. If it wasn't for a freak encounter with the doctor over there, I would still be pulling wagons for the needy. If there is a specific reason for me being here, I have yet to recognize it. I am here now and will do anything I can to help. But, what can I do specifically? I have no idea."

"Thank you for being honest with me, Porcene. I can tell you this; you are one of the most striking Horses I have ever encountered. Even Jak here can't take his eyes off of you. Your strength and spirit shine like the sun even though you travel almost completely covered with pack. I have no reason to doubt your being here. In time, your fate will be known to us all. Jak, do you have anything to add?"

"No and thanks a lot for overstating the obvious there, friend." Jak awkwardly turned to Porcene, "But what she says is true, you are an amazing creature and, like Belle said, I cannot gaze at you without it turning into a stare. I do hope you will forgive my being forward."

In the short time among their company, Porcene's countenance was slowly evolving from a bewildered, shy draft animal to a much stronger version of her kind. Her once banal mannerisms no longer portrayed a lack of confidence. With each moment that passed, her eyes widened, flickers and sparks of determination began to quietly dance. Belle saw a future much different than the past in those dark brown orbs. Beneath everything Mariel had tied to the Belgian's flanks and the years of humbly toiling ahead of wagons and menial carts, doing only as she was told, another personality lay dormant. Belle could not make any assumptions on the matter, at least not now, but she had her intuition and it had always been correct. Belle and Jak were hypnotized as they looked beyond the Horse they saw before them.

Tofur broke the trance when he excitedly came running to them. Held high in his clenched hand was a now refurbished, polished and finely tuned musical instrument. "Belle, Jak! Look at this! This is my whistle. Mariel is a genius! Look at it, would you? Just look at it. I had no idea it was this magnificent! He says it is solid gold with a pure platinum sounding ball. He has no idea where it was made or how for that matter. Isn't it beautiful? Well no matter what you say, I know it is. Belle, I'm going to blow it now. Cover your ears if you need to although I can't imagine the sound will be as shrill as it used to be. It always had an odd twang to it, but it always worked. I have to see what it sounds like now."

Mariel fastidiously cleaned each tool before carefully placing them back into the bag. After securing them to Porcene's side, he joined in with Tofur's youthful excitement. "I have never seen any instrument made with such detail. It took a bit of study to discover exactly what to do since it seemed so perfect on the outside once I got it cleaned up. I wish I could make its equal."

"Please, Belle may I blow it? You should cover your ears if you must." Tofur gave each legger a fair opportunity to position themselves for the blast. "Ready. Here goes!" He blew into the whistle with an enthusiasm known only to first timers. The sounding slit released an even, mellow blast which actually calmed those who heard it. "Whoa!" Tofur had no words to describe how he felt. Instead, he inspected every detail of the whistle again. He held it up to watch the sun reflect from the polished metal. He blew the whistle a second time, a long, soothing note. Again, no shrill, scratching shriek escaped, only a pleasantly loud blast. It covered those near as would a warm quilt on a nippy morning. Tofur was in shock.

Belle waited nervously in anticipation of the dreaded, ear-shattering shriek that never came. She uncovered her ears. "Tofur, blow it again. I want to experience it without muting my ears."

"No problem!" Tofur blew the whistle again. "Well?"

Belle smiled. "That was beautiful. How about the rest of you? Did the sound come out as wonderful as I perceived?"

Jak, too, was pleasantly surprised. "Sounded fine to me."

Porcene agreed as she moved closer to Jak's side, "I haven't heard it many other times, but I'd say more soothing than alarming. Mariel?" Nothing. "Mariel?"

The next voice came from the two-legger, but it was not the same voice they heard before. "Blow the whistle two more times son, short, crisp bursts."

Tofur, as the others, was shocked, not afraid, but shocked by Mariel's transformation. He did as instructed. He blew two short bursts. He then turned to where Mariel has stood, "Will those do?"

Instead of answering Tofur, Mariel was busy rummaging through small boxes packed inside bigger packs on Porcene. "Oh my, I know it has to be in here." He looked up to see four sets of eyes inquisitively following his every move. "Oh my, where did all of you come from? Have you met my Horse? Porcene, please...introduce me to your friends."

Porcene bent her gaze in Jak's general direction. "Oh my."

***

"Did you hear that, Whistler?" Taytay's head jerked around so abruptly, he almost flew into Motrey's second.

Whistler did hear the same thing; a whistle…once, twice…then two more times. "What call was that? I can't remember that progression, do you?

Motrey signaled for a right turn, "We are there. Come in on my tail. It will be tight going down through the trees." He pivoted his body on a tight axis making a very graceful change of altitude for such a rough looking winger. The trailing wingers did as told. Motrey dropped to the ground with a high degree of agility that, like his in-air pivot, portrayed a completely different flying technique than the Falcons would normally associate with a winger of his build. He whispered, "Careful now, we don't want to disturb the memorial here."

Each winger lit with precision and control, landing softly beside Motrey forming a short line. Motrey and his second bowed their heads reverently. The Falcons assumed the reason for this and bowed their heads accordingly, watching out of the corner of their eyes as the bald winger led them in. Within a short period of time Motrey raised his head slowly and nodded to his second.

Softly, came a reply, "Father, the covering is there, in that tree there, shall I get it?"

Motrey answered in a still subdued voice, "Yes, son. Please retrieve it for them." He looked ahead of him at a pile of drying leafy branches. "Your messenger lies over there, beneath that greenery."

The son swooped down with a well-worn, but sturdily made cloth tube held in his beak. He placed it in front of Taytay.

Motrey added, "If you want to see the other memorials, we can take you to them."

Whistler did not answer. For a while he and Taytay silently stood where they lit, gazing at the pile of branches, imagining what lay covered beneath them. Whistler whispered, "This is so very sad. I would love to visit the other places, Motrey, at a later time. We have to get this covering back to our group, It is very important to our mission. I can't think of how I will break this news to our friend. We have to make positive identification of the remains, if that is permitted?"

"Yes, yes, absolutely. Son, come with me." The wingers quietly moved to the branch pile. They began removing branches one at a time. The Falcons moved in between them to help the process. "Are you two ready for this? It seems to me you were very close to this dead 'un."

Taytay placed a branch to the side, "No, Motrey, we are not ready for this. I don't believe any creature is ever really ready for something like this. However, we have to know, so let us please continue."

"I understand completely."

After a few more branches were removed, Motrey signaled for his son to step back, leaving the final two branches for the Falcons. Whistler and Taytay each lifted a branch simultaneously exposing a stack of sturdy, drying bones. In the middle of the stack rested a large, robust canine skull. A black tail-feather with a satiny sheen covered the eye sockets.

Motrey noticed the inquisitive look in the Falcons' eyes. "That is a ceremonial gesture on our part. The dead 'un's eyes are shut from our world at death. They have no need to see here anymore. We place the feather so they can focus on their new life beyond. We struggle sometimes with what we do, but it is what we do."

"That is very kind of you, Motrey." Whistler was impressed with the depth of the collector's character. "Taytay, is there anything here that absolutely identifies these remains, beyond any shadow of doubt?"

"Yes there is. See the notch on the hip bone?" Taytay pointed the location out to Whistler. "See here? I remember the day this happened to him."

"Oh no." Whistler's eyes were filling with tears. Still, he saw the unquestioned damage to the hip bone. "Oh no...all three of them? Those who did this will pay a serious retribution for their actions. I have seen enough. Motrey, accept our deepest gratitude. When we come back through we will need to transport these remains and the others back with us. Will that be possible?"

"I see nothing impossible with that request. You know where to find us."

"Thank you. Taytay, we need to get back."

Like Whistler, Taytay was remembering the days shared with the three young Dogs. With tears dripping from his eyes, he agreed. "We must get back. Thank you, Motrey." He respectfully nodded to Motrey and to his son. "Cousin, follow me."

The Falcons rose swiftly into the sky, tears streaming off behind them. The past events weighing heavy on them, they raced back to join the group with full pursuit beats.

The second asked, "Do you think they were truthful with us, Father, or did we just make a mistake?"

"Son, they were truthful. I saw it immediately in each of them. Their pride and hurt were not hidden behind an egotistical front or evil cloaks. They are on our side. Our mistake, if one can call it that, is fanning the flame against those leggers that committed these despicable deeds. We may be collecting them very soon."

"I think you are correct, Father. I could not agree with you more."

***

"Mariel," Tofur was baffled. "Are you once again only Mariel? Not the doctor, not the professor and not whoever that was who told me to blow the whistle twice?"

The bemused two-legger answered back, "Whatever are you talking about, dear lad? Did you happen to repack my packings? Someone did a very good job of tying a few of these bags back on. Why were they off? Oh dear, is someone in need of something?" Mariel spun around to face the group. He held his hand down to Belle's nose, "You are a beautiful Dog. A Rottweiler, I think. Yes, that is exactly what you are. A Rottweiler, a Mule, a young man, Porcene and me. So there are five of us, is this all? Where are we going?"

Tofur raised the whistle to his lips. "Watch this." He blew four short times. The sound filled every nearby crevice of silence with a pleasant tone. Tofur watched Mariel intently to see if his theory was correct. The others in the group watched Tofur.

"Tofur, why are you not reading? I thought you were reading my book. Does it not interest you anymore? You are smart to read, lad. You must finish that book. I have several more you must read as well."

Tofur was smiling. His theory may be correct after all. He raised the whistle again. He blew three times once more and watched. He did not have to wait long for the evidence of change.

"Ah, the whistle, do you like the improvements? I have never seen a gem like that one before. Very fine craftsmanship, it must be worth a large fortune. Belle, do you have our plan to proceed yet? Porcene, you and Jak, why do you have those strange looks on your faces? What have you seen?"

***

The Falcons were winging back to the group as fast as they could fly when they heard the whistle blasts. "The whistle again, this time the emergency pattern, am I correct?"

Whistler agreed, "That is what I heard. We should fly faster."

Taytay could not fly any faster. "Faster? We are flying as fast as we can right now and we have a tail wind. We can't fly faster. How far have we come? That call sounded very close to us. It seems like it came from everywhere. Do you think it is Tofur? The sound seems different."

"Who else could it be? It has to be him. Why is he blowing that call? We need to hurry."

"We are hurrying. Let's hope the group can handle any situation until we get back!"

***

Tofur wanted to blow the whistle again. The only reason he didn't was because he knew who would appear next. He was not sure if the next one of Mariel's personalities was going to make a good traveling companion. He whispered to Jak, "Should I call the next Mariel to the stage?"

"I'm not sure that is a good idea. Can you skip back to the nutcase?"

"I don't know. I just know that by blowing this whistle, it triggers the changes in him or them right now. There must be a pattern to the transformations, shouldn't there?"

"I do hope so."

Belle could not help but notice the conversation between Jak and Tofur. "What are you discussing in your extra loud whispers?"

"Well, I was telling Jak that I know how to trigger Mariel's personality changes now. We were wondering if there is a certain pattern to call up each individual one."

Belle understood now, "Yes, I am putting it together now. Can we determine if there is a pattern or is it completely random?"

"So far, I think the key is four blasts."

Jak added, "Well there were the initial two blasts before you were instructed to blow two more."

"That's right Jak. Is it possible that the number of blasts triggers which switch takes place?"

Now Porcene was beginning to see the light too. "The blasts unquestionably trigger the switch. You have blown randomly most of the time, right? Two once, I think, what if you blow three times or just once or five times?"

"Wait, we don't want to get as confused as Mariel is right now." Belle hoped to put the events in perspective.

"I understand what you are saying, Belle, however, we may need one of these personalities at some time or another, it would be wise to figure out what stimulus triggers which personality." Jak certainly was smarter than he let on earlier. "I'm thinking that the current personality is a waste gate, sort of a collection of the confusion that is inherent in each of the other personalities. The best move, and I'm simply putting this out there, is to find the way to unite all of the personalities. Surely they were all the same person once in their lives, do you not think so?"

"Geesh, what kind of brain do you have between those tall ears, Jak?" Porcene was impressed again with Jak's hidden intellect.

"Nothing too complicated really," Jak answered. "It should be obvious to each of us that the four separations came from a united whole somewhere in the past. How he has lived or how long he has lived divided inside himself is not only a pertinent question, it is also up to us, I feel, to reunite them or him, if possible, with his other selves. Does that make any sense?"

Belle did not process information in the same way as Jak. That was one aspect of their friendship which allowed them compatibility. "It makes sense in a way that makes you so stubborn. It requires a deep thinker to reason that and a short thinker like me to want to complete the process. So, when can we fix him?"

"Belle, I don't think is will be as easy as that. I will need to get back with you on the first part of that."

Porcene was tiring of the discussion. "Tofur, I can tell you this much, I would rather have any of the other Mariels with me right now. This one is making me nervous with his ways. Can you please get any of the others back as soon as possible? And just for fun, will you blow the whistle just one time? I'm curious."

"Sure, Porcene. You have dealt with him longer than the rest of us." Tofur once again raised the whistle to his lips, this time he blew once. The change was instantaneous. In between strapping down another pack and adjusting the collar of his jacket, a different Mariel was in their midst. Just as he flipped the collar up to seal the crease, his eyes hardened.

"Here we are again. Have we not moved a step since I was last here? What are we waiting for?" Mariel number four braced himself against Porcene's side with one hand, the other stretched across his eyebrows to massage his forehead. "I have this headache that I can't get rid of." He sighed. "Who is in charge here? Is it you, lad?"

Tofur was surprised. "Well not exactly sir. All of us bring out own strengths to bear here."

"That won't work. The task is too complicated. There must be one sole leader and who else are you talking about? All I see is you, your animals and my Horse, if this is my Horse. Honestly, I don't remember where I found her. Are there others with you?"

"No sir, just us. We have come this far on our own."

"Okay then, you must be the one I am looking for. Who are you? And, how would you know what your animals bring to the chore? Am I to assume you chat with them? That would be a great trick."

"You mean you can't talk to animals?"

"Ha-ha, you are the one I'm looking for. You are a Talker! No lad, I do not profess to be a Talker. I have heard of them, but never met one before you. I remember a little more now, are you or are you not Master Christofur Polinetti? Your family comes from the south peninsula a ways east from here or from where I am from...originally. For all of my good thoughts lad, I am finally pleased to meet you."

"You know so much about me, who are you?"

The observing four-leggers did not know what to think. At first they were confused, then a little more confused and finally totally confused. They all watched closely and listened intently as Tofur carried on the conversation with Mariel's latest personality. The problem with Talkers communicating with non-Talkers was that four-leggers and wingers could only understand what the Talkers said. Half or less of any conversation was heard as gibberish, unintelligible noise. About now, the four-leggers were feeling left out. Not to be left out of a left-out group, Taytay and Whistler appeared above the trees as a flash. They were landing on the backs of Porcene and Jak just as Mariel was about to introduce himself…again. They lit silently and listened.

"Sure lad, I am Leiram Fraunchesca. I have no title. I am from common stock. My family has long been in the indebtedness to the hierarchies of the worlds. We are favored by the good and feared by the bad. We have had a few important people in our family and many say I have the qualities of them all."

The four-leggers were whispering amongst themselves somethings that sounded to Tofur like…"I knew that was coming." "Huge understatement." "What?" and other wise and not-so-wise statements.

"I have noticed that about you, sir. I am not positive that you know how true that is."

"Oh I wouldn't say that now, lad. I have heard people say that I sometimes have the mind of three or more men and the ingenuity of at least two men. Me? I think they are mostly lunatics talking crazy talk. I am good at what I do. In your case, I am here to protect you at all costs. You may well be the leader of the group, but you can't lead if you can't breathe. I am here to make sure you stay breathing. You have quite a task in front of you. Do you have any idea what it is? If not, I have a wax-sealed letter for you somewhere in that mass of gathered oddities astride that marvelous Belgian."

"This task is getting more convoluted with every passing moment. What do you…?"

Whistler dropped the map case on Porcene's back then interrupted Tofur. "We have to talk Tofur!"

The youngster glanced at Whistler and nodded his head. He placed the whistle to his lips and blew it four times. "What is it, Whistler?"

"We have the map cover or case or whatever it is. And there is more." He looked over at Taytay. "Lots more."

"You are still not reading my book, lad. Please tell me it did not bore you that badly."

Belle was relieved to be hearing all of the conversation again. She looked up to Jak, "I heard that."

Porcene made a mental note, four blows of the whistle recalls the doctor, one blow beckons to Leiram, two personalities down and two to go. What do three blasts do? And two?

Jak laughed.

15

Lemeer and Hazzell, two of the more respected Badgers of the area, busied themselves near the largest of the arms storage pits. A large Eagle with a distinguished white head oversaw the procedure. "Lemeer, do you really think it is worth the trouble to unearth all of these ancient weapons? Can this problem not be worked out with a good dose of civility?"

The Badger grimaced, "One could only hope so, Vincen. One could only hope for a genteel ending to what we don't even know has begun."

Hazzell agreed with her mate. "Vincen, this will be a last line of defense. If your diplomacy fails, we will have our weapons. I do not want to give up the Great Forest without giving the effort everything I have. My family will do whatever is asked of us."

"I know you will, Hazzell. Let us hope it does not come to that. I must find your son and his companions. We can't fight this upcoming battle stretched as thin as we are."

Lemeer agreed. "Vincen, it would be a great help to have Lightning, Mystic and Bubba here, but...they are not here and we have no idea where they are. I only hope that wherever they are, they are safe."

Vincen shook his head solemnly. "My wishes are the same as yours, Badgers."

A black Crow landed at Vincen's side. "We followed him as far as you asked. He seemed to be doing as you wish."

"Did he know he was being tailed?"

"Vincen, what kind of question is that? Of course he knew. I imagine he was flying in fear, because he did not waver one bit once he took wing. I want him to find the Falcon Master, but, if he doesn't come back, I won't lose any sleep for the rest of my days."

"I'm sure the rest of the Great Forest inhabitants think the same as you, Arlis. Have you heard from your kin?"

"No, Vincen, I sent the message to him with Absaroka. When she locates him, they will make their own plans. Do not doubt their intelligence or their fact-finding strategies. They are extraordinary examples of our kind. For all I know, Corvus may have heard as much or more than we have. He keeps up with everything in his part of the world."

"I believe that, Arlis. I am more concerned with how quickly she can find him."

"Rest easy, Vincen. She will find him and we will meet up with her later. She will not let us down."

"What about Karone? Is he putting the sentinels on extra alert? When I flew for Tine, I saw no other sky-travelers until I returned here."

"There is a concern of that being talked about."

"Arlis, we cannot afford to lose any of our sentinels. Keep them hidden in solitary groups. I do not want any large flocks congregating in one area. That will draw attention to us and could be our downfall."

Arlis nodded in agreement. "Vincen, can we get the more, um...skilled creatures out to the perimeter posts pretty soon?"

Lemeer heard what Arlis did not say. "Arlis, we will be ready by moon time. I will take charge of that deployment personally. You will still need to give me as much scouting as possible without causing any undue or unneeded attention."

"Then, Lemeer, I will rest easy. We could ask for no better protection than what you can offer." Arlis tipped her wing to the Badgers. "I will spread the word among the sky-travelers."

Vincen nodded to Arlis, "Be careful, friend."

Arlis looked at Vincen, "You can believe I will be, sir."

Vincen smiled. He turned back to the Badgers. "Lemeer, Hazzell, you two are in charge here. Do as you see fit, call on whoever you need. I must locate our missing trio of friends. How will I do that? I can't say, but I will try and I will return." Vincen took wing. He would fly back to the site where the well found Mystic and then plan his next move.

***

Frederick took his bag from Madaliene. "Madaliene, all I need are the letters. You keep this bag with you. You need it more out there than we do in here."

"Frederick, why are we back here? I told Lightning's ax thing there to take us to Burg One. Why didn't it do that? Lightning..." Madaliene looked up and down the corridor. "Where is Lightning? Where is Sig? Sig? Sig, come to me right now!" She began to wander down the corridor.

"Madaliene, come back here now." Frederick shouted loudly. "You can't stay here any longer. You are needed elsewhere. Sig is busy down below." He lied. "We must meet and get you on your way again. You need to take Bubba and Mystic this time." He looked at Hemoth, "You, Grizzly, must stay with me. You are the only one who knows anything about what is in this place. There is no other option I can think of. Will you do it for us, for the world?"

Hemoth was not used to being talked to in this way. "Two-legger, you must have a reason to be speaking to me in that way. Given what you have been through, I will stay with you…temporarily. As soon as I can, I will return to Madaliene's side. Is that clear?"

"Very clear, Hemoth."

Bubba and Mystic were trying to figure out what was happening around them and couldn't. Mystic asked, "Frederick, where are we to go?"

"Mystic, you two take Madaliene to the Great Forest, then to Nuorg." Mystic looked confused. "It's not the ax-pike that is doing the transporting, it's you."

"Me?" Mystic was surprised at the least.

"Yes, Mystic. It's you and each of the others. You are being carried to where you need to be. You don't need Lightning's ax-pike to take you places; you just need to let it be known that you are willing to go. It has something to do with the globing and the purification process we went through. I don't have the time, the reasons or the words to explain it. Please, you three go to the Great Forest and meet up with Vincen. You will know what to do once you find him."

Bubba was a creature of faith, still this was a lot different, or so he thought. "How do you know this, Frederick?"

"Bubba, please. Let's not get into this now. I think I know what I am talking about, so please be on your way. You are needed elsewhere. Be careful."

Mystic looked at Bubba, "What can it hurt?"

The Cheetah returned the Wolf's quizzical gaze. "Let's see, Prince." Bubba moved close to Mystic's side. "Princess, are you coming?"

Madaliene looked to Hemoth for assurance. "Hemoth, do you think this is wise?"

"Yes, Princess, I do. It needs to be done."

"Okay then." She knelt in front the Wolf and the Cheetah. "Give the word, Prince."

"Gladly." Mystic winked at Frederick. "We will see you soon. Oh, to whom should I direct this command?"

Frederick shrugged his shoulders, "I don't know the answer to that, Prince. Just say it."

Mystic raised his eyes to Madaliene. "Ready, Princess? Hold on to the both of us." Mystic steadied himself, as did Bubba. "Here we go. Take us back to the Great Forest." Immediately, the group of three vanished.

Hemoth nudged Frederick, "So, where is Sig…really."

Frederick's eyes fell to the floor. He sighed then crossed his arms before making eye contact again with Hemoth. "Follow me." He led Hemoth down to the corridor to the memorial chamber. "He's in here, Hemoth."

"I'm not liking the tone of your voice, Frederick."

"Believe me, Hemoth, I wish things were different." Frederick walked over to where the ornate rug covered their friend. Respectfully, he uncovered Sig's body so Hemoth could see.

"How did it happen, Frederick?"

Frederick's eyes brimmed with tears as he retold the entire story of the rigged doors to Sig's old friend. Hemoth shed a few tears as well.

"You are correct, Frederick. Sig died a hero. One day we shall memorialize him, but not today. You say the Nuorg water avoided him?"

"Yes, it did."

"I think maybe the water saved him, Frederick. Sig was an old winger, very old and very courageous. His death saved your life…and by dying to save you, he might have served a purpose he could never have performed while alive. He has moved on. He has been saved from the turmoil that we face ahead. He has served our cause well." Hemoth nuzzled the feathers covering Sig's head.

Frederick had to ask, "What cause is that, Hemoth? What cause are all of us so tightly bound to now?"

"Do you have to ask that question?" Hemoth glanced around the colossal room. He had not been inside it in many years. "You know,

Frederick, a lot of these creatures were my friends. Lots of them worked side-by-side with me as we created this fortress. Each has a unique story to tell. But our cause? That is an easy question to answer. Maybe one day you will figure it out on your own. Now, we have more work to take care of." Hemoth reverently stepped out the door. He swiveled his thick head back, "Are you coming with me or not?"

Frederick was startled for a moment. He was waiting for the answer to his question that never came. "But...the answer? What is the answer to my question, Hemoth?" He hurried after the lumbering giant Grizzly Bear.

***

They appeared near the thick hedge row where their last attempt at entering the Great Forest had failed. "I don't believe this!" Bubba exhaled. "It worked! Wait, why did we end up here again?"

Mystic had exactly the same thought. "Princess, I bid you almost welcome to the Great Forest."

"What do you mean by that, Mystic?"

"He means the Great Forest is through that hedge there and on a ways. We were right here before we made the detour which led us to you." Bubba stopped trying to figure it out.

"Is that a good thing or not so good?" Madaliene was up for anything.

"It depends on how we fare from here, Princess. If we can find the correct passage through here, I would say good. If we can't find the correct passage, then...I would say not so good."

"You know what I think?" Madaliene put her hands on her hips. "I think what we think really doesn't matter. Let's get through this green wall and move on. What is the worst thing that can happen?"

"I really wish you had not said it quite like that, Princess." Bubba grimaced.

"But she did, so in we go." Mystic walked slowly toward the hedge. He hoped a grand idea would come to him soon.

***

Vincen flew in the general direction of the South Quarter. He was not flying fast, though he was flying steady, probably a nice, efficient leisure beat. Myriads of ideas played in his head, none sticking around long enough to be plan worthy. He passed the edge of the Great Forest and laughed about the time Lightning had discussed building a fort here. Maybe it had not been such a bad idea. What he spied below him nearly dropped him from the sky. "This can't be! Why are they over here? Where is the Badger? Who is that two-legger?" Questions, questions, questions. He dove on his target.

Madaliene was taken by surprise. "Ahhh! Who is this?"

Vincen softly landed in front of her, albeit dramatically, and behind the four-leggers.

"Don't be alarmed by me, miss. I am Vincen of the Great Eagles. You should be much more worried about those with whom you travel!" He then addressed the excited pair of four-leggers coming up behind him, "Mystic, Bubba, who is this you have brought with you, where have you been and where is the Badger?"

Madaliene shook her head, "You too?"

"You too? You too what, miss?" Vincen seemed perplexed.

"You call Lightning a Badger too! For goodness sakes, he is a Bear! A big, furry Bear!" Madaliene looked to Bubba and Mystic for affirmation of her announcement.

"Well, miss, if you say so—I guess he may be." Vincen rolled his eyes to Mystic, "What do you say, Prince?"

"What do I say? I say where have you been? How did we get separated in the first place? How long have you been here? Better yet, how long have we been gone?"

"Wait, I was speaking first!" Madaliene jumped in, "There is no maybe! Lightning is a Bear!"

"Okay fine, miss, Lightning is a Bear. Now are you happy?" Vincen winked at Bubba.

"Finally!" Madaliene huffed. "A creature with the brains to know that."

"Oh, Vincen, why did you let on? Why agree with her? We had her fooled this entire time." Mystic feigned heartache. "How can we break it to his parents? Oh, mercy."

"They might take that very badly, Prince." Bubba played along.

"Ugh, you never had me fooled! Are you crazy, Mystic?" Madaliene didn't know what to think. "I am old enough to punch both of you, you know."

Vincen enjoyed the banter between them. "Mystic, who might this young lady be? Is she friend or some two-legger we must deal with in our normal way? I see you have the Staff secured in a comfy holster as well."

Madaliene's eyes cut instantly to Vincen as she awaited Mystic's answer. "Whoa! What is the normal way you deal with two-leggers?"

Vincen knew he was getting the best of her. "Never you mind that now, miss. Mystic, introduction please."

"This, sir, is Madaliene O'shay. She is a princess in her world and a cunning master of the bow and arrow. She is somewhat arrogant as a tweenst can be, a bit off at times, very inquisitive, loyal, intelligent, brave and...let me see...the main reason we came back here."

Madaliene couldn't figure out if she should thank Mystic or whack him with her bow. "Excuse me? A bit off? Arrogant for a tweenst? What on earth is a tweenst?" A bit off? Did you really say that about me? A bit off?"

Bubba walked to Madaliene's side, "Don't worry too much about what they are saying, Princess, after all, they are both a lot older than us. You know how older ones can be." He grinned.

"Yes, Bubba, I guess so. But a bit off? Really."

Vincen studied the young princess. "She looks rather young, Mystic, to be a master of the bow and arrow. Can she prove it?"

"Sir," Madaliene answered the question, not waiting for Mystic, "I have been to Nuorg earlier today or yesterday or whenever it was, and single handedly removed eight threats to the security and future of that weird land. If Lightning, the Bear, were here he would attest to what I am saying."

Vincen was interested. "Uh huh, Mystic, can you verify this story?"

"No, sir, I cannot. I was not with her. Bubba and I were with Frederick in Madaliene's mountain fortress tending to other business."

Vincen closed his eyes to shake a few cobwebs from his mind. "What did you say, Mystic? She has a mountain fortress? Why was Lightning with her and not you two?"

Bubba began to fidget. "I know there are lots of stories to tell here, but, I want to go home right now. Can we elaborate on these stories...I don't know, when we get inside the Great Forest maybe?"

"Absolutely, Bubba. I can't wait to hear all about this. What I must have missed!"

"Vincen, I hope we have time to share it all. Can we go home now?"

"I'm sorry, Bubba, of course we can. Follow me. I'll take you to where you first entered this area."

Mystic didn't understand. "Vincen, is this not the place where we entered the South Quarter?"

"Oh no, Mystic. This is much further south. Just follow me."

Bubba looked at Mystic while Mystic looked at Bubba. Just exactly where were they? Everything appeared the same.

***

He soared high. He had been waiting for some good news. As he watched the reunion below him, he knew his wait was over.

***

Mystic trailed Vincen. Bubba and Madaliene followed on his heels.

"Mystic, how far off do you think we were when we got back the first time?"

"Don't ask me! I thought we were right where you thought we were."

In the distance, Vincen began flying in a circle, waiting for the leggers to catch up. Madaliene saw him, "Is that where we need to be? Way up there? It looks like your friend is a long way from here."

"Mystic," Bubba asked, "She is correct. Can we not just want to be there?"

Mystic paused briefly, "I don't want to try that. What if Vincen wasn't there when we got there? How smart would we look then?"

"Do you think that could happen?"

Madaliene popped Bubba on his hindquarters, "Bubba, do you have to ask that question?"

Bubba laughed, "I guess not. On we go."

Soon enough the leggers were beneath Vincen. He landed as they neared. "You will find your way to the Great Forest right through that narrow opening. I will wait for you at your dwelling, Mystic."

"No, no, no! Not so fast, Vincen. We are not getting separated again, thank you. You lead us through here. I'm not taking chances anymore, not this day-round anyway."

Vincen scratched at the ground. "You know I don't like walking in that thickery. It ruins my feathers."

"I know that, Vincen, but if you don't lead, we are not going." Mystic stood his ground.

Reluctantly, Vincen gave in. "This way please." He walked into the hedge row upright as did the four-leggers.

Madaliene had more trouble. On her hands and knees with Frederick's bag dragging the ground, her curly, blond hair snagging at every chance, her bow tangling with her arms; she slowly backed out of the thicket. "Wait a minute all of you! I can't do this yet. I need to get a few things secured before I go crawling through here."

Bubba adeptly reversed his direction to help Madaliene as best he could. "How can I help you, Princess?"

"Thank you, Bubba, I have to get out of here and rearrange a few things. It shouldn't take long." She continued backing out on her hands and knees. It was a struggle at best.

Bubba froze. Very quietly he whispered, "Princess, don't make another sound or move another muscle. I hear something out there, some kind of creature and I don't know what it is. It doesn't sound friendly."

She whispered, "How could there be something out there? Would Vincen have not already seen it?"

"It doesn't matter now, does it? I'm telling you, Princess; I don't like the smell of it.

Mystic nosed his way next to Bubba. "So, you smelled it too?"

"Yes, Mystic, I did. What is it?"

"I don't know, but I think it is waiting on us to lead it somewhere. We are not going to do that."

"It doesn't smell familiar to me at all. Does it to you?"

"Nope."

Madaliene was nervous, "What is it? What does it smell like?"

"Princess, it smells a little like death." Mystic and Bubba had smelled this odor not very long ago.

"You are kidding, right?" Her eyes were opened to their limits. "Right?"

"No, I am not." Mystic tensed up. "It knows we are in here."

"Is it coming after us?" Madaliene began shuffling away from the hedge.

Bubba cautiously took a step closer to the entrance. "Princess, you need to find a way to continue through here. It may not be comfortable, but you need to get out of here the other way. It's not that far to the next opening. I'll wait here and watch or I may make my presence known. This bothers me. Mystic, do you think it was watching us before?"

Madaliene gathered her hair and twisted it into a knot under her chin. She pulled Frederick's bag close to her chest and held her bow in her left hand and her quiver in the right. She glanced at Bubba. "Will you be safe?"

"I don't know, Princess. Now go! Mystic, get her out of here!"

Mystic did not know what to do. "Bubba, why you? Why should you stay?"

"Because, you have the Staff and she has everything else. I am the expendable one here! Anyway, whatever is out there cannot catch me. You two are easy prey. Now go! I will wait it out here. I will catch up to you. I want to know what is out there. Remember, the whole Cat and the curiosity thing?"

Madaliene was not nervous anymore, she was angry. "Bubba, I shouldn't run from this. I am not a coward. I will stay with you." She returned to the Cheetah's side. "I'm climbing this tree. Whatever is out there, I can deal with it from up there. I am not running away!"

Mystic shook his head. "No, Madaliene, you are coming with me! Let's go…now!"

Madaliene was resolute. She was not going anywhere. "Uh uh, Mystic, you go if you must. The Staff is not glowing. There is no danger to it. Whatever is out there is only interested in us or what we are doing."

"You know she is correct, Prince. The Staff seems uninterested in whatever is out there. However, I am very interested. Has Vincen not noticed our absence?"

In the tree, just above them came Vincen's voice. "Yes, I noticed your absence. Once is enough for me! I'm not letting that happen again."

"Vincen, do you have any idea what is out there waiting on us?" Mystic asked without diverting his eyes from where the noise and smell were coming.

"No, I don't. I saw nothing earlier. I will tell you this, it won't take an instant for me to fly out there and see what it is. I'll be right back."

"Wait, Sir Eagle, I will climb up there and watch out for you. Hold on." Madaliene quickly climbed as high in the tree as she could. She took a few arrows from her quiver before waving Vincen on.

Mystic and Bubba slowly nosed their way to the edge of the thicket. Whatever was out there had moved...somewhere. "Do you see it, Bubba?"

"No, Prince, I do not. It must have grown bored with us, or maybe it didn't even know we were here."

"I don't think that is the case, Bubba. It was searching for something. Do you see anything, Princess?"

"I haven't yet. I can't see the Eagle either. Mystic, I know the Staff is not glowing or anything, but, do you think you might unholster it just for grins? You really never know what might happen."

"I will do it because you requested it, Princess. Bubba, can you pull it out of the holster?"

Bubba backed up slightly, "Sure." He pulled the Staff out and laid it in front of Mystic, then got back to watching. "I hope we don't need that."

Mystic, with fluid motions, loosed the globe from the Staff. He set a paw down on the handle and held the globe in his mouth. He nodded his readiness to Bubba and Madaliene.

Not wanting to give away Mystic's position, Vincen looped around behind the group and came in from a different spot along the hedge row. As soon as he crossed the imaginary line that separated the Great Forest from the South Quarter, a furious chorus of wild animal noises and high pitched screams drowned out the previous quiet stillness. Vincen immediately turned back to the Great Forest's boundary. He almost made it untouched. Two large, thick-bodied sky-travelers flew down on him, digging sharp talons into his wings throwing him off balance. No sooner had they grabbed him when precisely aimed arrows began to tear into their feathered bodies. The attacking wingers went down instantly. Vincen struggled to fly. He was dazed and out of control, spiraling to the ground. Another pair of the same type of wingers came for him again; like before, two well aimed arrows took them down. Vincen was now hurt, barely able to stay airborne. He was upside down, fighting a valiant fight with gravity. Two more sky-travelers came at him, except this time, they came from the

Great Forest side. They were fortunate that Madaliene noticed where they had come from or they too would have been shot out of the air. Instead, she let them carry Vincen into the thicket.

"Mystic, Bubba, what is going on down there?" Madaliene was still watching the sky.

"I can't believe what I am seeing, Princess. Look down here. There are hundreds of them!" Bubba stood bravely in front of Mystic as a herd of four-leggers amassed in the clearing in front of them. "Where did they come from?"

The largest four-legger was backed up by hundreds more like him. They flanked him on both sides readying for a charge into the thicket. Whether they were after Mystic or Bubba did not seem to be a concern. More imminent was a bold attack on the boundary of the Great Forest.

Madaliene dropped her eyes from the sky, and what she saw annoyed her. "What are they waiting for? They will charge through this thicket like it was a tall stand of weeds. Are those things your fellow inhabitants?"

"No, Princess, not anymore. They left of their own accord a long time ago. I have no idea why they are back now."

Mystic stood at Bubba's side, the globe was in front of his right paw and it still was not glowing. "Bubba, why is this globe not glowing?"

"I have no idea, Prince."

"Why have they come back?"

As each of them watched the amassing herd of four-leggers in no particular fashion, a lone, thick-bodied sky-traveler swooped down onto the lead four-legger's sharp shoulder.

"Oh no, Mystic, the warnings we received are now becoming very clear to me."

"The intelligents?"

"Yes, Prince, the intelligents."

"But why?"

"I have no idea. Princess, stay where you are. This is about to take a turn for the worse."

Behind Mystic, a familiar voice called to him. "Mystic, is my son with you?"

Mystic swung his head around to the new voice. His eyes nearly popped out of his head when he got a good look at the creature. "What kind of adornment is that you are wearing, sir?"

"More on that in a moment, where is Lightning?" Lemeer stood at Mystic's side expecting an answer. "Well, son, where is he?"

"Uh, he was with us earlier. We were separated just before we appeared in the South Quarter."

"Was he alright?"

"Yes, sir, he was fine. Now, what are you wearing?"

"These are called armors. I am wearing a set put away by my great-grandfather." Lemeer crawled closer to Mystic's head. "We have unearthed the stocks and supplies from the Terrible Years. I don't know how we will fare this time, son, but we are ready for what's coming."

The more Mystic studied what Lemeer was wearing, the more frightened he became. "Sir, what do you plan on doing dressed like that?"

"Isn't that obvious, son? We expect to fight a battle. The Great Forest will not be overrun by these tuskers or any other creature without a fight the likes of which they have never seen." Lemeer was nothing if not sincere.

"How did you know they were here?"

"Some of Karone's scouts picked them up as they gathered a ways out."

"Who else is with you?" He finally managed to get a good look at Lemeer and his armors. He was shocked. "Where did you say all of that came from again?"

Bubba took his eyes off of the intimidating herd of four-leggers to get a look at Lemeer for himself. "Whoa!"

It was not difficult to imagine the perplexed look on Mystic's and Bubba's faces or the baffled thoughts in their minds. After all, Lemeer's persona was not that of a chronic worrier, as all of the younger creatures had been told. Lemeer knew of the description and never saw the need to correct it. The side of him everyone saw now was on the farthest possible side away from a worrier. His front paws were now sheathed with well-crafted spurs, much longer and sharper than those he was born with. His rear claws wore a slightly shorter spur with the same sharpened edge. Layers of finely-woven mail wrapped loosely around his ample body leaving no area unprotected. A half-helmet exaggerated his snout ending in another sharp spur curved upward. None of the armors were polished. There seemed to be no shine on them of any kind, there was only a dull, pasty coating of something.

Bubba was intrigued. "Who else came with you, sir?"

"Son, we are everywhere. We are in the trees. We are on the ground. We are in the air." Lemeer motioned around him. "Take a closer look, Bubba."

Lemeer grabbed Bubba's full attention with those last statements. The Cheetah scanned the area on both sides of him. He noticed the trees and the thicket were now brimming with sky-travelers and furry leggers of most all types of Great Forest inhabitants. Each small or large legger was outfitted with armors suited to their particular strengths. "How many are left near the dwellings, sir?"

Lemeer shook his head, "Not many, son. Mainly the young and the tweensts stayed back. A few of the elders too old for battle also remained safely hidden away."

"But, sir, there is no way all of you can stop a pillage by those tuskers out there. They will run us over. We will hardly slow them down."

Lemeer blinked his eyes. "Maybe so, son. However, if we do not try, we have already failed. Where there is no effort, therein lies defeat."

Mystic could not help over hearing the conversation. "Lemeer, where is Arlis taking Vincen?"

"I'm sure she is taking him to your dwelling, where a healing chamber has been set up."

"Oh." He looked in the tree for Madaliene. "Princess, is there any Nuorg water in Frederick's bag? He had some at the barn. Please find it and toss it down here."

Madaliene sat in the tree, fascinated by the resolve of the Badger. The concern on their faces was evident. She reached into the bag and found the water container. She handed it down to Mystic. "Mystic, in case you didn't know, that legger you are talking to...that is what a Badger looks like."

"Yes, Princess, thank you for bringing that to my attention. By the way, this is Lemeer, Lightning's father. Lemeer, sir, may I introduce Princess Madaliene O'shay."

Lemeer looked up in the tree. "Nice to meet you, Princess. Maybe soon we can have some informative conversations about my son,

Lightning." Lemeer stumbled a bit, "If, if we make it through the next few clicks alive."

"It is a pleasure meeting you too, sir. I will make sure we get to talk about him. I have lots of questions to ask you." She turned back to the herd of tuskers. "Mystic, get your globe ready. It looks as though we are about to get very busy."

The sky became agitated as hordes of large, heavy sky-travelers appeared over the tuskers, waiting for the signal from their leader to approach the skies over the thicket.

Mystic dropped the water container on the ground near Lemeer. "Sir, will you please call a Crow to take this back to Vincen? If he is breathing, he will know what to do with it."

"What is this, son?" Lemeer saw no worth in the container.

"This contains water from the Land of Nuorg, sir. It is miraculous water. It has saved Vincen's life once already."

"So you have actually been there, have you?"

"Yes, sir, we have. Please, have a Crow carry this to him. He needs to only drink what is needed to revive him. I'm afraid we may all need to drink from it if this goes badly."

Lemeer pondered the statements. He shouted to the trees. "I need a Crow down here immediately!" His call was answered by a Crow similar in size to Arlis, maybe a little bigger. "Glad you are here, Eboni. Take this to Vincen's side at once!"

"Yes, sir. Are there any instructions I should give your mate?"

"Thank you for asking. Tell Hazzell to use this to heal the wounds of any that come to her, starting with Vincen."

"Yes, Lemeer." Without further chatter, the Crow grasped the container with one talon and took wing.

"Princess, what do you see from up there? Are they about to charge? What are they waiting for?" Lemeer motioned to the leggers around him. "Pass this down. We will take them as they enter the thicket. Do not expose your whereabouts to the tuskers. They could very likely take us all, but we will get our fair share of first strikes."

Bubba shook his head boldly. "No, this can't happen. No, no, no. Lemeer, sir, what are you thinking? If they rush in here, we will all be trampled, the Great Forest will be pillaged and whatever reason you are here to fight will be wasted. Those left near the dwellings will not survive either. Let me try something first."

Lemeer studied Bubba's words. "What you say does make sense. What do you say we do?"

"Let me run out there. Maybe they will betray their secrets if I charge first. We may be able to figure their next move."

"What if you get taken?" The Badger thought of all Lightning's friends as his own children. "What then will be gained?"

"Sir, they will never get me. They will never catch me. If they come after me, Madaliene will take them out one-by-one."

"I will guarantee that, little Cat!" Madaliene packed another hand-full of arrows from Frederick's bag, still hanging at her side, into her quiver before arming her bow. "You just say the word, Bubba."

Lemeer rubbed the bottom of his chin with a spurred paw. "So you think you two can trigger a response from them?"

Bubba slowly nodded his head. "Yes, sir, I do."

"And you, Mystic? Do you see anything wrong with their plan?"

"No, sir."

Lemeer relented, "That is good enough for me. Bubba, let's see what you can do."

"Very well, sir. Princess, are you ready?" Bubba edged his way to the front of the thicket.

"I won't shoot first, Bubba. But, if they make any attempt to attack you, they will pay as those wingers did when they attacked your Eagle friend." She focused on the lead tusker and the winger on his shoulder. She had already decided they were not on her list of favorite things.

Bubba crouched for his start. He hoped to run across the field in front of the tuskers. Maybe, he thought, it would startle them into making a wrong first step. If they moved, Madaliene would remove them from their mission. He spoke to Mystic, "Prince, should anything contrary to my being healthy happen, stride out there and roll the globe! Any questions?"

"That, I assure you, will happen. If the globe will rid the Great Forest of these predators and save the lives of all of those at our side, I will certainly use it."

"What are you two talking about? The globe? Surely not the one on the end of your wand-staff? What can it possibly do?" Lemeer soon doubted his approval of Bubba's plan. "The globe?"

"Trust them, sir Badger," Madaliene answered from the tree, "Just trust them."

Out in the clearing, the large sky-traveler was holding court from atop the lead tusker. Several like him perched on the tuskers close by as if their very existence hinged upon his every word. "Fellow champions, we are here to rid this area of these mundane creatures who would very likely grovel at our feet given the chance. For too long, they have had the chance to become more than they are, more than drivel chastised by our far superior minds. They have no reason to exist with us. They have no reason to eat food meant for us or breathe air that is rightfully ours to do with as we wish. It is now up to you. It is up to each of us! It is up to me to urge you on to eradicate this pestilence from a very fertile ground we need populate with our kind, to raise our offspring with our degrees of thinking. Are you ready to carry out our arrangement? Have we not prepared for this since the end of the Terrible Years? Is this not what our fathers dreamed of? We are the rightful rulers of all we can see. The two-leggers are here to help us. We will guide them as we see fit. These tuskers are here to do our bidding as we see fit. They have seen our light. They have come to our aide. Fellow champions, it is all about us! It is all about the intelligents. Shall we make our first valiant move to reclaim everything we should have anyway? I say yes!"

The lesser chosen wingers were goaded into a frenzy by words thrown together for no creature's benefit except the one sitting on the lead tusker's shoulder. None of them seemed to exhibit the superior thinking skill granted them by their leader. If any of them possessed any thinking skill at all, maybe they would have changed their minds. The lead winger with his ranting and magnificent posturing came clearly into Madaliene's focus. By doing so, he, without question, put his name on one of her first arrows. The first to go would be any creature that attacked Bubba. Her second arrow would be for him.

Bubba patiently waited as the rank and file positioning of the tuskers slowly broke down as the wingers became excited. He stalked the entire herd in front of him. He needed just the right break in the action. His wait was rewarded. The lead winger turned his back to the thicket to garner more attention of his fellows. By doing so, he gathered every eye. Bubba pounced from hiding. He ran directly at the lead tusker then cut sharply to his left, slightly bumping the leader's front leg as he turned. Immediately, the lead tusker broke rank to see what had hit him. He saw the Cheetah's tail bouncing above the backs of the tuskers on the group's outer fringe. He was confused. Why would the attack come from just one pathetic, weak creature? Were the others assembled in the thicket sending this poor creature out as a sacrifice, thinking they would take him and be on their way? Suddenly, the Cheetah came racing in front of the group again. Blazingly fast, no tusker could get a bead on the Cat.

"If that Cat comes around again, one of you gore him!" The leader shouted.

Again and again, Bubba circled the group. Not one tusker could track him fast enough. The entire herd began feeling dizzy as they strained to hone in on the fast moving Cat. The lead winger became furious. "One of you champions attack that Cat!"

There had been no direct attack on any creature aside from the brief encounter with the lead tusker. Still, that winger wanted action. One of his champions did make a move to attack Bubba on his next lap. As Bubba raced into sight, this winger made his last flying move. He rose above the herd as his prey moved closer. He dove on Bubba as he passed by. He had no chance. The arrow pinned him to the ground. The second arrow loosed removed the ranting winger from the lead tusker's shoulder. The archer waited the herd's next move. Several of the wingers took wing when their leader fell. Many tuskers began pawing the ground anxiously. A few grunted. Two made a fatal mistake of charging the thicket. Both of them fell within steps of each other. Within the thicket, Lemeer and the other Great Forest creatures could not fathom what they were seeing. Two more tuskers burst toward the thicket. They too, fell within steps of each other. The remaining herd was nervous. Bubba raced around again, faster. Deliriously distracted wingers tried to take wing after the Cheetah with no success. They could not get a bead on him.

Out of the thicket, Mystic stepped brazenly toward the maddened crowd with the globe held tightly in his jaws. Lemeer followed. Madaliene watched, from the tree, every move made at the same time.

Out of sheer disbelief, most eyes sought out the large grey Wolf as he approached, leading a short parade of much smaller, odd looking creatures. With the ranting winger out of the picture, some calmer thinkers prevailed. Yells of attack were heard interspersed through the herd of tuskers. Dirt flew from beneath the nimble hoofs. A stampede erupted, heading directly at Mystic.

The grey Wolf stopped. He dropped the globe in front of the storming herd. Nothing happened. Bubba came zooming by again. He paused to see Mystic standing dumbstruck as the herd charged.

"Mystic, run!" Bubba pleaded. "For the sake of the Great Forest, Mystic...run!"

The Prince of the Great Forest did not run. He did not move. He stood still as a stone. "Bubba, why is the globe not doing what we thought it would? Have I made a tragic last mistake? Have I doomed all of these creatures at our sides?"

Bubba reacted nervously, "I don't know, Mystic. I can't answer those questions at this moment."

"What do we do now?"

Madaliene came running to the impending melee. "Mystic, what are you doing? Get out of there!" She nocked an arrow and let it fly. It felled the closest tusker. Those behind him tripped over his carcass, somersaulting them into each other. She took down another and another. "I can't keep this up!" She yelled. "We need more help!"

Above, the intelligents had regrouped. As best they could, they dove on the many armored smaller four-leggers around the Cat and the Wolf. Though the armors appeared clumsy, they inflicted serious damage on more intelligents than ever imagined. Quickly, they determined the need for the upturned spur worn by the Badgers. With one strong, upward flick of their head, the spur sank into the intelligent's mid-section as they settled to maim with their talons, mortally wounding any and all that came in range. The Crows flew down upon the intelligents' backs; their sharp talons ripping many wings apart. Raptors of all kinds, although not in great numbers, flew bravely into the fray. Madaliene stood her ground between Mystic and Bubba. An intelligent came in high, aiming for Madaliene's bow. Bubba swatted it out of the air with claws extended. Another came for her left hand, with Mystic stopping that threat.

Everywhere in the South Quarter witnessed some type of attack. The planning went terribly wrong, which was fortunate for the Great Forest. The well thought out plans of the intelligents fell apart as their pompous leader orated to his champions. Had they not listened to that egotistical monologue, the outcome may have turned in their favor. Thanks to that short interlude before the attack, the Great Forest was saved, for the time being.

The globe sat harmlessly beneath Mystic as he growled menacingly under his breath. From the far end of the South Quarter, a Horse and rider made their way to the front lines of the fighting. The tuskers scattered as the thundering hooves of the Horse pummeled the ground. Atop the Horse, a slender two-legged figure rode wearing no ornate costuming, no armor, no regal drapings. As he approached where Mystic fended off the tuskers Madaliene did not place arrows into, a light began to appear at his feet. The light rose to knee height and stayed there. The rider guided his Horse directly at Madaliene. He pulled tight on the reins. The Horse reared up in protest. The fighting around them never slowed. The Great Forest creatures, though holding their own, were taking a fair share of losses.

The two-legger stared a hole through Madaliene. "Little girl, where is your captain? Who leads this ridiculous bunch of soldiers you have here?" Then he saw it. "That is what I am after. There at your feet. Give me that globe and the staff that holds it. You grant my request and this battle will be over for now. If you refuse, all of your laughable army will be wiped out."

The glow began to recede back into the globe. Madaliene reached down and picked it up with one hand. "This is what you want? This globe is all you are after?" She yelled over the noises about her. "Then you shall have it." She raised the globe to him. She held it as high as possible. "Mystic, I think this will do it!"

Mystic, Bubba and Lemeer looked at the globe as she held it for the rider, their faces holding different levels of all emotions at once. The rider defiantly reached for the globe, at the same time screaming to the assembled intelligents and Tuskers, "Kill them all!"

The light was brighter that anything Lemeer had ever seen. The creatures of the Great Forest would forever talk about that brilliant blast of light. Within the time it takes to blink an eye, the rider was gone, the Tuskers were gone and the intelligents were gone. The remaining creatures stared mystified at each other. What just happened?

***

Arlis perched at Vincen's side. "Hazzell, it's not that serious. His wings were torn badly by the attackers' talons. I say he will be fine, right, Vincen?"

"You are telling the truth, Arlis. I will be fine. We need to get back out there. Where did those tuskers come from?"

"I may be going back, but not you. I doubt you will see any flying for some time."

"I won't have it, Arlis. I have to fly. We have to fly! The Great Forest is counting on us."

"Hazzell, talk to this molt, will you?"

"I understand your desire to fly Vincen, but you can't. Your wings can't hold air right now. You must allow then to heal properly."

"We have no time for that!"

"It doesn't matter, Vincen, you can't physically fly!" Arlis flew to the open window. "Can't you understand? Your wings are broken!"

Eboni flew as fast as possible with his cargo. He saw Arlis at the window and cawed to her, "Incoming. I have something to use on Vincen's injuries." He landed next to Arlis.

"What did you say you brought, Eboni?"

"That archer pulled it out of her bag, gave it to Mystic, he gave it to me. They told me to use a little of it to heal Vincen's injuries and to save the rest for those who are injured in the battle."

"Really? Vincen, do you have any idea why your new friends sent this package with Eboni?"

"Of all the bad luck in my life, finally a touch for the good. If that is what I think it is, bring it over here. Quickly now!" Vincen's mood suddenly changed.

Eboni flew to Vincen's side. "Here you go, sir."

"Thank you, Eboni. Hazzell, do you think you can finagle the top off of this container?"

"Certainly, Vincen." Hazzell used her agile paws to loosen the container's spout. "There you go."

"Wonderful job. Now, can you tip it so that some of the water inside spills on my wings? Wait, wait, just spill some onto this table for me." Hazzell did as instructed. "Not too much. We will need the rest of this soon enough."

Hazzell let the container tilt until a small amount of water puddled beside him. He bent his head to it and sipped as much as he could. After feeling the water pass down his throat, he flipped himself over to wet his wings in the remaining puddle. The three others watched astonished at the transformation.

One of them asked, “Vincen, what is that?”

“It’s hope. It’s miraculous, healing hope. It’s water from the river running through the Land of Nuorg!” Vincen hopped to his feet and flew around the room. “Arlis, Eboni, we must get back to the South Quarter at once!”

Hazzell argued, though she couldn’t figure why. Vincen was healed.

From the window sill, Vincen asked, “Hazzell, seal the container. We will need it for the wounded. I will carry it back with me now. Be ready. We will know soon enough how much healing will be required of you. I will send Eboni back.”

“I can’t believe your wings are healed, Vincen. I will certainly take your word to heart.” Hazzell waved them on. “Get out of here, you two. Go do your duty.”

“As you ask, ma’am.” Vincen took wing. He was followed closely by Arlis and Eboni. Both of the crows still marveled at the power of that water Vincen carried snuggly beneath him.

***

Madaliene took a big sigh of relief. “I didn’t know if that was gonna work or not!” She looked around at all of the creatures staring in her direction. “Oh, for those of you who haven’t met me, I’m Madaliene O’shay. It’s nice to meet you.”

“Excuse me. That would be Princess Madaliene!” Mystic was not going to let Madaliene or anyone else forget that small detail. “I had no idea what you were about to do, Princess. I’m glad it worked out.”

“Remember, Mystic, Frederick told us if the globe was not threatened, nothing would happen. As long as we were fighting to protect it, it stayed dormant. When I offered it to that two-legger, well…that changed everything. I was certainly hoping it would work.”

“You and me both, Princess. Do you see anything else here that is strange?” Bubba moved away from Madaliene. “Where are the bodies of the creatures Madaliene took? Where are any of the attackers?”

Mystic scanned the area around them as well. "I guess they were taken with the living ones. That saves a lot of clean-up and it's really weird."

"Wait, I see one tusker laying over there and one of my arrows at his side." Madaliene noticed the bright pink arrow feathers above the yellow and green striped shaft. It was stuck in the ground approximately a full step away from the motionless tusker. She ran to get a closer look.

Mystic focused his attention back on his fellow Great Forest dwellers. "How many have we lost here? How many do we have wounded?"

Lemeer scurried here and there amongst the downed creatures. "Mystic, they are all breathing. Did the light save them or did it trade their lives for the ones that disappeared? I have too many thoughts to even ask questions right now. This is all very strange for me to comprehend."

One by one, every creature injured in the skirmish struggled to get on their feet. For several of them, that was not a possibility. The surviving sky-travelers took a few practice runs above the crowd and the four-leggers that could, walked around aimlessly stretching their muscles and offering help to those less fortunate.

Lemeer walked cautiously over to where the globe laid, its light fading away. "Mystic, please tell me more about this."

"All in good time, sir. Bubba can you fetch the handle for me? I'd like to put the Staff back together again. I feel better with it in the holster."

"You want me to fetch the handle? Fetch it? Really? Cats don't fetch, Prince." Bubba laughed. "With all that has happened, you can tell a joke. Not bad. Tell you what; I'll go retrieve it for you if you wish."

"Hmm, that sounds fine. So Cats retrieve, but they don't fetch? Is that correct?"

Bubba quivered and then shook his entire body from the front of his nose to the tip of his tail. "Whatever...Prince."

Mystic smiled. "Lemeer, let us go see what Madaliene is up to."

***

Madaliene bent down to get a better look at the tusker. “So, what are you, creature? Around here they call your kind a tusker. Is that what you are? Why were you not taken with the others?” As she ran her hand down the creature’s side, she was taken back by the coarseness of its hair. As her hand passed over its ribcage, she jerked one hand back and pulled the small knife from her waist. “Creature, did you just take a breath?”

“I’m sorry, Princess; I held my breath as long as I could! Please don’t kill me.” The tusker rolled his eye at her and gasped for breath.

“That is harder than it would seem!”

“Mystic! Bubba! We have a live one here!”

“Princess, they will have you shoot me with one of your magic arrows. Send them away, please. I need to talk to you.”

Madaliene looked at the poor creature with pity. “Magic arrows? How do you know I’m a princess?” She stood up waving for Mystic to slow down. “Were you not with the others?”

Mystic trotted the rest of the way to Madaliene. “What is it, Princess?”

Lemeer arrived a little later, “What do you need, Princess?”

“This tusker here is alive! Why was he not taken by the globe?”

Bubba sprinted to the impromptu meeting. He dropped the Staff’s handle at Mystic’s feet. “Here you go, Prince. One retrieved staff handle.” He looked at the downed tusker. “Who is this?”

Madaliene giggled. “You are a Cat, Bubba. Cats don’t retrieve.”

“Princess, you seem to have a finite grasp on stating the obvious. Where did you acquire that annoying skill? Really, who is this?” Bubba glanced curiously at the sole remaining tusker. While Mystic reassembled the Staff, Bubba began to chat with it. “Speaking of the obvious, you were not a member of the attacking herd, were you?”

The saved four-legger clamored to his feet, shaking off much dust and several other things even he wasn’t sure about at the same time. “I tried to be, Cheetah. But so many things weren’t working out. I could not bring myself to believe even half of the rubbish we were being told. I find it hard to believe any creature a quarter past stupid would fall for that malarkey.”

Mystic nudged Madaliene while holding the assembled Staff securely to the ground with a paw. “Princess, would you be so kind?”

"Sure, Mystic." She placed the Staff back in the holster. "There you go, Prince." She turned to the new legger, "So, tusker, I presume you have a name, yes?"

"Yes, I do. I am called Gullinbursti."

"Gullinbursti? Did your mother or father not like you? A name like that sounds like a cruel trick to play on someone." Madaliene usually said what was on her mind, right or not. "Well, I'm not gonna call you that. I'll come up with something a little less ostentatious."

"Yes, Princess, please do. One of my brothers is called Hildesvini and another Ottar."

"Whew, those names sure sound Greek to me." Madaliene laughed.

"Tell me about it, Princess. Try to spell a name like that early in your life. You will grow to despise it."

Mystic listened as the conversation drifted to asinine edges. "Let's get back to the point here, if we may."

Bubba jumped into the conversation also, "It seems that you, Gullinbursti, were not of the same mind or intent as those you were running with. My question is why? I have a few thoughts on the matter, but, would rather you tell me to save my guesses for a later situation."

"He's correct, you know." Madaliene added. "If you had been of the same mind as those you were with, you would be trapped with the rest of the tuskers in that globe."

"In the globe? All of those that were with me are now captured inside that globe? Is it heavy?"

"No, it's not heavy. Where did you come from? Why did you invade my forest?"

"They did not invade the Great Forest, Mystic. They invaded the South Quarter." Bubba corrected.

"Gullinbursti, nah...that won't work for me. Tusker, you need a name easier to shout out. I'll come up with something." Madaliene continued on her thinking tangent.

Lemeer could do nothing but listen. So, he listened intently to every word from every creature.

Vincen and the Crows passed over the edge of the thicket. To their amazement, the invading horde was gone. "Arlis, you and Eboni take the water and have those who are wounded drink. Dole it out as needed. No creature should need very much of it. It's all we have, we need to retain as much of it as possible. It really doesn't take very much to do the job. I am flying out to that get-together there in the middle."

"Yes, Vincen, we will take care of the wounded." Arlis never missed a beat of her wings as Vincen passed the water container to her in flight. "Eboni, who looks like they could use this first?"

"That would be that group yonder. Follow me." Eboni took aim on a small group of four-leggers wearing armors similar to that which Lemeer wore. "We should give those a drink first."

"Yes, I see them now." Arlis followed.

Vincen lit on the ground near Mystic. He spoke to them all, "I see evidence here to suggest you rolled the globe. Am I correct?"

Mystic answered, "Not necessarily, sir. You see, I did try to roll the globe, but nothing happened. The result you see here is the work of the princess. She made the decision to offer the globe to the two-legger who came seeking it."

Vincen cocked his head slightly, "Two-legger? What two-legger? There was a two-legger leading this attack?"

"No, Vincen, a two-legger rode to the front from far in the back during the skirmish. He demanded the globe, so I offered it to him. Obviously, the globe was not thrilled with him."

Bubba added, "Or everything else that was here. Vincen, it took the living attackers and cleared this entire field of the few dead ones. Why would it do that?"

Vincen was, again, stymied with the actions of the Staff's globe. "Who knows? Who is this? The very fact he is standing here would lead one to believe he is not of the same mind as those who were about to attack us. Lemeer, please go assist Arlis and Eboni as they care for the wounded. They will tell you what to do. They need someone with paws."

"Certainly, Vincen, I will help them. When I return, you will tell me how you were able to fly back here after I saw you carried back to the dwellings without a working wing."

"I won't need to do that once you realize what Arlis has in that container she needs you to open."

"Alright, I will see for myself." Lemeer hurried to where Arlis and Eboni were studying the wounded.

Vincen watched as Lemeer began a conversation with Arlis. To no one in particular he said, "That could get interesting." He looked up to Madaliene, "Princess, we haven't met formally. I am Vincen of the

Great Eagles of the Great Forest. It is true honor to meet you. Albeit, I know nothing about you, where you are from or your intentions, but still, it is a pleasure. I hope these two sons of mine have not been too much trouble."

"Thank-you, sir. I heard you while I was in the tree earlier and I have heard these two speak volumes about you. We have needed you with us, but, I see you have been busy with your own preparations here." Madaliene stood surveying the meadow around her, both hands on her hips. Where are my arrows? I can maybe understand, and that is a very cautious maybe, the bodies of the creatures I shot disappearing, but my arrows too? I may need them again."

Bubba asked her one question. "Princess, have you checked in your quiver?"

"In my quiver? Bubba, why would I check in my quiver?"

"Simply because it looks full to me, I guess. The only arrow I see is this one that respectfully missed this tusker."

"Bubba, I don't miss." She walked around continuing her search.

Vincen strutted around behind her. "Princess, why do you say you never miss?"

"Oh, that is an easy question, Vincen, because I never do, never have that I remember."

"That is a remarkable story to tell, Princess. So every shot you took hit its intended target?"

"Yes, sir. I shot four of those intelligents that were after you and numerous other tuskers and wingers. Every shot brought the intended target to the ground."

"How do you explain the lone arrow?"

"I don't know. It hit its target, I know it did."

Vincen folded his wings tightly to his side. "What if that arrow," he stopped walking to look back for emphasis, "What if that arrow hit its target, but didn't kill it? What if it passed completely through its target, doing no harm, then continued on to the ground?"

"I guess that could have happened. I'm not really sure why, but, at this point, why not accept that proposition? Further, that scenario would leave only one clear explanation; whatever I targeted had, at some point in time prior to then, experienced a globe purification. Oh my! Mystic! Bubba!" She turned and ran back to the others.

"I wonder why she is in such a hurry?" Bubba watched as Madaliene came running.

"Bubba, Mystic, ask this tusker what just happened. Never mind, I'll ask him. Gullinbursti, that name is so long, have you ever seen a spectacle like this," she waved her arms wildly about her head, "before?"

The tusker paused before answering. He patted his hooves on the ground, nervously. "If I say yes, Princess, will that be a good thing or a bad thing?"

"Don't bother about that right now. Yes or no?"

"Well, I may have witnessed something like that before."

"What does that mean, may have witnessed?"

"Okay, Princess, yes. Yes, I have witnessed a living light before. It was not of the same brilliance, but, my answer is yes. Yes, I have."

Madaliene gasped. "Where? Where was it? Who did it? Where are you from?" She sat down on the ground in front of the Tusker, grabbed his tusks and shook his head. "Where are you from?"

16

Hemoth took Frederick back to the main library. "Frederick, you know we could have used a two-legger like you when we started this place. What have you found out so far?"

"Hemoth, why do you say that as if I don't know the answer? I have found that out at least."

"Ah, so you have. What was your first clue?"

"Something I discovered in the memorial chamber."

"Was it a clue someone left for you?" Hemoth guessed.

"Yes, it was a clue I left for me."

"What else do you know?"

"These books I wrote. I left clues in each of them in case I forgot... which I did." Frederick continued in a haltingly excited manner.

"Did Mystic or Bubba catch on?"

"No, I don't think so."

"Frederick, how is all of this happening and where is it supposed to lead?"

"Don't ask me, you're the one who should be telling me that!"

"Fine, we need to look at these letters Madaliene brought back. I don't think I wrote these also, did I?"

"No, I am almost sure you did not write them."

Frederick sat in the chair he was becoming familiar with at the spot he was beginning to call home. Hemoth sat to his side. He laid the two letters out in front of them. "Why are there two letters? Why not write just one to tell the whole story?" He tapped his fingers over the yellowed paper. "Hemoth, do you know this Karl or Zachary Clermoneau?"

"I can't say for sure, Frederick. Nothing rings a bell."

"Will you do me a favor?"

"Sure."

"Will you go to the memorial chamber and search for any and all names such as these? Who is Karl and who is his father? Should we know this?"

"I will go check it out for you. Where will I find you when I finish? Here?"

"No, I need to go check the other libraries for clues as to who this Clermoneau character is. What if he has nothing at all to do with any of this? Why did he need to find Princess Madaliene? How does he even know of her? What does he expect her to do? And the code, did you see any code on the letter? In either of them? I need to take a walk. Maybe something will click. Let me know if you find anything? Okay?"

"I absolutely will. You know how big that chamber is, it might take a while to check all of the names."

"I know. I am pretty sure we have the time, if not, I think we can find it…if you know what I mean."

"Aha! If you can figure out how to do what only you could do before, then maybe we can. If not, we will have to fit all of these pieces together upside down." Hemoth chuckled to himself as he lumbered out the door.

Frederick said to himself, "Now what did that mean, big fellow?" His attention returned to the letters lying in front of him. One sentence kept bothering him, the last one…*There will be one among your group who can decipher the code.* "Is that me?" He stretched back in the chair, one hand scratching his head, while the fingers on the other hand began tapping again.

***

The Horses patted the ground with their strong hooves nervously, their riders contemplated the next few decisions, the Osprey and Crow busied their minds silently as they all gathered one last time before going their separate ways.

Evaliene was very curious to know any information the Crows might have. Curiously, she asked, "Corvus, what do you know of the situations? Are they dire? I feel guilty for some, if not all, of the confusion, if there is any. I was coerced, rather blackmailed, into sending ridiculous letters out on several occasions under extreme duress. I was told to write letters to nearly every ruling two-legger I have ever heard of and more, most of the letters, actually, went only God knows where. I did not address but one myself. The greeting on that one did not even list a name. I addressed it to P.M. It should have been sent to my sister's domicile via a secret network of messengers. I have no idea if it was a successful delivery or not. Do you know anything about it?"

Corvus nodded, "There was talk of the letters before the onset of the slaughters. There is no way of knowing which letter ended up where. All of the communicators, well, most of them anyway, are no more. There have been wholesale eliminations of wingers or sky-travelers or what-have-you over the past several clusters of moons. The savagery of the attacks added to the explicit planning has confounded even the most fluid thinkers of our kind. I'm sorry, ma'am, but in order to track down this letter, I'm afraid you will have to divulge as much as you know of the secret network. We will need to scrutinize it from every possible joint. What can you tell me about it?"

"As much as I want to tell you, Corvus, I cannot."

"And why is that, ma'am?"

"Because, dear Crow, I don't know anything about it. It was set up that way for our protection – me and my sister's."

"But...someone has to know. Someone somewhere has to know."

Evaliene continued, "The details were left in the hands of our Protectors. Sean here is one. I doubt his level of confidence is great enough for that burden to have been set on him. Sean, can you add anymore to this?"

"No, Princess, I can't. As you noted, my level is not that great."

"Who has attained that burden, Sean?"

"The only one I know of is your messenger, Princess. She was one of the last to know. She may know of others, I don't."

Evaliene grimaced at his response. "That is a truly horrific bit of information. What about my messenger? Was there any notice of the Rider's bag during Broanick's initiated clash? That tyrant normally rode with that bag he imprisoned her in secured firmly to that saddle horn you sit behind. Broanick, did you notice losing the bag?"

Sean loosed the reins in his hand slightly. He was at a loss to explain why he had not immediately searched for the bag. "No, Princess, I failed you and her. I did not think about her. My only thought was protecting you from this beast on which I rode here. That, as is turns out, was a grievous mistake by me. I can't go back now. My hope lies with my brothers. Surely, they located her."

Evaliene breathed out a miffed breath. 'What of you, Broanick? Did you notice the absence of the bag before you came after me?"

"No, Princess."

"Well isn't that wonderful to hear!" She hopped off Rhiannon's back with ease and grace. She spoke to the black Horse and rider while she looked at the throng of wingers about her. "You can watch me, but don't approach me. I need to walk this festering anger out of me before I say something I'll immediately regret." She whirled around, staring at Sean and Broanick. "Or do something I may regret tomorrow!"

"Yes, Princess, as you command." Sean felt about as solid as a spoonful of jam. He looked at his steed, "Horse, we have made a terrible mistake." Broanick only heard garbled sounds. Still, he sensed Sean's remorse. They both watched her every move as she walked through the flocks of wingers, each one bowing as she passed.

Rhiannon swung her gaze to Broanick. "What do you suppose happened to her messenger?"

"I honestly don't know." He pointed his nose to the ground and snorted.

Corvus clicked his eyes to each individual legger left not walking heatedly away. "Alright, I take it this Protector here is not a Talker. Why do you suppose that is?" He continued to click his eyes around, "Anyone? Do you have anything to add, Osprey?"

Pandion shook his head. "I know nothing of the happenings around here. If you would like, I can send a quartet back to the village, wherever it is, to inquire about this messenger. I assume it would be safe enough. I saw nothing to the contrary while flying in."

Corvus thought a moment, "I tell you what, Osprey. What if you and I flew back to find this messenger or her whereabouts? Are you up to the task? We should take some scouts with us, just in case. I see you could be a fast flyer if pushed."

"I would welcome the challenge, Corvus. And yes, we need scouts and I am, most definitely, a fast flyer." He looked to the white Horse.

"Dear, which direction do we go and how far?"

"Fly to the east past the river. Turn north to the low hills. Fly their feet until dawn. Turn north again, to catch the southern sun. You will see the main road, ignore it. Behind the lake, take to the east once again. Look for the small forest of spindle pines, cross the gap to north. There you will find the village. Be careful, the Protectors are on edge. They are marksmen with the bow. Use my name, tell them you seek Kelly. He will help you. Wait a minute, he is not a Talker." She groaned. "There are no Talkers in the village!" Another groan. "Ask around for Pewny. She will stir the oats. She will locate the messenger."

"Ask for Pewny?" Corvus wanted to make sure of the name.

"Yes, you are correct."

Pandion sighed. "Rhiannon, those directions would be perfect if we were running as you did. We will be flying. Is there one direction we could aim for, say... as the Crow flies?"

Broanick laughed. "That was amusing, Pandion."

Corvus looked away and slowly shook his head. "Go ahead, make the Crow jokes. I can take it. When you are finished with your humorous attempts, we can be off."

"What did I say?" Pandion innocently replied.

Broanick's laugh turned to a mild chuckle. "You need to fly northeast. You will spot the village. Fly high. The trip should not take you far into the night. You need to get on with it. Are there any instructions we need to heed while you are away?"

Corvus nodded. "Yes, Broanick, there are. Do not let Evaliene out of your sight for one instant. The Crows will stay with you. They will be out of sight, but, if they warn you, even in the slightest, take action to hide. Do you have a safe place already picked out?"

Broanick answered. "Yes, of course."

Corvus acknowledged a look of agreement from Pandion. "We both think you need to get there as soon as you can. You can never be too careful. Send the wingers to the trees as you await our return. There is no need to expose our whereabouts to any prying eyes."

Pandion added. "The sooner you arrest the princess' movement, the better for us all."

"We will take care of that right now. You and your group, be careful. Return quickly." With that said, Rhiannon trotted over to retrieve Evaliene. "Princess, we have to go."

She had not completely walked out her anger, yet she remained sensible. "Where to?"

"We have to get you hidden away. We have been out in the open for too long."

Evaliene climbed into the saddle with ease. "I am all yours, Rhiannon. Take me wherever you see fit."

As Rhiannon brought Evaliene back, Broanick came running to her with Sean in saddle. "Rhiannon, follow me. The wingers have their tasks laid out for them. They will disappear into the woods until we call for them. The Crows have split the flocks up into smaller groups to await further instructions. Pandion's scouting groups will follow us. They will be our lifeline to the world until our next plans are made. I hope Corvus and Pandion return quickly. I had no idea the Crows were so wise. Corvus is a fine winger. It's too bad we judge them based on hearsay and appearance."

Rhiannon pulled into a medium gait alongside Broanick. "Princess, did you hear all of that?"

"Yes, I did. Sean, we are heading for our safe place. How I wish you were a Talker. It would make this so much easier."

Sean kept his focus on the path ahead, "I'm sorry, Princess. I have no say in that matter."

***

Pandion and Corvus flew northeast at a steady pace. Pandion had never flown with Crows before. He was very impressed with their speed and endurance. It seemed they could fly this pace for days on end. "Corvus, how are you involved with the princess?"

"Pandion, I was soon to ask you the very same question. I would say we are participating more out of a need to keep our world from being overrun with creatures who would prefer to dictate our lives to us rather than letting us live them as we see fit. We are not willing to fight this fight solely for one life. We are willing because there is so much more at stake here than Evaliene and her sister. If it comes down to one point of contention, it would be survival of all creatures and all ways of life. Yes, Pandion, in a nutshell...life and freedom to live it."

"Very well said, Corvus. Your kind, are they all as wise as you?"

"I would say, that generally speaking, they are...well, we all are. I can't say as much for some other wingers. We do tend to discriminate as a general rule. I'm not saying that is a proper attitude or way to live, but, let's face it, it is a pretty universal way of behavior."

Pandion agreed. "I would say most species discriminate, Corvus. Although, as it is well documented in the transcriptions, most don't or won't admit to it."

"I wholeheartedly agree."

"Corvus, what do you know? I am brimming with information from my world, but I was told to trust no one other than Evaliene, her Protectors and her sister."

"Sir Osprey, I received those exact instructions. There was also one statement which was brought to the forefront of every conversation..."

"Was it presented to you by a very large winger of few words?"

"Yes, it was and it was always at the very end of the warnings."

"Beware of the..."

"Intelligents. That was it." Corvus shrugged his wings.

Pandion continued. "And your interpretation of that? Could it be the same as mine?"

"It very well could be, Pandion. Have you seen any of them in any shape or color?"

"No, I have not."

"None of us has seen a single one either. They are a secretive species, although for a while, they were everywhere."

"Corvus, we have taken one captive on the coast. We cannot get it to divulge anything. She condescendingly perches there, right at the tip of our beaks and laughs. Several want to kill her off, but we are hoping that one day she will tire of our stupidity and tell all!" Pandion managed a laugh between strong beats of his elegant wings.

"You are joking with me, are you not?" The Crow's eyes lit up.

"No, I am not. It was quite entertaining since they are so much smarter than the rest of us. They are quite doltish on occasion."

"Really? You have captured an Owl?"

"Yes, Corvus, we have and she is very high up the chain of command."

"Really?"

"Yes, really."

"We need her brought here immediately after we find Evaliene's messenger."

"I hope we can make that happen. Why Corvus, what do you have in mind?

"What do I have in mind? I'm going to make her talk!"

They flew on in silence, each wise leader's mind astir with minglings of coming strategies.

***

The Horses proceeded with a steady gait up a non-existent path to the safe place. Hidden in the trees under a thatched roof, completely invisible from the sky, sat the refuge. Not overly big, the structure was adequate to comfortably house six individual creatures. The stores were plentiful and contained within the structure. Once in, no exit would be required for several passings of the moon. It was not built as a dwelling or royal residence; instead, it was carefully constructed to conceal and protect those that lived within. Broanick stationed a few small groups of wingers in the trees surrounding the haven, then he and Rhiannon, with their riders, continued on.

***

Pandion was blessed with greater vision than any of the Crows. He saw the outskirts of the village first. "Corvus, we are approaching Evaliene's village. It should be coming into your view shortly. What do we want to do first?"

Corvus tilted his head down a notch, "I will take your word for it, Pandion. I suggest we perch near the edge of it. Surely, we will meet someone who can lead us to Pewny. I find it hard to believe we failed to ask what kind of creature she was."

"Yes, quite a blunder on our part. I will not blend in well here. Ospreys never venture this far from our coast. I will keep watch while you take the lead in finding our liaison."

"I agree. Pandion, your vocabulary…you tend to use words not normally associated with the ordinary trappings of mountain or forest life. What are you? What were you trained to be?"

"Ah yes, I was afraid that would become apparent. I am from a family of…let me see, how do you put it politely? We…uh…"

"You are an operative, a warrior?"

"No, those words lean too much to the harsh side of what we do. I rather like to describe myself as a fixer."

"A fixer? What on earth do you mean by that?"

"Corvus, with your high degree of acumen, I will let you come to your own decision on that. You can count on this one truth, friend; I can protect myself, you and any other creature under my wing from just about anything."

"That sounds very suspicious, Osprey."

"Yes, it does, Corvus. It certainly does. We are not evil creatures. We operate only for the good. Sometimes good needs its own protection, we are able to provide that."

"Well, you did capture an Owl."

"That we did, among other things." Pandion focused ahead. "There, just past that sprinkling of fir trees, there is a fence running away from the main path, we will perch there while you do your reconnaissance."

"See, a perfect example. That word is not used much around here..."

"Noted." Pandion led his group down to the old fence. "This should be an inconspicuous perch, should it not? Corvus, do what you need to do. We will wait here."

Darkness softly enveloped the landscape as Corvus searched their surroundings for any clues to the whereabouts of Pewny. He blankly glanced at Pandion, "Anything you can add here?"

Pandion noticed the village was void of any and all traffic. "There must be creatures here somewhere. They should not all be resting yet. I suggest we position ourselves in several spots closer to the dwellings. If this is where the princess came from, there has to be some activity about."

"I'll take the lead. I will check out that first larger dwelling, then, I will make my way down the main path." He nudged the winger next to him. "Come with me."

Corvus flew around the back of the large dwelling. A light flickered through one of the open shutters. Inside a group of two-leggers were seated at a long table. From his vantage point, he couldn't tell how many were assembled, but there were several. He thought aloud, "I wonder if there are any Talkers among them?" He perched in a bush beneath the window. All he heard was gibberish. "Hmm, I guess not." He flew to the next building and so on down the wide central path. Something did not seem natural with the inactivity as he searched the dwellings for a Talker. There were creatures here. Where were they? That was the most important question on his mind.

The Crows were seen. Two small four-leggers tracked their every move. Scampering along behind them, they planned to introduce themselves at the next stop. When the Crows eventually settled on their next perch, the questions began. “What are you two doing here?” “Do you know it is not polite or safe to enter here without introductions?” “Who are you?” “What are you looking for?” The questions were not asked cruelly, more matter-of-factly. The Crows were a little surprised.

“We were hoping this place was not deserted. I am Corvus, this is my second. We were sent by the princess to seek her messenger. She believed the messenger to be imprisoned in a bag which Rhiannon, Broanick and Sean failed to secure when they made their escape earlier. Do those answers serve us well?”

As one of the four-leggers pondered Corvus’ answers, the other said, “Yes. Come with us.”

Corvus was pleasantly pleased with the short answer. “Can you take us to Pewny?”

The same legger answered again, “Yes. This way. We had a little skirmish here. I don’t know how much you were told, but we have control over our village again. The Visitors are…I’ll say it nicely, contained.”

“I am afraid we were not privy to much information regarding the circumstances here. The princess told us to only gather information about her messenger.”

“That is understandable. Rhiannon whisked her away before the containment took place. The Protectors have things well in hand now. There should be no more trouble from the Visitors that remain here.”

The second four-legger spoke. “And by ‘that remain here’, we mean to say those that remain alive. The Protectors did not take kindly to those two-leggers. They have several imprisoned and the Visitor’s lead Rider is, um…not doing well.”

“I see,” answered Corvus. “I commend the Protectors for a successful clash. Do you know where the messenger is?”

“Yes we do, but she is not well.”

“Do we need to see Pewny?”

“At your service, sir Crow.”

“Oh, so you are Pewny.”

“Yes, I am. Evaliene’s messenger is in the care of Paddy’s mate. She is a well respected care-giver in our village. We will take you to her. She is not a Talker.”

“Is there a Talker left here?”

"No."
"Wonderful!"
"Not really."

***

"Rhiannon, why are we not stopping there?" Evaliene asked as they passed by the shelter, attracted by its utilitarian coziness. "Looks fine to me."

"Princess, that is a decoy. There is no way we would hide you away out in the open like this."

Evaliene was surprised. "That is out in the open? I am afraid to ask where we are going then."

"Leave that little bit to us. We will get you where you will be safe and secure for years if need be."

Evaliene dropped her head to her chest, rolling it back and forth to ease the strain of the day's adventures. Suddenly, she jerked straight up, her eyes wide. "Rhiannon, you can't possibly mean..."

"Yes, Princess, that is exactly what I mean. We are taking you to the fortress built for you by our ancestors. It is the only safe place now. We pray Madaliene has reached hers as well."

"Do my Protectors know of its location?"

"This current group does not. The location died away with the last Protector of two generations ago. The location was not passed on to any two-leggers. Sean will be the first to see it again."

"Will he know how to navigate it? I remember hearing it was a massive place."

"There are volumes of books and maps, Princess. You and Sean will have a lot to study once we arrive."

Evaliene took several deep breaths, "I never imagined actually visiting there. Are things out there that bad?"

"From what we hear, yes... and getting worse."

Evaliene sat tall in her saddle, "I would have never imagined this."

***

17

What is it, Whistler? I see you retrieved the map's covering. Was it difficult to locate? Did you see anything else of note during your assignment?"

"Yes, we saw more than either of us wanted, that's for sure. We need to speak in private, Tofur, the sooner, the better."

"I can see by your actions this is serious, Whistler. Very well, then." Tofur excused himself from the group. "I apologize, Doctor, I need to chat with my Falcons about an important matter that arose during their absence. That will be alright with you, won't it?"

"Yes, yes, you go right ahead, boy. Should anything come up, I will alert you."

Tofur walked with the Falcons until they were just outside of the four-leggers' hearing range. "What is so important, Whistler?"

"Tofur, the map covering was left back to cover the eyes of a four-legger that attacked those two-leggers we are following. Not only did they kill that four-legger, they killed two others just like him."

"I am very sorry to hear that, Whistler. How does that concern our group?"

"Tofur, the four-leggers were all Rottweilers! They did not wait. They did not do as Belle told them."

Taytay could not keep quiet any longer. "Tofur, he is telling you the truth. It was all three of them. We are certain of that beyond any shadow of doubt. All of Belle's sons, Tofur, are dead. The two-leggers we are following killed the three of them at different times. We can't even venture to guess why they separated."

Whistler added, "Tofur, it was horrible. We have to let Belle know. She can't keep on thinking they are waiting at home for her. She will be devastated either way."

Tofur's young eyes became misty, his breathing difficult. "I, I don't know what to say." His head began shaking from side to side. "I don't think we should tell her now, Whistler. What if she doesn't take it very well?"

Taytay ruffled his feathers a few times before speaking. "Tofur, either way, she isn't going to take it well. There is no right way or good way to tell her this news. I suggest you tell her sooner than later. I can't assure you of it, but I believe she needs to know now and make her mind up whether she wants to continue with us or not."

"Taytay, we have to have her with us. There is no other option. None!" Tofur was much too young to deal with this kind of emotional dilemma. "I have known her my entire life. No matter if we tell her now or tell her later, she will not leave me. I know she won't. I think we should tell her now and see how she reacts. I hate to, but I guess I need to be the one to break the news to her."

The Falcons looked past Tofur's eyes. They looked into his emotions. What they saw pleased them both. Taytay told him so. "Tofur, you have what you need to tell her wisely. Take her to the side and tell her what we told you. Do it in a way where you don't draw out the misery."

Whistler added, "But don't take it too lightly, either. She will have a reaction. You need to be prepared for it. Go now and tell her."

Tofur agreed with both of them. He solemnly acknowledged their instructions and walked over to where Belle, Porcene, Jak and the doctor were making plans to continue the journey. "Excuse me all of you. Belle, I need to talk to you right now."

"Tofur, you can tell me whatever it is in front of our friends. Please, what is it?"

Tofur stammered a little, "Well, I think it would be better..."

"No, Tofur, tell me now. Whatever you need to tell me they can hear. It won't hurt. Go ahead. Say what you need to say."

Jak noticed the hesitancy in Tofur's actions. "What is the problem, Tofur? You are turning ghostly white."

"Jak, I have bad news." He turned to Belle. "I'm sorry, Belle, it is very bad news. While the Falcons were retrieving the map's cover, they learned some tragic news." Tears began to mount in his eyes. "Belle, it's, it's the trips. They followed us. You told them to wait, I know you did. They...they were attacked." Tears were now flowing freely. "They were all three killed coming after us. Those two leggers we are following killed them all, Belle! I am sorry, I am so sorry." Tofur collapsed to his knees beside Belle and hung on her neck as she absorbed the news.

A disturbed scowl appeared on the Rottweiler's face; her eyes, confused, clouded over. Disbelief instantly manifested itself over her entire body. As she solemnly stood beside Tofur, Jak and Porcene remained silent. The doctor knelt in front of her. “Dear Belle, who were these…these trips?”

Tofur answered for her, his words muffled, “Doctor, the trips were her sons. Three brave Dogs who loved life and each other beyond their good senses.” Tofur was angry at the trips. “Why didn’t they do what they were told?”

All emotion faded from Belle. Her poignant resilience impressed the doctor and Porcene. Jak knew it well. One tear was allowed to roll from Belle’s big brown eye as she nuzzled Tofur. “Master, we have a job to do. I will grieve for my sons when we accomplish what we have set out to do. My resolve is hardened even more against the ones who have caused us to leave the safety and comfort of our homes. Now please, cry if you must, but if you allow this horrible circumstance to fog your eyes, it will also fog your judgment. I am now, more than before, determined to stop whatever is coming and bring a swift and just judgment to those who have brought it on us.” She took a deep breath. She looked at those around her. “It is time to plan. We will not delay another instant.”

Whistler and Taytay closed their eyes. They expected this. They had not known Belle as an emotional creature. She was hurting, they knew, but more than that, those about to be in her way would hurt more, a lot more.

“If that is what you wish, Belle, then let’s get to it.” Tofur wasted no time in attending to Belle’s wishes. “Jak, Porcene, have you two formulated any plan yet? You need to say yes.”

Jak’s eyes took on a steely glare. “Tofur, we do have a plan and we have decided we need Leiram here to make sure it goes off without a hitch. We can’t trust the other personalities Mariel is accommodating. We mean no ill-will to them, but Leiram is our choice to lead this motley band of creatures.”

“I can understand that. You do remember Leiram is not a Talker, right?”

“We have discussed that and can’t find a problem with it as…eh, long as you are around to interpret for us.”

“Okay, Jak, what if I am not around? What if something tragic happens to me leaving you without an interpreter or a way to toggle between Mariel’s personalities? What then?”

"Well, young sir, that would open a new set of complications for us." Jak looked to Porcene for affirmation of his statement. "Would it not, dear Belgian?"

Porcene smacked her lips together as she looked to Belle. "Belle, do you have anything to add to Jak's answer?"

Belle shook her strong, square head left to right. "I'm sorry, Porcene. I have nothing to add."

Mariel's current personality was taking in not only the conversations audibly taking place, but also the other unspoken ones. In other words, he heard what each of the other creatures did not say. He rose from Belle's side to address the group. "If I may, I have something to say I feel is important to you all. I can't help but think that each of you, in some way, feel these personalities of mine are changed by outside stimuli. While that may or may not be true to an extent..."

Each of the creatures within the sound of Mariel's voice became suddenly interested in what he was about to say. Tofur crossed his arms in front of him with the newly refined whistle lightly clasped in one hand. The Falcons lit on each of his shoulders. Porcene, Belle and Jak all turned to give the zany two-legger all of the attention he deserved.

Mariel continued, "I have my own theories as to why they switch."

Tofur whispered to Jak, "Which Mariel is this?"

"I don't know if I remember this one taking the last one's place."

Porcene overheard, "Neither do I."

Belle barked at the noisy leggers, "Let him speak. After all, does it matter which one of them is sane?"

Jak answered, "Actually, Belle, it matters a lot."

Tofur toyed with the whistle in his hand. "I see your point, Jak." He blew it three times.

Mariel immediately took on the persona of the inventor. "Whatever are we doing? Isn't it time to be leaving here?"

Tofur blew the whistle once more.

The look on Mariel's face turned cold and hard, "I see you have no plans for us to follow lad. This is how this group will proceed..."

All eyes and ears stayed attentive as Leiram spoke.

***

Gullinbursti could not help staring directly into Madaliene's dark eyes. "I am from a place far from here. It has taken me half of my lifetime to get here. Does that answer your question?"

"No, it does not. Where exactly are you from? And I mean exactly. How did you happen to experience the light from the globe?"

The tusker continued staring deep into Madaliene's questioning eyes. "I was little and very young. I can't remember the details. I don't know where we were or even who was with me. I saw the light explode and it scared me. I ran away from it. When I came back, I was all I found. Whatever caused the flash of light was gone. I had no idea what it was or why it happened. It left me alone."

Madaliene looked around for Mystic. "Mystic, come here."

The Prince of the Great Forest trotted over to Madaliene's side. "Yes, Madaliene?"

"Mystic, he's with us. Find something for him to do. We need as many warm bodies as we can get." She hurried over to Bubba and Vincen. "And just call him Gulli." She continued walking, "That will at least be easier to say."

Mystic did not question Madaliene's order. He nodded to Gulli, "I guess that means you'll be coming with us, tusker." Mystic motioned toward the retreating Madaliene and the others, "Shall we?"

Madaliene rushed passed Vincen and Bubba heading straight for the thicket. Lemeer, after turning the nursing duties over to a surprised fellow inhabitant, scurried over to Vincen as he and Bubba took chase after the princess. "Vincen," Lemeer called, "Hold up, please. What was in that bag you gave me?"

"It's a long story, friend. Inside that bag is a gift we brought back from Nuorg. All that we have left is in that bag. Use it wisely. Get this place cleaned up and follow us back to the forest at once." Vincen turned to again chase after Madaliene who seemed very intent on bull rushing into the thicket.

Lemeer paused, "Nuorg? All that is left? Oh my!" The Badger summoned all the speed he had and returned to his last patient. "Excuse me", he exclaimed to the other four-legged creature administering the miraculous water. "It seems we don't have much of this left. Use only one drop if it will suffice. If one drop won't do it, use two, but no more if you can help it." He received a nod in agreement before heading back after Vincen and the Princess. He ran as best as a Badger could.

***

The field awakened as many of the Great Forest inhabitants felled in the skirmish got their legs back under them or were again able to take flight. Their healings were appropriately called miracles, although no one had, of yet, realized there was a limit to the Nuorg water's healing power. Several of the previously wounded survivors flew back to their respective dwellings with too much euphoria and not enough reality filling their heads. Who could blame them? More than a few were nearing their last breaths when the Nuorg water wetted their tongues. In complete death throes, some of them even fought off the liquid, more than willing to take their deaths in stride with the coming battles. Some dreamed they had passed on and did not want to return. Some fought the foggy feeling of no sensation at all - through a fleeting moment of terrific pain - then the stark realization that they had returned to the living.

The life-giving water from Nuorg, in Nuorg, never lost its potency. However, once it began to absorb the contaminants of the worlds in which these creatures lived, it too became slowly tainted. The reason for its purity rested within filters made of many forms and substances not of this world. In due time, thoroughly purified drop by drop, it collected to form the Hopen River that flowed tantalizingly clear throughout the land of Nuorg, giving life to those as needed.

Upcoming trials would sincerely hope for a replenishing of, at least, that one container of water.

***

As Madaliene stormed into the thicket, Bubba, Mystic, Vincen, Gulli and Lemeer eventually caught up to her. Very determined, she swatted and kicked limbs, thorny branches, small trees and rocks out of her way. Nothing was going to stop her. Her aim was the Great Forest and she was going to get there, the sooner, the better. Those following her could only guess at what had set her off. But, although none had tried, there would be no stopping her. "These cursed thorns in my side!" she hollered as she managed to fight her way through. "How much further? Anybody?"

Mystic mumbled an answer no one could understand. Vincen nipped him on the ear.

"Not now, son. Let her have her say. There is a lot of pressure on that young one right now."

Madaliene's rants continued growing stronger and more profane as her struggles with the intertwined mat of vegetation increased. "If I ever get back to my fortress, I will burn every last thing those posers ever touched. The very idea of tricking me is an abomination of good sense." She let a loud, stress-relieving scream escape her lips before continuing. "If I get my hands on the creature instigating this whole…pile of…rotten, stinking berries, I will personally see the last breath come from their body!" She fought with a particularly stubborn vine, "Get out of my way!" Onward she stomped.

Vincen rode on Mystic's back, marveling at Madaliene's continuous stream of harsh words. "Mystic, this two-legger is not to be messed with."

Mystic agreed, "You are telling me! I certainly agree with you. I hope she lets all of us live!"

Gulli walked beside Bubba. He asked, "What do you creatures know of this princess?"

Bubba rolled his eyes, "Obviously, not as much as we need to. What did she ask you back there? I'd be lying if I didn't say I am more concerned with the answer you gave her than her question."

Gulli nodded, "She asked where I had seen the light cloud or whatever it was."

"And? What did you say to her?"

"I told her I experienced it long ago, nearly half of my life ago. I also told her it was far from here. Can you figure out what I could have said that would have made her go crazy like this?"

Bubba stopped walking momentarily. He glared at Gulli, "No. No I can't. Not only does that confuse me, it also makes me angry. Why now? What is on her mind?" Slightly up ahead they heard a good word for now.

"Finally!" Madaliene shouted as she burst out of the thicket.

18

The Eagle and Rakki had every intention of flying directly to Burg One in order to be there waiting for Karri and Hugoth to ascend from the caverns. Mystic prodded Rakki to take a short break to rest before they flew past the protective wall surrounding the Burg. All of the seven Burgs were built in this way. The wall was only one of many measures taken to guard the inhabitants of each Burg. Against Rakki's more impetuous nature, they stopped several clicks from the entry bridge. Both of them, being types of raptors, possessed keen eyesight which allowed them to view the Burg from their perch should anything out of the ordinary happen. The big trees on either side of the gate were alive with winger activity. Neither of them could see inside the wall since the bridge had been drawn under Hugoth's orders. They had no reason to suspect anything out of the ordinary, so they rested on perch without much being said.

Far beneath them, a noisy Horse-drawn cart containing four two-leggers casually made its way to the worn out, rock-hard spot where the bridge would soon drop to allow entry. A trio of big cats was approaching the cart at high speed.

"No! Stay away from the Bridge!" The larger one shouted.

The lead Horse swung his head around to see who was calling out the warning. Atop the cart, a two-legger urged the Horses to keep pace.

"What do you think the commotion is all about, Nathan?" Lewis asked from the passenger side of the bench type seat, located ahead of the smallish cargo area. "Should we pull down and check it out?"

"You know, Lewis, I sure wish there were more Talkers in this Burg. We have a standing order to get these prisoners of ours to the Keeper. I say we shouldn't dally 'bout that."

"You do have a point there. The Horses seem very upset." Lewis spun around to check on the prisoners and, maybe, catch a glimpse of what the lead Horse was trying to see. He grabbed Nathan's sleeve and tugged hard. "Pull down, Nathan, we have company."

Nathan immediately commanded the Horses to stop with a constant pull on the reins. “I do hate to override the Keeper’s orders. What is it, man?”

Lewis pointed to a spot behind them. Two exceptional Tigers, Cirrus and Duister, and one black Leopard, Luiperd, were now in clear sight, coming quickly out of the trees. All three of them ran in unison, strong muscles nearly exploding beneath brilliant coats of fur. The Cats were not the problem. The throng of angry men on their mounts was the problem. Greatly outnumbered, any chance of eluding the invaders was non-existent. One of the prisoners raised his head to Nathan, his gag had worked loose. He spit it out.

“I warned that girl back there that all of you would soon be in for more than you could handle. From the panicked look on your face, I would say that you now agree with me?” He turned to his fellow prisoner. “See, I knew they were not far behind us.” They both laughed out loud.

Nathan did not know what to do. He hopped down from the cart and unhitched the team of Horses. Lewis followed and began removing the harnesses. “We will have to make a break to the mountains, Nathan. It will be our only chance, if we have any chance at all.”

“Lewis, I agree with you. Why haven’t they lowered the bridge? We could have at least been more protected inside.”

“I can’t answer that, Nate. Take the mare. I’ll take the stallion. We will meet up at the Sweet Gulley drop…if we make it. Stay hidden, maybe they won’t come after only two of us.”

It did not take long before each two-legger was astride a different Horse, headed deep into the mountainside forest. A plan had been in place, as long as anyone could remember, for this very reason. Of course, no Nuorgian ever dreamed this reason would ever come to be.

The prisoners were still tied in the cart, but they laughed louder as the two-leggers galloped out of sight.

“Cowards! Come back here and bring your fight to us!” He spat on the ground. “That is what I think of this place!” He spat again.

The Cats saw the two-leggers ride off. “Cirrus, should we not follow the Horses?” Duister was not one to go against steadfast rules.

“We may follow them after we determine what is going on. This army behind us wants something they think we have. As soon as they recover our prisoners, they will know much more than they do now.”

The third big Cat, a black Leopard, agreed. "Cirrus, what you just said makes too much sense. These invaders cannot discover what the prisoners know of Madaliene."

"Luiperd, what are you saying?"

"Cirrus, you know very well what I am saying! These two cannot be allowed to tell what they know. They already tried to get answers from the dead ones we left behind."

"Yes, I remember that very clearly, Luiperd. It was a brave move on Duister's part to bring the satchel of that wildly dressed one. I wonder what secrets it contains?"

Duister agreed, "It may have been very brave or very stupid. When I ran back and took it, you'd have thought them ready to rip me to pieces."

Luiperd grinned, "Duister, the dead tried to rip you to pieces? Back to my point..." He looked back at the approaching army, "These two can't be allowed to talk, Cirrus. You know that."

Cirrus, a large, exquisitely marked Tiger, solemnly nodded her head. "I agree with you, Luiperd. Let us please try to take them with us first."

Duister kept looking toward the approaching horde then back to the cart, "Alright... Cirrus, how will we accomplish that?"

Cirrus leaped onto the cart with a terrific roar. She slashed at the ropes holding the prisoners securely to the sideboards, slicing them neatly in half with her strong claws. She bit down firmly on the collar of the prisoner's thick overcoat and leapt off of the cart as if she was carrying a small cub. Duister knew what to do next, but the ropes holding the talkative prisoner were not as easily cut. He fought with the bindings while Luiperd stood watch.

"Hurry, Duister!" Luiperd was getting more nervous as he watched the army of invaders head their way.

"They won't let go, Luiperd!" He tore at them some more.

Luiperd had enough. "That's all the time you have, Duister! Go now!"

"What are you going to do, Luiperd?"

"I am going to make sure this legger answers no further questions, now go! Now!"

Duister hopped off the cart to follow Cirrus. He turned back once, acknowledged a wonderful friendship with the Leopard by swatting a paw across his face, then, shaking his head, he was gone.

Luiperd jumped back on the cart as the first of the invaders neared. His life up to now had been normal, or so he thought. It would never be thought of again in the same way by any surviving Nuorgian or Tiger. He crouched beside the terrified prisoner, talking to him with a horrific series of roars and growls. A line of invaders pulled to a stop no more than a few Leopard leaps from the rear of the cart. Luiperd heard a voice call to the legger beside him.

"Willem, don't move. What can you tell us?" A rider decorated in the same style of adornment as the satchel carrier moved forward. "Draw your bow on the Leopard's left side. Loose your arrows when you have a bead drawn. Do not shoot Willem!"

Luiperd noticed the sly movement by the archers. He knew what was next. Willem was trembling terribly at his side, he knew too. The legger attempted to answer his leader. A powerful swat by a brave black Leopard with claws fully extended prevented any words from coming out of Willem's mouth. The prisoner immediately slumped over, the bindings still holding him to the sideboard. Six arrows pierced Luiperd's body simultaneously in places that would never heal. The Leopard fell beside his prisoner; neither of them would ever breathe again.

A teary-eyed pair of magnificent Tigers watched as the events unfolded before them. Cirrus jerked hard on her prisoner's coat, rendering him unconscious. She and Duister proceeded deeper into hiding without uttering a word. Cirrus did not take great care with her baggage, if he was broken or bleeding when they got where they were going, then…so be it.

Willem slumped in the cart with the Leopard at his side. The invading squadron's leader rode up to the cart. He was noticeably furious with this outcome. He yelled, "Someone did not shoot soon enough!" He seethed at his fellow invaders. "Blow the horn! I want that bridge lowered. We still have some house cleaning to do. We will work extra hard to get our answers now." He pointed at the Burg, "Someone in there will have them."

A slight man on the ground raised a battered silver horn which was sloppily tied to a worn piece of cord encircling the man's neck and chest. He blew a feeble warble that sounded anything but meaningful.

Inside the raised bridge, two invaders heard the horn and quickly fumbled with the bridge lowering mechanisms. To their delight, they found the levers in good condition and easy to understand. The bridge began a slow arc to the worn spot where the cart still sat along with its cargo.

Before the bridge was completely lowered, the irritated leader of the group charged hard towards it. He spurred his mount up onto the heavy planking and on between the Forever Trees. The rest of his men followed at a normal pace once the bridge was completely lowered.

The leader dismounted. He challenged the two working the bridge. "Where are the prisoners?" He looked around excitedly. He was expecting a whole Burg's worth of terrified prisoners and a few stupid animals. He received no answer. Again he ranted, "Where are my prisoners?"

One of the men stepped near him holding his own floppy hat in his shaking hands. "Sir, there are no prisoners. This entire place was deserted when we came through the crack. There is not a soul here."

"Not only that," the second man said, "Our entire squadron was caught in the crack and destroyed. Their screams alone nearly did me in, sir."

The leader was livid. "Did that idiot Owl make it? Please tell me he did. I have quite a surprise for him."

***

Lightning motioned toward the large mass of tree roots in front of them. "Perrie, inside the roots of that tree is a large bucket. We can use it to enter Burg One. Are you up for it?"

"I can't see how I have any choice, Lightning."

"Well, you are correct there. I suppose I was just being polite."

Lightning moved around to activate the hidden lever. The opening emerged just as it had on his earlier visit. "Perrie, if you would be so kind, hop on my shoulder. We need to take a ride."

Neither of them knew who to expect when they arrived at their destination; they just knew they needed to hurry.

"Who will we find up there, Lightning? Do you think Hugoth is there?"

Lightning's neck stiffened as his ears suddenly perked up. He raised high on his back legs to peer over the large clump of roots at his side. Instead of climbing into the large bucket, he motioned for Perrie to perch back on his shoulder. He pulled the lever back into its original position and watched as the opening disappeared.

"What is it, Lightning?" Perrie showed a little discomfort with the situation.

"Something is coming through the tunnels," he told her. "Stay quiet." He concentrated on the barely audible sound emanating from the other side of the cavern. "It's almost here, Perrie."

She nuzzled closer to Lightning's huge head, her eyes glued to a medium sized area, she assumed, where Lightning was already looking. The feathers on her head rose slightly as a shaded figure appeared.

Lightning let out a cleansing sigh and walked around the foot of the roots. "Hugoth! What brings you down here?"

Hugoth kept walking towards them. "Lightning? How did you get in here?" The Grizzly Bear was surprised, as can only be expected.

"It wasn't us that brought us here, Hugoth. We were brought here by this!" He held his ax-pike high for Hugoth to see.

"Really?" Hugoth's size was exaggerated by the scant light in the cavern. "But, why would it bring you here? Where are Princess Madaliene and the rest of your bunch?"

"With a question like that, you could open several hives of bees, sir. I fear that just a short story detailing our latest adventures would take too long to tell and the chances of you believing it are doubtful at best."

"You don't say? You do realize where you are, do you not? Is anything even the least bit dubious in this land not lauded as completely possible?" Hugoth grinned.

"I can almost see your point, Hugoth. Let me say this much. I don't know how many day-rounds have passed since we have been here, but we have, so far, been haunted twice by ghosts…the same ghosts each time, been transported back to Madaliene's fortress and now we find ourselves here, right smack under the Forever Trees of Burg One. What have you been up to?" Lightning looked to Perrie. "Have I left out any details, little Falcon?"

Perrie chuckled, "Maybe about a short book's worth there, friend."

"Uh, maybe so, Perrie, maybe so." Lightning held his paws out to Hugoth. The large Grizzly's head was hanging with lower jaw agape. "Questions?"

Karri spoke from Hugoth's shoulder. "Did you say you were haunted by ghosts, Lightning?"

"Yes ma'am, I did. Twice."

Perrie nodded her head, re-affirming Lightning's story.

Karri continued. "And then you traveled back to Madaliene's fortress before coming here?"

"Yes, Karri. Yes, we did." Lightning answered, nodding his head politely.

Hugoth's head was twitching. "Ghosts? Real, live ghosts?"

Lightning turned to Perrie, "That seems a little contradictory, but I'd say they were real, live ghosts—wouldn't you, Perrie?"

"From what little I know about ghosts, I would say yes to that question, Lightning. A definite yes."

"Wait a tick here." Hugoth stood, lifted a paw to his giant head and knocked it around a little. "Where is my brother? Where are Mystic and Bubba? Where is Frederick? I still haven't seen him during all of this."

"We don't know for sure. We left the fortress with Madaliene, Mystic and Bubba. We assumed we would be traveling with them. We didn't. Frederick and Hemoth were staying on in the fortress with lots and lots of mysteries to unravel there. We were sent, obviously, in different directions to take on different tasks."

Karri tilted her head, "Obviously. Now what are those obviously different tasks? Hugoth, you got anything?"

"Uh…no. Not right now. Let's get to the Keeper's dwelling. Surely something will manifest itself for us."

Lightning once again manipulated the hidden lever, revealing the enormous bucket hidden in the shaft. He and Hugoth climbed in with the small wingers clinging to their shoulder fur. The ride up was silent except for a few grunts and groans here and there from the large creatures as they toiled to lift the heavy contraption to its resting spot just below floor level of the gate house.

Karri unabashedly eyed Perrie for the entire trip up. "Perrie, have you had time to realize what is going on here?"

The young Falcon answered. "No, I haven't. Why do you ask?"

"No real reason, I guess. You and the princess are so young. What would any sensible reason be for two as young as you are to be up to your necks in whatever is happening here? It seems like such a waste." She focused the conversation to Hugoth. "What do you make of it, Keeper? Do you think the princess or her Falcon have any idea the perils that might lie ahead of them or, should I say, do lie ahead of them?"

Hugoth was put off by this questioning. "Karri, we have discussed this, have we not? I told you I would not intentionally put any of us in danger."

"Exactly my point, Keeper. How can you look at these young ones and not realize that whatever your plans are, your best intentions have nothing at all to do with what may happen? I simply think they should live while enjoying their young lives rather than fighting for them. That's all." She looked upward, "Perrie, follow me." Karri took wing.

The young Falcon was torn. Should she follow Karri or stay with Lightning?

"Go ahead, Perrie, fly with her. She means you well. I will be with Hugoth. Surely you will be able to find us with little or no trouble."

"Yes, sir."

Perrie took off after Karri. They flew out of the gate house and high into the Forever Trees, before heading out to find Mystic, the Eagle and her brother, Rakki.

Lightning continued to tug on the strong rope turning the gears that, in turn, lifted the bucket. "What do you suppose that was about?"

Hugoth answered. "I'm sure it has something to do with Karri's motherly instincts. She came here a long time ago, unable to hatch birdlets of her own. We saw eye to eye most of the time...that is until recently. She had a small issue with me after your group left the first time. I think she misses being a mother and sees the young princess and Falcon through the eyes of a mother. She is concerned for their future as I am concerned about all of our futures. I just can't break it down into stipulations regarding age. I have to think of it as a whole. We really have quite a dilemma coming at us. Here we are."

The bucket gently nudged against the receiving platform. Hugoth tied the rope off before climbing out. Followed by Lightning, they made their way up a short flight of stairs ending in the main room of the gate house.

"It seems like forever since I was here," Hugoth said as he continued toward the door.

The two large leggers stepped into the bright light of the yellow ball hanging brazenly in the sky. Lightning squinted as he caught a glimpse of it. "Is that thing getting brighter?"

Hugoth shrugged his shoulders and sighed. "Yes, my friend it is." He took a few steps toward the bridge and looked around. It was too quiet. He scanned the trees, which revealed nothing. He looked at the shutters on the buildings. They were all open. Everything seemed normal except for the silence and total absence of living creatures. "Lightning, something is wrong. This bridge should not be down. I left instructions to leave all Burg gates closed. We need to slip back to the bucket and cut it loose. We can't leave the lower caves accessible from here."

"Stay here, Hugoth. I can do that. Keep an eye open for strangeness." Lightning hurried back to the bucket and broke the peg and a few other structural pieces off where the rope was tied. The bucket began a hasty drop to the roots of the Forever Trees. He was back at Hugoth's side in an instant. "I sent the bucket down. It won't be coming back up without a lot of work."

"Thank you, Lightning. Now tell me this, how can creatures our size become invisible?"

A wry grin was visible on Lightning's face. "With this." He held up his ax-pike.

"Very good," Hugoth whispered. "How fast can it work?"

"As fast as it needs to."

"Wonderful, keep it ready. We will head to the Keeper's dwelling. If we need to disappear, I will let you know."

"I will stay alert." Lightning was a little nervous, but he didn't show it.

Down the main path they went, side-by-side, retracing the very steps Hugoth and Hemoth had taken not so long ago. The Burg was silent everywhere they looked. Their steps grew slower and shorter until they were just barely creeping along. As they passed a short row of buildings where the two-leggers usually worked or milled about, a double blur exploded to their left. Racing at them from behind an overturned wagon, they had no chance to use the ax-pike to avoid the collision. Instead of knocking them down, the two disturbances took up guard on each side of the Bears.

"Luiperd is dead, Hugoth. We have to get out of here now. Burg Seven may be safe, but it won't be for long."

A voice came from the other creature. "They have our prisoners and every other creature that lived within these walls. I have never seen so many vile creatures in one place."

Hugoth and Lightning listened in shock.

"Duister is correct. We couldn't fend them off fast enough, so we had to run for it. Luiperd tried to be the hero. They got to him before we could."

"He was the hero, Cirrus. He allowed us to escape."

Hugoth could not believe what he was hearing. "Cirrus, what are you saying?'

"Hugoth, this Burg was attacked. No one knows how they got in. The bridge was drawn. The attack came from everywhere at once."

Lightning scoured the areas around them, "Where are the victims?"

"That's what we are asking ourselves, Lightning. They aren't here," Duister said confused.

Cirrus added, "And that is too strange for me to understand."

Hugoth was becoming very angry. "We have to check out my dwelling."

"It's no use, Hugoth. They ransacked it looking for the staffs." Duister kept his eyes focused behind the closest building to them. "I refuse to believe this attack was only for the staffs. I think they want the princess also."

Lightning roared, "They will not get her!"

Cirrus growled, "I didn't think they would get Luiperd either. We have to go. Burg Seven may be next on their list, or... what am I saying? Who knows what is next?"

Hugoth nodded to Lightning. "Get us to Burg Seven, now!"

Lightning didn't bother lifting the staff or any other showmanship. He whispered, "Burg Seven, if that is where we belong." The group disappeared.

From behind the building Duister had been watching, a two-legger stepped out with an Owl on his shoulder. He was dressed in attire that might suggest he was partaking in a hunting party. Heavy pants tucked into well-worn riding boots, a rugged coat with several pockets, a brown shirt and a belt holding several small knives and a sword to his side. His blondish hair was pulled behind his head and secured with a string attached to a rounded, floppy hat. "So, you said it would be so easy did you?" The two-legger grabbed the Owl with a strong gloved hand then slammed it flailing to the ground. "I was to follow you? I was told you would lead me to the staffs? If I was a Talker, I would tell you why I am about to do this, but I am not!"

The Owl's eyes were wide open with fright. This was not supposed to happen. There was no use trying to reason with the two-legger, he would not understand. The Owl's body was soon lifeless and mangled beyond recognition.

"Serves you right, you despicable, feathered rot!" The two-legger took a last kick at the carcass and stomped off toward the bridge. "Now what?"

Karri and Perrie circled back and came in from behind the Burg. They didn't see everything, but they saw enough. As the two-legger stood at the bridge's edge with his gloved hands on his hips, they dove. Four razor sharp claws and two beaks capable of tearing the flesh off of bones were aimed at the vital areas around the legger's upper torso. At the last minute, Karri screamed. The legger spun around to perfectly catch all four talons with his wretched face. What happened to his eyes will remain unsaid. The legger screamed in pain and terror. He threw his arms madly about, tossing the heavy gloves from his hands, covering his face in agony. As he blindly staggered around patting his face, he found the very place where the bridge stopped. A knot in the cord binding the large bridge timbers together snagged his boot, causing him to plunge off the bridge. On the ground, a large rock broke his fall and, ultimately, his neck. The two wingers flew high into the sky then turned for a second attack. They saw the gloves as they were flung from the legger's arms and the fall that took him from Nuorg.

"Karri, we need to collect those gloves. They may reveal some clues as to who is attacking the Burgs." Perrie was already heading for the first one she saw.

Karri spoke to herself, "I don't know where this young Falcon came from, but I am glad she is on our side." She spotted the second glove, swooped down on it and carried it off in her talons. She caught up with Perrie. Together, they headed to Burg Seven as fast as they could fly.

It was not on Karri's mind to question where or how Perrie came up with the plan they had just completed. It was not on her mind to start an inquisition as it would pertain to her earlier training. It was on her mind, however, to never doubt the survival instincts of this young Falcon again. Where did she learn the quick thinking, the tenacity, the voracity with which the plan was formulated? Those were questions she was not sure she wanted answers to. Maybe Perrie should be taking Karri aside to have a talk and not vice-versa. Either way, Princess Madaliene and Perrie were born for each other.

***

In Burg Seven, Jahnise fell to the ground, tripped up by something unseen. "Bongi, it is happening!"

Bongi was immediately at his friend's side. "What is happening, King?"

"The attacks on Nuorg have begun. I felt them like blows to my stomach. I saw them as clearly as I see you right now. I must try to act against this evil." Jahnise braced himself on his stick.

Bongi nervously scanned the area around them. "Did you see where they came from?"

"Yes, Bongi, I did. However, I am not familiar with the lay of this land, so I can only describe what I saw to you. If I do, do you think you can tell me where it was I saw?"

"I can only try, King. Please, describe it for me."

Jahnise stood once again. They were just past the cave's entrance. Jahnise looked at the yellow ball that seemed to be watching their every move. Jahnise changed the subject. "Bongi, you never answered me. What is that ball that hangs there in your sky? It is not the sun, for it never moves, and the sun never appears to mean me harm as that thing does."

As Jahnise awaited Bongi's answer, the yellow ball began to sizzle and pop. A few arms of yellow, evil energy began to circle around the sphere, whipped into a frenzy like long willow branches in a whirlwind. Jahnise stood patiently studying the phenomenon, Bongi still at his side.

"King, we should step back into the cave immediately. What we are seeing is not an everyday occurrence and not a pleasant one at that. The yellow ball, King, is captured evil. What is inside wants out. I can only assume it wants to find you and the other staff bearers."

Instantly, a bolt of scraggly light hit the ground a mere hoof length from Jahnise. He jumped away from the smoking bare spot in front of him. He rushed into the cave with Bongi close behind, nudging him through the entrance. Jahnise was not one to panic and he hardly ever became afraid, but now he stood in the dark cave trembling. Jagged yellow strikes were slamming the ground outside of the cave, pelting the innocent earth as if it were at war with the yellow ball.

Inside the cave, Jahnise removed the small knife from his waist belt. He slipped to the edge of the cave's opening and held the knife blade out in the open. As he twisted the blade back and forth the shiny blade dulled. It became as black as the darkest spot in the cave. He pulled it back in and showed it to Bongi. "This, my friend, is as bad as it gets. It is time for me to reveal another of my staff's little secrets." He took the small knife and stuck it in a slit near the rounded end of the staff. The blade immediately returned to its shiny brilliance. All evidence of the dullness vanished as Jahnise pulled the blade from the staff. "The one who gave me this staff had heard of this peculiar arrangement of the pieces years before my birth, but he had never tried it. Let us hope, good friend, that it delivers as that one said it would."

Bongi had almost nothing to say. "Let us hope? Jahnise, all we do is hope. Is it not?"

Jahnise smiled, "Maybe not Bongi. Let us say this stick of mine is hope, this blade, faith." He held the stick to Bongi. "Now hope can stand alone as this stick held in my hand is capable of doing. It can do wondrous things as you have already noticed." Jahnise moved the small knife closer to the stick. "Now, let us say this small knife is faith, two separate entities standing alone, each completely happy on its own. But wait, my friend, if we take hope and inject it with a good portion of faith, what we have then can amaze us all. Or, at least, I am told. Hah! Let us see what we get here."

Jahnise took the knife once again and slid it back into the slot on the staff. He grasped it with both hands and slammed it into the ground. For an instant nothing happened, which was evident in the look on their expectant faces. Jahnise attempted to lift the stick off the ground for another try, but, it would not budge. He looked at Bongi, his eyes full of questions he couldn't ask for answers they could not fathom.

"Bongi, I can't lift this up! Does it look stuck to you?"

Bongi cautiously eyed the bottom of the stick. Warily, he scanned up and down the stick and paid special attention to where it was stuck to the ground. "I'm sorry, King, I can see nothing to cause that."

The area beneath their feet began to lightly vibrate. Their eyes met, this time widened by surprise. Light began to seep from the stick.

More and more light followed as it swirled its way upward, toward the knife. The knife blade glowed brightly, seeming to soak up every trace of light on contact. This could have lasted for eternity, as both leggers were sure it did, but it did not. Mesmerized by the light's spiraling path, Jahnise and Bongi lost track of time. Eventually all of the light emitted from the stick was contained somewhere in the knife. Jahnise stepped closer to it, Bongi took a step or two back.

"This is a very odd tool, is it not, Bongi?" Jahnise looked around and found the Okapi peeking in his direction from the opening of the cave. "Not one for heroics, are we, friend?" He smiled and turned to the staff once again. "What mystery do you have for me this time?"

All at once, a tiny spark flew from the blade's point toward Burg One. Jahnise watched as doubt etched itself into his face. Bongi stepped out from hiding.

"Was that it, King? Is that all there is?"

"Like I said before, I have never tried that out."

"Hmmph. Maybe you should have."

"I think you may be correct."

Suddenly, Nuorg went black. The yellow ball was extinguished, casting the entire land of Nuorg into total darkness. There was no other light to be found. Jahnise fell to the ground praying – for what, he did not know. Bongi, motionless, stood silently by. Little did they know of the calamity unfolding in Burg One.

The black-out loitered around for only a few ticks longer, although the time in darkness crept by at an agonizingly slow pace. The yellow ball soon resumed its previous state, casting its familiar glow throughout the land once again.

"King, what do you think just happened?"

"Bongi, I wish I could tell you." Jahnise shook his head as the stick fell into his hand. "I have no idea. No idea at all."

***

Stewig stood guard outside of the Keeper's dwelling as Oliviia was attended to inside. A small group of Nuorgians were there to comfort and care for her. The young lady's way of dealing with her parents' death was a private matter as far as Stewig was concerned. Her safety, however, was not. He stationed himself at the door to make sure no creature he was not totally familiar with gained entrance. As word spread, several leggers came by to give her their condolences, all leaving with the same question. How did this happen in Nuorg? Stewig could give no answers. As he acknowledged the questions, he could only shrug.

Oliviia came to the door. “Stewig, must we stay here any longer? We have options, you know.”

“Options?” He asked. “What kind of options are you speaking of, Livvy?”

“Sealing the crack options. I could stay here forever, lamenting the loss of my family...but what good would it do me or anyone else? We have work to finish that my mother and father started. I don’t intend to shed another tear on the matter until their job is complete. Are you going to help me or continue standing there like a breathing door post?”

Stewig did not know whether to be stunned or saddened by Oliviia’s remarks. “Door post? I look like a door post? Very well then Livvy, what do we do first?”

She did not answer. Nuorg became abruptly dark.

***

For some inexplicable reason, the ancient Eagle and the young Hawk stayed on perch and helplessly watched as the encounter happened below them. There was nothing they could do at this point to change even one infinitesimal detail of the scene. They mourned the loss of Luiperd, at the same time heaping silent praises on his selfless devotion to Nuorg. When all went dark, they too were at a loss for an explanation.

***

Ciruss and Duister silently stopped in their tracks. The Horses they had caught were also still and unsure. The two-leggers, Nathan and Lewis, held tight to the Horses’ manes. They did not utter a sound.

“Duister, I have no reason to think you will believe this, but I have a strange feeling we should head to Burg One immediately.” Ciruss paused, waiting for his answer.

"I have no reason not to believe you, Ciruss. What do we do with the prisoner?"

"We will leave him with the Horses and their riders. They will figure out what to do with him." She spoke in the general direction of the lead Horse, "Please take this legger with you. Your riders will know how to treat him."

"We will do that for you, Ciruss. Is it just you and Duister now?"

"Yes, it is."

"How sad. I thought a lot of Luiperd and I think even more of him now."

Ciruss nodded in the dark. No creature could see any movement whatsoever; each could only assume the actions of those gathered. "Me too. Duister, follow me."

The Tigers were off. An innate ability to hunt guided them in the pitch black darkness. They knew where they were going and hoped they would arrive in time to help in whatever way was needed.

***

The Nuorgians of Burg One had heard the news concerning the going-ons in Burg Seven and the surrounding areas. They had raised the bridge at first warning from the winger on Hugoth's orders. Those in the know suspected he would be making his way back through the tunnels. While the normal business of securing the Burg was underway, everything went dark. Leggers and wingers were caught midway through their preparations. Every action ceased as the ominous shade of night befell Nuorg. The only object visible to the naked eye was a tiny spark racing high through the darkness like a falling star that failed to fall – that is, until its path took it within the Burgs tall protective stone border. It arced to the ground without a sound. Dozens of creatures witnessed as it landed along the main path leading to the Keeper's dwelling.

None of the onlookers expected the next unexplainable incident. As the spark hit the ground, common sense told all observers the spark would fizzle out. It did not. From the spark, hundreds of dazzling rays of thin light reached out for every dweller, wrapping around whatever appendage it could locate, forming a shimmering web like no spider had ever spun in Nuorg or the lands above. The strings of light showed no particular interest in binding the Nuorgians, so there was no panic setting in--it simply wanted contact. Once every creature on the ground, in the trees or in the air was securely located, the light exploded in one small, succinct, almost indiscernible pop. Suddenly, without any further fanfare, Burg One was empty.

***

Stewig was afraid to move for fear he might crush Oliviia's feet should he misstep. "Livvy, are you still here?"

"Yes, I am. What is the cause of this?"

"I can't say. It's never happened here before to my recollection."

"I say we wait it out. If we need to run, we might as well be able to see where we are running to. Do you agree?"

"Absolutely. Should we need to run, you climb aboard my back. I will get you back to the tunnel."

"Good idea. I will do just that."

As was felt everywhere in Nuorg, the darkness seemed to linger much longer than it actually did. Before much apprehension could set in, the yellow ball once again ignited, bringing light back to the land.

Oliviia batted her eyes as they readjusted to the brightness. "Stewig, is it just me, or was that very weird?"

"It is not just you, Livvy, it was weird."

It didn't take long for every Burg Seven dweller to recognize the influx of new Nuorgians. This Burg was now alive with new faces. Conversations broke out on every corner and every gathering place possible. A two-legger aimlessly bumped into Stewig's massive flank as he stood next to Oliviia.

"I'm terribly sorry about that." The new face blurted out, his actions not hiding the confusion he was feeling. "What Burg is this?

Stewig answered for both he and Oliviia. "Is that a question for me or the young lady?"

The new face answered, "Well, I guess either of you, actually. It matters not to me which one of you answers."

"This is Burg Seven. Where do you mean to be?" Stewig did not hide the fact that he and every other Burg Seven dweller were just as bewildered as the new faces.

"No more than a few shakes ago, I was preparing Burg One as per Hugoth's instructions. All at once, I and, from the looks of the others here, all of my fellow Nuorgians from Burg One were transferred here. I have to say, nothing quite like this has ever happened before, in my memory."

An eerie feeling hit all three of them at once.

Stewig asked, not totally understanding his intent, "You were where?"

The new face answered. "I know it sounds implausible, but I had just raised the bridge. I was walking back to gather my um…security devices in order to return to the gate house. I was filling in for Donkhorse while he was visiting here. Anyway, it got uncomfortably dark, a spark fell from the sky and well, here we are. I got nothing after that." He shook his head in disbelief. "Where is Donkhorse? Have you seen him?"

The information was bludgeoning Stewig's brain. "I can't say where he is. I know he wasn't allowed to leave. Take this path. It will lead you to our gate house. If you don't see Donkhorse, ask around. He should be near there."

"Thank you. I will do as you say."

The two-legger walked briskly, following the path just as Stewig instructed.

Oliviia scanned the gardens in front of the Keeper's dwelling. A look of foreboding began to veil her lovely face. "Stewig, I don't like this. Something is far too coincidental." Suddenly, the beauty fell from her face like a heavy curtain, "The cracks in Burg One, Stewig. They were the next ones my father was to repair. They were showing the highest chances of failing. It has something to do with some crazy importance quotient and predictability of the knowledge to be gained upon its fall."

Stewig had no way of interpreting what Oliviia just said. "I'm sorry. What was that?"

"I'm sorry too. It is some of the technical language my parents were working on. He explains most of it in his book. What isn't good for us is that I am not the one who was working with them on that particular part of the problem solving. Emiliia was!"

"And that is a bad thing." Stewig stepped away from the door, looking in the direction of the tunnel in case Jahnise may be making his way back. "Livvy, we need to get back to the tunnel. You have to find that book!"

She agreed. "Let's go!"

"But..."

"Stewig, I know my parents have been killed. I know their bodies may still be there. God rest their souls, I can't help that. I have to do what they trained me to do. As I said before, I can cry later!"

She climbed onto the Rhinoceros' back. Together they thundered back to the cave, hoping Jahnise and Bongi could help sort this out.

***

"Patrick," Emiliia whispered, "We need to find somewhere away from these men to regroup."

Emiliia's eyes sparkled a lovely shade of green whether she was laughing, working, or, in this case, running for her life. She got the green eyes from her father, Ian. Oliviia and Patrick both got their mother's crystalline blue eyes. Their hair was all the same color, black. That attribute would help them blend in more than their cousin's hair, which was a deep, bright red. They never totally understood why she left all of those years ago when Patrick was no more than a baby crawling around under everyone's feet. Their cousin was the same age as Oliviia, a few years older than Emiliia.

"I'm right behind you, Mili," Patrick whispered back. "In which direction should we head?"

"Well that would not be such a big problem if you hadn't...done what you did. I am pretty sure they want your blood in payment for what you did back there. It was very brave and one day may prove very valuable to ending this, I don't know...this thing we are in, but really, could you maybe have done something a little less... oh... inhospitable?"

"Come on, Mili, it was our only chance to give our father something to identify these creeps with. That ring and that bracelet have to have some kind of markings on them. Some clues? No?"

"I guess they probably do. Still, what you did... They are really, really mad at us now."

"Serves them right. I'm not afraid of any of them. If they give me the chance, I'll treat them all equally as badly."

"This is just great. I have an eleven year old warrior on my hands. Just to let you know, if we ever get back, Mother is going to hurt you!"

"What do you mean, if we get back? We will get back. Where were we anyway?"

Emiliia could only shake her head. She crossed her arms tightly across her chest. She was shivered just a little. Wherever they were, it was cold. The breeze blowing past them right now was not just cool, it was very cold. Nuorg never got cold and it never got hot. At one point in time, they had all missed the changing of the seasons, but now she was thinking how silly that had been.

"Follow me, Patrick. We have to get to the top of this hill. You can keep up, right?"

"Lead on, sister."

"Keep your ears alert. If you hear something, whatever it is, tug on my vest. We will stop immediately and sit deathly quiet until we either discover what the sound is or it goes away. Got it?"

"Got it."

They walked silently for half of the day. It was obvious to Emiliia the soldiers had gone in another direction for they neither heard nor saw any sign of them. She was silently saying prayers of thanks for that.

Patrick was feeling the effects of being young. He was hungry, tired and irritable. "Mili, why haven't we stopped yet? I need to eat sometime today!"

"We will stop when I feel it is safe to stop… and not until then. Keep walking."

"But…"

"Keep walking!" Emiliia said sternly.

The hill they were climbing was a mountain. They reached the top of the tree line as the day neared an end. Out of their sight, a silent observer watched as they emerged from the trees. "What are they doing here?" This was not in the plan. Why were these youngsters on this mountain anyway? How were they not seen by the soldiers earlier in the day? Did they escape somehow? Several questions peppered his mind. He decided to get a closer look and, if necessary, question them. This situation was too far from what was expected not to get more information.

He floated down behind the leggers in an attempt not to alarm them. Not sure of what they had been through, they may be skittish.

His wing brushed a closing ray of sunlight, casting a foreboding shadow across Emiliia's path. She froze.

"Patrick, don't panic. We have company."

Her brother yanked his head skyward and caught sight of the huge winged creature as it silently glided over them. The creature was large. Its entire shadow seemed to pass over them for an eternity before settling down a short distance in front of them. The bird lightly perched on a broken tree trunk from long ago. The winger's size alone would have frightened older humans, but not these two youngsters. Their interest was only piqued. The huge bird stared at them through large, beady eyes that projected wisdom and concern. Its voice was not cawing or scratchy. It was fairly deep and pleasant, like a grandfather's voice.

Patrick and Emiliia stood tall as the winger addressed them. The older sister took hold of Patrick's hand and pulled him close to her.

"Good day, young ones. May I ask why you are where you are?" The winger stood almost as tall as Emiliia. The wings folded to his side could hide large banquet tables from sight. A crest of feathers waved slightly as a breeze blew up the mountain's side.

Emiliia took a deep breath. "Sir, first I must ask, do you mean us any harm?"

The winger answered, "No, child, I do not. It is not in my character to do so. I have several assignments to carry out and I am afraid you now have thrown a kink in those plans at the moment."

Patrick moved in closer to their guest. "What does that mean?"

"My tasks have been many but simple. I am one of the "warners". I..."

Patrick's manners had not developed fully, something that often caused serious lapses in judgment. "What is a "warner"? Don't believe I've ever heard of that before."

Emiliia stomped on his foot. "Patrick, manners?" He looked up to her and smiled.

The large winger chuckled. "I understand, young lady. What I was saying is that one of my tasks consists of spreading the most important news we have accumulated to the ones we have deemed key role players in this wicked maelstrom as it develops. I do hope you two are on the side of the good or else I will have to do away with you both." He looked over the treacherous terrain lying directly above them. "I'd say an unfortunate fall from any one of those sharp precipices up there would be sufficient. What do you two think?"

Emiliia replied in a mildly astonished tone, "You wouldn't dare to do away with the both of us!"

"Alas, you may be right. I doubt I could get both of you up there at the same time. Maybe I'll take you individually." He cocked his head and winked at Patrick.

Patrick quickly fell in behind his older sister.

"Wait a second here, sir!" Emiliia's voice became stronger.

"It was only an attempt to lighten this moment. No need for excitement. I have no ill will towards either of you. My life lately has been rather uneventful. I have been doing a lot of watching and waiting, not much else. What do you say? Can I enlist your services?"

"Okay, that is better. Eh...services? To do what? You still don't know who we are." Emiliia was beginning to warm to this old fellow.

"Oh, right you are. Who are you?"

"Sir, I am Emiliia Mecanelly." She pulled Patrick from behind her. "This is my brother, Patrick."

"Are you traveling alone? Do you have parents? More siblings?" He nodded with short easy strokes of his head.

"Yes we are. Colleen and Ian Mecanelly. Our sister is Oliviia."

"May I ask where they are now?"

"Presumably, they are still in the land of Nuorg. We had started the process of sealing the cracks that have been appearing at an alarming rate in the caves and tunnels below there. Strangely enough, the first crack we started to repair happened to rupture on us before our work really began. A few invaders were waiting on the other side to gain entrance and attacked us as we worked. We fought them off as best we could. It was apparent that the first of the invaders was not expecting a fight. They got one! We forced them back into the crack and Patrick was grabbed by one of the last ones out, which enraged my mother. The one man released Patrick, but he was carried out by another. I went after him. Patrick found use of the man's sword and I started in on the beastly thief with my own sword." She pulled back the corner of her vest exposing the handle of the utilitarian weapon. "I began stabbing at anything I could draw a bead on. Patrick escaped and ran back to the crack where one of the invaders' leaders was escaping from my parents just as the crack was closing. Patrick managed to inflict some considerable pain on him, and the goon was not able to run off with his squadron. We were not able to squeeze back into Nuorg. So, here we are. Where are we?"

"That is a terrible tragedy. The cracks are already weakening? How did your attackers know where they were located? No one is supposed to know that on this side of Nuorg!"

"My father had not found the answers to those questions yet. Mother had some ideas, but nothing definitive."

"Your vocabulary is very broad. I am quite impressed. Once you escaped the attackers, is that when you tried to re-enter the crack?"

"Yes."

"Exactly what happened when you returned to the crack?" The winger was very intrigued.

"It was closing rapidly. We heard some voices coming from the inside; not our parent's voices, but other voices. They were concerned for our safety. I thought the attackers were returning, so our conversation was short. Patrick did toss a clue that may lead to the thugs' identities through the crack before it sealed completely though."

Patrick nodded slowly and very dramatically, "Yes I did!"

"What Burg were you working under?"

"Burg Seven, definitely Burg Seven. There had just been a meeting to discuss a new visitor there. A King from somewhere. He was very tall and dark. I heard his name...it was, it was..." She closed her eyes attempting to force the name from her memory. "Jahnise, yes, Jahnise Equa...Equa...something. I'm sorry, every one of us but Father left early to begin our work."

"That is good news. Jahnise is needed there. I am glad the timing worked out as it did. We have not heard a report from his land in some time. Did you happen to spot a large Bear other than Hugoth during your visit?"

"No, I did not."

"Fair enough. At least Jahnise is on schedule. This mountain sits above Burg Seven. You are not as far away from there as you might have imagined. I can get you to the window, but I can't get you in Nuorg."

"Really? If you can get us to the window, I can get us in!"

"I will take you up one at a time. While I am airborne, the one I leave must stay out of sight. I feel like I am being watched. Nothing can harm me here, but they can harm you. Let's not let that happen."

Patrick's eyes opened wide. "You are going to carry us to the window? You mean we are going to fly? Me first!"

Emiliia agreed, "Yes, Patrick must go first. But when you get there, Patrick, wait for me before you do anything, understand?"

"Yes, Mili, I understand. I'm not hopeless, you know!"

"So, it is settled."

"What is your name, sir?"

"Please forgive me, Emiliia. I am called Rhodoch." The winger took to the sky. He made a large graceful loop, then circled back to pick up Patrick by clamping strong, blunt talons lightly to his shoulders. "Stay out of sight until I return."

With that Rhodoch flew off with Patrick marveling at the scenery passing beneath them.

"I'm flying, Rhodoch. I'm flying!"

19

Frederick's fingers continued to roll in a steady, rhythmic tapping motion as he pored over the information laying neatly scattered around him. He had no idea where Hemoth had wandered off to, but wasn't overly concerned with it. The Grizzly knew more than he was letting on, Frederick was certain.

He began talking to himself, repeating question after question after question. What, when, why, how, all of these words of purpose, when would the answer become obvious or even the least bit apparent? Not prone to worrying, he continuously made a concerted effort to avoid the many lingering feelings of doubt that crept into his head. Had he been here, in this mountain fortress before? The correct answer, he was beginning to theorize, was yes. Yes, he had been here before. But when had that occurred? For what reason or reasons was he here now? It was more than circumstantial or coincidental. There was an underlying current of something yet unexplained which urged his mind on.

The letter from Evaliene lay to his right. The letters Madaliene brought to him lay in front of him and to his left. The Nuorg tomes were stacked all around the table with the pages of Staff notes mingling here and there, neatly arranged in the order of significance Frederick assigned each of them. One book he kept returning to was the first one he picked up in the library. Maybe there were more answers in it than he had initially thought. He once again began reading it from page one.

***

Hemoth made his way to the fortress' lower levels. He had not been inside in ages. Still, he found his way around with no problem. He was headed to the armories. There were a few things stored away down there he felt Frederick must have. Shafts of light illuminated gathering areas every so often which made daytime journeys possible without the need of torches or candles. A clever use of mirrors and everyday items polished to a fabulous sheen reflected much of the available light around otherwise dark corners. The legger behind the maze of light shafts was a wonderful addition to the original association. Who would have known the genius hidden behind his thick eyebrows and bulging eyes. Hemoth fondly remembered him and regretted the day he fell from the mountain. When he returned to the memorial room he would have to pay his respects again.

As he made the last turn before entering the armory, Hemoth noticed many sets of footprints leading in and out of the entrance. Upon closer inspection, he realized the prints were made by only two different two-leggers. The size of one print never changed, while the other print followed the growth of a small two-legger from its very early years to its middle tween years. He smiled. "So, Madaliene, you have made this trip many times I see."

Hemoth entered the armory and, to his pleasant surprise, everything was just as he left it. He noticed no signs of tampering with any of the crates or cases. The posers must have spent most of their time in the upper levels looking for whatever they were looking for, not knowing, thankfully, that the real important stuff was packed away in these non-descript looking boxes. He noticed with amusement the arrows sticking into nearly every crate residing on the front rows in the room.

After a short rest, Hemoth plodded back to the main entrance. To his right was a stack of the largest crates in the room. As he neared the first crate, he kept his nose low to the ground, sniffing for the trip wire which had been lubricated with fish oil then covered entirely with a thin joint of mortar. Using his very capable sense of smell, he discovered it right away. Scratching along the mortar with one claw of his massive paw, he broke out the mortar and lifted the buried wire from its long hidden trench. As he pulled on the wire, mortar popped out of the joint, until the wire went taught. Hemoth followed the wire to its end where he found it embedded in a heavy trim board that was part of a smaller crate in the second stack.

"I hope I am remembering correctly," he said to the empty room.

Hemoth raised both front legs to the top of the smaller box. He braced the majority of his bulk on one paw as he pushed the top of the trim board gently away from him, trying not to push hard enough to snap the board in half, but hard enough to separate it. His effort was a success. The side of the crate pivoted open, revealing a crank and a pulley with one end of the trip wire already wrapped around it. He began to turn the crank.

***

Back in the library, Frederick was not having any luck at all. The immense amount of information he had collected was now weighing down any thought processes he could start, giving him an awful headache.

"Maybe I need to clear my head. Get away from this for a while." He stood and stretched his legs by bouncing up and down on the balls of his feet and reaching his arms high over his head. He took a walk around the room, opening as many light shafts as he could figure how to. The room slowly became bright enough to recognize intricate details he had never noticed before. "I still say this place is a palace, not a fortress." He spoke louder, "If anyone has another opinion on that matter, please make it known now!" Fortunately, he did not receive an answer.

In the back of the room, a heavy, dark set of curtains was now noticeable stretching from one side of the room to the other. He quickly hurried to one side in search of a rope or cord with which to open it, if it did open. The left side yielded nothing. He trotted over to the right side and pushed back the edge of the curtain. There it was. A rope woven from several smaller cords of twine spanned the distance from the floor to the top of the curtain. Frederick hesitated for one moment, hoping something, or at least another clue, resided silently behind the vast cloth. He tugged downward on the rope. Nothing happened. Again and again he pulled, begging the rope to move. Nothing. His muscles ached. Breathing hard, he released his grip on the rope and bent over to rest, putting his hands on his knees. He spoke directly to the curtain.

"What are you concealing, you stubborn curtain? What more can this place confuse me with today? Why are you playing these games with me?"

He stepped over near the center of the wall where the pair of curtains came together. They were tall, almost reaching the ridiculously high ceiling in the room. From where he stood, his neck would not bend far enough back to see their tops. He stepped backward until he could comfortably see the curtains' top and bottom. He folded his arms across his chest, yet still nothing happened. He was tempted to sit down and wait the curtain out, but he feared he would be standing there for a very long time. Then, suddenly, an idea raced across his mind so vividly he could see it. He ran back to the table and grabbed the heaviest book he could easily run with. Arriving back at the very spot he used to admire the curtains last, he set the book down. He did this again and again until he completed a stack of books that stood as tall as he was. He ran back to pull on the rope again. With hope glowing and sweat rolling from his face, he once again pulled downward on the rope with every ounce of strength he could coax from his body. He waited. Again, nothing happened. He sank to the floor exhausted. He muttered, “That was brilliant. What was I thinking?”

***

Hemoth turned the crank as the thin wire coiled around the pulley, removing any and all slack. He knew if anything had been tampered with, continuing to turn the crank would be disastrous--at least for him. Memories of the original members of the association and the parts each played coursed through his big Bear mind. Pressure began building on the pulley as the strong wire began to stretch between the assortment of gears and pulleys that comprised this machine. At the end of the wire, a heavier cord followed closely and then an even heavier cord until finally a thick, smooth rope came into view. Hemoth paused for an instant. Was this the right time? Nothing could be undone now. The rope could not be pushed back into storage. All the years of planning, all of the work, now it was all up to him. He turned the crank vigorously. The rope began to spool onto the pulley, dwarfing the wire and cording that had come before it. Hemoth heard noises. It was working. After all of these years, it was working.

Farther under the mountain, many machines began to toil. Pulleys and gears and pinions and rings threw the many layers of dust aside as they began to turn in a well rehearsed performance. The direct link between Nuorg and the world above was about to be re-opened.

***

Frederick banged his head against the room’s hard rock wall, sweat rolled from his chin. He was tired. Instead of hopping to his feet, he had to place his hands down on the floor behind him to push up. Instantly, one hand slipped due to a slick, wet spot on the floor. That hand rammed into the wall with a crack. Frederick flinched in pain. The other hand slid in the opposite direction stopping slowly as it came into contact with what one could assume to be a man-made object of some design. With one hand throbbing in pain, Frederick had enough wits about him to notice his second hand had not hit rock. He spun around to face his latest discovery, gently holding his injured hand at his chest. When he realized what the object was, he shook his head in dismay. “Why, of course. You have been there the whole time, haven’t you?”

Frederick lightly tugged and pushed on the object to feel its direction of movement. Once he felt almost sure of the object’s intentions, he pulled it toward him. The rope at his side became looser. “I can’t believe that!” He said out loud. “Of course the rope had a brake on it.” He needed to get to his feet and he attempted to pull up on the rope. It came free in his good hand and offered no help getting him up. Instead, Frederick used the wall to inch himself into a standing position once again. Standing on two good, but tired feet, he pulled the rope downward one arm’s length at a time. After what seemed to be, in his mind, a very long time, the rope abruptly stopped. He was out of energy again though he did manage to stumble his way back to where the stack of books still stood. He nimbly balanced his weight on the books and looked up where the drawn curtain had not drawn at all, nor had it exposed its secret.

His eyes nearly popped out of his head at the sight he beheld. “You have got to be kidding me!”

***

20

"I want each of you to know... Wait, lad...Tofur is it?"

"Yes, sir."

"As you recall, I am not a Talker. Please repeat everything I say so these other creatures will understand what I am about to say."

"Yes, Leiram, I certainly will."

Belle nudged her master's pant leg. "What is he asking you to do?"

"He wants me to repeat to you everything he tells me."

"Oh, that's fine then."

"As I think I said before, I am here to protect this young lad. I am not to be toyed with. I am very capable of doing whatever is necessary to insure his survival, as I trust, each of you are as well. Now, with that being said, we will leave immediately. Staying in one place for too long at a time is never a good idea when you are being hunted."

"Hunted? Who is being hunted?" Jak was twitching a little.

Tofur repeated Jak's question to Leiram, "Who is being hunted, sir?"

Leiram looked directly into Tofur's eyes, "You are, lad. I was assigned to you before you were born. The association which my family has served for generations has you and three others under our perpetual observance. You have never known of us before and I dare say you will very likely forget us once life returns to normal around these parts."

Tofur struggled to repeat everything Leiram said to those gathered about him. He found it confounding to speak of himself in third person.

Leiram continued. "Many call us Protectors, but we are so much more than that." He walked to Porcene's side. "I must find the letter. You need to read it and share its information with your friends, if you please." Leiram opened pockets and bags, slits and slots, flaps and sacks. "I know it is in here, lad."

Tofur raised the whistle to his lips and blew three short bursts. "Can you find it, Leiram?"

"Leiram? Leiram is here? I haven't heard from him in a while. Oh, well, what is it, young man? What am I looking for?"

Tofur never missed a beat and the others could now follow the conversation. "You were looking for a letter addressed to me. It is hidden somewhere in those saddle bags. We desperately need to find it."

"Oh, I know that letter. Don't know why I am carrying it around, but I have it right here." Mariel detached a group of sacks and set it on Porcene's back. The next row of compartments had a row of belts and buckles across its bottom hem. He unbuckled the belts and lifted the contraption's top piece up giving it the appearance of a butterfly's wings. Laying it over Porcene's back as well, he then took a knife from his pocket and slit a few of the stitches holding the bottom piece together. Prying it slightly open, he was able to coax the letter out, little by little, by placing the blade of his knife on the corner of the letter and tilting his hand ever so slightly. After a tedious amount of time and energy was spent, Mariel handed the letter to Tofur. "Is this you?"

The envelope was addressed with a heavy style of handwriting unfamiliar to all of those gathered around.

"I have never seen this type of writing before, Mariel. Do you know who wrote it?"

Mariel shook his head. "No, I do not. It has always been that way."

"Hmmm." Tofur flicked the envelope against the palm of his hand and pondered the moment. "Have any of you seen this type of writing? Can anyone of you read it?" He held the envelope in front of each and every creature in the small group. "Anyone?"

Belle's ears perked up. "Shhh. Everyone quiet. I hear something. It's in the air." She moved her body around so that she was pointing in the direction the sound was coming from. "That way! Whistler, Taytay, check it out."

The Falcons were aloft like they were shot from a bow. It wasn't long before they spied the commotion in the air. They swooped in on their helpless, unbalanced target with Whistler snatching it out of the air in mid-flight. Without uttering a word, they urgently flew back to Belle.

Whistler gently slowed down as he dropped to Jak's back. Flapping his wings softly, he tenderly placed his catch at the base of Jak's mane. Taytay landed at his side.

"He doesn't look good."

Tofur and Mariel rushed to Jak. There was nothing they could do. They looked on helplessly.

"I got too close. They are bad…they have watchers. They know…you are here. You…must stop them…tell Vincen I kept my word. He may not forgive me…but I kept my word." Tine closed his eyes for the last time.

It was difficult for any of the group to outwardly feel sorry for the ill-mannered and condescending Dove. Privately, they each felt a blow to their armor. For the sake of the group, pity was not an option. Belle had just dealt with a larger emotional blow than the death of a near-stranger, so while Tine's passing was not expected, it was promptly dealt with.

"Should I bury him?" Tofur asked.

Belle sighed, "Yes. Do it quickly. We must get out of here and, Tofur, we need Leiram back."

***

Barth stood in the middle of the road, shocked. "Is this bird following us?"

Ligon had no answer. In front of them, a menacing grey bird stood, its smallish, yellow eyes casting a very condescending stare their way. It was a bulky creature, its head nearly as large as its body. Barth took a step toward the bird to scare it off. It did not budge. The bird tilted its head, toying with the pair of leggers. Behind the first bird, two more landed, their coloring similar, their beaks much sharper and pronounced. They continued staring at the surprised two-leggers.

The first bird turned his head in a nearly complete circle to address the others. "Are these the idiots that we are supposed to meet with? Did you kill that wart of a Dove that was trailing them?"

The second bird nodded. "From the messages we have received, yes."

The third bird added, "The Dove will not live long enough to perch."

"Fine, where is the translator?"

The smaller one answered, "In that group behind us. The ignorant Dove was leading us right back to them. We will need a greater number of us to take out his group and take him prisoner."

"Fools! We are it! Go get him!"

"He is not traveling alone, Bulos. He retains a formidable contingent of companions."

"I will have to trust your judgment there. Find a way to separate him from his assembly. These leggers are useless to us if we have no translator. From the looks of them, I'd say they are ill-equipped at best for the rest of the plan. We will rid ourselves of them when we exhaust their information. Both of you, go locate the translator and take out any members of his group you can. Make the others miserable. Scare them. We must have the translator!"

Barth and Ligon watched the three birds with amusement. They heard nothing but screeches and hoots. Two of them flew off, one remained. They were not certain, but it seemed this bird was sizing them up. They were correct.

***

Tofur quickly buried Tine in the soft ground beneath the trees where they slept the night. No fanfare, no kind words, just the actions of a caring young man. As he tamped the moist ground with the sole of his boot, he glanced at his friends. How was this group going to travel with any stealth at all? One of the biggest Horses known to the two-legger's world, a Mule that didn't give away much to the Horse in height, a Rottweiler who nearly weighed as much as he did, a handsome pair of Falcons and a fellow, though eccentric, human who carried multiple personalities beneath his utilitarian clothing. Where would all of this lead? He gave the ground one last firm pat, wiped his hands on the seat of his pants and re-joined the group. The envelope containing the letter was secured inside a buttoned-down pocket inside his jacket. He decided not to get it back out for the time being.

"I guess we need Leiram back, huh?" Tofur stepped to Jak's flank and blew the whistle once.

Mariel was fastening the final buckle back into place when his countenance instantly changed and Leiram took over. "Well, this should about do it. Lad, did you find the letter yet?"

Tofur replied, "Yes, sir, I have it inside my jacket. Do you need it?"

"No, lad. That is your burden to bear, while you are my burden."

"Okay, well just know that I do have it now."

"As you say. Now, I think I would like us to saddle up these fine equine mounts. We won't look as out-of-place riding them as we would walking them everywhere we go. I'll take the Mule, if you will hop up on the Belgian."

"I can do that. Thank-you."

"Oh, can you tell the animals what is going on here? Tell them we are heading after our targets. And, if you will be so kind, warn the Mule that I am quite the equestrian. Don't know what made me say that. Oh well...eh, have the Rottie walk to your left, I'm on the right. If the Falcons can fly a rotating scout...that would be good too."

"Gladly, sir."

Tofur relayed Leiram's plans to the leggers. They had no problem with the immediate plans. Whistler and Taytay decided to fly together instead of rotating the duties. Tofur released them to fly. He and his Falcons were wise enough to know that when separated, their survival chances dwindled.

***

Up ahead, the birds left Bulos to deal with the two-leggers. They were doing as he instructed, coming after the translator. Never before defeated, reckless abandon became their calling. The truth be told, they had never battled with an adversary when they weren't the strongest, meanest and the biggest. For all of their accumulated intelligence, bullying dispositions had taken over. They came in low, expecting to frighten the young two-legger off of his Horse.

Taytay and Whistler both saw the silvery-grey wingers beneath them.

"Those two seem in a hurry." Whistler noticed.

Taytay was looking far ahead. The two low-flying wingers passed below his field of vision, but that is how it was supposed to be. He left it up to Whistler to observe medium and short ranges. "What? Did you see something, Whistler?"

"Yes, I did. Two wingers passed below with a quick wing. Looked a bit like silver Eagles."

"Should we roll back and observe them?"

"Yes. Our group will be coming out of the trees soon. I want to make sure we see trouble before they face it."

The Falcons wheeled around beautifully in tandem, reversing their direction without losing a single beat.

***

Tofur rode atop Porcene as if he owned the world. The packs behind him allowed him to recline as much as he wanted. He was just about ready to unpack one of Mariel's books. He figured he needed to start reading again soon. Leiram and Belle had everything in the immediate vicinity under control.

It came at him from the back. Talons extended, both birds aiming to knock him off the Horse then scatter the remainder of his party. The first winger caught Tofur completely off guard as he leaned onto Porcene's backpacks. The second winger's talons hit Leiram in the back of the neck, inflicting a sizeable gash that began bleeding immediately.

The Falcons could not believe what they were seeing. "Are those wingers attacking Tofur?" Taytay asked.

"And Leiram!" Whistler dove from the sky like a falling boulder. Taytay dove at his side. There was no time for decision making.

Porcene reared on her hind legs as Tofur yelled and clung to strapping. Leiram pulled hard on the reigns, his teeth grinding in pain. Jak jerked to a stop, his head swinging around to steady Leiram should he fall from his back. Belle ran circles around the larger four-leggers with deep, loudly violent barks penetrating the quiet stillness.

"Where are they?" Belle yelled.

Jak answered, "I never saw them!"

Porcene dropped back to the ground, her front legs pounding the earth in anger. "Where are the Falcons?"

The attacking wingers quarter-circled to the east in order to make their next attack out of the sun which would make it difficult for any member of the group to spot them.

Porcene positioned herself facing West, Jak faced East with a wounded rider clutching at his neck while sitting on his back.

Belle barked, "Tofur! Get on the ground under Porcene. Tell Leiram to get under Jak! Now!"

Tofur did as he was told, but not before helping Leiram climb down from Jak's back. He clamped his hand over the bleeding gash in Leiram's neck, stemming the blood flow temporarily. He pushed Leiram under Porcene, covering him like a shield.

Jak never saw them coming. He was too late to protect himself. He lowered his head to keep his eyes sheltered and braced for the impact.

The winger hit the top of his head, ripping a chunk of hair and flesh from his mane. The second winger dug his talons deep into the side of his neck.

Taytay drew a bead on the first winger striking it squarely in the head, his talons crunching trough bone, feathers and tender flesh.

Whistler hit the second winger with the same amount of viciousness. He was able to embed one set of talons in the grey neck feathers and the other set into an extended wing. His momentum never ebbed as he slammed the larger winger into the ground where Belle dispatched it with one vice-like bite from her powerful, square jaw.

Taytay flew his victim high past the tree-tops. He looped over and dove again, racing toward the ground at Belle's feet. He released the winger from his talons and watched it fall limply to the ground.

Belle eyed the winger for movement of any kind. "Tofur, are you alright?"

"Yes, I am, Belle. Leiram is bleeding profusely. If I keep my hand clamped around his neck, I hope to stem his blood loss. Oh Belle, I can't let anything happen to him."

Belle looked around. There was no traffic on the road; still she wanted off of it. "Can he walk, Tofur?"

"Not right now, Belle. We will have to wait here until the bleeding stops."

"Very well then." She saw the Falcons flying wide circles around their position. She knew she would not have to worry about another attack given the mood those two were in right now. "Porcene, stay where you are. Jak, block the other side."

Jak nodded as droplets of blood dripped from his neck to the ground. "Which one of those cowards has a claw full of my mane?"

"I'm not sure. What kind of wingers are these? I've not seen their type." Belle studied their markings. "They look very similar to Eagles."

Jak shook his head. "They are similar, but an Eagle's head is not that big."

Porcene stepped away from Tofur for a moment. She looked down at the winger's carcasses. "Those are some type of Owl, Belle."

"Owls?"

***

Ligon was getting antsy. "Barth, why won't that bird fly off? I'm about ready to make it fly off."

"Don't let me beat you to the punch." Barth jumped at the confident bird as it firmly stood its ground.

Suddenly, the bird opened its wings, which were at least as wide as Barth was tall, and flapped them enough to rise to the two-legger's eye level, hovered momentarily directly in front him, then suddenly lunged at him for good measure. Barth ducked as the bird's sharp claws barely missed his balding scalp.

Bulos flew off to check on his aides. As he left, he shouted, "Idiots!"

To the two men watching the bird fly out of sight, the shout sounded like a screeching hoot.

Barth was shaking down to his cheap boots. Ligon's eyes and neck were twitching.

"Barth, I'm liking this job less and less."

"I agree with you, Ligon. Let's do what we have to do and get back where we belong."

***

"These are Owls, Porcene?"

"Yes, I think so."

"Tofur, we need to get off this road."

"I agree with you. Let's try to get out of here now." Tofur helped Leiram to his feet. "Come on, sir, we need to get out of sight again. Walk with me. I need to keep pressure on your neck. You have a deep cut on your neck."

"I believe you, lad. I feel a bit woozy. You think a tourniquet would work?"

Tofur straightened up a little, "A tourniquet on your neck?" He looked at Belle. "Did you hear what he said?"

Leiram laughed out loud. "It was a joke, laddie. Don't take everything I say so seriously now. Help me away from this infernal clearing."

Tofur let out a deep breath. "Let us do just that."

Belle led them into a free-standing grove of trees. Jak followed with Porcene bringing up the rear. The Falcons were flying mad.

***

Bulos flew steady. He had no reason to fly fast. Time was on his side. Time was on the side of the intelligents. The rabble making up the rest of the world would soon know the new world would have no time for any of them. The new world would be governed by the intelligents and a select group of humans capable of living up the high intellectual standards that would be set. He knew his spot on the roster would be high, but not the highest. That honor was reserved for someone different than him, but he didn't mind. Simply ridding the world of ignorance in command would suit him just fine.

What he saw stopped his heart. Had not been flying low to the ground, as only his arrogance would permit, he would have never seen them. Just ahead, he focused on the grey clumps in the middle of the road. The closer he came, the more his blood simmered. He spread his wings to slow down and landed merely footsteps away from the lifeless carcasses of his next-in-command.

He screamed at them, "How dare you end your lives in this manner?! Here you both lie, taken down by creatures with levels of intelligence woefully short of that required to fill one vein of your tiniest feather. You deserve what you received! It is strangely a pity I know not the whereabouts of these useless creatures that have wasted my time with the taking of your incompetent lives!"

The hits came in rapid succession. The blows to Bulos' ego did not compare with the blows his body absorbed. He tumbled over, his feathers roughed up by the pebbly surface of the road. Before he could regain his balance, he was hit again and again. His sight grew foggy, his mind hazy. Soon he found himself lying on the ground, his yellow eyes desperately trying to focus on two wingers standing over his beaten body. One apparition per wing held him stationery.

"Who are you? He demanded. "Are you responsible for the deaths of my servants? I will have your eyes blinded and your feathers plucked!"

"Whistler, is this who I think it is?"

The Falcons stood over their prey, ready to devour every tasty morsel. Their dark eyes locked in stares of hatred at the downed winger.

"Strix Nebulosa, I believe, Taytay."

"I do think you are correct, cousin." Taytay spat the next words, "Bulos, what evil strategies have you concocted now? Why are you not dead?"

Bulos' head was clearing. The voices he was hearing were becoming familiar. He batted his groggy eyes. "My favorite cast of heroes. You two disgust me!" His eyes closed as if to make the ghosts from his past vanish.

"You shouldn't even consider dying on us, you miserable moron." Whistler knew the fastest way to irritate the Great Grey Owl was to berate his intelligence. "It is hard to believe two Falcons will be your undoing, is it not?"

Bulos' eyes glared at both Falcons. "I am not beaten by any stretch of your puny imaginations! No cast of Gyrfalcons will ever undo me! Cousins! Hah! One of you is a half-breed and the other is a wretched mistake of nature! Please yourselves if you must with bravado over your cowardly attack of a superior creature, it will not help you live any longer once I escape!"

"Whistler, is he talking rudely about me or you?"

"I think he is doling the rudeness around very evenly, Taytay."

"Escape? Bulos, did you say you were going to escape? What a ridiculously stupid thing to say. Whistler, you'd think he was a cave Bat uttering nonsense such as that."

A stern look came over Bulos' face. "Cave Bats are not birds, fool!"

Whistler chuckled, "Look who is the fool now, Bulos."

"Is this the winger that was after my master?" Belle stepped boldly over Bulos. She placed one heavy paw on the humorous bone of the Owl's wing. "Is he making at attempt to escape, Whistler?"

"He certainly has made mention of wanting to, Belle."

"Oh, pity he won't be able to do that. I hope he is not overly distraught when he is prohibited from exacting that plan."

Bulos' eyes burned with abhorrence. "You will let me go, Dog, and it will be soon. You will not hold me against my will. You let your guard down for one instant, I will be gone...spreading the news of me finding you far and wide...alerting each and every army of ours to your exact location."

The Rottweiler feigned a swoon. "Please, you wouldn't do that!" As a half smile tried to surface on Bulos' face, Belle put her full weight on her paw that pinned the Owl's wing bone to the ground.

Snap.

Bulos' cry was muffled as Tofur put a heavy hood over his head. "That was brutal, Belle."

"It was deserved. Bring him back to the trees. We need to silence him after we get as much information from him as we can. If we have to torture him to death, well, I'm not opposed to that." She sauntered back to Jak's side.

Under the hood, for once in his life, Bulos was terrified.

Taytay caught Whistler's eye. "That's a side of her I have never seen."

"I think in light of the past events…losing her pups, this attack… she is not to be messed with by anymore."

The Falcons flew back to regroup with the others.

"Tofur, I want to speak to Mariel. Make it happen." Belle demanded more than asked.

"Which one of the Mariels do you wish to speak with?"

"Get me the doctor first so he can bandage himself, then I want the inventor. I need a cage for our Owl. One from which he can't escape or be heard."

Tofur blew his whistle four times. "Doctor, you need your help. You have a terrible gash on your neck inflicted by an Owl's claw. I have the bleeding under control, but you need to bandage it."

"What are you saying, boy?" Mariel removed his hand from his neck, eyeing the drying blood covering it. Rubbing his fingers together he was relieved to see no dirt forming clots on his skin. "Oh yes, I see the problem now. Tofur, there is a bandage kit in the saddle bags, left flank, third layer. Bring it to me. Will you?"

Tofur stepped over to Porcene. The bandages were easy to find with explicit directions. He took the entire packet to Mariel. "Are these the only bandages you have?"

"No, boy, they are stashed all through those bags. Get me some water. You will need to help me." Mariel fumbled through the bags contents with one hand while he kept the other pressed to the wound. "You say it was an Owl, was it?"

Belle told him the story. "It looks like you are cut badly. Will you be okay?"

Mariel smiled. "Yes, Belle, a little deeper…a little further to the front…it could have ripped my jugular vein. Now, I would not have survived that. I would have bled out before you moved me here. I'm pretty sure that's what they were aiming for. Owls are smart, you know."

"Here is the water." Tofur handed Mariel a damp sack.

"Thank-you, boy. Now, press this moistened bandage over my wound while I fold another fresh one. I'll need to wrap a kerchief around my neck to hold the bandage in place until the blood clots, unless you can stitch it up for me."

"I can do that, sir. It shouldn't be anymore difficult than sewing the Falcons' hoods. I'll give it a try anyway."

"I think it would be best if you did. Let me get what you need out of here."

Mariel handed Tofur a sharp, curved needle and a length of thin, black thread. "If you make Falcon hoods, this will be an easy task for you. You don't mind the sight of a little blood do you?"

"No sir, I don't...as long as it is not mine!"

"Fair enough, boy. I will hold the skin tight for you. Try to get a stitch or two under the top layer of skin if you can. Oh, wait..." Mariel handed a wet rag to Tofur. "Here, you'd better clean it first!"

"Oh, right." Tofur swabbed sweat, dirt and dried blood from his patient's neck. "Doctor, this cut is very deep."

"No need to worry, boy, I'll talk you through it."

Tofur steadied himself while he threaded the needle, "Is this going to hurt you?"

"Oh yes, it certainly will. But it will feel so much better when you are finished."

"I guess it will at that." Tofur placed two fingers over the wound to spread the top layer of skin. "So I just sew this sinewy stuff together first?"

"Yes. What you see are my neck muscles. Use two or three stitches there placed evenly apart, tying small knots. You can dab it with the wet rag to remove the excess blood. When you finish with that, sew the skin together with a row of pretty, tight stitches. I don't want a big ugly scar back there."

"Right." Tofur laughed to himself. "Right you are, sir."

Jak and Porcene watched Tofur closely as did Belle and the Falcons. Bulos was giving them no problem. He had passed out earlier from the pain in his wing.

"He is doing a very good job, isn't he, Porcene?" Jak was proud of the youngster.

"Yes, he is. Maybe he should look at your neck when he is through with Mariel's."

"I don't know. I don't stand a lot of pain. It looks like that hurts."

Mariel grimaced with every stitch. Tofur was performing admirably, but, the fact is, with nothing to dull the senses, the pain was very intense.

"You almost done, boy?"

"Yes sir. I should be closing it up soon."

Mariel looked at Belle and winced. "Wonderful boy you got here, Belle, very mature for his age. Tofur, how old are you?"

"I will be 10 years and 7 this coming fall."

"Well you aren't that young after all. You are almost a grown man."

"Yes sir. That's what they tell me." Tofur inserted the needle for the last time, pulling it through smoothly before tying the thread off close to the skin with a reef knot. "There we are, doctor, all done and the bleeding is controlled. How do you feel?"

Mariel lightly rubbed his hand over the stitching. "Well done. Maybe I should be calling you the doctor, boy."

"I'm just doing my part, sir." Tofur looked around at his friends with his arms raised high in the air, grinning as wide as he possibly could.

Belle admired her master proudly. "Now, Tofur, I need the inventor. Whistle if you will, please."

Tofur was brought back to reality with Belle's no nonsense disposition. "Yes, certainly." He blew three bursts. "Mariel?"

"Yes?" Mariel turned. "What can I do for you, Belle?"

The transformations from personality to personality were becoming seamless. Whether it was the whistle or Tofur's practice that caused it, everyone was adjusting to the two-legger's many different personas.

"I need a cage to store our latest guest in." She motioned to the hooded winger beneath Taytay and Whistler. Each Falcon employed death grips on the Bulos' feet and wings.

"Is our guest injured?"

Belle nodded her head. "Yes, he is. Don't bother with that. We need a cage or crate to secure him. He is evil and plans to escape at his earliest convenience. Of course, he has one broken wing as of right now and if he tries to escape, he will have two. I don't want passer-bys to hear him screeching for help. Can you accommodate my request?"

Mariel studied the situation with one arm across his belly and one hand to his chin. "I think I can do precisely that, ma'am." He attempted to roll a recent stiffness out of his neck only to find himself in severe pain the instant he lowered his head. "Oh good Lord! What have I done to my neck?" He quickly threw his hands to the stitched area. "What is this?"

Tofur stepped to Mariel's side with a tightly folded kerchief in his hands. "Here, sir, you need to wrap this snugly around your neck. You had an accident, but, no need to worry, we buttoned you back up."

Mariel did not know what to think. "I did? You did?"

"Yes. You have a wound in your neck inflicted by instructions from our guest over there. So, the sooner you build a cage to keep the mugger in, the safer we will all be."

Mariel acquiesced, "I suppose so. I will have you something shortly. Will you explain to me what happened?"

"Yes, we certainly will." Tofur shook his head, "We definitely will."

"Thank you." After fitting the green, plaid kerchief around his neck, Mariel wandered off to begin converting several miscellaneous pieces on Porcene's back into a holding cell for Bulos.

"Tofur, as soon as he is finished, we need Leiram back. Okay?" Porcene cut her eyes to Tofur.

"Yes, Porcene, as soon as he is finished."

The hooded winger began to stir.

"Belle, our guest is waking up." Taytay tightened his grip on the Owl's feet.

"Tofur, can you tighten the hood around his neck so he will pass out?" Belle asked.

"I guess I could. Is that the most humane thing we can do right now?"

"I'm not worried about being humane at the moment. Would you rather I kill him?"

Tofur shrugged. "Won't we need to question him at some point?"

"Yes, of course we do. I'm not actually going to kill him…yet."

"I'll see what I can do then." Tofur reached into his jacket pocket and pulled out a bag. He emptied the contents into his pocket before placing it over the original hood. "The second bag will reduce the amount of air he is breathing, which should keep him out until we want to wake him."

Belle inspected his work. "That will be fine." She raised her large, brown eyes to her young master. "I hate to subject you to this kind of barbarianism. Please understand it is not our normal nature. We are being forced into this."

The entire group, except Mariel, who was busy fitting parts together, solemnly listened to Belle's explanation. The polite, fun-loving proclivity shared among the group was being violated by necessity. The extremes to which they would eventually be forced to go were not pondered or discussed. As the needs arose, the actions to offset would be equally or excessively proportionate. Survival mode is an untamed beast, as they were all beginning to understand.

***

21

Jahnise pulled his knife from the end of his staff, placing it back in the belt around his waist. "I was expecting much more than that, friend. It was a much grander scene in my head."

Bongi continued to quell the trembling shakes from his body. They were working their way up his neck. He hoped they would shake themselves out soon. "King, where are Ian and Colleen?" The Okapi no longer felt the burden of their weight.

"I do not know, friend. They may have been taken by that tiny spark. It is not for us to be concerned. Maybe they have moved on as we should. Shall we follow this path to the Keeper's dwelling?"

"Yes, King, this is the only path that will take us there. Shall I lead the way?"

"Please, after you." Jahnise bowed his head and waved his hand in a low gracious sweeping motion. After a few minutes, Jahnise posed a question. "Mister Bongi, how did you arrive here?"

"That, King, is a very long story."

"Ah, so it is. Bongi, should we have even the shortest of time left, I still am very interested in your story. Where shall you begin?"

Bongi kicked at the ground, "I suppose there is no better spot to begin than the beginning, but since we have no time for that, I will start by saying that I was lured here. At least, I was lured to the window and then I was sucked inside it. I was carried here through some kind of tube, filled with very colorful water. I have since found out most of the newer Nuorgians have arrived in the same way."

"That sounds very familiar, Bongi. I too was brought here by that colorful water you speak of. What is that? I breathed it into my lungs as I do air. I haven't even spoken of it since I have been here. Wasn't everyone brought here the same way?"

"Not at all, King. There are native Nuorgians, creatures who have known no other home. Colleen Mecanelly, for instance, and her son Patrick."

"So the girls and Ian were born above?"

"Yes, they were. Ian was from what he called a big island. He was summoned here long before me. Once he met Colleen, Hugoth sent them back up to collect information for us. They were married up there and Livvy and Mili were born during their time of discoveries. They arrived back here, and shortly thereafter, Patrick was born. They have lived here since that time. Their travels back up were often, though not as prolonged."

"Did Mister Ian learn of the cracks in Nuorg or in the lands above?"

"I'm sorry. I am in the dark about that. Most of us are. Hugoth was rightfully troubled about too many knowing the cracks existed. He assigned Ian and his family to the tasks of observing, mapping and sealing them. Lately, they have been opening everywhere. Ian and Colleen were very concerned about the fracturing. They were on their way to discuss their findings with Hugoth in Burg One when the Wolf and his companions arrived for the first time. Mystic's arrival threw Hugoth in a tizzy. The Staff had to be dealt with in order to stabilize the age-old theories."

Jahnise walked stride-for-stride with the long-legged Okapi. Occasionally, he would pause, wrap both hands around his walking stick and reflect on what had happened in light of what Bongi was telling him. "So the Staff's timing trumped the plans made over the years by others like Hugoth?"

"Yes."

"That intrigues me, Bongi."

"Why is that?

"Isn't it obvious? The Staff knows a lot more than we do about everything."

"I have a problem believing that, King."

"It's not so difficult to believe, Bongi. There is something working through the Staff, almost demanding obedience from all of us. My staff falls somewhere in the lesser workings of the Wolf's Staff. I have to think there is one greater reason for all of the Nuorg activity."

"I am growing more confused by the day, sir." Bongi caught a glimpse of a growing crowd of creatures ahead of them. "King, we have a welcoming party."

Jahnise studied the crowd. "Was your Burg so crowded when we left, Bongi?"

"No, I don't believe so. Where did all of those new creatures come from?"

Jahnise shrugged his shoulder. "You don't know?"

"No, I do not."

Stewig stood crossways on the path, partially blocking the throng from Jahnise and Bongi as they neared the Keeper's dwelling. Oliviia sat on his back. She motioned to them with both hands outstretched. "Sir, did you have something to do with this?" She waved her hands over the assembled crowd.

Jahnise stepped to her side, "Oliviia, are these not regular dwellers of this Burg?"

Bongi licked his lips. "I will answer for her, King. They certainly are not!" He reared up, putting his front hooves just behind Oliviia on Stewig's back. Scanning the crowd, he addressed the newcomers. "From where have you all come? Are the gates not closed and the bridges drawn under Hugoth's order?"

Oliviia pivoted around to face the crowd behind her. Her eyes fell immediately to new face. "Sir, what shall we call you?"

"Miss, I am Kirch Meadeau. I am one of the few Talkers from Burg One."

Oliviia eyed him sternly. "Please, Kirch, explain to us who you are and why you think you are here." She was being as polite as she could muster under the circumstances.

"Thank you, miss." He stepped around Stewig's broad flank. "Keeper, King...we are all inhabitants from Burg One. We were following Hugoth's instructions which we received from a winger. Suddenly, we were plunged into darkness..."

Jahnise nodded, "I am aware of that, go on."

"When the light from the yellow ball returned, well...we were here, all of us! Every dweller over there was transported over here. Our question is simply... why?" It was then he noticed Jahnise's wrap. "Is that a Cat on your shoulders?"

Jahnise contemplated the questions. He perused the faces staring anxiously at him. "What was happening in your Burg when the darkness fell?"

"Like I said before, King, we were following Hugoth's plan for defending our Burg."

"I understand." Jahnise began walking through the crowd, tapping his stick on the ground, studying each and every face attentively. He made his way to the middle of the crowd. He gently persuaded the gathering to ease back enough to give him room, some breathing space. "Now, I must ask each of you a question. Can you pass the test?"

Jahnise raised his stick and slammed it to the ground as he had done for the last gathering. He surprised no one. The light puddled near the stick's bottom, appeared a little interested, then, taking no further actions, returned silently to its resting place. Jahnise smiled a wide, toothy smile. His eyes lit up. "Very well then, we are all on the same side! That pleases me!"

Kirch looked around the group. "Did you not trust us?"

Jahnise looked down at the man who stood more than a head shorter than himself. "Honestly, I did not. I'm afraid my discerning abilities have decreased many times over here in Nuorg. There is a greater power watching over all of us now. I have faith that power will bring us triumphantly through our coming dilemmas."

Oliviia stood up on Stewig's back and looked down on the crowd. "Jahnise, please, let's make our plans. We will reconvene in the Keeper's meeting room immediately." She looked directly at Kirch. "Who will Burg One send as a representative?"

Kirch closed his eyes to think. "In Hugoth's absence, it must be the ancient Eagle, Mystic." He opened his eyes. "Have you seen him?"

***

After the attack, Vincen and Rakki took wing to Burg Seven. Rakki followed the Eagle with no word spoken between the two. The scene they had just witnessed was too dire for inane conversation. Rakki followed the old winger closely, flying in the wake of the Eagle's larger wings. Vincen did not head directly for the Burg. He led Rakki on a significant detour which put them over the pre-set rendezvous point where all survivors of any incomprehensible incidents in Nuorg would reunite. From far below, both the Cats and the two-leggers felt hopeful as the wingers acknowledged their progress with tilted wings before setting their sights on Burg Seven.

***

22

Evaliene peered directly ahead, watching as the cleverly marked trail emerged before their party. The going was treacherous. Loose boulders and slippery rocks littered the pathway as the climb became ever steeper. The air was thinning.

Sean remained silent. He was along for the ride now. There was nothing he could add or take away from their current situation. He was close at Evaliene's side and that was all he could honestly convince himself of. The Horses knew much more than he did. He was not sure if he had already failed at his mission or had never really known its extent. His eyes were alert, smoothly focusing on every detail. Every miniscule change in scenery was vividly stored away in case an escape was ever required. Alternate routes to and away from their final destination were categorized then committed to memory.

"Rhiannon, I feel we are nearing the entrance." Broanick spoke lightly and breathed hard. They were traveling too high on the mountain and breathing air much too thin to waste talking loudly. "Do you have your clues?"

"I feel it too, Broanick. Yes, when the time is right, I will do what is needed. Did you arrange for Corvus or Pandion to find us?"

"Yes, my dear, the wingers know as much as we do. They will not fail her."

Evaliene bent down to hear the conversation. "I'm sorry, who will not fail who?"

"The wingers will not fail her, Princess." Broanick did not waver.

"Her? I thought I was her?" Evaliene laid her hand on her chest. "Am I not her, Broanick?"

"Princess, you are her sister. Madaliene is who we all are protecting. In order to protect her, we must also protect you and your heirloom." Broanick's large, dark eyes took on a hardened glare.

Evaliene gulped. Her temper simmered. "You mean my little sister plays a bigger role in my own destiny than I do? Why...how is that?"

Broanick continued with a stern voice. "Princess, you are the bearer of the staff, but she is the wielder. Her role is much more dangerous that you can imagine. Had the staff not been separated from her, as were you, you would have very likely both been dead long before now." He let his words soak in. "Any more questions will be answered when we are safely hidden away. We are being followed."

Evaliene's temper quickly died away. She heaved under the stress of the moment. "Rhi, what is he saying? We are being followed? How does he know?"

Rhiannon spoke softly. "Princess, they were waiting for us as we neared the tree line. There was no way we were going to cower and retreat. Please tell Sean to be prepared for anything."

Evaliene turned nervously to her Protector. "Sir, I need to inform you that we are..."

"Being trailed. I know, Princess. I was waiting for the Horses to sense it, but it seems they already have. They are an amazing pair of animals. What are we to do?" Sean's hands rested at his hips. Broanick's reins dangled around the saddle horn. There was no reason to guide an animal that knew more than the rider.

Evaliene seethed under her outward calm. She asked through clenched teeth. "Why are you not a Talker? You need to be conversing directly with them, not through me!" She smiled, awaiting his answer that never came.

The Horses drew tighter together, breathing in sync with each other, every step practically choreographed. Ahead, the trail turned sharply to the left and ended with a vertical drop equal to the height of hundreds of trees stacked vertically, root to top branch. An eerie quiet enveloped the meandering silence about them.

Broanick and Rhiannon both took the left turn before pulling to a dead stop, overlooking the deadly drop-off. They moved together as tightly as their physical stature allowed. Very carefully, they performed a beautifully executed pirouette, bringing them face-to-face with their unseen pursuers.

From behind perfectly concealed cover, several two-leggers emerged with small Owls perched on their dusty shoulders. The sun was racing for cover behind the western ridge of mountains, leaving the Horses and riders silhouetted against the orange and pink-tinted sunset. The pursuers gained in numbers, standing patiently as they awaited the next move. An average sized two-legger stepped in front of his cohorts, eying the Horses and riders with a combination of admiration and disdain.

Evaliene could not help but notice the man. She confronted him. "What do you plan to do now? One more step toward us and over the edge we go. Is that what you want?"

"Lady, we want what you are carrying. We want the staff. We know you have it. We have waited for it for several lifetimes. Had we known of its whereabouts sooner, you would have never needed to make this arduous trip. You don't deserve to bear its burden."

Sean sat completely still. He said nothing, his eyes searching for any way out of this predicament.

"Sir, you know I will never relinquish anything to you. I would rein my Horse over this cliff and die with her before I turn anything over to you. Whether or not my servant goes with me is up to him." She nodded to Sean. "But for me? You will never take possession of that which I have been birthed to protect."

"That seems to be a dire tune, lady. Would you rather your steeds die first? With a wave of my hand, they will be dropped beneath you."

"You move any part of your body again and over we go. It's really up to you, I guess."

"You do not look the type to sacrifice yourself for a cause such as this. Would you rather not give up the staff and live with us and the riches it will bring? You are still young. You will make quite the stunning bride for any number of future leaders. Why throw away such a beautiful package as yourself? Seems like a waste."

"Your words are to woo me, stranger? Is that all you have?" Evaliene's knees applied pressure to Rhiannon's strong sides. She remained strong, her hands searching for the heirloom. She whispered to Sean. "Be prepared for anything. Follow the Horses' lead." More theatrics on her part produced what the pursuers were after. She held it loosely at her side. Again, she addressed the conniving two-legger. "You know...I am thinking...this ugly thing may not be worth the trouble for either of us." She began to toss it, very adeptly, back and forth from one hand to the other. It really wasn't much to look at after all.

Broanick and Rhiannon began to think that maybe Evaliene knew more than she let on about the staff. Each of them felt for the edge of the cliff behind them, being very careful not to give their intentions away. Eye contact between them was crucial right now.

Broanick neighed quietly to his beautiful mate. "Is she about to do what I think she is about to do?"

Rhiannon pulled on her reins, her head nodding up and down in graceful arcs. She nervously patted her hooves against the hard packed ground beneath them.

Sean felt the movement of the mount beneath him. He stayed outwardly calm while his heart beat thunderously loud beneath several layers of clothing.

Evaliene threw the staff higher with each hand. She would catch it and make large, pendulum type swings with it gripped in her hands. "Or, I could just toss it over this cliff and charge my steed through your group as you rushed to save it from disaster, mauling as many of you as I could by doing so." She spoke to Sean. "How many of these men can we trample into jelly if we make a break for it?"

Cleary getting nervous, the thief in charge spoke again, not sure he read the lady correctly on first glance. "You may take some of us with you, but you would not get far. As for the staff? It is indestructible. Nothing you can do to it will harm it in any way. We will find it at the bottom of this mountain. You can die knowing we will. That would be nothing more than a bump on our quest."

Evaliene caught the staff one last time. "As you wish!" She slung it high over her head, out into the thin air filling the empty space behind her, between the valley floor far below and the sky above.

Both Horses exploded backwards off the cliff, taking both riders with them. Instantly, a bright light burst around all of them. A warm cocoon of serenity cushioned them from their world. The fall was painless.

The pursuers rushed to the cliff's edge, watching in horror as each one of them, in whole or in part, vaporized as they came in contact with the blinding light. Many recoiled in agony, throwing themselves on the ground, tortured by unbridled pain. Those unfortunate enough to lag behind stood mesmerized by the tormented screams coming from deformed bodies that were once fellow robbers and pillagers. Many clumsily staggered around in shock, eventually finding themselves falling off of the mountain. Those wise enough to hold their ground watched as many of the surviving Owls raced off into the sky, heading back to where they came from. This was not planned. The survivors never fought again. Questions pelted their minds. What was this cause anyway? Why were they a part of it? Why was it their fight? For the few that survived...the answers were forever burned into their reasoning.

Rhiannon, Evaliene, Broanick and Sean held tightly to the hope that they had done the right thing.

***

Pewny scampered through front yards, under bushes and fences, over cobblestone walkways as she led the Crows to Paddy's dwelling. They managed to follow her around every turn and obstacle. It was not long before they saw her stop at the back stoop of a nicely built cottage with a well-tended garden in full bloom. A dim light oozed through a slit between the closed, wooden shutters and the stone window sill.

Corvus lit at Pewny's side. "Is the princess' messenger beyond those shutters?"

The spry Numbat answered. "Indeed she is. What I hear is that she was in very bad shape. I have not heard any update on her condition. I have had quite a lot of happenings to record."

"Is the healer a Talker?" Corvus asked as he searched for a higher perch.

"No, I am afraid not. You're about as lucky as the messenger is healthy. If she can talk, then you will get answers, if not, then...I'm afraid we will know nothing more."

Corvus continued searching for a better vantage point. "Can you find your way in there to check on her or should I wait for the shutters to open?"

"I tell you what; the night is still young, let us listen to what the two-leggers are saying about her. There is much to learn by simply listening. Do you have the time?"

"Yes, we do." Corvus then told the second Crow to go get Pandion. "I will wait here with you, Pewny."

"Certainly."

Inside the dwelling, two voices were clearly heard, though a problem remained. Neither two-legger was a Talker. Gibberish and more gibberish were the only discernable noises.

Pewny rolled her eyes. "I have to get up there. I'll find out what is going on in there."

With no further chatting, she nimbly raced up the rough, stone wall of the house, pausing just long enough to leap onto the window sill.

She glanced back at Corvus and winked an eye. Carefully, she pulled on the closest shutter and, as her luck would have it, it opened silently. The room was now quiet.

From her vantage point, she could see the entire layout of the room. Directly opposite the window, a pair of two-leggers sat in matching rocking chairs, between them stood a small table with a dimming candle burning down its wick. Pewny's beady eyes noticed serene looks on both leggers' faces. As one sat puffing on a pipe, small clouds of sweet-smelling smoke floated over his head while he skillfully carved a pointed stick with a small knife. Pewny assumed, incorrectly, that this legger was Kelly. The other legger was fully engaged with a set of long slender sticks, tapping them together as they transformed a ball of yarn into a garment of some kind, she was also taking light puffs on a pipe of her own. The two made a handsome couple.

Pewny scanned the room, finding everything organized and tidy. A cloth covered a substantial portion of a squarish table of some kind in the far corner of the room. From what she could tell, something was hidden beneath it.

"Excuse me. Excuse me," she whispered softly. "Is there a Talker among you?"

The lady never missed a beat as her fingers continued clacking her sticks and yarn together. "Paddy, dear, I believe we have a visitor."

The solidly-built man raised his eyes to the window. "Yes, Jeenay, I believe we do. Do you suppose it is here to check on our patient?

"That would be a good reason for it to be snooping up there, would it not?"

"Invite the little creature in."

"And how do you suppose I do that?"

Jeenay laughed, "Offer a bit of food. That usually gets their attention."

Paddy set his bit of whittling on the table, swapping it for a half-eaten slice of breadfruit. He gently rose from his chair so as not to startle their pointy-nose guest. Offering the tempting morsel with one hand, he swept the room with the other in a universally accepted wave of welcome.

Pewny turned back to Corvus and gave him a quick nod before hopping into the room. She sat on a high wooden chest, scanning the room once again. Her intuition kept taking her attention to the cloth and what may or not be under it. She nibbled the breadfruit graciously and curtsied to Paddy. He smiled.

Corvus wanted to see for himself what was going on, so he flew to the window sill, landing softly beside the open shutter. Jeenay noticed him too. "Paddy, we have another guest."

"Aha, so we do." He gave Corvus the welcome sign. "Please, come in, Crow."

Corvus jumped to the wooden chest. "What do you think, Pewny? Is the messenger in here?"

She motioned to the cloth, "I think there is something breathing under that. Can you hear it?"

Corvus tuned his ears. "Yes, I hear it. It sounds like a rather normal breath, does it not? Would a sickly messenger sound worse to you?"

'"I agree, whatever is under that cloth is on the mend."

Corvus took the liberty of giving himself permission to inspect whatever was under the cloth covering. He flapped his wings once, just enough to travel the distance needed to land near where the cover stopped. He delicately pulled the cloth back with his beak. What he discovered both elated and sickened him.

Pewny climbed to his side. "Is that the princess' messenger, Crow?"

He studied the breathing creature below him. "I am not certain. I have no idea what kind of creature the messenger is. I was never told. I was only directed to find a messenger. I suppose this could be it." He shook his head nervously. "I don't understand this, Pewny. Why is this creature in such bad shape? It looks morbid, yet it breathes peacefully with no sign of struggle."

Pewny studied the creature with growing interest. "I believe this winger has been plucked, Corvus. Look at the scars all over her. There must have been no way to assess the damage to her body beneath a full plumage. It looks like this healer has done a magnificent job putting her back together."

"I can only guess to understand what you are saying. I am excited to see her, if she is the messenger I seek. If not, I need to get back to looking again."

"Shhh, she is stirring. Let's see if she wakes."

Both the Crow and the Numbat watched in silence over the next few moments. Several times they would look up to see the two-leggers eyeing their every move.

"Jeenay, I wonder if they know the Eagle?"

"I'm sure they do, Paddy. At least they know of her. I have seen the little Numbat many times since we arrived. I think she is in the know around here. I am pretty sure she knows who she is looking at."

"When that bird awakes, I hope she understands why her feathers are missing. She looks as if she could be very menacing."

"Especially towards people, Paddy. The Rider must have nearly killed her on several occasions. There is no way of telling what she has been through. If only we were Talkers."

"Dear, I think the times are drifting away from all of the Talkers. We may see a time soon when there are no more of them. I don't look forward to that time. These creatures have so much courage, so much resilience. I'm not sure we will ever have as much."

"I know, Paddy. Has there been any word from Sean lately?"

"No, no one has heard a thing from him. I have prayed my brother well on many occasions over the past several days. His only task is to protect the princess. Beyond that, I can't worry for him. He will do what he needs to do."

"My, you sound so distant, so…uncaring."

"It's the way we were raised, dear. Had it been he born first, he would be wherever I am now. Don't get me wrong, I love my brother, but he has a job to do. If he needs my help or any other Protector's help, all he needs to do is let us know."

"I understand. These days are surely changing and not for the better."

Paddy turned to the crib that held the Eagle. He walked cautiously over to stand beside it, being careful not to startle their guests. "Jeenay, maybe one day this crib will hold our sleeping baby." He grinned.

"I wish for that day, dear. Maybe one day it shall."

Paddy offered his hand to the Crow. "How about you Crow? What have you got to say for yourself?"

Corvus used his beak to tap on the well-muscled forearm of the kind two-legger. "Pewny, is there not a single Talker in this village?"

The Numbat shook her head.

The three continued to watch as the messenger began to stir.

"Jeenay, I think you need to see this. I think she is waking up. She will probably be hungry and very sore."

Jeenay was at her husband's side instantly. She held a basket of cut fruits in one hand and a bowl of strong-smelling Echinacea tea in the other.

"You are really going to make her drink that stuff? It was hard enough forcing it down her throat!"

"Just stand there and watch me." She nudged him to the side. She had work to do.

Corvus and Pewny both reeled when the tea's strong odor hit their nostrils. "I have never been so unfortunate to smell a concoction like that before."

Pewny nearly fell into the crib with the patient before catching her balance. "That is certainly a foul-smelling brew there." Her eyes watered as she tried to shake the aroma from her nose. "I'm afraid it's of no use. I might as well get used to it."

Corvus stayed focused on the messenger.

Paddy gently wrapped the cloth around the Eagle to settle her if she woke with a start, making sure to avoid her sharp, powerful beak. Jeenay waved the tea in front of the Eagle's face.

"There now, girl, come back around. You have some visitors. Hold her firm, Paddy."

The Eagle's head began to teeter. Her eyes fought to pry themselves open. She began to flex her talons, but without enough strength to completely close them. When she willed her eyes fully open, she caught Corvus staring at her. Her head rolled sloppily a few more times, her eyes opening and closing with greater consistency. Then, suddenly, she spoke directly to the Crow.

"Who are you, Crow? Where am I? I feel a blink away from dead." The Eagle spoke with a sluggish clarity that did little to hide a high intelligence. "Is she, I mean the lady, a healer?"

Corvus immediately noticed great pride in her voice. "You are in a village, but I am a visitor and do not know where we are. You are on the mend. You must have taken quite a beating. Yes, the lady is a healer, but she is not a Talker. We have been communicating with sign language, if you can call it that. From what I've gathered, they are good-hearted two-leggers."

The messenger closed her eyes. "That is a wonderful thing to hear. What do they call you, Crow?"

"I am Corvus. My little friend here is Pewny. We were sent here to find you by Princess Evaliene. She left rather hastily and neither her

Protector nor their Horses had the time to retrieve you. They are dreadfully sorry for that mistake."

"That is quite alright. I forgive them for that. There is so much to do, Corvus."

Jeenay and Paddy marveled as they observed the birds conversing with each other. They said nothing. Jeenay tended to her healing and Paddy held the Eagle snugly in the soft wrap.

"Corvus, why am I wrapped in this piece of cloth?" The messenger had not seen her condition.

The Crow was not one to obscure the facts as they were presented him. "You are wrapped up to keep you warm...I assume. If I can read the obvious, the damage you suffered to a massive amount your body left only one option for the healer. She had to remove most of your feathers to facilitate sewing you up."

The Eagle did not flinch. "I understand the need for that. Fortunately, our feathers do grow back."

"Yes they do, but, until then...you will be grounded."

"Yes, obviously. I feel remarkably well, given the circumstances. I have been confined to that horrible bag for too long. If I may, what has become of the Rider who imprisoned me?"

"From what Pewny here has to say, he is not doing very well. She can take it from here."

"Good to finally meet you, ma'am. I know almost everything that goes on in this village. The village know-it-all, I do not think of myself in that way. I prefer to call myself the re-distributor of village information. I am extremely trustworthy as well."

"Glad to finally meet you too, Pewny. I have heard of you...well, not directly, but I have picked up on many conversations here and there."

"My pleasure. By what name shall we call you? I'd rather not keep saying messenger. Quite impersonal, if I may say so."

"Yes, I agree with you. My given name is Mustanghia." She noticed a droop in Pewny's pert face. "Very well, it is difficult to say...Tanghi will work splendidly."

"Thank you, ma'am. Tanghi, it is. The Rider, I hear, is in a secret location constructed by the Evaliene's protectors. He was nearly dead the last I heard and no one was too eager about him being anything better. Our host's brother is in charge of him. He is not a kind man when it comes to that human."

"As much as I want him to suffer, Pewny, I think he should be kept alive, if possible. He may know something that we do not. Is there some guarantee that he will never escape until we have extracted everything he knows from his infinitesimally narrow mind? Mind you, that may not take that long."

Pewny smiled. Tanghi showed no signs of her past struggles and, as she slowly adapted to her weakened condition, her mind and sense of humor became enthusiastically apparent.

"I will leave right now and find out what I can. Corvus will be a much better guardian for you right now." With that said, Pewny jumped back up to the window sill, climbed down the outside wall of the house and scampered off.

Corvus chuckled as the Numbat scurried out of sight. "Quite a character, that one. Tanghi, there is someone else with me you need to meet. May I go fetch him?"

She looked at him, her eyes beginning to regain their sparkle. "Absolutely. I'm going nowhere."

Corvus excused himself, bowing to his hosts, and went for Pandion.

Jeenay stood close by with the cooling bowl of tea. Paddy laid Tanghi back in the crib. The tea was offered to Tanghi and she sipped freely of it. There was never any sign of apprehension seen from the Eagle. She was happy to be alive and she knew it was because of these two-leggers. She would do nothing but appreciate everything they did for her.

It was not too long before Corvus lit again on the window sill. At his side, Pandion landed softly with a look of concern etched across his feathered face.

Corvus hopped to the crib. "Tanghi, I wish to introduce you to another friend who has come seeking to aide the good side. This Osprey is called Pandion."

Pandion took a spot on the side of the crib. He bowed. "I am pleased to meet you, Mustanghia. I have heard about your accomplishments for years. It is without a doubt an honor. I wish our introduction could have come at a better time, but we all know that such a wish would be unproductive."

Paddy and Jeenay returned to their rocking chairs, giving the birds some room. Jeenay watched Tanghi closely for any sign of distress; if necessary, she would cut the visit short. Paddy was a highly-trained

Protector who never quit watching anything having to do with Evaliene. And this meeting still qualified very much as pertaining to that particular princess.

Mustanghia continued to rest, snuggly wrapped in her cloth cocoon. "Pandion, the pleasure is mutual. How did your sons fare in their task? The last I heard, they were gaining on a victory for us all."

Pandion's aura darkened slightly as he answered the question. "Indeed, they were gaining ground there at the end..."

Mustanghia interrupted. "At the end? At what end? There is no end yet."

Pandion shook his head. "There was an end for them, Mustanghia. They gave all they had, but in their end, it wasn't meant to be. I am proud of my sons. They made the ultimate sacrifice for our cause." His head dropped a little more.

"You can't mean this, Pandion!"

"I am afraid I do. All five of them were killed in the last days of their flights. Killed by Owls or the evil men, I can only assume. To make matters worse, my two daughters also suffered the same fate. All of my offspring are no more. That, in a large part, is why I am here. After what happened to their mother, what did I have left? I did take it upon myself to capture Pariah. I wanted to kill her so badly, but I could not bring myself to do it. I had her in my grasp, clutching her so tightly in my talons I could feel her wicked heart's every beat. At the last instant I took no blood. I held her long enough to cage her. Then, I reluctantly turned her over to the association. There is much to learn from her. Now all we have to do is persuade her to talk."

Mustanghia recoiled slightly as Pandion spoke. "I am so sorry for your losses, Pandion. These times will be hard on us all. I doubt many will escape with no losses. But still, all of them? I am so sorry...Pariah, where did you find her? How did you take her? Were you accompanied?"

"Mustanghia, losing my family in the way I did was unforgiveable, but their mother warned me of this end before she was taken from me." The Osprey turned to the wall. Once he regained composure, he continued. "Yes, I went after Pariah myself. There was to be no stopping me. That Owl had to pay dearly for my losses. I was not going to risk any lives but my own. I tracked her for nearly a full year. I did away with her minions as I trailed her. I was a desperate creature, giving in to no danger or toil to reach my goal. I killed a good many creatures and I am not proud of it, but I got her. I finally got her. I admit I may have discovered much more had I not been so impetuous upon putting my talons around her throat. I should have trailed her to the top. Looking back on my reasoning, I feel I was justified in what I did. I would have never escaped with my life or hers had I not found her when I did. At least she won't plot anymore evil deeds." His eyes turned hard.

Corvus had no idea exactly who the characters Pandion was speaking of actually were. All he could fathom was a new and greater admiration for this Osprey warrior. He perched in silence.

"How long will it take for my feathers to return? Would either of you know? It is certain I can do no flying for a while. I hope these two-leggers will keep me fit here and not mind us using their dwelling as a gathering room of sorts." She couldn't see either host from her positioning, but if she had and if they could have understood her, she would have been assured that they were planning on such a future for her.

Corvus racked his brain. He hadn't ever thought of this before. Typically, if he lost a feather, he had no recollection of it. Tanghi's circumstance was different; she had lost hundreds at the same time. "I would say it will be winter before you are able to fly again."

Pandion agreed. "Unless you possess some miraculous healing agent in your body, I'd have to agree. You are sure to be here for a very long time."

"Thank you both for your candor. As much as I would love to disagree with both of you, I can only assume you are correct." She sighed. "I need my rest, fellows. Please keep me updated with the news as you hear it. Might you both be on your way back to my Evaliene? She needs you now. I will do nicely here, although it may be a bit too hum-drum for me. If you see Pewny on your way out, tell her to come see me when she has any news of the Rider."

Corvus nodded while Pandion said their goodbye. "Mustanghia, we will leave you now and keep you updated as you ask. I look forward to the day we can fly together once again."

Both birds turned to their hosts and bowed deeply and graciously. Their bid for respect was returned with polite and sincere nods from Jeenay and Paddy. They were soon to the window ledge and off in search of Pewny. Finding her as they surveyed the quaint village, they spoke briefly with her on their way out. She had yet to make it to the

Rider's prison, but she had nearly filled her small brain with random bits of gossip and fact.

"I'm sorry, Pewny, we haven't time for that right now. We must be off to the princess. Pass all of your information through the Eagle. She will instruct you further."

Pewny admired the Crow and the Osprey as they flew out of sight. She quickly returned to her business.

23

Madaleine was disgusted with the recent series of events. The whys, hows, whens and so forth were sizzling onions in a hot, black skillet. Her mind raced like a strong gale blowing through a tight, twisty canyon. "Where do we go from here, Mystic?"

He heeled to her side. "We have a good walk from here. These are our stomping grounds, but our Great Forest is a very big place."

"Okay, when will we get there and how fast can we go? If we encounter anymore obstacles like that blasted thicket back there, I will not be happy. And if I'm not happy, no one is going to be happy!"

Mystic laughed, "Well said, Princess, however... forgive my laughing, it's just your choice of words... well, it seems like I have heard it before...many times."

"Really?" Madaliene trudged onward. "So what?"

"I'm sorry, Madaliene, I can see now your sense of humor is long gone. I can understand it too, but why now?"

Madaliene took a deep breath, exhaling slowly. "I'm sorry, Mystic. It's really the culmination of things to blame. I never grieved before. My first chance to do so found me too young to know what it was and this time, with the loss of my fake grandparents seeming to overshadow the loss of my real grandparents and my recent participation in killing several fellow humans... You know, I really should not be sorry...I am only 16 years old, for goodness sake! I can get mad if I want to!"

Vincen flew to her shoulder. "We understand your losses, Madaliene, we really do. We are all victims of similar losses. Granted, ours did not happen as recently as yours, but still, we can help you through this time if you will allow us."

Madaliene never broke stride. In fact, she was speeding up. She was nearly at a trot now. "Forgive me, sir. We haven't the time for me to take you up on your offer. At some point in the future, I will lean on your experience. Now, we are going to lean on my lack of it!" She began to run. "How much farther must we go?"

The small army of creatures followed closely to the energetic teenager. Her pace settled down somewhat, allowing those behind her to keep her well within sight.

Vincen flew ahead just in case anything was out of the ordinary closer to the dwellings. He called for Arlis and together they scouted the immediate vicinity around the Great Forest's central hub. All inhabitants were on alert, some making their way to where the battle, to their knowledge, was still going on. With great relief, each of them sauntered back to their dwelling to wait the next batch of instructions.

As Mystic's group turned the last corner, a welcoming party lined the path on both sides. Nothing was said, but it was easy to tell they were overjoyed to have their leader back. The length of his absence was irrelevant. As far as they were concerned, Mystic was back and that was worth celebrating. As the smaller four-leggers brought up the rear behind Gulli, everyone joined in the parade to Mystic's dwelling.

"So, Mystic, it seems you have quite a following around these parts." Madaliene was forgetting her surly mood for the moment.

"Of course I do! I'm the prince around here! Are you jealous, Princess?"

"No, not in the least. I'm thrilled that someone else has the world on their shoulders right now. Mine needed a rest."

Bubba added, "I do enjoy being back, but it feels as though there is only a small comfort in being home. Are we letting down the others depending on us if we enjoy it?"

"I'm saying yes." Madaliene's thoughts drifted back and forth frequently. It was difficult for her to enjoy anything right now. Hopefully, in the near future, she could enjoy her life once again with no regrets. "I need to see Sig. He always knew what to say to me when I needed to hear just the right thing." She paused, considering her words. "I'm sorry, that sounds so redundant."

"Now don't take it too hard, Princess. We are doing our best. Can anyone ask anything more of us?" Gulli was new to this group, but felt very comfortable in their midst.

Ahead, Mystic's dwelling loomed over their path. For as long as most creatures could remember, nothing was ever said about its size or significance, since no inhabitant really cared, except for Hazzel. She thought it in desperate need of upkeep. That is, no creature did until Madaliene got a good look at it.

She stopped dead in her tracks, her eyes staring up at the tall spires, the ornate cupolas, the two massive round towers topped with exquisite corbels which beckoned even larger round turrets atop them, merlons attaching each to the other before stretching backward along the side walls.

"Mystic, this is not a simple dwelling! This...this...this is a small castle! The only things I see missing are the moat and the drawbridge. Who built this? And why?" Madaliene began to walk the perimeter of the dwelling in staggering awe.

Bubba shrugged his shoulders for Mystic's benefit. "Who really ever thought about it? Did you?"

Mystic did not have much to say. "Uh...nope."

Madaliene, in due course, found her way to the back of the dwelling. There she saw a back yard that stretched forever before it ended in another large building that stood two stories tall while spanning nearly the entire width of the yard, bordered by a chiseled stone paved walkway. The front side of the building consisted of many large wooden doors set on strong wooden hinges with large arches at their tops. As with the main building, several turrets sprang from the corners. She walked to the back of this building and was not surprised to see a stone barbican jutting out approximately 20 of her steps which hid a well protected postern gate. As she shielded her eyes from the sun, she observed another parapet wall running along the roof line, broken only by the curvature of a drum tower. She continued in a mesmerized state.

Vincen and Arlis were returning from their fly-around when they saw Madaliene stumbling around the back guardhouse. "Arlis, I think our newest visitor may have some questions," Vincen told her with a wink.

Arlis agreed. "Yes, Vincen, I'm sure she will. Let's answer what we can for her."

The two wingers landed at Madaliene's side without startling her. "Madaliene, excuse me, I would like to introduce you to the matron of the Great Forest."

Madaliene came to a halt. "Vincen...what is this place?" She remembered her manners. "I am so sorry." She looked down at the wingers. "Vincen, who would this be?"

"Very good, Madaliene, this is Arlis. She is the second in command around here; it's me, then her."

Madaliene bent down on one knee, stretching her hand out to Arlis. "It is a pleasure to meet you Arlis. Wait, Vincen, if she is second, and you are first, where does Mystic fit in?"

"Oh, young one, you picked up on that very astutely. Mystic is the Prince of the Great Forest. I guess we are his first and second in command. We comprise his advisory council, you could say."

Madaliene laughed a soft, comfortable laugh. "I get it! He gives the orders and you two obey them if you see fit, right?"

Vincen slid his eyes to Arlis. "I…I guess you could say it like that."

Arlis quickly changed the subject. "So, young lady, what have you to say for this dwelling of Mystic's?"

Madaliene started to reply then caught herself. "Oh my, that was very smooth, Arlis. I'll let it go for now. My first question for you two is... what was this place? In my opinion, it is a small castle, only it's a very big small castle." She held both arms high and wide to accentuate her bewilderment. "What's the story? I think I have seen a picture of this place before, unless I dreamed about it."

Vincen began to pace in a circle similar to the one he walked when he and Mystic stood at the brim of that hole over in the South Quarter, wings folded tightly to his side, looking much like a two-legger with his hands clasped behind his back. His eyes darted in many directions, his head bobbed. "That is interesting, Madaliene. This dwelling has been here as long as any of us can remember. It has never, in my lifetime, been inhabited by two-leggers. How about you, Arlis?"

"Me?" The Crow was very surprised. "You are much older than me, sir. If you don't remember anything, you can rest assured I don't."

Vincen nodded. "Yes, you are probably correct. As a matter of fact, Madaliene, none of us has ventured much further than the front room of the place. I know Mystic has never had any desire to go deeper in than the front room where he sleeps."

"That is odd, Vincen. Do you think he would allow me to lead an expedition? We could wander through the entire place. I'm sure we can find something in there worthy of our interest!"

"Well then ask away, Princess." Mystic stood at Madaliene's side with Bubba in tow.

"Aha, the Prince has arrived!" She excitedly pivoted on her heels. "Do you mean to tell me you have never explored this palace of yours? And, if the answer is yes, why not?"

Mystic fumbled for an answer. "Uh, I uh, I uh…I really never had the interest. Princess, we...uh we four-leggers don't…well, we don't really care about the extravagances your kind seems to depend on.

Nothing meant by that, except to say, why do I need 78 rooms in my dwelling when one will do nicely?" He cut his eyes directly at Bubba.

"In reality, Princess, the main dwelling only has 48 rooms. The guardhouse, where Mystic sleeps, has seven, the garden dwelling has 16 and the barn back there contains five small rooms and two very big rooms." Bubba's face instantly became flushed, at least as flushed as a four-legger can appear. His eyes squinted, his lips pursed, his jowls inflated.

"Well, it seems to me the old saying still rings true there, Bubba, does it not?" Madaliene laughed for the first time in a long time. "Had your curiosity killed you, we would not be nearly as entertained." She plopped to the ground between the Wolf and the Cheetah, grabbed their necks and wrestled them each to the ground. "When was the last time either of you had a bath?"

Arlis emitted a few clucking sounds from her beak, while Vincen rolled his eyes.

***

Near the top of the wooden ramp leading into Burg Seven, two Bears and two Tigers appeared with no fanfare.

"Well, this looks like Burg Seven to me. How about you, Lightning?"

"They all look alike to me, same gate, same big trees."

"Do you see a river in front of this one Badger?"

Lightning peeked over his shoulder. "No... no, I don't."

"Then how can you say they all look alike?" Cirrus grunted.

"Figuratively."

"Hmmph!" Hugoth banged on the heavy gate with his front paws. He yelled into the trees. "Hey, is there anyone in the gatehouse?"

Much to their surprise, there came no reply. Looks of concern etched their way onto the large, furry faces.

Duister seemed worried. "Hugoth, is that silence a bad thing?"

Hugoth was even more determined to get inside now. "Help me, Lightning. We will never break this gate down, but we can cause enough ruckus to maybe get some creature's attention. In tandem, the over-grown Bears promptly began banging on the gate with reckless abandon as the Tigers watched. The disturbance did not go unnoticed.

"What are those two doing down there?" Karri saw the commotion before she heard it. "And how did they get there before we did?"

"The ax thingy of Lightning's. That would explain it." Perrie was confident of her answer.

"I think I need one of those myself!" Karri led the dive on the gate. She pulled up just before driving herself into Hugoth's shoulder. "You two sure are making a lot of noise!"

Hugoth never slowed his attack on the gate. "Nice of you to join us, Karri. Welcome to Burg Seven!" He continued ravaging the large timber planks.

Lightning saw Perrie land near the gate's base. "You think one of you fine feathered beauties could fly over this thing and ask someone to open it?" He kept up his assault as well.

Perrie pondered the question for a moment. "Sure. I would be glad to. Karri, shall we?"

"If they will cease their noise making, I will gladly join you."

Hugoth turned his back to the gate. "Fine!"

The Bears fell into heaps, exhausted. Cirrus and Duister settled between the weakened Bears and the ramp, alert for any threat.

"There is no creature in this land who could have made me believe that what we just did, to no avail mind you, would have made me feel so worn out." Lightning dropped his head down onto the hard ground. "Ouch."

"I completely agree with you, Badger. Why did your ax-pike not take us beyond this gate?"

"I have no idea."

The four intimidating four-leggers laid there waiting, two of them somewhat exhausted, for the wingers' return.

***

On the other side of the gate, neither Karri nor Perrie saw any creature immediately available. They flew several clicks along the main path towards the Keeper's dwelling before noticing any sign of activity. Up ahead a thick mass of leggers and wingers were crowding around a tall, dark man and a lovely young lady standing on the back of a Rhinoceros.

"Karri, that assembly up there may be the reason no one was manning the gate."

"You must be correct, Perrie. Let's go right to the source." She led Perrie to the gathering's center, where they delicately lit on Stewig's neck. Karri whispered to him, "Stewig, what's this all about? Hugoth is waiting at the front gate. Someone needs to allow him entry and soon!"

Stewig's eyes shot wide open. "He is here? Oh my." He carefully searched for Bongi. "Bongi, it's Hugoth, he's waiting at the gate. He wants entry."

Bongi immediately excused himself from the others. "Oliviia, Jahnise, Hugoth is at the gate, please excuse me." Stepping past Stewig, he said, "I will get right on that." He noticed the wingers, "Karri, would you like to come with me? Maybe fill me in on some things?"

"Yes, please. We will both accompany you. Come with us, Perrie."

With the wingers hopping onto his back, Bongi made his way clear of the throng, the Okapi recognizing his Burg dwellers and the Hawk recognizing her fellow dwellers from Burg One. "Bongi, what is going on here?"

"I was so hoping you could tell me, dear."

Bongi left Stewig to explain the quick exit and select those individuals whose presence would be requested in the Keeper's gathering room.

***

"So, Bongi..." Karri asked, "You have no explanation as to why dwellers from Burg One are now attending a meeting at Burg Seven when all gates have been ordered shut by Hugoth, who now stands outside of your gate? What has happened?"

"At first glance, it would seem to appear as some kind of problem, certainly. However, it may not be problematic at all. There may be some easily explainable, very logical reason for it...it's just that...well, I have no idea what it is. How about you? How have you been?"

"Hold on, now, you odd shaped Horse or whatever you are. You're not evading her question that easily!" Perrie could be very feisty at times. "And, thank you for asking. We have been peachy." The young Falcon nipped at Bongi's tall, round ear. "Are you joking? Tell us the truth, Bongi!"

Karri leaned closer to Bongi's other ear, "You need to answer my question, as she tends to get rather defensive."

Bongi shook his head. "I will not argue that point with you. She has a very sharp bark and a very painful bite!"

"Trust me, Bongi, you have no idea. I'd hurry if I were you, she is a meat eater."

"Oh dear." Bongi broke into a hasty gallop. "I'm hurrying, little Falcon. Please, no more biting."

"That wasn't a bite, Bongi…that was a taste test!" She stood up straight and winked proudly to Karri.

Bongi hurried around to the back of the gatehouse where he pushed the lever which set the ropes and pulleys, cogs and gears in motion. Soon the gate was slowly swinging open. Outside, Hugoth and Lightning felt the rumble, forced themselves to their feet and moved out of the way as the gate lowered over them. As soon as an opening large enough to accommodate the Bear's bodies appeared, they climbed through. Hugoth yelled for the gate to be drawn once again. Obediently, Bongi pulled the lever to its starting position and the mechanizations reversed. Cirrus and Duister leaped through the narrowed opening with room to spare.

Word of his arrival spread quickly. Hugoth stood looking up the main path as a horde of Nuorgians rushed to welcome him. They were all hoping he could explain the recent string of events. Unfortunately, their questions would only prompt his own. Those in charge swiftly decided to curtail the questions and answers in order to return to the Keeper's dwelling for the planned meeting and subsequent discussions. There were many answers to be shared and much planning to do.

***

"What do you mean you were all transported here?" Hugoth sat on the floor at the head of the table, speaking to Kirch who sat in a chair to the left of those used by Jahnise and Oliviia. Lightning sat to the other side. "Where are the ancient Eagle and Rakki? And Cirrus? Where is she?"

In front of the dwelling, Cirrus was instructing Duister to help Stewig with whatever odd jobs needed to be done. After experiencing the failed attack on Burg One, she made it clear to all within hearing distance that if anyone had any knowledge of the developing cracks, they needed to speak up or face severe consequences. She left it to Duister to explain what had happened. Satisfied with his willingness to take charge, she slipped into the meeting just as Hugoth was shouting her name.

"Hugoth, I am here. I have instructed Duister and Stewig to find out what they can about the attack on Burg One. They will question those from your Burg and report back to us." She circled the table in a menacing way. She had no ill will toward any of those in attendance, but regardless, she was a large, aggressive Tigress and that alone demanded much respect and attention. When she was in her protective mode, menacing was normal behavior. Many attendees felt the glare from her piercing, yellow eyes. Many too, were unnerved with her low, reverberating growls. As she circled the table, no living creature was spared her complete attention.

"I can't explain any of this, Hugoth. Where were the cracks in your Burg?" Cirrus was too agitated to stand still. Hugoth let her continue. "How do we even find the cracks? What constitutes a crack? Are they occurring naturally? Someone educate me on this matter!"

Hugoth turned to Oliviia. "Livvy, where is your father?" There had been no time to tell him of the attack that took Ian and Colleen's lives. "Tell us where he is and what you know. You are young, but you have been at his side in all of his research."

Jahnise stood. "Hugoth, Mister Ian was killed in an earlier attack on this Burg. We arrived too late to help him."

The look on Hugoth's face was one of complete shock and sorrow, not only for the immediate cause, but for those that would be coming without the guarantee of his expertise. "What did you say, Jahnise?"

"Mister Ian and Colleen were..."

Oliviia stood. She grabbed Jahnise's arm, prodding him to sit back down. "It's alright, sir. Thank you, but I will take it from here."

She began to tell the story leading up to that tragic, life-altering moment.

"We awoke this morning earlier than usual. Mother wasn't able to sleep much the whole night. Father asked me to take Patrick and Emiliia to get breakfast, while he and Mother had a theory they wanted to check out. We spent the last three days and nights in the cave with only a short break to come meet Jahnise, so it was a relief for the three of us to get out for a while. Patrick filled his backpack with fruits, Emiliia collected the vegetables from our stores and I refilled the water bags. We met back at the cave's entrance. We walked to the exact location where we spent our restless night and neither Father nor Mother was there. Patrick called for them. We heard them call from deeper down. Of course, we were famished and didn't feel any reason to continue to their sides... They were always so wrapped up in their work, but in a good way. It didn't bother us. So, we sat down to eat figuring they would come find us if they got really hungry. That mistake..."

Cirrus interrupted the brave youngster. "That mistake more than likely saved you children's lives. I'm sorry, please go on."

"As you wish, ma'am. We ate our fill, I don't know...for maybe twenty or thirty minutes...can I use minutes? I don't know how to convert minutes to clicks..."

Hugoth nodded, "It's quite alright. Go ahead, Livvy."

"Thank you, sir. We were putting the food away when we heard Mother running up the cave, yelling for us. She was calling for us. She said, 'Come quickly, come quickly!' All three of us dashed towards her. She told us they had found the answer they had been looking for all of these years..."

Hugoth raised his head, "Livvy, do you mean they found it?"

"Yes, sir. They found the way to seal the cracks. Mother was so excited she could hardly speak. We ran with her all the way to where Father was waiting to show us the complete method to close the cracks up forever. He was giddy with excitement."

"Well, what happened?" Cirrus was locked into the story now.

"Father sat us down in a semi-circle to explain to us in detail what each of us would need to do to heal the crack."

Hugoth interrupted again. "Excuse me, Livvy, did you mean seal the crack...?"

Jahnise continued Hugoth's question. "Or heal the crack?"

"I said heal the crack. Father explained to us the cracks are living things. They change with the climate of good and evil in the world. I don't know how my parents figured that out, but they did. The cracks...I know this will sound silly...they run from evil, which allows them the ability to not be found. Ugh, I can't believe I'm telling you this! It's still hard for me to fathom. Patrick caught on to it immediately. He is the smart one in the family. Sorry, I veered a little off track." She scooted her chair back and began to walk around the room.

"Say, for example... Oh, how did Father say it?" She reached across the table to grab an apple. "This might work." She held it up and pointed to section of it. "See this yellowish spot here? Why is it not red? It's not red because it wasn't in direct sunlight. This is the part hidden by the tree's own leaves. The tree did not mean to hide this part of the apple...but, it did. Or did it?"

"Oliviia, you are losing me. We haven't time for an explanation such as this." Hugoth wanted simple answers for complicated questions.

"Whatever." Oliviia blew out a long breath intermingled with loads of frustration. "Okay, the cracks move on their own. One day they might be here..." She slammed her open palm against a flat spot on the wall. "The next day they could be here..." She slapped another spot as she continued walking. "And those two spots may be the same crack, Hugoth! What I am trying to say...well, I don't know. Father understood this phenomenon and mother was beginning to, but I don't. Patrick does, we need to find him. Emiliia and I have...well, we have other strengths."

Hugoth stood. He pressed his paws on the table, consequently lifting the other end off the floor. "I apologize to you, Oliviia. I do, but we need answers! Where will the next crack materialize?"

Oliviia became angry. "Did you not hear what I just said? The cracks move on their own!"

"That is impossible!"

"They do, Hugoth. They do!"

"If they do and we can't track them, how are the invaders tracking them?" Hugoth slammed his paw against the table, nearly shattering it.

Oliviia's face became blood red. "Because someone from here is tracking them too! Jahnise is the only one here who can locate that creature and dispose of him. His staff is described in my father's diary." She turned to Jahnise. "King, do you still have the book?"

Jahnise stood. He pulled the Ian's diary from a pocket and laid it on the table, pushing it toward Hugoth. "This is the book I found with Mister Ian. He was pointing to the "E" on the cover when he breathed his last. It was a clue."

Oliviia sprinted back to the table. "Are you sure he was pointing to the 'E', King?"

"Absolutely, Oliviia. I am quite sure of it."

Oliviia picked up the diary and quickly skimmed through the pages. "E. E. E. E..."

"What are you looking for?" Hugoth asked.

"It was a clue! E is the first letter of the name and the name will contain five letters as well."

Jahnise looked puzzled. "I thought his clue referenced Evaliene?"

Oliviia never looked up as she continued skimming through the book. "No...no...no..."

Cirrus moved to Oliviia's side. "Five letters starting with an "E"... It was Eekay, wasn't it, Livvy?"

"Yes! Cirrus, it was Eekay. She was spying on us the whole time! Father often wondered why she would mysteriously show up at the most inconvenient times. The whole time!" She closed the book with both hands and patted the top of her head with it. "This is bad!"

Hugoth tried to calm Oliviia. "Livvy, Eekay is dead. We heard from the Storks of her demise."

"Storks! No, they can't be here!" Oliviia was frightened. "Where are they right now?"

All of leggers in the room looked around for someone to speak up. No one did.

"They are in it up to the top of their stupid long necks!" Oliviia was nearly screaming her words.

Panic began to set into each creature in the room. Bongi was standing watch halfway out the door, listening to everything going on inside and outside the dwelling when he felt a live load land on his back. "Excuse me?" He turned to see Oliviia settling in as if he wore a saddle.

"Bongi, get me to the last place the Storks were seen." She quickly called for Cirrus and Hugoth. "Follow me! If the Storks are in the cave, we have a real problem. Be ready to combat an awful enemy!" She dug her heels into Bongi's side. His hoofs slipped on the hard floor of the stoop as he fought for traction. Oliviia relentlessly urged him on.

"Let's go, Bongi!"

Cirrus and Duister were at Bongi's side immediately. Hugoth trailed slightly behind with Lightning. Karri and Perrie flew at Oliviia's ear.

"Karri, please go find Stewig. Tell him to be ready for anything. Perrie, you are our only scout. You must fly ahead solo until Karri returns."

The Hawk peeled off beautifully to head in the opposite direction as the young Falcon flew her route.

Jahnise walked to the doorway. He looked longingly at the fading cloud of dust trailing his new friends, staff in hand. He scanned the room looking for a leader in those remaining. “Kirch, gather your bravest fighters. We have a problem. Meet me back in this room as quickly as possible.”

Kirch did not ask questions. He excused himself through the doorway and immediately spread the word to the Burg One dwellers. Soon, a small group was once again assembled in the large gathering room. Mostly made up of non-Talker two-leggers and a few four-leggers, Jahnise felt an overwhelming sense of calm among the group.

Jahnise stood where Hugoth had once sat at the table’s head. “Nuorgians, I have something to share with you I did not want to burden Miss Oliviia with. I was given this through the crack in the cave where Mister Ian and Colleen were attacked. Look at it closely. Can any of you gain any information from it?” Jahnise reached into another of his side pockets to pull out the object in question. When he laid it on the table and un-wrapped it, a hush fell over the crowd. All eyes opened wide at the sight of the clue. “Come in closely. Each of you needs to examine every small detail.”

The calm demeanor was interrupted by several gasps and a few grunts.

Kirch reached past some of the gawkers to get an even closer look. He picked the object up as carefully as he would pick up a cup or a saucer. “I’d say this came from a man of not much wealth. The wear and tear are obvious indicators of a rough style of life.” He turned it over. “These markings across the back are permanent though hastily done.” He gently tugged on a smaller object attached to the larger. “If I can get this off…maybe we can look even further into this man’s past. There we go.” The smaller object came off with a weak popping sound. He laid the larger object back on the table holding the smaller shiny one in his fingers. Kirch walked to the large window to hold the clue to the brighter light outside the dwelling. After studying the object from every conceivable angle, he called on a knowledgeable fellow also from Burg One. “Stephane, what do you make of this? Is it what I think it is?

A shorter, rounder two-legger stepped to the window. “Let me see it, Kirch. It is a ring, I know that for sure.”

"Here you go. Yes, it is and a fine looking one at that. Look at the engravings, do they tell anything besides the obvious?"

"I'm not sure I follow you... What is the obvious?"

"Of course, man! The obvious!" Stephane held the ring to the light, then grabbed Kirch's arm. "The obvious, man!"

Jahnise and the other attendees watched the pair as they argued back and forth. There was no reason to interrupt their conversation, for in all probability, it was headed somewhere.

"What do this ring and that hand have in common?" Stephane pointed to the first object on the table. "I will tell you…nothing, nothing at all. That hand never earned this ring. Whoever was attached to that hand at one time stole this ring from its original owner. Are your eyes too weak to see that?"

"Oh, is that what you were implying? I knew that much. That hand came from a common thief or ruffian, if you will. This ring is a fine piece. When it was purchased or made, it was very costly. I want to know what you make of the engravings. You crossed paths with the higher-ups when you worked the law? This insignia seems to be not unlike one of the association's symbols that I have seen before. Take a closer look."

Stephane glared at Kirch with an unhappy look. "Are you insinuating something here?"

"For Nuorg's sake...no! All I want to know is if you have seen this insignia before."

"Why did you not just say that?"

"I did just say that!"

Jahnise loudly cleared his throat to get the quibbling pair's attention. "Ahem!" The polite, though loud attempt to stop the arguing did not succeed. Jahnise smiled as he walked around the table to the window. He tapped Stephane on the shoulder with his stick. "Thank you both for your attention to this matter. Give me the ring back. I will hold it until one or both of you have a remembering of this item you see. I can't have it causing so much bickering."

Kirch laughed. "My apologies, King. We have known one another since birth in the land above. I guess this is the way we talk to each other all the time. I never really paid any attention to it."

Stephane nodded in agreement. "He is correct, King…all the time."

"That is your business, sirs, but when I ask you to do something, it will be discussed or performed in a civil manner. There is enough to rile us already." He took the ring and returned to the head of the table.

"King, that ornate symbol on the side of the ring is a variation of the 'association's' standard. If we can discover which camp it belongs to, we will be closer to discovering where this group of invaders originated." Stephane chose his words carefully and spoke tranquilly.

"I wholeheartedly agree with my friend here, King. Is there a scribe in this Burg with access to any historical documentation?"

Jahnise tapped a long finger on his lips. His eyes lit up for an instant. "Where is Grendl? She should know of this inquiry." Jahnise looked around the table at the many grim faces of those wanting answers. He noticed Perrie at the window. "Perrie, go ask around, I want to see Grendl and Kohlyn at once!"

"Yes, King." She flew off to find Stewig. He would be the one to ask.

Jahnise regained control of the meeting. "While we await the arrival of our small scribe, give me some ideas. Kirch, who among your Nuorgians is the battle monger?"

Kirch was perplexed by the question. "Battle monger? King, I am not sure what that means."

Jahnise explained. "Yes, mister Kirch, who among you plans your battles? Who is your fiercest warrior?" He studied all of the faces blankly staring back at him. "Why do you look at me as you do? Did I say something wrong?" Again, he looked over the crowd.

Stephane stepped forward. "King Jahnise, none of this group has ever fought in a battle. We certainly don't have a fierce warrior among us. Maybe some fierce conversationalists, but no warriors."

Jahnise closed his eyes, stretching his fingers across his long face. "No warriors? How were you to protect Nuorg? How were you to protect each other?"

Again, Stephane answered for the group. "King, we are those considered to be too meek for the lands we left. We are do-gooders. None of us have ever lifted a finger toward another individual. We have scholars and teachers, thinkers and sayers, but we have no warriors." He held his hands up. "Feel these hands. They have never known rugged work before."

Kirch stepped to Stephane's side. "He is telling you the truth, King. We don't know how to fight. That was not a part of why we are here. The animals are here to protect us. They have the natural tools."

An incredulous look took over Jahnise's face. "Are you telling me that no man here can swing a sword, shoot an arrow or throw a spear?"

"We are saying exactly that, King." Stephane stood proudly with his fellows.

"However," Kirch picked up with where Stephane was headed. "There are more ways to protect Nuorg than by merely raising weapons."

Jahnise managed to let a smile creep back on his face. "And what might that be?"

Kirch returned the smile. "Give us some time to prepare a plan. If you will go assemble the four-leggers, we will formulate something that may surprise you with its intricate complexities and shock you with its ruthlessness. May we have three quarters of your next hour?"

"However long that is in this wonderful place, so be it. I will be outside. I need some quiet time myself. There is much for you to do and much praying on my part. Please excuse me."

Jahnise stepped silently through the door as the two-legged Nuorgians began to scheme. Once outside the Keeper's dwelling, he began to stroll the main path taken earlier by those under Oliviia's direction, his stick jabbing the ground on occasion. He had no idea what to expect. He simply felt he needed to expect anything and everything. He prayed silently as he walked, his eyes studying this lovely Burg more efficiently than before. "Creator, be with those who have gone before me. Protect us as you will."

Jahnise had never needed to come to terms before with all of the differences he knew existed between man, animals and birds of the sky. Up until now, there had been no need to. Where he had come from, no man went out of his way to be exceedingly kind or hurtful to the four-legged creatures. He knew of those tribes who hunted animals for food and he had lost some friends years ago, but that was their business. Suddenly, it was becoming his business too. The treatment and respect of animals was never discussed. Around his parts he was the only Talker. There was never a need for another. Until Kirch mentioned "natural tools", Jahnise had never brought that detail into any of his thinkings. As he kicked small poofs of dust from under his feet, he wondered what kind of situation the creatures ahead of him were about to get into. He continued to pray for guidance and understanding... Lots of understanding.

24

Mariel completed the cage for Bulos. As per Belle's instructions, it was escape proof. It was built around the prisoner, so no door was necessary. The absence of a door made the prospect of escape even more improbable. From what Mariel noticed of the Owl's condition, an escape was not something to be concerned with. He was hoping Belle stayed a safe distance from the cage. She was in no mood to be messed with. Her mood actually seemed to get more aggressive as the day passed. While she struggled to stay social with the group, everyone knew to tread lightly.

"Belle, this cage is complete. You will not need to worry. An escape is out of the question."

Belle immediately studied the portable prison. "Yes, I can see that as well. Thank you." She called to Tofur. "Leiram, if you please."

Tofur checked the kerchief around Mariel's neck. It continued to hold the bandage snug. He placed the whistle to his lips and blew one short blast. "That should do it."

"What is this pain in my neck?" Leiram gingerly touched the bandaged area.

"It is a long story, sir. We were attacked and you got the worst of it. The attackers were killed and their leader is now locked in cage. I sewed you up. Please, don't disturb the bandage if you can help it."

"Whatever you say, lad. Why are we not on the move?" Leiram could have asked more questions, but he refrained.

"As I said, sir, we were attacked. In order to take care of your immediate medical needs, we had to delay our start. My Falcons are flying. Shall I call them in?" Tofur readied his whistle.

"Yes. Absolutely. I want a scouting report. I want to know where our quarry is. I want to know the lay of the land. I want to know everything all of you know about our attackers." He paused for a moment to rub his neck while walking over to study the cage and its captive. "Everything!"

Taytay and Whistler heard the four short bursts. Without questioning the reason, they headed straight back to Tofur at an alarming speed. Tofur spotted them shortly as they circled above him. He placed the gauntlet on his left arm, offering it to the obedient cast and blew one short blast to counter the effects of the four blast call. Leiram was very impressed with the practiced precision.

"Welcome back to the both of you." Tofur gathered the group together. "Let's all get closer, please. Leiram is taking the lead of our group. I will relay to you exactly what he tells me and to him exactly what you all tell me. Taytay, what is the lay of the land? Whistler, are those we pursue still out there? Those two questions should get us started. The time has never been more right for us to move forward."

Taytay answered first. "Master, the land ahead should allow for quick travel, although there is no cover until we reach the foothills." He nodded to Whistler.

"Those two-leggers we are following remain out there, but they are opening the gap. We will struggle to catch them by nightfall."

Tofur told Leiram what the Falcons reported as the other creatures listened closely.

"Tofur, please instruct your cast to continue scouting ahead of us. What bothers me is another attack from the rear. We don't have the resources we need. I would enjoy having a second cast behind us. For now, we will have to make due with what we have. Ask them how far ahead our quarry has gone."

These conversations went on until no questions or answers were left unknown. Leiram walked back to the road, his fists beating on his hips. He stepped into the middle of the road before turning around, his hands now firmly clutching the belt loops of his pants. "Are you going to stay over there all night? Let's go!"

Tofur translated for the group. "He's ready."

Belle ran alongside Porcene as the beautiful Belgian galloped to Leiram's side with Tofur hanging on. The Falcons raced upwards. Jak initially stumbled, but regained his poise before anyone saw him. The wound inflicted by the Owls was hurting Jak more than it should. Leiram soon climbed atop the Mule as they led the way. If any creature had been watching, they would not have guessed the weight pressing down on each of those brave travelers.

***

The group traveled in silence. Eye contact was the only form of communication used for the remaining portion of the afternoon. As the sun began to set, Leiram spoke softly.

"Tofur, the absence of life around us is chilling. There is nary a bird in the air or mouse in the grass. If I didn't know it to be true, I would wonder if we were actually breathing. What is happening?"

"Sir, I was kind of hoping you would be telling me. We were only told to follow those men once we found them. Now, I'm of the mind that we need to capture them and find out everything they know. I can't believe I'm even saying that. It's really not in my nature, if you know what I am trying to say."

"I know what you mean. I am not understanding everything either. I don't even know how I met up with your group! I don't know why I travel with one of the most magnificent Horses I have ever laid my eyes on while she is hidden beneath a never-ending load of baggage I have never seen before." Leiram paused for a breath and then laughed. "I only realized a short while back that we have no weapons other than the teeth of your loyal Dog and the talons of your trained Falcons. Well, maybe the hooves of these creatures we ride, but that is it! Explain that to me! What a perfect time to be loyal."

Tofur didn't know how to react. "Sir, what are we to do next? If by some stroke of luck or genius we do catch our quarry, what do we do with them then?"

"Not if, young man, when. Check with your Falcons. Can you call them down without the whistle?"

"I'm sure I can try, if they are flying the area. Why no whistle?"

"Merely a precaution, lad. If we can hear the whistle, so can the enemy. No?"

"Point well taken, sir." Tofur searched the sky for his faithful companions as Porcene continued stepping regally down the road.

The group did not make a scene as they steadily made their way toward an unsure goal. A draft Horse completely concealed by her load, what looked to be a tall, red crop Mule and a large black and tan Dog accompanying two unassuming two-leggers, possibly a father and his son, did little to stir curiosity…had there been any living creature around with any curiosity to stir.

Tofur wondered aloud as he continued scanning the sky. "Porcene, do you have any idea where we are? It is not an idyllic land, but it still looks hospitable to me. Leiram, there…" Tofur pointed to his left at a dark, silhouetted dot moving towards them. "That is Whistler coming back. I'll try waving him down." He waved politely to the incoming dot so as not to startle him.

"How can you tell the difference in them, lad?" Leiram watched the dot grow more discernable as it approached.

"Because they are mine, sir. I have studied their flight styles since they were young birdlets just off the nest." He turned to his right, "There, just over the trees, that will be Taytay. Notice how much tighter he flaps his wings. He is much more driven to speed than Whistler. Whistler grew to be a lazy flyer. He is the swifter of the two, but he has the potential to be so much faster."

Leiram nodded. "I'll have to take your word for that. I will admit, they make a handsome cast."

Porcene tried her best to spot any landmarks which could give her a clue to their whereabouts. As a matter of fact, she had been trying ever since they left the last small, inhabited outpost. She came up with nothing.

"Tofur," she said, "Ask the Falcons what they have seen. I can no more tell you where we are than the rocks under my hooves."

Jak swung his head around to her. "Porcene, you know these rocks can tell us more about where we are than you might think." He faced forward again and kept walking.

Porcene seemed amused. "Figures you'd be the one to say that."

Whistler spotted the gauntlet Tofur held out, his arm stretched out on his left side at shoulder, bent 90 degrees at the elbow. A slight nod of his chin was the only signal needed. Whistler dove on the gauntlet without hesitation, landing as gently as a feather with a few braking beats of his wings.

"Yes, master?"

Leiram looked on with a great deal of respect for the years of training these Falcons and their master must have experienced. The obedience to Tofur's every command and the nuances learned over the years as the personalities wove themselves together into a remarkably tight cord were very admirable. Spying Whistler's landing prompted a brief circling by Taytay. Soon, with another slight movement of Tofur's chin, he too, was perched next to Whistler. A smile spread from ear to ear as the young Falcon master greeted his cast.

"How was the flying, Whistler?"

"I must report that I don't like what I have seen far ahead in the direction we are heading. We must find an alternate route. It looks to me as if a war is escalating."

Taytay affirmed Whistler's doubts. "I agree, Tofur. There is a gathering ahead of us the likes of which none of us wants to be involved with. The leggers we are trailing are headed directly for it."

"If we are to question them…we need to get it done quickly," Whistler added. "They are a good five hundred pursuit beats away. About that same distance further is a party we don't need to run into."

"Yes, Tofur, we are terribly outnumbered."

Tofur's demeanor changed from an ear to ear smile to a dour, grim look of consternation. "Leiram, we are heading directly into a big problem. The men we are following are between us and a gathering battle group. We must reach them before they reach that group. I don't know exactly what we are to do, but I scarcely believe we are to take on a large group of soldiers."

Leiram frowned, disturbed by the news. "Is that what they told you?"

"Yes, sir, it is. Seems the trouble we are looking for is about 10 miles ahead of us."

"You are correct, lad. That is not the news I wanted to hear. I agree. We must catch our quarry before they meet up with that larger group. Let me think."

Tofur called to Belle. "Belle, what is your take on this matter?"

"I'm not sure. I was waiting on a decision from Leiram. Do you want me run ahead and take care of those two-leggers?"

Tofur entertained the thought. "I'm not sure you could take them both down in a controlled way that would leave them available for questioning."

Belle seemed perturbed. "Oh, you want to question them? I'm afraid that would not be possible if I had my way."

"That's exactly my point, Belle."

"What is your Dog thinking, Lad?" Leiram heard Tofur's side of the conversation and was curious.

"Sir, she wants to run ahead and take out the ones we are after. And when I say take out, I mean take them out permanently!"

"You are right to tell her that is not acceptable. We need to catch them. You say they are on foot, correct?"

"Yes, sir. What are you proposing?"

"If these creatures we ride can run for any distance, we must try to overtake those we are after. We need to hide these provisions and return to them if we are able." Leiram looked into the fields to their sides. "Over there, see the clump of tall grass? We will head there to hide all of these bags we can. Once we are relatively certain our packages are safe, we will take off after those two men. Send your Falcons to scout them. Tell them to harass them if necessary. Do whatever it takes to slow them down. We will be on their trail shortly."

"Yes, sir." Tofur relayed Leiram's orders to Taytay and Whistler. "You two fly after our prey, stall them in some way. We will follow soon once we unload Jak and Porcene. We must do that to allow them to run, as they must to catch those leggers. I hope there is nothing we will need in what we leave behind."

Whistler answered, a tone of concern shading his response. "We will do as you ask, Tofur. Please hurry. We can't hold them too long without causing serious damage to the both of them. We certainly don't want to be spied by that large group beyond."

Tofur's face turned cold. "Whistler, I will say only this…do what you must. There is no option for failure. Taytay, take care. If all of your plans fail, return to me at once. I will see you before morning.'

The Falcons bowed politely and took wing.

"Leiram, sir, I hope you know what you are asking of those two. They can be very vicious if need be."

Leiram led the draft animals off the road. "On that I am hoping, lad."

Tofur followed the older legger's lead, his face awash with equal amounts of anger and hope. Leiram could not help but notice Tofur's ever-changing demeanor.

"Lad, what seems to be the major trouble you're having? By the looks you are showing on your face there, you'd think your whole world is crashing down on you at once. Tell me what's bothering you."

"In a word, sir, fear. I am afraid of what is coming. I may have been too sure of our little group's possibilities. I'm wondering why we set off on this adventure at all. Belle has already suffered a tremendous personal loss. I fear what may be coming for the rest of us. We can't take on an army posed against us."

"Lad, you're being too hard on yourself. Forget about the army ahead of us. You can't be for sure they are out to get us, can you?" Leiram pulled Jak up alongside a tall clump of reedy grass that reached nearly over the tall Mule's ears. "This will do nicely, I suppose."

Leiram and Tofur climbed down from their mounts to begin loosing all of the large four-leggers' burdens. They worked diligently, arranging each load in the order it came off. Several bags came off Porcene full of contents none of them could imagine a use for. Boxes full of bags, bags full of boxes, tools, trinkets, everything and more than anyone could imagine.

"Tofur." It was Belle's time to question Leiram. "What does he plan for us to do once we catch those two-leggers we are after?"

Tofur continued un-strapping heavy cases from both Porcene and Jak as Leiram stacked them in the reeds. "I honestly can't answer that, Belle. He has offered no opinions on that matter. I rather think he will come up with the plans as we need them. Anyway…how can you really plan for something you know nothing about?"

"Fair enough, Tofur. Fair enough." Belle sniffed curiously through the growing stack of everything. "There are so many different smells in these bags. I smell food, clothing, oils, tools…just about anything you could imagine is packed here."

Tofur let the last bag fall from Porcene's back. "Leiram, what is this?" He had uncovered four cylindrical sacks buttoned along their long sides. "Have you ever seen anything like this before?"

Leiram moved in for a closer look. "I think not, lad. Unbutton one of them and let's see what we have there."

Tofur slowly loosed each of many buttons holding the wrapping taut. "Porcene, do you have any idea what is held in these last containers?"

"Yes I do, Tofur. Those have been with me since before Mariel was thrown at me." She began looking somewhat curious.

"Really?" Tofur continued unfastening the buttons. "If I'm not mistaken, I'd say you were set out on a specific journey as well!" Tofur unbuttoned the last button on the first sack. "Oh my, Porcene, you are not a draft animal at all, are you?"

"What do you mean, Tofur? Many in my family have served as draft animals for as long as I remember."

"Yes, but what I am seeing here has nothing to do with drafting in the least!"

"What on this earth are you carrying on about, lad?" Leiram stacked the last of the many heavy bags before covering them with loose reeds and heading back to Porcene's side. "What has this marvelous mount been hiding from us all?"

"Have a look for yourself, sir." Tofur began rolling out an exquisitely woven silver mesh over the Belgian's large flank. "If I am not incorrect, this will be chainmail. I have never seen anything that comes close to the craftsmanship required to make this. Have a look!"

Leiram's jaw dropped. "Well, this Belgian has been keeping a secret from us for sure. I knew she was of pedigreed stock." He felt the smoothness of the armor and the hardness of the metal. "This work compares favorably to the best mail I have ever seen anywhere in my world! Look, there are two layers of it."

He completely unrolled the first layer which was made of small metal loops as thick as strong twine. The second layer was much finer than the first. The second layer was loosely woven as a fine woolen blanket with strands of metal no thicker than standard cording.

Porcene chuckled. "Tofur, you may want to open some of those cases over there marked 'just in case'. You may be very interested in what they contain."

"What are you telling me, Porcene?"

Jak walked to their side. "I suggest you open them, Tofur. I knew there was more to this old nag than meets the eye!"

Porcene feigned shock. "Old nag? Is that what you said? Why that's very apropos, coming from a genuine a..."

Belle barked loudly. "Tofur, we have company coming!"

***

The sky became crowded with large clouds of medium-sized, dark winged creatures. They traveled in silence, thousands of them stretching as far as a two-legger's eye could see. From where they had materialized was a mystery for another time and another day. Leiram felt useless. There was no hiding from this throng of birds. Should their goal be exposing Tofur's whereabouts to all creatures around, it would not be a demanding task. Tofur froze at the sight of the endless cloud of silent birds.

"Everyone quiet," Leiram whispered.

Each of the animals and Tofur cut their eyes at their current leader incredulously.

"Why would we need to be quiet now, sir? I believe we have been spotted already. What are those things and why are they flying so high? If they want us, why have they not dived on us already?"

Leiram stared at the continuous cloud of birds. "I don't think they are after us, lad. Who? I don't know, but certainly not us."

They spoke too soon. After the lead cloud passed, a second cloud appeared much lower in the sky, heading directly for them.

"Tell your friends to prepare for anything, lad." Leiram took a defensive stance in between Tofur and the approaching flock of birds.

Porcene's thoughts and directives were calm and orderly. "Tofur, I suggest you two-leggers open those bags quickly. You may need what they contain. Oh, we need the inventor back."

Tofur fidgeted nervously. He found the whistle in his pocket and blew three barely audible blasts. Immediately, Leiram's personality changed. Mariel looked to be confused.

"Now what is going on here?"

Porcene took control of the conversation. "Mariel, we need to unpack the supplies. Get me ready for…well, you know what."

"You mean for battle, Porcene. Has it come to that already? Where are we? Where have I been? I remember building a cage for the Owl, then nothing. What is going on?"

"Rig me up, Mariel!"

"Yes, yes…of course. Where are the satchels?"

"Tofur, show him where Leiram hid my packs."

"This way, Mariel. Everything is right over here. We had to hide it. We are about to begin a chase. We must travel fast, so we hid the stuff here."

Mariel was aghast. "Here? Do you not realize that you will most likely need everything you are leaving?"

"But…but, we are coming back for it all."

"You mean if you survive, you will be coming back for it! Our survival depends on having all of this with us at all times!"

"Mariel, there is no way we can travel with any speed if Porcene and Jak are weighed down to the pace of a slug."

Mariel snapped back, "Speed? Again, if you don't survive, what difference does it make?" He focused all of his attention on the unloaded stacks. "Porcene, come over here at once."

Porcene did as she was instructed. Soon, Mariel had found the bags. He meticulously picked through them, finding in each one exactly what he needed. Effortlessly and without much sound, he rigged Porcene for battle from the last hair of her tail to the broad face plate running the length of her entire head. Once he finished with her, he called for Jak.

"Jak, you are next. Shake a leg and get over here immediately."

Jak had no idea what to expect and no intention of not following the instructions coming from the current Mariel. He stood in awe of Porcene's transformation. He was soon adorned with what looked to most observers to be Porcene's outgrown armor.

Belle watched, slightly mystified. "Mariel, how was all of that packed on Porcene's back? Are you a magician of some kind?"

"No, of course not, Belle. I am a proficient packer. I could have packed the entire contents of my home on her strong back, had I a home to pack. It truly is an art. Thank you for noticing."

Soon, Jak was rigged to look like a miniature Porcene, the only differences being his size and color, and his long, pointy ears. He was outfitted for battle, but he wore his armor poorly. Porcene carried her adornments with honor and strength fit for royalty. Jak simply wore his.

"Tofur, I feel like a fool dressed up in this costume. Must I actually wear it?"

"It is not up to me, Jak. Ask Porcene. I think she is second in command here."

Jak humbly raised his eyes to the lovely Belgian mare. "Well?"

"Jak, you look stunning. If I didn't know better, I'd say you were born for a moment like this."

Jak then looked to Belle. "What say you, Rottweiler? Do I look like I was born for this?"

Belle cocked her head two or three times while she looked over Jak's dress. "Yes indeed, Jak, you carry it well. Stand proud."

Mariel stepped from behind the reeds carrying yet another bag of goods. "Belle, if you will? Please step this way."

Tofur hoped this time would come. "Mariel, do you have armor for her as well?"

"Yes, I do. I also have some for each of us…uh, two-leggers also."

"Really? How did you know what to expect?"

"That was easy. I did not pack all of this. It was given to me some time ago. That is another story. Let me get Belle suited up, then you and me. Here you go, open this bag for me."

"Certainly."

For the next few minutes Mariel dug through the remaining boxes and bags, retrieving just what he needed before returning them to the stash hidden in the reeds. Too soon the leading edge of the second living cloud was right on them.

"It looks like we finished in the nick of time, did we not?" Mariel took a moment to admire his handy work. "Where are the Falcons? I have something for them too."

"They were sent ahead by Lei…uh, by me, sir. I told them to stalk the men we are after and stall them by whatever means necessary."

"Oh, very well." Mariel clutched a short stack of interesting garments in his hands. He forced them toward Tofur. "Here, put these on underneath your outer clothes. I do not want anyone to assume you to be someone you are not."

"These are for me? What are they?"

"Do as I say, Tofur. We have no time to argue the point. Do it now. That flock of birds is swarming above us."

Tofur raised his head, as Mariel stated an innumerable flock of birds circled high above them. The youngster could not help but feel overwhelmed. What did all of this mean?

25

Frederick found the curtain's refusal to open difficult to believe. He was nearly positive the stack of books would do the trick. Did the opening of the curtain require two individuals? Why the weighted stack of books had not worked befuddled him even further.

"I have to get those curtains open," he muttered to the empty room. Once again he stood to walk and think. He circled the books with one arm across his chest and the other firmly planted over the first. His chin rested in a tight vice made with his thumb and fore finger. As his head tried to turn, it found too much resistance from his fingers' tight grip.

"What simplistic process have I failed to account for?"

Hemoth entered the room from an entrance Frederick had not previously noticed. "So, my friend, the curtains have you stymied, have they?"

Frederick was not afraid, only shocked. "Where did you come from, Hemoth? There are no openings over there. At least, not any in plain sight."

"Oh, ye feeble minded two-leggers. Just because you can't see something doesn't mean it doesn't exist, now does it?"

Frederick smiled, "Once I might have thought that, Hemoth, but not anymore. I take it there is yet another concealed entrance in that wall behind you?"

"Sorry, but no."

"What? Surely there is."

"Fret not, friend. The opening is in the floor. Actually, it is not close to the wall at all."

"The floor? Of course! Where else would it be?"

"Take a seat, Frederick. I need to let you in on a few secrets. You have come with me this far, I might as well trust the remaining secrets I have to you since there is no guarantee either one of us will survive what is coming."

Frederick was honored to be privy to the secrets, but not so much the end of Hemoth's sentence. He took a seat next to the stack of books. "What have you got for me, Hemoth?"

"Let me get comfortable here first." The Grizzly took a glance around the room before plopping to the glistening, hard floor. "I just started a string of events that will either prolong or curtail the existence of "The Land of Nuorg". Whether that land survives what is to come or not will depend heavily on how our little groups play out our uncertain futures."

Frederick made no attempt to hide a myriad of emotions. His face contorted as he progressed through feelings of surprise, disdain, uncertainty, frailty, anger and several others not important enough to name. "What…what…huh? Why…how? Hold on now. What exactly are you saying, Hemoth?"

"Frederick, we…those of us in the original group or guild, rather…we have lived an extraordinarily very long time nurturing Nuorg. We have also built this fortress and another just like it strategically placed over entrances to Nuorg. The day will come when our kind and the systems we have put in place will be no longer relevant in this world. You have noticed, I'm sure, those like you – and I mean Talkers – are reaching a point of extinction. That is not because of a lack of need, but it extends from a world that is running away from itself. In the coming years, well…things are going to be different." Hemoth sighed.

Frederick's attention was captivated by the calm and sincere presence encapsulating the huge Grizzly Bear. He watched as Hemoth reached to his side and placed his enormous, heavy paw on a barely noticed outlined square so finely crafted that it would have never been noticed at all, had not all the weight from Hemoth's paw been applied to it. He was sure he had stepped on the very spot numerous times in his quest to open the curtains. Beneath the floor a feint trace of turning gears caught Frederick's ear.

"Oh, so that is the secret to this room. You have to be huge in order to press the right buttons so they will do your bidding?"

"Hah, Fredrick, a wise observation. Although it is not the complete method, it would certainly help you out. You would never make anything in this place happen that you have not already made happen."

Frederick was growing used to the double meaning in most of Hemoth's statements to him. "Are you talking about this time or the last time?"

Hemoth smiled. "So, you are figuring it out after all? How many times have you been here?"

Frederick laughed himself. "Well, using my best deductive reasoning, I have concluded that I have been here, in this fortress, three previous times."

"Very clever of you, two-legger. You are close. You have been here six times previous. This is your seventh and last visit. This is also my seventh visit, although several of my stays have been for much longer than any of yours."

"Did I write the books, Hemoth?"

"Yes, you have written several of them. You also wrote the notes to yourself in the books you authored. Then you hid them away for you to find now. Did you note the progressive nature of your clues?"

"Yes. At first I thought nothing of them. After spending a good time pondering only the notes, I figured it out. Why is the writing so different with each progression?"

"Now that, I don't know. It was said you did it that way to confuse anyone else into thinking there were more authors involved. Do you not remember it that way?"

"Hemoth, I actually remember nothing of any of it."

"Perfect, then your theory was correct!"

In front of them the large curtain finally began to open. Inch by inch the curtain yielded the hidden wall to the two observers. A note written on a small piece of paper fluttered down directly to Frederick, landing on his lap.

Listen and learn! You should already know this by now. F.M.

"Hemoth, am I at it again?"

"Funny way of saying it, but yes. You are indeed at it again."

The curtain was nearly open as much as it was going to open.

Frederick stood to study the exposed wall. "Hemoth, is this it? I don't see anything worthy of the secrecy. In fact, I see nothing at all."

"You are not looking in the correct place, Frederick."

"What can you possibly be talking about now. I must admit, the riddles are becoming very annoying."

"As they should. Frederick, what you see is not a riddle. What you are seeing is what is happening. Nothing we have done has affected the big picture yet. Go over there and pull the curtains back at the edges. I'm sure you will see something then."

"What on earth are you talking about?"

"Frederick, it is bigger than the two of us. Please, just do as I say."

"Very well then." Frederick walked over to the edge of the right curtain and pulled it back slightly. As he stared at the spot on the wall, very slight colors making up very small drawings began to emerge. "Am I seeing history in the making or am I seeing the emergence of a mural painted with invisible paint?"

"Neither."

"I'm afraid I don't understand at all, Hemoth."

"Be patient and what you are looking for will appear."

Frederick stood patiently waiting as the colors ebbed into an actual scene. Suddenly he saw it. "Am I seeing the Staff of Hewitt in this corner?" His stare grew with intensity as not only the Staff, but the creatures bearing it came into focus as well. He turned to Hemoth, "Is the perspective correct here? This detail is so small! If this entire wall is to show the end results, the staff bearers have so much yet to do."

"That is correct, Frederick. We must find a way to help each one of them. How do you propose we get started?"

Frederick raced to the other open curtain and pulled it back as well. His eyes began to fill with tears as the weight of his responsibility bore down on him. He watched as another staff appeared carried by what looked to be a young lady on horseback, surrounded by hundreds of birds and one more two-legger on horseback. "Hemoth, how am I to see the upper corners?"

"Hold on just a moment please." He pressed another square area in the floor. Within a few seconds, a ladder slid toward Frederick from a side wall. "There you go."

As the time spent in the mountain fortress accumulated, Frederick became less and less surprised should anything odd happen. He took the ladder sliding toward him as merely another in a long line of occurrences he need not bother with trying to understand. He stopped the ladder at the curtain's edge and quickly climbed as high as he dared. Again, he pulled the curtain back hoping to reveal some kind of further hint of what was going on. "Hemoth, what is this wall? Is it some kind of device to see the future?"

Hemoth shook his head. "No creature can see the future. That would not be something I would like to know. It is a story wall. Anything you see there has already happened or is happening right now. The unfortunate part is you, or we, have no control of anything happening. We can't change anything you see there whether it be good or bad. Do you still wish to watch it?"

"Of course I do!" Frederick squinted his eyes. "Hemoth, more characters are appearing up here. Are they for us or against us?"

"If they are against anything, it's not us. This coming battle is not between creatures. It is about what all creatures do or do not believe."

Frederick turned away from the wall. "What? Are you trying to tell me what I saw in the basement of that barn was not a bad thing? It wasn't evil?"

"I'm sorry, what exactly did you see? If you told anyone, I was not aware of it."

Climbing slowly down the ladder while keeping his eyes on every square inch of wall passing before him, Frederick answered. "At one time, Hemoth, I was not expecting a moment when I could rationally speak of what I saw. You were not there to experience the smell, the sights or anything else my little group went through while we were there." He reached the bottom rung, held on with one hand to steady himself and continued. "I am not sure what I saw. Other than unidentified bodies laid out like cord wood, evidence of horrible endings, signs of unimaginable pain...trinkets strewn about...I really can't explain it to you. My mind fought to comprehend it then as it fights to now. I thought maybe the shock of it would wane with time, but it has not." He slid off the ladder to the floor. He slowly scooted backwards until his back pressed firmly against the wall. "What is all of this, Hemoth? What are we doing? Why am I involved? Where is this going? What did you mean when you said this battle was between what we believe?"

The wise Grizzly Bear rose to his feet and began pacing. He remained silent, trying to choose his next words carefully.

"Frederick, I have not prepared a statement for a time such as this. I suppose I could say it succinctly by telling you this, when we wrap ourselves too tightly in our own ideology, it becomes far too easy to find evil in another's good." A steady sound of plodding paws continued. "Does that make any sense to you?"

Sitting against the hard wall, Frederick studied Hemoth's words while folding both hands across his lap. "Let me think about that for a little while. Are those your words?"

"No they are not. That is only one of several verses written within these walls by others wiser than me. I could go on, but that one was the first to jump out of my memory." He paused a moment and raised his eyes to the wall. "Uh oh!"

The uncertainty in Hemoth's voice jerked Frederick to his feet. He stepped away from the wall to watch it and Hemoth's actions at the same time. Hemoth watched as the upper right corner and the lower left corner burst to life with much activity.

"Hemoth, what are we watching? What is happening? Is this a mirror of something that has already happened or events about to happen?" Frederick hopelessly tried to watch everything at once. "Well, what is it?"

The giant Grizzly Bear stood on his hind legs frantically trying to follow the action. "Yes!"

Frederick was dazed. "Yes to what?"

"Catch up here, Frederick! These actions have happened. I told you we can't see the future. If we could, you would have already written the responses we are to make at these turn of events! Yes! These happenings have already occurred and they are not good." Hemoth raised extended claws pointing to various jagged lines appearing in the wall. "These lines here..." He moved across the wall, "and here are cracks in Nuorg's defenses. I had no idea there would be so many all at once. The foundation's fabric is fraying. Come with me, quickly!"

Hemoth raced into the corridor leading down to the lower levels, down to where the irreversible gears were already turning.

"It could all be my fault, Frederick. If I can't stop the sub-tunnels from opening...Nuorg and our friends are doomed!"

***

Early morning brought out the best in Jeenay. Outside, the sun was about to rise, the quiet sounds of morning piddled about beneath the open window. She stepped to the window to catch a breath of the sweet early breeze blowing down the road now traveled by no invaders or heathen if you will. She was pleased beyond measure with the overthrow of the Rider as was every other villager.

Pewny scampered up below the window and sat silently awaiting any acknowledgement from Jeenay to bid her entrance. The night had been short, the Crow and the Osprey were now well on their return trip to wherever they had come from. It was now her job to not only keep up with the daily talk, but also keep tabs on the Eagle's healing.

Jeenay waved her up to the window. "Come on in here little Numbat. We can check on your Eagle friend together."

Pewny did not understand the greeting; however, the signal to enter was unmistakable. Jeenay was a caring two-legger and made no indications otherwise. They both peered into the small bed where the Eagle lay comfortably snug, wrapped in a soft damp cloth. Tanghi awoke after sensing the two care-givers hovering over her.

"Is it a good morning, Pewny?"

"A good morning it is, Tanghi. That is your name, correct?"

"Yes, that will do. I rather like the sound of it."

"How are you feeling?"

"Surprisingly, I feel astounding. There is not one pain this morning. Rather odd, actually."

"You don't say?"

"I had a dream last night. I dreamt something came through that very window and cried over me. The tears were not salty. They were alive. My entire body tingled as they fell upon me."

Jeenay noticed the dampness. It had not been there the night before. She looked inquisitively to Pewny, shrugging her shoulders. "Paddy, did you come in here last night after we put our patient to bed?"

From another room came the answer. "No, I did not. I did step out earlier today. I went to the keep. I had to make sure the prisoners were still awake. We don't want them getting any sleep until they start running their mouths. Why do you ask?"

"This cloth is very damp. Did it rain it the window?"

"Not that I know of. Hasn't rained in a few days now."

"It got wet somehow."

"Maybe the Eagle sweated. Was she wrapped too tightly?"

"No, never mind. Some answers don't want to be found. I'll take it this is one of them."

"Alright then."

Pewny wished furtively for a Talker about now. "Tanghi, do you have any understanding of what she is saying?"

"No, Pewny, I do not. Well, maybe a word here or there."

"I have my doubts that you were dreaming last night. Your bedding is damp. Something did drip on you. Do you not feel wet?"

Tanghi glanced around. "No, I can't feel any dampness at all. And…this cloth is much tighter than when she wrapped it around me."

Jeenay carefully reached down to remove the cloth. The wounds needed air this morning in order to properly scab over. The healing would take time. Only then would the feathers begin to grow back in.

Paddy heard what seemed to be a startled cry from his wife. He was instantly at her side staring profoundly at the Eagle. "How is that possible?"

Jeenay looked at Paddy then Pewny. Both creatures were dead-faced, staring in amazement at the very cause of Jeenay's cry. As the cloth slowly peeled away from Tanghi, vibrant, although slightly damp, gray feathers burst forth from the Eagle's head. The feathers turned a darker gray as the more of the cloth was removed. Soon, after exposing a snowy-white underside, the cloth fell loosely from two gray and white striped legs before finally giving way to two large, muscular deep yellow talons.

"I would have never imagined that for the world, Paddy."

"Dear wife, what kind of potion have you applied to this towel?"

"It wasn't anything I did, husband. It was nothing I did."

Pewny attempted to shake the amazement from her eyes. "You are quite a stunner, Tanghi. Who would have thought a few feathers would have made you so regal?"

The Eagle was confused. "Feathers? Are you saying I have my feathers back? Already?"

"Yes. I am saying exactly that. Your dream must have been more than a dream. Whatever happened here last night was real."

"I told you earlier I felt no pain, nor did I feel the dampness from the cloth. My feathers must have been insulating me from it. I feel well enough to fly, Pewny. I feel wonderful."

"Take it easy now. Your outside is well. How about your inside?"

"I will never know until I try it out."

Jeenay and Paddy watched the two creatures chatting with each other. "If that Eagle is ready to fly, we shouldn't stop her. I have a feeling she has a lot of catching up to do with her duties. I'm sure they haven't waited on her."

"I totally agree, Paddy. If she must go...I, I...I just don't understand how this transformation happened. I have never seen her in this glory. What kind of Eagle is she?"

Paddy thought for a moment, "I am thinking a Harpy. Not real sure, but I am thinking Harpy."

"I've never heard of a Harpy."

"Largest Eagle known, as I hear it."

"She is magnificent." Jeenay helped the Eagle to her feet, steadying her as she regained her balance.

Tanghi appreciated the assistance. She curtsied to her hosts, spreading her wings so wide Pewny ducked for cover. She perched on the side rail of the child's bed, softly flapping her wings, stirring a wind inside the room. She looked to Pewny. "I need to go. I have so much to do. Tell everyone I will return as soon as I can. Keep up the good fight."

Without another word Tanghi hopped to the window sill. She immediately took wing, rising regally to the clear sky.

Jeenay looked to Paddy. "Where do you suppose she's off to?"

"I have no idea, wife. She is a better bird than I am man. I would want my revenge on the Rider before I did anything."
"I think she will take care of that when she returns, if it still needs to be done. From what I hear, the Rider may not last that long."

"You may be right there."

***

She rode the high wind for most of the day. Her travels took her far across the very widest of the big water. Alone, she flew. Her endurance had yet to be tested. She had never felt so completely alive. Through the night she soared, diving on swimmers when her appetite requested. It was a long flight back to the Great Forest. She hoped she would find a welcome once she arrived. She had been a very long time gone.

***

Madaliene wrestled the two four-leggers valiantly. She needed the release. As Arlis and Vincen watched on, Lemeer made his way back to Hazzell's side, Gulli rooted around in the neighboring field and the Princess attempted to toss Bubba and Mystic around like large pillows. They played along. The grass was lush, the air cool and the sky a brilliant blue. They all laughed without a care of embarrassing themselves or a fear of laughing at another's expense. Soon, the three of them lay exhausted on their backs looking straight upward, big smiles on each face. Necessity found Vincen and Arlis doing the same. Karone came out of the sky first.

"Mystic, we have a visitor flying in. I can't be sure who it is. I flew here at first sight of it."

Both Vincen and Arlis were up in a flash. Vincen spoke up. "Do you have any idea what kind of sky-traveler we are talking about?"

"Like I said, I don't know what it is. The scouts are watching it now. Should it become hostile, what shall we do?"

"If it becomes hostile, wound it so it can't fly then bring it to us. We will be in the courtyard."

Karone was off in an instant.

Mystic looked to Vincen. "Who do you suppose it is, sir?"

"Prince, I have no idea. I only hope it is here to help and not hinder our efforts."

"Yes, sir."

Arlis offered a suggestion. "And speaking of efforts, Madaliene, have you spent enough time there on the ground? Would you like to get up and maybe tour this old place?"

The princess raised her back, propping herself on both elbows. She shook the grass and debris from her shiny golden mane. "Arlis, I believe I have. I would love to tour that old place. Of course, we will request Mystic's permission of course." She laughed.

"Why of course," said Arlis.

Vincen turned to Mystic. "Prince, will you be so kind to allow us entry?"

The Prince of the Great Forest rolled his eyes. "Sir, you know I only stay in the guard dwelling up front. I don't have a clue how to gain entrance to the main dwelling. Won't it be locked or something?"

"Do tell, maybe we should consult Bubanche. He seems to know his way around in there fairly well. What have you got to say there, Bubba?"

The young Cheetah grinned, "I usually jump through the side window over there. It's never completely closed."

"Madaliene, I suggest you follow this Cheetah through that window and unlock the doors so we can enter correctly. We don't want to gain entry like a gang of hooligans, now do we?"

As Madaliene pursed her lips, her forehead crinkled. She threw a glance at the front windows. "Bubba, how high am I to jump?"

"Princess, you may be climbing to the window."

"Hmmph, that sounds doable. Let's get to it. I can't wait to see what is in there!"

Bubba led the way as the party returned to the front of the expansive dwelling. Behind the guard dwelling was a heavy gate no one had opened in recent memory. The latch was ornate and well-crafted. Madaliene easily manipulated the opening mechanism. With no fanfare, she slowly pushed the gate open. To the surprise of those gathered, there was not a squeak emitted from the hinges as the gate opened wide to its stop. The wide, stone paved walkway beckoned them to the main entrance where a series of tall, round columns awaited their arrival, perched on square, dark granite bases. The elegantly built front door dwarfed them as they approached. Madaliene could not help but notice the regal style with which the dwelling was built. From the spot they were standing, the dwelling looked smaller than it actually was.

Madaliene lightly took hold of the dull metal handle. "Vincen, can I try the front door first before I have to climb in the window?"

"I can see no reason you shouldn't, Princess."

She looked at Mystic, "What do you say, Prince?"

"By all means, be my guest."

Madaliene hesitated for an instant then pushed the handle down. Like the gate latch, it worked flawlessly. The door gave a slight shudder as she pushed it open. In what was to become a story passed down for the ages, the dwelling came alive in front of her. Dull, listless metal objects transitioned into brilliant pieces of craftsmanship. The colors on the walls returned to their original rich hues. Dust was blown out windows that opened on no command. Rugs that had lain unused for years suddenly looked as they had just been woven from the finest wools available. Chairs, couches, tables, everything in the dwelling became as new. The living spaces erupted with welcome.

Bubba pounced ahead of Madaliene. "This is exactly what I expected!"

Madaliene was mesmerized by the transformation. “This place is mind-boggling.”

Bubba bounced around madly. “Princess, follow me! There is much to see!”

Madaliene slowly turned completely around several times as she tried to take it all in. “Give me a moment, Bubba. Vincen, am I dreaming this? Mystic, steady me, I feel a swoon approaching.”

Vincen cocked his head. “A swoon? Really? We are past that sort of thing, Princess. Take charge here. This place was obviously built for you.”

Madaliene attempted to respond. “What? What makes you say such a thing, Vincen? This place was built for royalty. Am I…am I truly that royal?”

Vincen nodded his head. “Yes, I think you truly are. If I am correct, and I usually am, the outside of this dwelling now looks as magnificent as the inside.”

Gulli trotted into the room, stopping as he bumped into Madaliene’s side. “Excuse me, Princess. I wish you could have seen what happened to the outside of this place when you walked through the door. It was as if something just brought it back to life. It’s not the same as when we arrived here and that’s the honest truth.” He joined the others in admiring the interior. “Wow! Who lived here?”

“No one has ever lived here that I can remember. I don’t know any stories of this ever being lived in.”

“What was that?” Madaliene quickly barged in. “What do you mean, Vincen? Surely, someone had to live here at one point. If not, who built it and why?” She walked away, not waiting for an answer.

Through the front room and to the left sat a large drawing room. Directly across the entryway was a room big enough to comfortably accommodate one hundred people. Madaliene walked slowly, her booted feet silently carrying her from room to room. Behind her trailed Mystic, Bubba and Gulli. Vincen stood on the Tusker’s high shoulder. They walked without comment. A fireplace sat majestically in every room with bulky, yet graceful hearths, mantels and chimneys accompanying them. Picture frames without pictures were hung sparingly throughout the palace, waiting for images to fill the now blank canvases. They followed the main hall to the end of the house where a wide staircase invited them to explore the upper floors. Before they made it up the first flight of stairs, a commotion near the front entrance sent the entire party running back to where they came.

Karone was arguing with one of his scouts about the visiting sky-traveler.

"I'm telling you it can't be her. There is no way she would simply show up after all of these years away. Surely you are mistaken!"

A smaller sky-traveler stood defiantly shaking his head back and forth. "I'm telling you it is her! She identified herself and asked that she be allowed to enter even though she also thought she did not need to ask, since she was originally from here anyway!"

"Oh, that is preposterous. Did you make her mad? Is she angry?"

"Not yet, but I can!"

"You won't!"

"Both of you settle down!" Arlis flew right between them. "Follow me. Now. Both of you!"

Madaliene nudged Vincen, "I wonder what that is about?"

'Princess, it seems we have a visitor that has not convinced Karone of their intentions or identification. No need to worry, Arlis will get to the bottom of it."

They watched as Arlis flew out with Karone and the scout to Mystic's dwelling.

***

"Karone, who does she say she is?"

"Arlis, the visitor introduced herself as Mustanghia. She purports to be one of the Great Eagles. Is there a Great Eagle with that name?"

"Oh my." Arlis looked away. "Mustanghia? Are you absolutely sure?"

"Yes, Arlis, I am sure. She was quite adamant." The scout was hoping this would be resolved quickly before the visitor became angry with her escorts. "She is the largest Eagle I have ever seen."

Arlis furrowed the feathers on her crown. "Yes...yes, if it is Mustanghia, she will be a large Eagle and at times, a very mean one. I don't know what Vincen ever saw in her."

Karone jerked his head back. "Excuse me?"

"It's a long story. We have to treat this very carefully or firstly, she will kill all of you and secondly, if she doesn't...Vincen might."

Karone and the scout began to shake nervously.

"Oh, both of you stop that! She's not angry yet!"

Those words did nothing to quell the scouts' fear. A large shadow appeared, swooping down with a silent beat of her wings.

The scout cried. "It's her! We're done for."

Mustanghia landed softly at Arlis' side. "It's good to see you, Arlis. I assume you are telling these young ones terrible stories about me?"

Arlis stared directly into the Eagle's eyes. "After all of these years? Are you serious? You've finally come back? For how long this time? You know how Vincen feels about you. Are you trying to rip his emotions to threads? He had long ago given you up for dead." She stomped around cawing angrily. "How do you think he is going to react to seeing you now?"

"Arlis, this is not about me and Vincen. I'm sure he will be...alright with it...eventually."

"Eventually? Eventually? There you go again. Can you not tell me what needs to happen? I'll tell him the visitor decided not to stay."

Mustanghia hung her head. "Arlis, I know I hurt Vincen. I was young. I wanted more of a life than I could get here. You know that. I have matured a lot since then."

"Young? You were older than I am now, and I'm old! What do you want?"

"Arlis, bad times are upon us."

"Wow! That's it? Can you be a little more precise?"

"Why do you have to be so difficult, you old Crow?"

"You remember Mystic, don't you?"

"Yes, I do, thank you. He was just a pup when I left the last time."

"And by that, I guess you mean the last time you were here but failed to tell Vincen?"

"Yes...yes...whatever. Go on!"

"Mystic, Bubanche and Lightning have just returned from a place called Nuorg with the same news."

Mustanghia nodded. "And...?"

"It seems Mystic's wand/staff is the Staff of Hewitt that those bad times are searching for."

"They went to Nuorg and returned? Why...why would they want to return from there? No one ever wants to return after they go there."

Gulli rounded the side of the dwelling. "Uh, if you don't mind…Vincen and Mystic are getting a little antsy. Can you birds wrap this up?"

Mustanghia spread her wings to defend the three smaller sky-travelers.

"Whoa!" Gulli backed off a little. "Calm down there, Harpy. I'm one of the good leggers, contrary to what you might have heard."

"Arlis," Mustanghia demanded, "Is he one of us?"

"Yes, he is. Mustanghia, this is Gullinbursti, a Tusker from far off."

Mustanghia did not relax. "I know he is a Tusker and I am not fond of Tuskers. They can be extremely problematic."

Gulli lowered down on one knee. "Madame Harpy, I apologize for the actions of my kind. Please understand I am not like most of them. I have a conscious. My conscious has caused me to forsake my fellow Tuskers. I joined the good side. I am terribly sorry for anything we have done to you."

Mustanghia lowered her wings. "You have been heard, Tusker. If you attempt to harm one feather or hair or whatever on any of the creatures in the Great Forest, I will personally make you regret the day your mother sow birthed you. Is that understood?"

"Yes." Gulli rose to his feet. "I will protect these creatures to my death."

"Very well. I will trust you until you give me reason to think otherwise. Now, please return and tell those that sent you it will be just a little longer."

"I will do as you ask."

"Oh, Gullinbursti, don't tell them about me yet. Arlis will take care of that."

Gulli made his way back to Vincen and Mystic. True to his word, he gave no hint of the visitor's identity.

"Arlis, you were saying?"

"No, Mustanghia, you were asking why they came back from Nuorg. Why wouldn't they?"

Mustanghia folded her wings. "How can I say this and not sound crazy?"

"Tanghi, nothing you can tell us about Nuorg will be any crazier than what we have already heard."

"Well, since you put it that way I'd rather tell everyone at once. We better call a meeting together. Can you please tell Vincen I am here?"

"No need for that, Mustanghia." Mystic walked around the corner with Vincen perched on his shoulder. "It has been a long time."

***

A meeting was immediately called. In due time, Mystic's back garden overflowed with Great Forest inhabitants. Arlis, Vincen, Mystic and Mustanghia stood side-by-side in front of the crowd. Arlis gave a welcome and briefing as Mustanghia readied herself to speak. Whispers mingled through the crowd as the younger ones asked the older ones about the strange Eagle. Several questions were not answered because many of the older inhabitants had never seen Mustanghia. Rumors were passed through the crowd, but none were malicious in any way. The listeners grew quiet as Vincen spoke to them.

"You all have heard, in one way or another, what is upon us. We have already fought one battle for our home and do not fool yourself, for as certainly as I stand before you, more will follow. We were fortunate not to lose any of you thanks solely to Princess Madaliene, whom some haven't met yet, and the water brought back from Nuorg by Prince Mystic and his fellow adventurers."

"Today we have yet another individual for you to hear from. She has come to us from several thousand pursuit beats away and I must think, in some way, her absence is what destiny wanted…for today she is back with news we all should hear. I have not heard anything she will be saying, so I am as anxious to hear what she has to say as you are. Mustanghia, if you will, please speak to us."

The hush stayed over the crowd as Vincen gave his position to Mustanghia. Several listeners pushed closer to hear every coming word. Madaliene, Bubba and Gulli were part of the closest group.

"Old friends and new friends, it is good to see you again. I have been gone a long time and some of you are new faces to my eyes and some of your faces are as comforting as my many fond memories of living here. The reasons are many why I have been gone and I apologize for any inconvenience that may have caused. When I left, Mystic's father was in charge. That was years before the Killing occurred. Mystic was not even born."

"One face I see here has no idea what she is in for." Mustanghia looked directly at Princess Madaliene. "Princess, I know about you. I know about your sister, Evaliene. I have been Ev's messenger since you two were separated. Up until recently, all of the letters she wrote were delivered by me until the Rider and his men came to our village. I was captured and Evaliene was forced to write letters and cryptic messages to you and several others, in order to flush you out of hiding. I realize there are only the two of you, but your support network is vast."

"I was taken prisoner many, many day-rounds ago by the Rider. I was kept imprisoned in a bag for un-numbered nights on end in order to break my spirit. It was hoped that torturing me would give up your location and that of the staff you are meant to wield. "For you see, your sister is only the bearer of the staff, she cannot wield it." Mustanghia smiled. "She has quite a temper and has tried on a few occasions, but the staff has refused to show itself completely. It was my job to protect Evaliene and I did until I was captured. She is now, I pray, with her trusted Rhiannon, a magnificent white Horse and Rhiannon's mate Broanick. They will be headed for the second fortress. We must return you to your fortress at once. It is only there where you will be safe."

Mustanghia relaxed to gather her strength again. The crowd remained silent. Vincen walked to her side. Madaliene fought to keep her tears from streaming down her face. Bubba and Mystic looked at each other with blank stares. The others bowed their heads.

"Tanghi, can you continue?"

"Yes I can, Vincen. Give me another moment."

"Absolutely." He turned to Arlis. "Will you get Tanghi something to eat, please?"

Arlis nodded her head and flew off.

"Vincen, I'm ready to continue."

"Very well, then. Arlis will bring you something right away."

"Thank you." She locked eyes with Mystic, then Bubba. "Prince Mystic, I hear you have been to Nuorg and back. You must answer one question for me."

Mystic nodded.

"Why did you return? Most creatures there are not given the chance to come back. You are one of the chosen ones, but when your time comes...there is normally no option."

"What are you saying exactly, Mustanghia?"

"Mystic, Nuorg is the first station of Blisomne."

The hush of the crowd grew more intense. None of the gathered even breathed.

"Blisomne? Is that not where the ainjils gather?"

Mustanghia bowed her head. "Yes it is. Nuorg is where the ainjils transition."

"Wait, Mustanghia." Madaliene moved on closer. "I have been to Nuorg and I was also sent back... Bubba too!"

Bubba spoke up. "And Lightning. He was there with us... as was Frederick."

Mustanghia bowed a full bow in front of them. "Princess, you have no idea then what this means?"

Madaliene was crying. "No ma'am... I... I don't."

Mustanghia raised her head. "Princess, you are indeed chosen. The ainjils did not want you. You have a higher calling than even them. Have you seen ghosts in your travels?"

Madaliene slowly shook her head up and down. "Yes, I have. We saw the same ones twice. I was given a note from them. I gave it to Frederick the last time I was in my fortress."

Mustanghia breathed a heavy sigh of relief. "That's good, child. We must get you home before you can move in to your new dwelling."

"My new dwelling?" Madaliene held her hands up to Vincen. "What new dwelling?"

All eyes gradually turned to focus on the main dwelling behind them. Mustanghia's eyes led Madaliene's.

"That is your castle, Princess. It was built long ago by the guild. The fortresses will be closed up during the last battle, the mountains sealed, the ainjils will complete their task and move on, the yellow ball will explode and Nuorg will be swallowed up by a never-ending fire."

Madaliene cried and shook her head is anguish. "No! That can't be true. The inhabitants of Nuorg don't deserve that!"

"Did you not hear me, child? All of the Nuorgians will move on. Their work will be done on this earth."

"Are you telling me that none of them will die?"

"No, that is not what I am telling you. You can't bother with that now."

Vincen stood by without uttering a sound. In his head, his thoughts were racing back through time and every story he had ever heard. It was all making sense to him now.

Mystic nudged Bubba. "We need to get her out of here. She can't be safe here."

"I agree. Let's get on with it!"

Mystic stepped between Madaliene and Mustanghia. "We will make plans to move the princess from here immediately. Gather our party. We will leave when you give the word."

Mustanghia addressed the crowd again. "Dwellers of the Great Forest, your time has come. Go to your dwellings and prepare for the worst. I am hoping the battles will center more toward the fortresses, but there is no guarantee of that. Be prepared for anything." She flew to Madaliene's shoulder. "Princess, take me into your castle. Vincen, Bubba, Mystic come with us. Leave someone here to tell Arlis where we are. She needs to be with us."

Arlis flew in just as Mustanghia spoke her name. "I heard you, Tanghi. I'm right behind you."

Madaliene slapped Gulli on his snout. "You are coming to, Tusker. This is what you signed up for... correct?"

"Princess, I guess it is now!"

26

Oliviia pushed Bongi hard back to the cave where her parents had lost their fight. Lightning and Hugoth kept pace as well as the two remaining big Cats, Cirrus and Duister. Karri had returned after locating Stewig, so she and Perrie circled between the leggers and the cave watching for any hint of trouble.

***

Inside the cave, the crack was opening again. Every now and again, the ground would vibrate and the partially sealed crack would slightly open. Much prying, yelling and scraping could be heard from the other side, wherever the other side was.

***

Near the entrance to the cave, two Storks hid beneath minimal coverage, their long spindly legs quivering from a combination of fear and nervousness.

***

"Perrie, right there in those low branches, I think we may find our prey. I haven't made an obvious dive on them in case they are waiting to meet someone."

"I saw them too, Karri. Two sets of very thin trees?"

"Exactly. We need to alert the others."

The pair of wingers headed back toward the others. They were able to slow the thundering herd of leggers near the halfway point.

"Hugoth!" Karri dove to the Grizzly's thick neck. "Stop here. We have found the Storks."

It took some distance and lots of energy to completely stop the heavy animals. Dust floated away on a light breeze as several sets of weighty hooves and paws became still.

The two big Cats stopped much faster than the heavier animals and were already discussing the next move. Cirrus trotted to Hugoth's side. "What did you find Karri?"

"Cirrus, the Storks are near the entrance, not in the cave. I'm sure…"

Oliviia interrupted Karri's thought. "I'm sorry for speaking here. If I am over-stepping my bounds, please tell me."

"No, Livvy, what do you have to say?" Cirrus could be very motherly.

"The Storks aren't in the cave because they can't get in. They have no means to move the stone and activate the mechanism. What that tells me is…"

Perrie finished Oliviia's thought. "They are expecting someone. They were supposed to open the cave to let whoever is in the cave out. Is there a way we can permanently seal it up? Is there another way out of it?"

"No," Oliviia answered. "There is no other way out of that cave except for the crack we were trying to seal."

Cirrus stared up the path. "The Storks are a ruse. Let me take care of them. I'll get some answers!" She called to Duister, "Follow me. The rest of you…" She looked at the anxious faces gathered around her. "Very well, everyone follow me, but try and keep up." She was off with Duister at her side and the others struggling to get up to speed.

***

Jahnise needed to find Stewig and Donkhorse immediately. The walk brought ideas to mind. He had a plan that would deviate from any other plan being formulated. He must leave Kirch and his Burg One dwellers to their own ends. If he succeeded, the other plans would not be necessary. It would however endanger the lives of two more brave leggers.

The Burg was, without question, alive at every turn with conversation and activity. The Burg One dwellers seamlessly joined tasks with Burg Seven dwellers as if Burg blending was a common occurrence. Kirch and his companions re-wrote old defensive plans. Every Nuorgian was given a task to perform and accepted it without question.

As Jahnise waded through the crowds, he asked of Stewig's whereabouts and if anyone had seen Donkhorse recently. Everyone was so consumed with their own duties they had failed to notice either of the large four-leggers. Jahnise kept his eyes roving with every long stride he took.

From behind a regular-looking dwelling, a clattering sound made its way to the clearing. Jahnise laughed before running to intercept it. "Oh, what do we have here, friends?"

Stewig was outfitted with layers of wooden armor and attached to a wagon sitting on wide, heavy wheels. More thick wood had been erected to form a protective shield around the driver. Hitched along side of Stewig was a taller four-legger, completely unrecognizable at first glance. Jahnise stepped up to the legger's flank to have a closer inspection.

"Donkhorse, is that you?"

A muted answer was barely heard.

"Ha-ha, if that is you in there Donkhorse, please twitch one of your long ears for me."

Stewig tried not to laugh. "It is he, King. I've heard a wet Cat that wasn't as mad as our friend Donkhorse is right now. He is not taking a liking to his role."

Jahnise stepped back as Donkhorse kicked and stomped at anything that approached him.

"Please be patient, friend. There is no time to question one's duties. I have been searching for both of you. It looks to me as someone has already seen my thoughts. Stewig, was this your idea?"

"No, King, it was his."

"Then, tell me why he is so angry."

"I think it is because we can't hear him. You know how he likes to talk."

Donkhorse erupted with whinnies, brays, stomps and more kicks.

"Take it easy, friend." Jahnise pulled a few pieces of wood from the barrier across Donkhorse's face. "Is that better?"

"Thank you, King! When this is over, I will have several words with our friend Stewig. He seems to think those horns are enough protection for him. He had them build a dwelling around my entire head!"

"I hope there will be time for those words, Donkhorse, and I hope we live to hear them. Why you were hitched to this wagon is not for me to question, but it fits my plan perfectly. I want you both to take me to every Burg in this land as fast as you can. I will ride in the wagon. You will stop for nothing. At the gate to each Burg, you must allow me time to get out and exercise the power of my staff. If there are any lingering creatures with ill will towards us, I must rid Nuorg of them immediately."

Neither Stewig nor Donkhorse questioned anything Jahnise told them. Without further conversation, Jahnise climbed aboard. The mismatched draft team needed no urging. They were off as soon as they felt the King settle in, racing unimpeded to the gate.

"Lower the gate!" Stewig shouted as they neared the gate trees.

The gate lowered, the wagon barely slowed as it was pulled through the entrance and down the ramps, heading for the nearest Burg.

Stewing swung his massive head around his shoulder, shouting to the temporary gatekeepers. "Raise the gate! Lower it only if you see me again!"

The pair of four-leggers pulled the wagon effortlessly. They made swift work of the distances. At each stop, Jahnise said a short prayer then let his staff do its work. Burg Three was the only Burg Jahnise's stick found free of evil elements. It was the only Burg Ian and Colleen found pure and free of cracks.

***

Cirrus had not needed to stalk prey for most of her life. Her lack of experience did not hamper her in the least as she and Duister came upon the Storks. The poor wingers had nowhere to turn, run or fly when the Tigers pounced on them. The struggle was minimal at best. There was no reason for it. The Tigers were simply the superior creatures. The Storks were initially relieved not to be eaten. That feeling would change when the little Falcon arrived to get the answers to many pertinent and unanswered questions.

Hugoth and Lightning arrived once the Storks were subdued, followed by a heavily breathing Bongi carrying a very irritated Oliviia. She jumped from his back.

"Bongi, thanks for the ride. Please rush back to handle the matters we have discussed. We will be fine here."

He obliged her. “Give me a short rest first. If anything happens to you, Livvy, I will find it troubling for the rest of my life.”

She slapped his shoulder. “Go!”

Bongi turned and trotted away.

“Cirrus?” Oliviia demanded, “Where are the worthless pieces of feathers and bones? If you haven’t broken their ridiculous legs by now, move out of my way!”

Cirrus looked to Hugoth as she and Duister shielded the Storks from view.

Hugoth took the cue. “Hold on, Oliviia. We need to get some answers first. We can’t hurt them beyond the point of talking.”

When Oliviia approached, Hugoth wrapped his massive arm around her and lifted her off the ground. She kicked and screamed at the Storks while dangling a few feet off the ground.

“Hugoth, maybe you should take her away from here until she settles down. You and Lightning take her and destroy the entry device. This cave does not need to be opened again…ever.”

Hugoth nodded his assent. “Very good idea, Cirrus. Will you question them?”

“Hugoth, from what Karri has told me, the little Falcon will get all of the answers we need.”

“Perrie?”

“Yes. Go, you have work to do.”

Karri was animatedly chatting with Perrie in a tree high above.

“You told me yourself you were a meat-eater.”

“But here? In Nuorg? Sure, I’d like a good meal right now, but those Storks aren’t what I had in mind.”

“Perrie, I don’t want you to eat them! I just want you to act like you want to eat them. I’ve seen you work, young one, and I am not sure I want to know everything you have been taught. However, I am giving you permission to use any methods you deem necessary to get answers from that pair. Do you understand me?”

“Yes, ma’am, I do.”

“Perrie, I know Eekay is ear deep in this and she got away cleanly before all of this started. She got out while she could. I think she is up above running around without a care in her world and these Storks know it. Find out everything! Is that clear? Everything!”

“Yes, Karri, I will. Whatever it takes…right?” She looked intently into Karri’s eyes.

"Yes, Perrie, whatever it takes."

Without another word the wingers swooped to Cirrus, landing between the two Tigers.

"Cirrus, Duister, we will take it from here. Please give us some room." Karri continued, her eyes focusing on the Storks, "This could get ugly. Perrie, do what you were trained to do."

Perrie violently spread her wings, a piercing cry wailed from her beak. She attacked the first Stork with talons sharpened to kill and maim, ripping feathers from its wings and back. The Stork fell to the ground with no chance of defending itself. The second Stork backed up into Duister's shoulder, terrified. Perrie began to pull dirty-white wing feathers out with her beak while clamping the Stork's long beak shut with her strong talons.

"Who sent you down here? Was it the Lioness? I am not like these other creatures in Nuorg. Where I am from, we eat meat. Do you want to answer my questions or get eaten?" Perrie yanked another feather from the Storks wing. "I'm running out of feathers. You will be losing flesh soon." Another feather floated to the ground.

The second Stork lunged away from Duister directly at Perrie, its long, pointed beak honing in on a vulnerable spot beneath a wing. The move surprised the Tigers as they helplessly looked on.

Karri was not surprised or amused. She flew into the Stork's side, knocking it off course. "Cirrus, detain that one!"

In the blink of an eye, Cirrus pinned the Stork to the ground with one paw and one terrifyingly low growl.

The trapped Stork yelled at the crowd. "Why did you pick the wrong one? He knows nothing. We only did what we were told!"

Karri was on him in a flash. "Then why are you in such a hurry to shut him up?"

"What?" asked Duister.

"He wasn't aiming to spear Perrie," Karri explained, "He was aiming for his partner. If he silenced him, then their secrets would be safe. He was hoping to end that poor winger's life and in doing so, lose his own to one of us."

Perrie was unfazed. She stared with emotionless eyes into the horrified eyes of her quarry. "I need answers. Don't tell me you haven't any, because your friend over there was ready to kill you to keep you silent."

The de-feathered Stork was trembling with good reason. "Yes, Eekay sent us. She has been sending us messages since she got here. She came through the window and sent us here with the story we told you."

Perrie continued the interrogation. "How involved is she?"

"She knows everything. She followed that family around, taking notes of her own and asking question after question. They were foolishly trusting of her. She knows where every crack is located and the approximate opening time. Nuorg, as you know it, is over."

"How can we stop her?"

"You can't only stop her. She is just one of several spies here. We followed the King before he passed over. We tried to get in behind him, but missed the opening. When Eekay didn't see us, she had to come up and she was not happy."

Oliviia stood close by, listening to every word. Words cannot express the rage and betrayal she was feeling. Several times, she willed herself quiet. At other times, she bit into her sleeves in hopes of temporarily quelling her feelings.

Perrie wanted more of an answer. "Go on."

"One army is coming through this cave, another through Burg One... It's no use, you can never keep them out."

Hugoth and Lighting walked up.

"Are you getting any answers, Karri?" Hugoth surveyed the damage. He also noticed a tiny drop of blood dripping from Perrie's beak. "Is that necessary?"

"I'm afraid it is, Hugoth. From what this one is saying, we are in serious trouble."

"Was Eekay involved?"

"More than you want to know."

Hugoth stepped nearer the Falcon and her captive. "Perrie, are you okay?"

"Hugoth, I was until I heard this one's answers. We have some problems."

"Well, the good news is no invaders will be coming through this cave. It's closed forever." He stepped back. "Do what you have to do."

Hugoth looked as if the very being of Nuorg was crushing down on his strong shoulders. Lightning stood close at his side.

Oliviia put her arms lovingly around his neck. "Hugoth, we need my father's book. We will have to set our defenses up according to his discoveries."

Hugoth agreed. "Cirrus, find out what you can from these two and then, if they are still breathing, drown them in the river. I must hurry back now this is dealt with."

Cirrus managed a grin. "I can read between the lines, Hugoth. Thank you. Perrie, that's quite enough. You can let that one go."

"Are you sure?"

"Yes, quite sure. Duister, grab that one. We are about to get wet."

Perrie released her grip on the battered Stork as Duister instantly clamped his jaws around its de-feathered mid-section. As the Tigers trotted off, Perrie looked to Karri for her own answers. "And what are you going to tell me now?"

"Maybe later, Perrie. Not now. Not now. Livvy, we need to get your hands on your father's book."

Oliviia nodded, "I agree, Karri. Lightning, you are with us now."

"Where we going, ma'am?"

"Let us catch up with Hugoth first. Then, I want to know more about that big, axey thing of yours."

27

Tofur fastened the last hook on the garments Mariel had given him. "Mariel, do I need to put my other clothes over these?"

"By all means, lad. We don't want to draw suspicion from unfriendly eyes, do we?"

Tofur was a bit perplexed. "But, sir, Porcene is dressed in the most regal armor I have ever laid eyes on. Jak is armored up. Belle looks like a miniature, tailless Porcene. Those helmets you have for my Falcons say nearly as much as a full suit or armor. You and I will stand out for our lack of protection."

"Let me handle that part, lad. What of our prisoner? Do we need to take him with us? Can we not question him then bury the evil creature?"

The sky was turning darker as hordes of birds circled above. There were flocks of birds several layers thick, each level a different type.

"Sir, what type of birds are we dealing with up there?"

Mariel was silent for a moment, pondering the sky. "To be honest, I hadn't noticed them yet."

"What? How could you have not noticed?"

"I have a one-track mind, lad. No lack of focus on the here and now. They are not attacking us, are they?"

"No, not yet anyway. But, that scenario does bother me."

"Enough of that talk. Let us be on our way. Jak, forward ho."

Jak snorted. "Forward ho? Are you kidding me?"

Porcene laughed at them both. "What's the matter, handsome? You got a problem with forward ho?"

Jak didn't answer her.

Before they could move a few steps, the ground became littered with landing birds.

Tofur pulled Porcene's reigns hard. "Whoa there!" He shouted to those around him. "What is happening now?"

The ground became as dark as the sky. A middle-sized winger stepped in front of Porcene.

"I take it, Horse, that you are in charge here?"

In order protect the others, Porcene answered affirmatively. "Yes. I am in charge here. What business is it of yours, Crow?"

The Crow did not budge. “What are you called, Horse?”

“Who is asking?”

“We can play these games well into the night if it amuses you. I have to know.”

“I am Willing and this is my Mule, Able. We can do anything we want.”

“Cute. I sense a hilarious sense of humor between you both. Who are you and you are your riders?”

Tofur spoke up. “I am Tofur Polinetti. I am a Falconer from the south. What is it to you and yours?”

The adamant Crow continued showing no emotion. “If you are a Falconer, where is your cast? Where is your gauntlet? Are they strangely absent or are you telling a falsehood?”

“I assure you I am telling the truth. My cast is coming back from the west as I speak to you. I warn you, they can be very protective when need be.”

The Crow whispered to a few of her like. They took wing heading west.

“I have sent my seconds to verify your story.” Hundreds of Crows moved closer to Tofur’s group. “Until then, tell me more of you. Do you carry any particular items?”

“What to you mean?” Tofur answered.

“I mean, do you have the staff with you?”

“What staff? What are you talking about?”

“Do you have an odd-shaped, ornamented stick or article with you?”

“I have no idea what you are talking about. Can you be more specific?”

“No.”

“Well then, let us pass. I’m sure there is not much you can do to stop us anyway, except get trampled on. Do you have a wish to get trampled?”

“Of course I don’t. That is a foolish thing to say.”

“Well, it’s your lucky day. My cast is on the horizon and I do believe they are clutching your seconds in their talons.”

The Crow spun around, horrified at what she might see. She quickly jerked her head back to Tofur. “Those two better be unharmed when your cast arrives or else I will have them plucked!”

Taytay and Whistler came in fast. Their cargo was miraculously unharmed and thankful for it. The Falcons set the two Crows on the ground near their leader then lit on Porcene's back in front of Tofur.

"Are either of you hurt in any way?" the Crow shouted.

One of them meekly answered. "Only our pride. You should warn us of potential dangers before you send us out from now on. Those two saw us coming, knew we were looking for them and grabbed us before we realized what had happened."

"It happened so fast, we had no time to be afraid!" The other second was more impressed with the Falcons' skill than his preceding predicament. "Mother, they are very good, just as we were told."

"You are not hurt? Not at all? I could not live with myself if they had killed you."

"Mother, we are fine. Go ahead, tell them what is going on."

The Crow looked at each one of Tofur's group, individually sizing them up. "My name is Absaroka. I am from the Great Forest. The legions you see about you are from all over the world. We went into hiding once the attacks begin to take place. For some reason we were overlooked while all of the birds of prey or fast flyers were decimated in forests everywhere. I was sent first to find Princess Evaliene and her party. Once I found them, I was sent to find you by Pandion, an Osprey from the shores. My cousin Corvus and the Osprey are searching for Princess Evaliene's messenger, who left the Great Forest long before I was born. It was told to that she is a member of an ancient guild of protectorates. While our mission has developed, we have gathered information which led us on a journey to find the Falcon master. We were told he would be traveling in a non-descript manner." Absaroka looked at Tofur. "Youngster, are you who we search for?"

Tofur was surprised. "You were led to believe that I am the Falcon master? Who told you that?"

"If I may be so direct, you have been shadowed by a very large sky-traveler, supposedly for some time now. He watches you from far higher than any of us can fly. He visited our flocks one evening after we passed the second line of mountains. He spoke of others like himself who are watching three groups such as yours."

Mariel climbed off Jak's back. Walking among the horde of Crows, he began to speak. "Tofur, you are the Falcon master she is speaking of. Porcene and I were sent to find you as well. The two men we are following are of major significance to your success. They must be stopped. I am not the bumbling crazy man as I led you to believe, nor am I the doctor or the inventor…I am all three. My name is indeed Mariel Fraunchesca. Your Rottweiler there is a descendent from the protectorate Absaroka speaks of."

Tofur looked down to Belle. "Is this true?"

"Yes, Tofur, is it true. Your entire life has been lived for this destiny. I was born to protect you to my death. My sons were to carry my task on if I was not able to see it through. As we know, that can no longer happen. I am afraid that if I can't see this through until the end, my life will have been for nothing."

Porcene huffed at the pessimism. "That is nonsense, Belle. You are doing everything you can. Do not speak again of failure. Our mission cannot fail."

Tofur cut his eyes to Jak. "Am I to believe you are not involved in what is going on here?"

Jak shook his long head and twitched his ears. "Master, I assure you I know nothing of this. Never have. Have I, Belle?"

Belle agreed. "That is true, Jak has no idea what is going on."

Jak recoiled. "You think you could have phrased that a little differently? Maybe?"

Belle laughed. "Maybe I could have, but I didn't."

Tofur looked to his Falcons. "And I suppose you two are innocent as well?"

They looked at each other with perplexing glances. "Well," Taytay began, "If we are spilling all of the beans right now, then…"

Whistler picked up, "Our great, great, great, great-grandfather…" His eyes rolled about in his head as he bobbed his head with each great and looked to Taytay for help. "That is correct, isn't it?"

"Yes, I think so."

"He was also a member of this same protectorate guild they speak of. His name is Sigourne. He was designated to mentor and protect the wielder of staff number two, the Staff of O'shay. You are the bearer of staff number three, the staff of…"

"Polinetti." Tofur turned white as blood drained from his head. "Where is this staff? I have never had a staff."

Belle corrected him softly. "Yes you have. It's the whistle."

Tofur disbelievingly shook his head. "It can't be! This?" He pulled the whistle from his pocket. "This is a staff?"

Mariel reached up and placed a strong hand on the young man's arm. "Yes, lad, that you are holding is the staff of Polinetti. I was sure of it when I cleaned it for you. There is no question about it."

"It can't be! All it is good for is…it…I just use it with Taytay and Whistler."

Mariel smiled up at him. "You also thought it changed my personalities, lad. Remember? Two blasts called the crazy me, three blasts called the inventor and so on? I know you believed that."

Tofur held the whistle in front of his face. "Yes, we all believed it did that. But one blast changes you into Leiram. Who is he?"

"Lad, Leiram is a part of me, but I am not him. I mean... it is very complicated. I am an ainjil. Leiram is who I will be when I completely passage through. One blast does indeed call him although I do not know him. What is he like?"

Tofur felt disoriented. "You don't know him? Passage through? What is an ainjil?"

Mariel patted Tofur's back. "It will all be known in time, lad. Let's take care of one thing at a time, shall we?"

Absaroka and her flocks stood quietly by as the conversation progressed. The sun was once again sinking to the west when it became obliterated by an approaching flock of wingers intently chasing a flitting and darting trio of Crows.

Absaroka cawed an order to her followers. "Protect them at all costs!"

The thousands of Crows shot skyward, surrounding the trio heading their way, confusing the pursuing mass of wingers. Absaroka flew directly for the lead winger of the trio. She called to her and they flew an arrow's course down to Porcene and Tofur amid the mass of beating wings. Several larger wingers chased her before they were shredded by the beaks and talons of hundreds of brave Crows.

Absaroka and her charges lit on Porcene's armored neck. Mariel rushed to their side and shouted. "What is happening?"

She shouted to him over the thunderous din of beating wings. "We have to protect these three! They are my spies. They know what lies ahead of us. Obviously they got too close for our good. Please do something!"

Mariel shook Tofur's arm. "One blast, lad. Blow one blast! Quickly!"

Tofur was now dazed. "One blast? Now?"

"Yes! For all of our sakes, yes!"

Tofur fumbled with the whistle while overhead one-on-one battles were being fought between Crow and attacker. The ground was growing thickly littered with winger carcasses of several varieties.

Mariel grabbed the whistle and forced it in between Tofur's clenched lips. "One blast, lad! One blast!"

Tofur blew the whistle hard. The blast spread across the ground like a shock wave. Mariel was transformed again. Without needing to take in everything around him, Leiram threw the front flap of his overcoat behind him and with one deft movement drew out a small sword hidden between many layers of clothing. He grabbed Tofur's hand, pried open the fingers then slapped the sword's handle into the newly exposed palm.

Tofur held the sword lightly, rolling it back and forth. He noticed a hollowed out void in the handle's side. Not having to think, he pressed his whistle into it. A precise clicking sound resulted. He looked back to Leiram. "Now what?"

"Hold it aloft, lad! Hold it aloft!" Leiram shouted.

"Is that all I do?"

"No, grab the blade!"

"The blade?"

"Yes, grab the blade!"

Under the cacophony of beating wings, Tofur responded with hesitation. "Is it sharp?"

"Yes," Leiram shouted. "It is very sharp!"

Tofur's eyes widened as he swung his head to Leiram. "How sharp?"

"Grab the blade, lad! Now! We haven't time to dally!"

Against his better judgment, Tofur grabbed the blade tightly with his free hand. He cried out as the honed blade's edges sliced cleanly into his fingers. As his blood spread along the blade, it collected in depressions left long ago from a fine engraving tool. On each side of the blade, exquisite details appeared as bright red blood filled the hollows in the finely crafted steel blade. Slowly words appeared on each side of the blade. Around Tofur's small group, wingers continued to fall with mortal wounds. The fighting in the air was ferocious.

"Can you read the words in the blade, lad?" Leiram exclaimed.

"Words? What words? Where?" Tofur asked.

"Look at the blade!" Leiram yelled back.

The roar around them grew louder as Porcene, Jak and Belle backed into a tight circle.

"The blade?" Tofur asked. "You want me to look at the blade? Now?"

"Yes! If you see any words, read them out loud!"

The roar moved closer to the small group of leggers as the Crows' losses continued to increase.

Tofur brought the blade before his eyes. He could barely make out the forming words. "Blis…blisom…blisomne…" He flipped the blade over. "Blisomne du apo…I can't read them yet, Leiram!"

"Keep trying, lad! I'm afraid you have to!"

Tofur kept trying while more blood from the deep slices in his hand ran down the blade. The excess blood dripped off the sword recklessly. With the wounded hand, he rubbed the blood into the blade's sides.

"Leiram, what else am I looking for?"

"Lad, you must read the other side of the blade! Blisomne du apo what?"

Again, Tofur tried to read the blade. He wiped a collection of sticky, black feathers from it to uncover the engravings. "Blisomne du apo Ha'vuhn…Blismne du apo Ha'vuhn."

"Louder, lad!"

"Blisomne du apo Ha'vuhn!"

A brilliant light cascaded over the leggers and continued to rush across the ground. At the edge of the farthest winger's carcass, it suddenly turned upward, racing into the evening sky creating a perfect circle around Tofur and his comrades. The loud roar was quenched, the Crows kept flying, but every other bird within the lit cylindrical wall fell dead to the ground, landing and disappearing at the same time. Shadows of fallen Crows left the ground, flying up the column of light and out the top. Each one turned transparent in color as they exited to the sky.

All at once, the ground was empty of fallen wingers while the light cylinder continued to glow brightly. Silence followed. The leggers were motionless. Each of them stayed that way for an undocumented period of time. As the evening made its presence known, the circular wall of light slowly made its way to the ground. Outside, the surviving Crows made their way to Porcene. Absaroka spoke for them all.

"Who are we to follow, Horse?"

"You are to follow the wielder of the staff of Polinetti, Crow."

Without a sound, every Crow bowed to Tofur.

"We are here to do as you command, young Falconer."

Tofur sat on Porcene's back, mesmerized by the incident.

"What have you to say, lad?"

Tofur remained quiet, slowly turning the sword over and over in his hands. He held the wounded hand tightly to his chest as blood continued to trickle from the cuts.

"Tofur," Leiram asked. "Are you still with us, lad?"

Tofur looked first to Belle, then Jak. "What have I unleashed? Belle, what is this?"

Belle answered succinctly, as only she could. "Our destiny."

***

Down the path and throughout their part of the world, the gathering armies saw the glow cast by Tofur's staff. Fear and indecision clawed at each individual as they carefully re-evaluated their commitments.

***

Not quite as far down the road, Barth and Ligon were lying face down on the ground. The blast of light knocked them several paces from their path, leaving them both temporarily unconscious. They would eventually come to, but it would be in the hands of a small band of leggers and wingers heading their way.

***

Needless to say, each creature now making up Tofur's growing group was at a loss for words. Leiram stared off in the distance. Taytay and Whistler perched on each of Tofur's shoulders, watching the horizon for coming dangers. Absaroka and her flocks silently counted their missing. Porcene and Belle eyed at each other, trying to fathom the reality they were experiencing. Tofur sat astride Porcene's back alternately studying his bloody hand and his new sword. Jak stared at Porcene because she remained the most beautiful thing in the world to him.

"Lad," Leiram broke the silence. "We must get going if we are to catch those men you are after."

Tofur did not raise his gaze from his lap. "I suppose you are correct, sir. What do you make of this?"

"I can't make anything of it until it's done with us. Then I'll give it some thought." He kept his eyes focused down the road.

Tofur surveyed the smaller flock of Crows. "Absaroka, are you still with us? I'm sorry I can't distinguish you from the rest. Please, if you are here, I'd like to speak to you."

Hushed whispers spread through the flocks. They found Absaroka softly de-briefing the trio of spies who had earlier escaped capture.

"I want all of you to come with me. We are being summoned. Remember everything you saw or heard. These are the ones we were told of. We have nothing to fear with them." She turned to her second. "How many did we lose?"

"Mother, that number is currently in the hundreds, could be thousands once our count is completed. Wasn't it glorious seeing our fallen ones depart?"

Absaroka closed her eyes. "Hundreds? Please complete the count. And glorious? I will save judgment until I know for sure where they departed to."

"Yes, mother."

She led the spies on a short flight back to Tofur.

***

"Jak, is our prisoner still lashed to your flank?"

"Yes, Belle, he is. I made sure he wasn't stolen or further harmed. From what I can tell, he is coming around."

"We will need Leiram to position him for questioning while we hear from the Crows."

"I agree. One day, will you tell me exactly what is going on with us?"

"One day I will, Jak…if that one day comes."

Jak returned his gaze to Tofur while Belle attempted to get Leiram's attention.

"Tofur," Jak whispered. "Can you switch Leiram for Mariel real quick? Belle wants our prisoner readied for questioning."

Tofur nodded, "I'll try."

"Laddie, you can try if you must, but it won't bring him back. Mariel is gone for good. He has passed on, bless him. I am all that you've got."

The look on Tofur's face said more than days of conversation could ever say. "What?"

"I'm telling you...you can't blow that whistle anymore. Take a look at the handle of your sword there. The whistle isn't coming back out. You are now wielding the staff of Polinetti. A much more powerful thing you have there. The combining of the sword I tossed to you, your whistle and the blood from your veins completed the forging. Now the staff can be tracked on the wall."

"I'm sorry, what did you say?"

"What voice is saying that?" Leiram looked around curiously.

"It wasn't me," Tofur answered.

"I know it wasn't you, lad. Oh, I forgot to tell you, I'm a Talker now. There will be no need for you to translate what your animals are saying to you anymore. I can understand them all..."

Porcene interjected. "Tofur, I can understand everything he is saying."

Affirmations came from all about.

Tofur took a deep breath. "It's time for some explaining to start. Who is going to be first?"

"Laddie, I'll tell you what's gonna happen first and it doesn't require lots of talking."

"Excuse me?"

"Those two men you're after...they are lying unconscious about a stone's throw from here. We are going to capture them, then we will have our discussions. Is that alright with you?"

"Really? You can see them?"

"My eyes are truly wide open now, lad. There is no end to what I can see now."

"What is your plan?"

"You and me, we're going to walk up to them, grab them by their coat tails, tie them up and throw them up on these draft animals here."

"We are?"

"Most certainly!"

"And we can do that? Like…there is nothing to it? I will be able to grab a fully grown man and toss him all the way up on either Porcene or Jak's back?"

"Yes, you will."

Tofur shrugged his shoulders. "Sounds good to me. Let's go."

Belle was more cautious. "Hold on here! Then what?"

Leiram's face became one big ear-to-ear smile. "Then, dear Rottie, it'll be whatever the staff wants. Look around you. Is this the same place it was before the staff was created?"

This question spurred the curiosity of every creature within hearing distance. Each one surveyed the surroundings then looked back to Leiram.

"What are you all looking at me like that for? Are we where we were or not?"

Heads shook everywhere. The trees were in different places. The road was headed in a different way, the ground a different color. The grass was taller.

"What each of you needs to understand right away is this; those of us continuing on this journey have been adopted by the staff. We are not invincible yet, but we are under its protection. We go where it takes us. It is controlled by a power you can only imagine. I'd say we are at least 30 kays, by my measuring methods, from where the incident took place. The staff not only took us closer to those we are chasing…"

Porcene again interjected. "It also took us closer to those chasing us."

"Exactly the point, lovely Belgian, I could not have said it better. So, what will it be?" He stretched out his arm, pointing his fingers down the road. "Do you want to pick up two more prisoners or wait for that entire army up there to come barreling down on us?" He put his hands on his waist. "Well?"

"Okay," answered Tofur, "Belle, follow Taytay and Whistler. They will lead you in. Do not let those two men off the ground." The Falcons were winging instantly with Belle giving chase. "Absaroka, if you please, I want you and yours to stay with us. We have much to discuss. I'm sure your spies have pertinent information we need to know regarding the army Leiram speaks of. Leiram, climb aboard Jak. Porcene, follow that Dog!"

Porcene reared on her hind legs, causing Tofur to grasp desperately for her mane. She thundered off in the wake of Belle's dust trail. It was an exhilarating ride for the two-leggers as Jak showed as much speed and strength as the larger Horse. The flock of Crows followed slightly behind, spread across the sky like a dark cloud as the solid, blanket of night covered the landscape behind them.

28

Evaliene, Rhiannon, Broanick and Sean followed the staff over the edge of the cliff. Wherever they were going was not of their doing anymore. They trusted the staff or whatever the staff stood for. Surrendering themselves without recourse was the correct act to perform and a second thought never entered their mind.

The fall was not far. None of them felt any sensation of landing properly or awkwardly. They moved as one, cushioned by hope. They succumbed to a long day and previous night of running. Sleep welcomed them. Their future was out of their hands and minds now.

When they awoke some time later, two pairs of bright eyes glared at each of them through a fake darkness. The Horses were standing near the walls with Evaliene and Sean lying comfortably at their feet. The staff of O'shay rested securely in its holster beneath the hem of Evaliene's dress. The unique journey had been kind to them all, bringing renewed vigor and an unquenchable thirst to succeed.

A voice behind the shorter pair of eyes addressed Evaliene. "Who are you, lady?"

Rhiannon stood her ground, thinking the staff would not have immediately landed them in trouble. She assured Broanick this was true with a flirty wink of her eye.

The voice behind the taller pair of eyes remarked. "You know, she looks very familiar to me, don't you agree?"

"How would I know, I can't see her that well. You tell me."

"Okay, I will. Ev, Evaliene…is that you?" The voice walked closer to the red-headed lady lying asleep on the floor. The voice lowered closer then asked again. "Evaliene?" Turning to the shorter pair of eyes, it continued. "It is her! I know it is! Evaliene!"

Evaliene finally stirred. "Yes, who is calling me? Is this a dream?"

"Evaliene, it's me, Emiliia. Remember me? I was much younger when you left, but it is me. This is Patrick. Remember my little brother? He was merely a baby when you saw him last."

"Emiliia? Is that really you?" Evaliene asked. "Where are we?"

"Yes, cousin, it is me. How did you get in here?"

Evaliene rose to her knees and sat back on her ankles. "Emiliia, let me look at you. You are no longer a little girl and you are beautiful.

You have hair like your mother. And you Patrick, the spitting image of your father. Where are they? Are they with you in..." She looked around. "In wherever we are?"

"No, no they are not with us. We were separated a while back. We were in Nuorg, studying cracks. One split open before us and we were attacked. We were taken while Father repelled the attackers."

Evaliene's memory was coming back to her in massive waves. "And Oliviia? Where was she?"

"She ran for help as we were being taken."

Patrick added to the story. "The crack began to close as we reached the other side. I kicked one of the guys in the stomach and he fell backwards into the closing crack and the crack ate him. All that was left of him was his hand. When that happened, the attackers ran off like scared bugs."

Sean awoke but didn't move. He remained motionless, listening to every detail. The Horses found no reason to become restless.

Evaliene's eyes opened wide. "Patrick, the crack ate the man?"

"Yes, it did."

Emiliia nodded in agreement. "Ev, it ate him. His hand fell to the ground."

"But Ev, later we heard a voice calling us from the inside of the crack after it opened up again...but, only a tiny bit though." Patrick held his hands up then pulled them apart. "Only about this much."

"What happened then?" Evaliene asked.

"The voice, a man's voice, spoke to us. He sounded nice. We tried to tell him what happened..."

"But the crack began to close too quickly, right?"

Emiliia and Patrick backed up, staring at the man speaking.

"Don't be afraid you two, this is Sean. He is one of my protectors. You can tell him anything you can tell me."

Emiliia continued. "How can you be sure?"

"I have heard my own stories."

"Yes, sir, it started to close so Patrick picked up the man's hand from the ground..."

"And I tossed it through the hole."

"That was a very brave thing to do, Patrick. It might help them figure out who attacked you."

"Well, I thought so. Emiliia yelled at me for it."

"Patrick," Emiliia looked at him awkwardly. "I did no such thing."

"Well, you talked to me real loud." He turned to Sean. "Who are you?"

Evaliene grinned, "Patrick, I told you this is Sean."

"Okay."

Evaliene turned back to the girl. "Emiliia, how old are you now?"

"I am twelve, Patrick is seven. Oliviia is old. She is almost 16 now."

"Oh my, that is very old." She motioned to Rhiannon. "This is Rhiannon and the black Horse is Broanick. You'd better get to know them too."

"All in good time, Evaliene." Sean needed an answer. "Do you know where we are? How did you get in here? I see no openings of any kind."

Patrick jumped at the chance to answer. "We flew here, sir."

Sean laughed. "You flew here? How am I to believe that, youngster?"

"He is telling you the truth, sir. Well, kind of. Actually, we were flown here. We were followed earlier today. At least I believe it was today, by a huge bird."

"Sir, it was gigantic. It was enormous!"

"Thank you, Patrick. I've got this." Emiliia continued. "It was very large. He asked that we call him Rhodock. He told us he was a warner."

Patrick interrupted excitedly. "He picked me up and carried me up the mountain. It was so fun! A little scary, but more fun."

"Yes, he did fly us to the top of the mountain where he pointed out a window to Nuorg we were to use."

"The window was not a real window though…"

"Patrick? Please? May I finish?"

"Sorry, Mili." Patrick took a seat by Evaliene. "Hi, cousin Ev, I'm Patrick."

Evaliene put her arm around Patrick and pulled him close to her. "Yes, I believe you are." Her eyes once again rose to Emiliia. "Go on, Mili."

"He is correct. It was not a window. Rhodock sat us gently down near the absolute top of this mountain, next to a vertical rock so tall and heavy no creature could possibly move it. But as he stood there watching us, he said something and the rock let us in."

"What did you say? The rock let you in?" Rhiannon moved in closer to hear everything. "How could that happen?"

"Oh good, your Horses are Talkers. You don't see that much anymore. In my whole life, I have only seen a few outside of Nuorg."

Sean and Evaliene shared a chuckle at Emiliia's expense. It was the way she said "in my whole life". She was only twelve years old.

"Anyway, the rock let us in and we waited here for just a little while when all of you showed up. Are you on your way to Nuorg also?"

"Mili, we don't know where we are going. These friends are supposedly escorting me to my fortress."

"Really, Ev? Fortress number two belongs to you. I am so excited!"

"Huh? What do you know about the fortresses?"

"I guess almost everything there is to know."

"Really?"

"Yes, Ev. The guild built them long ago. One for you and one for Madaliene. They..." She pointed to Sean. "The protectors were to take you there once you left us. You were to live there safely secluded from those set out to get the staff. How do you still have it?"

Evaliene stared at Sean. "Is this true what she says? Why have I been moved about so much?"

Sean picked at the floor with one hand. "Yes...yes, it is true. But we couldn't take you as planned. The plan was compromised. We fought desperately to get you there but it was not possible at that time. Since then, hundreds of protectors have waged skirmishes much like we would have been involved in outside had you not tossed the staff over the edge of the cliff."

"What did you do with the staff, Evaliene?" Emiliia's face could not hide her horror.

"Mili, it is fine now. I have the staff. It took care of us. It brought us here...to you."

"I have to sit down. Ev, you scared me so. You have no idea, do you?" Emiliia sat straight down where she stood, holding her hands to her chest. "You almost have me a heart attack."

Sean laughed again. "How old did you say you were, Emiliia?"

She pursed her lips to stare at him. "You were saying?"

"Oh yes, back to my story. Evaliene, we did what we had to do to keep you safe. Moving you around was our only option. When the Rider showed up...well, we thought we had lost you for good. It was fortunate for us all that he was ignorant and solely bent on his own gain. But those men outside, I didn't like what I saw in them at all."

"What does that mean?" Evaliene asked.

"It means the look in their eyes unnerved me and the Horses. They were dangerous and we were badly outnumbered. Tossing the staff was genius on your part."

Evaliene blushed. "It was nothing really. Just a hunch."

Emiliia's stare bore straight through Evaliene and Sean. "When you two love birds finish chatting, we can get on with this. Please, tell me when you are ready."

Sean laughed again. "You said you were twelve?"

"Ugh! Men!" Emiliia jumped to her feet. She pulled a candle from her front jumper pocket, scratched the nearest wall with a brittle piece of flint and lit her small torch. "You had better follow me. Patrick, come up here with me. You Horses, watch our backs. I'm gonna find out where we are!"

Patrick hurried to his sister's side. "You want me to light my candle to, Mili?"

"Did you bring it with you?"

"Of course I did!"

"You know, little brother, we may be the most mature people in here." She spun around. "Are the rest of you coming with us?" She lit Patrick's candle, took his hand and led the travelers down the long, dark path ahead of them.

Sean whispered to Evaliene. "Is she really twelve years old?"

Evaliene smiled, "Yes, she is, in our years."

Sean's face contorted in a perplexed way. "What does that mean?"

"In time, protector, all in good time."

***

Rhodock flew with an uneasy feeling deep inside. He saw the flash of light far below him, which told him what he had hoped for had indeed occurred. As things go, he was doing well. His tasks were progressing nicely. He hoped the others were faring as well as he was. Rodahn was following the Staff of Hewitt, Rohdyne oversaw the staff of Polinetti, he had the staff of O'shay and Nuorg now had the staff of Equakembo. It wasn't time to return to his home... At least, not yet.

***

"Look for some writing on the walls or something, Patrick. There have to be some arrows or something else pointing the way."

"Yes, Mili."

She did not turn around, but shouted instructions to those stragglers behind her. "If you have anything to help light this place up, now would be a good time to use it. We have to find something to tell us where we are."

Sean searched his pockets. "Evaliene, I left too quickly…wait, let me look in my bag. Kelly packed it for me. It should have something in it we can use."

"I hope you find something. I am sure I have nothing to use. I escaped through my window with only the staff."

Sean rummaged through his bag tied to Broanick's saddle horn. In the bottom he found a candle of his own. He held it out for Evaliene. "Do you think you could get her to light this for us?" He pointed to Emiliia."

"Can't you do that? I don't think she will bite you."

"Are you sure?"

Evaliene took the candle. "Give that to me. Mili, I have this. Will you light it for me, please?"

Emiliia did as Evaliene asked while glaring at Sean. "I suppose you have nothing to offer here, sir?"

Sean held up his empty hands. "I'm sorry, lass, I brought nothing."

Emiliia took Patrick's hand again. "I hope you grow up to be a smarter man than that one back there. I don't know what she can see in him."

Evaliene walked back to Sean and the Horses. Once she was close enough, Sean whispered to her. "Has she always been like that?"

"Oh, Sean, wait until you meet her sister."

From up ahead came an observation. "I heard that, sir! You'd think you'd know how well sound travels in a cave!"

Sean and Evaliene laughed... Very, very quietly.

***

"Mili, what is that?" Patrick pointed to a wooden, dust-covered box of some kind, still in excellent shape, placed to the side of the widening area directly ahead.

Emiliia rushed to the box just fast enough to get there without blowing her candle out. Falling to her knees, she immediately sat her candle to her side and began fiddling with the latch that held the box securely closed. "This latch has no lock, Patrick. Is this a welcome home present?"

"I don't know, open it!"

It did not take a highly-skilled locksmith to unlatch the very simplistic design. She carefully pivoted the top open on the hinge running along the back. Inside were books and a scroll tied tightly with a ribbon woven from silk and hair. "Patrick, this must be for her." She took the scroll gently in her hand and ran back to Evaliene. "Ev! Ev! This is for you! Unroll it. We need you to read what it says."

Sean stepped in front of Evaliene. "Emiliia, what if this is a trick? What if it is dangerous? I must open it for her." He took the scroll.

"Ev, he can't open it. It's not for him!"

"I'm sure it will be fine, Mili."

"It won't, Ev!"

Sean slipped the ribbon from the scroll and began to unroll it. As he did, a small blast blew him across the room. He crumpled as he slammed against the wall.

Emiliia and Patrick watched. It was their turn to laugh out loud. "Sir, she told you it wasn't for you!"

Sean crawled slowly back across the floor, shaking the stars from his eyes. He fell on his stomach before he agonizingly rolled over on his back. He laid there staring up at the ceiling without saying a word.

Evaliene bent to his side on one knee. "Are you alive, Sean?"

Emiliia tugged on her sleeve. "He will be fine, Ev, as soon as he learns to listen. I told him not to open it. Read what it says out loud."

Dear Evaliene,
We are overjoyed to have you home. We trust this finds you well. It was not known to us who would deliver you here, yet here you are. We are thankful for that alone. We are very distraught that we could not welcome you to your home or your sister to hers. Fate held other plans for us. We have included everything you need to settle in here. You will even find your fourteenth birthday present.

We so wished to give it to you in person. But enough with the sentiment, the more you read of the books we left for you, the more you will understand. We love you with all of our hearts.

Read the final words slowly and enunciate very carefully. You might enjoy what we have built for you.

Emiliia was bouncing on her toes. "Well, Ev, read the last words."
"Mili, is this really happening? Is this truly my home?"
"Yes, yes, now read what is left!"
"Alright, here we go...

Blisomne, Blisomne du apo Ha'vuhn."

The candles went instantly dark. The cave became so quiet no creature could hear its own breath. The stillness became overwhelming. They began talking to each other, but all voices were silenced. The cave, in essence, died. It considered nothing to be living within its walls. The silence wore on for what Sean considered to be days. The Horses fell noiselessly to their knees before keeling over. The two-leggers slowly sunk to the ground without a fight. They slowly stretched out prone and still on the rough, hard rock. Sean reached for Evaliene's hand as she reached for Patrick's and he for Emiliia's. They held each other's hands tightly and fought bravely to breathe until even the smallest of breaths ceased completely.

***

Outside, the uneasy feeling deep inside Rhodock disappeared. It was replaced with a feeling of accomplishment he had not felt in ages. His eyes twinkled, his feathers smoothed to his body and he made one final turn for home. His work was almost done. He looked forward to seeing his family once again.

***

29

Madaliene followed Mystic as he led a short parade back through the over-grown gardens leading to the large dwelling's rear entrance. Gulli followed with Arlis, Mustanghia and Vincen perched on his back. Bubba lingered slightly behind.

The Great Forest was soon consumed with activities directly related to Mustanghia's closing comments. Every dwelling found its hidden storage spaces not previously opened and unlocked them as armaments of every type were again readied for action. Those inhabitants not included in the earlier skirmish were fully aware their time to action may be nigh.

***

Mystic, for whom Prince Mystic was named, and Rakki had every intention of flying to Burg Seven after winging their way over where Cirrus and Duister had met up with Nathan, Lewis and their prisoner. Shortly after the rendezvous point, the Tigers were again seen galloping across open ground in the direction of Burg One. Mystic and Rakki thought nothing odd of that, but just in case wanted to assure the cart tenders, Nathan and Lewis, that they were still under watch care with the Tigers' decision to leave. They returned to offer any help the two-leggers may require. Upon their arrival, they were terrified at what they found. They lit high in a tree overlooking the unexpected assembly.

"Mystic, what is happening down there?"

"Rakki, that small army of two-leggers...where did they come from?

"Sir, I can not fathom an answer to that question. How many are there?"

"More than plenty. Do you spot either of the cart tenders?"

"No, sir. Do you suppose they are in with the others?"

"Absolutely not. Those two came in with me several hundred moons ago. They were friends since birth; they would give their lives for each other. They are not involved with the others in any way."

"Where have they taken them?"

"Rakki, you know what cannot happen to them here. However, some vile methods of torture would be difficult to tolerate."

"Would they know to question them in such a way?"

"Highly doubtful...unless." Mystic saw what he did not want to see. "Rakki, look behind the boulders near the tall hickory." Rakki spied where the older Eagle alluded to. "Oh no, she came back."

"Yes, she is obviously not dead and she is not being very kind to our fellow Nuorgians. We must do something and soon."

"Mystic, she knows she can't..."

"Yes, Rakki, I'm sure she knows that. Still, she is up to something smelling of the wickedness she embodies."

"Why was she allowed to stay here, Mystic?"

"Rakki, some things are allowed to happen for a greater good."

"So, what good are you speaking of?"

"I have no idea." Mystic stared at Eekay as she swatted Nathan around like a rag doll, a group of the invading two-leggers looking on.

"Your highness", one of the animals within the group asked, "are you trying to kill these men? If they haven't answered your questions by now, will they ever?"

"Never you mind. I've owed these Nuorgian two-leggers a beating since my first day here! They hated me and I them."

She swatted Nathan so hard he bounced into Lewis who was laying unconscious near his side. Her methods produced nothing but rage within her. The answers to her questions would not come from these two.

"Rakki, I know this is dangerous, but they desperately need a drink of water. Please, find a way to retrieve enough to revive both of them. Fly the long way. Wait," Mystic called him back. "Do you see any wingers with them?"

"Sir, I haven't yet. Why do you suppose that is so?"

"If my theories are correct, wingers cannot come through the cracks. They can only come as Vincen did through the viscous portals."

"I would say that makes sense, but seeing that I have no idea what you are saying, I will just take your word for it."

Mystic shook his head. "Very well, get the water."

"I will return as quickly as I can. You will be here watching, correct?"

"I can't answer that truthfully, Rakki. I hope to still be in the area."

"Sir, do not do anything foolish. This is not your battle alone."

"Go quickly, son."

Rakki flew for the river away from the invading army. Before he made the river, he changed course. He headed for the Forever Trees of Burg One. If he knew Donkhorse and Hugoth at all, he was sure to find a freshly-filled pail of water near the gate. He flew at full speed.

***

Mystic watched in awe the hatred Eekay released on the cart-tenders. They didn't deserve to take this beating alone. Something had to be done now. Although Rakki sternly warned him not to get involved, his instincts were hard to overcome.

***

As fate would have it on this day, Rakki found exactly what he expected in the exact place he expected it. Slowing his beating wings, he hovered for a short instant above the bucket. He found it unnerving that absolutely no creature had welcomed him back, escorted him in or called his name. Had the time been available, he would have at least circled the main path. After he grabbed the full pail in his talons, he set off for Mystic. He noticed an out-of-place two-legger napping below the bridge. Now was not the time to inquire as to the whys.

***

Eekay took another swipe at Nathan, sending him sprawling over Lewis. A low growl seethed between her teeth. The invaders watching the spectacle turned away, fearing the worst.

Eekay whirled around to them. "What is your problem? Can you not watch and learn?"

Not a word was given to answer her question.

"Weaklings! Every two-legger I have ever met has been a weakling!" She stalked around her prisoners, wordlessly daring anyone to say anything. "So? Are neither of you brave enough to answer a simple question?"

***

Rakki flew faster. A frightening scenario kept running through his head. Mystic was not going to wait for him to return. The old Eagle was intending to take on the entire squadron of invaders.

"Mystic, you can't do that!" Rakki screamed.

Rakki flew even faster. He flew as fast as he could, clutching the water pail with every bit of extra energy he could spare.

***

The Eagle was getting more upset with a long-gone decision than he was with the current situation. Although, the Lioness' despicable actions made him nauseously angry, opting earlier to allow Eekay entrance to Nuorg bore the brunt of his frustration. What had he and the others been thinking? Her history was questionable, her attitude worse at best. What was it he told Hugoth that day...Nuorg was created to charge the souls it could and change those it could not? What it all meant was lost somewhere between anger and remorse. It would more-than-likely never become crystal clear again...a mere stepping stone to Blisomne for chosen ainjils? Ainjils chosen for what and by whom? Nothing made sense to him.

Several times he tried to turn away, leave the scene to be watched by another. He failed epically whenever he tried to distance himself from his incorrect decisions. He must make restitution for this unfortunate decision immediately or have his fellows continue to suffer at his behalf.

The decision was made. He dove from his high perch at a speed he never reached before. Aimed squarely at Eekay's head, it was too late to turn back. It was almost over.

She never saw Mystic. She felt the thud as the Eagle's weighty body slammed into the top of her skull, beak first. The impact sent Eekay dead to the ground. The several invaders viewing Eekay's relentless tormenting never grasped what happened. For all they would ever know, the Lion suffered a literal and deathly collapse.

***

Mystic also suffered mortal damage. One of the first Nuorgians had passed on. Rakki caught a glimpse of a translucent figure approaching him from below. The figure was not in any hurry to escape. As it moved gracefully by the Hawk, it nodded and winked. It continued a gentle climb until it was no more, vanishing from Rakki's sight.

Rakki and all other Nuorgians knew their stay wasn't permanent; still, one's heart skipped a beat when a passing occurred. Mystic had completed what he was destined to do. He would meet up with him again. He was sure of that.

Nathan and Lewis were able to see Mystic attack Eekay. They also witnessed his transformation and passing. Small, sincere tears were shed. The crowd around them dispersed to spread the word of the Lion's sudden collapse. There was no more they could do. The prisoners were lying unconscious, beaten surely within an inch of their lives. Leaderless, the invaders were left aimless.

***

Rakki flew in quietly as the last invader's back was turned. He set the pail down within a comfortable reaching distance from both two-leggers. He looked at them, his eyes scanning the damage to their bodies and the glaze covering their eyes. Figuring them comatose, he used his wings to dip water from the pail. He flicked the healing liquid at them until their skin and clothing glistened from the fine covering of droplets. Soon, they were awake. Within seconds, they were formulating an escape plan.

Rakki knew they weren't Talkers; a fact Eekay failed to grasp. He would need to leave them on their own, but needed the pail to complete his own ongoing plan. Motioning for the leggers to drink the remaining water succeeded. They drained the pail, immediately jumping to their feet. As they watched, Rakki picked up the pail to fly over the largest group of invaders. He made eye contact with Lewis. He tilted his head the direction opposite where he would be flying. They understood completely.

Rakki flew straight up behind the invaders. He leveled off just slightly and let the pail drop from his grasp. It fell hard like a small boulder, exploding as it hit one unfortunate invader solidly on the head, scattering fragments of water soaked oak into and about the group.

Many panicked, sending errant arrows skyward and throughout the trees. Some ran for cover. Several found themselves gashed by the many shards spread among them. However, the wounds healed as quickly as they occurred. Oddly enough, those who survived the wounds also experienced a drastic change of heart.

Nathan and Lewis made a run for it as soon as the pail dropped. Rakki continued on his way to Burg Seven. A scraggly string of light shot unceremoniously from the yellow ball in the sky streaking to the ground landing in the midst of the invaders. It crackled as it searched for its target, burning ground and flesh as it meandered across rocks, bodies and dirt. Multiple thin strands fanned out, all searching for the same prize. The two-leggers were terrified as they watched the menace locate Eekay's body, swarming over it, devouring without taking a bite. Strand after strand melded with its twin, creating a glowing silhouette of the dead Lion. All at once, the string of light stretched taut. A small explosion triggered the capture's violent return to the yellow ball. The onlookers instinctively shielded their faces, some of them a bit too late. Without question, their mission was becoming scarier with each passing tock of the clock.

Nathan and Lewis cared nothing about watching Eekay's end. They blazed a new trail to the "Beaten Path". There they paused briefly.

"Serves her right. She had no business here anyways."

"What is our next move, Nathan?"

"We have to get word of this group to Hugoth. Which way did Rakki head?"

"He looked to be heading to Burg Seven."

"I'm sure he will tell of this to the first available Talker."

"What are we going to do?"

"Lewis, you and me? I have a plan. From what I could see, these invaders are not very organized without their departed leader. I'm sure the yellow ball taking Eekay to her hereafter caused quite a stir as well."

"You think they are vulnerable now?"

"Very."

"What's the plan?"

***

Rakki traveled to Burg Seven slower than planned. His speed was now slower due to a randomly placed arrow sticking through his chest. "How did this happen?" He asked knowing he was the only one present to answer. "You just had to be a hero." He carried on this one-way conversation until he met an escort from Burg Seven.

"You look a tad uncomfortable, Rakki." Linnaeus noticed the limping flap of the Hawk's wings from several beats. "Shall I carry you in or help you pass?"

"Yes, to both if you don't mind, I would appreciate it greatly."

Linnaeus gently clasped his talons around Rakki's back.

"I have you old boy. Are you going to make it?"

Rakki shook his head. "I don't much think so. I believe my time has come to pass over. Mystic did so earlier today."

"That old bird. Why did he stay as long as he did?"

"Unfinished business, I presume."

"I hate to see you go. I'm really going to miss you for a while."

"Linnaeus, you know better than that."

"Did you not hear me, I said for a while."

"Maybe I missed that part. That old Eagle sure looked happy when he made his way out."

"They say it's the happiest part of living."

"If I don't finish the trip, tell my dear sister I will be awaiting her and love her dearly."

"You can't pass yet, friend. Tell me what happened."

Rakki's voice was becoming softer. "It was Eekay alright. She came back through one of the windows with another band of invaders. She was torturing the cart-tenders when Mystic and I spotted them. Mystic took care of her. I ran interference for the tenders to escape. Thus, the arrow in my side."

"Uh, it's not through your side, Rakki."

"Hah! Dear friend, I am speaking metaphorically of course."

"Of course." Linnaeus knew the Hawk would not last much longer. "Are you ready?"

"One more thing, please locate a two-legger Talker and then find the cart-tenders. They have much to tell."

The Golden tenderly squeezed Rakki's body. "I will consider it an honor to perform that task for you, sir."

"You know I will appreciate it." Rakki took a few more deep breaths. "I think I'm ready now, friend."

"As you wish, Hawk." Linnaeus adjusted his wings allowing him to fly straight up into the blue. Several eyes caught the marvelous sight. He increased his speed as he separated from the ground, creating a wake in the air behind him. He flipped over on his back and released Rakki to the sky. "Good-bye for now, friend!"

Rakki's body rolled over and over, tossed with care. Just as it happened with the ancient Eagle, the Hawk became a translucent mirror of himself. As the partly physical being met the complete spiritual being, it righted itself in flight. It came back to Linnaeus, smiled and flapped its wings. Soon the old-friend vanished from sight.

"Good-bye again, Rakki."

Linnaeus headed for Burg Seven to fulfill his obligation to Rakki. He was thinking he would probably need to see Karri as well.

***

"Why is this latch so much different than the one on the front door?" She asked.

The troupe somberly entered the back entrance once Madaliene figured out the latch.

"Once I start living in this place, I'm changing the latches on every door! Where do you want to meet, Vincen? This room looks big enough. Well, if you want to know the truth...every room in this place is plenty big enough for us to meet in." She noticed Mustanghia shaking her head. "Are you shaking your head because this room isn't big enough?"

"No, princess, it is not the right room."

"You mean we have to meet in the right room in order to have...the meeting?"

Mustanghia answered. "Yes."

"Bubba, you've been through this place, lead the way."

"Mustanghia, what does this meeting room look like?"

She shook her head. "I won't know until I see it."

Madaliene grimaced. "Bubba, now many rooms did you count?"

Bubba thought on this. "Let me think. 48...7...16...5...and 2."

"Are you kidding me?" exclaimed Gulli. "That's a total of 78 rooms! That is preposterous!" He made a large circle with his head. "Bubba, are you serious?"

"Uh huh. You added that up pretty fast."

"Yes, we are pretty smart you know…my kind, that is."

Madaliene was writing the numbers in the air beside her without a pen or paper. "Yes, that adds up. Nice work, Gulli. Mustanghia, any hints about this mystery room? Any at all?"

Mustanghia groaned. "No, princess. I have no idea. I'm not sure I like your tone either."

Madaliene scratched through her invisible drawing. "That doesn't surprise me."

"Young lady, may I ask which part doesn't surprise you?"

Madaliene did not answer. She stood silently studying her drawing. "You know…that room would not be in this building. We need to try the barn out there."

"Again, princess, what did not surprise you?" When asked, the question did not sound like a question in the least. It was more of a demand. "I'm waiting."

Vincen, Bubba, Mystic, Arlis and Gulli pensively waited and watched for Madaliene's answer.

"I'm sorry, ma'am, were you speaking to me?"

"I certainly was. What did I say that didn't surprise you?" Mustanghia stood as tall as she could on Gulli's coarsely haired back. She did not like waiting.

Madaliene, on the other hand, did not have a clue what Tanghi was talking about. She was lost in her drawing. She kept drawing shapes, then erasing them. To the others, it was curious thing to watch with the exception of Mustanghia. To her, it was disrespectful.

"Princess," she said. "I am still awaiting an explanation from you."

Madaliene did not respond.

"Princess."

Madaliene erased her work and started again. This time she was drawing every building on the property, moving around as if she was drawing on large canvasses set on easels all around the room.

"Well, I have never been ignored like this before." Mustanghia was beside herself.

"Tanghi, calm down. She is barely old enough to get angry with. I should be the angry one, not you."

Mustanghia raised the fine feathers above her beak. "And what are you saying?"

"I'm saying you left without a word to me. I even hear you have been back since that fateful day and decided I was not worth seeing. Is that true?"

"That is not what we are talking about, Vincen."

"Why? Is that because you didn't bring it up?"

Mustanghia looked around the room nervously. "Can we talk about this later, Vincen?"

"I think I want to talk about it now. The princess may not be ready to move for some time now. She looks to be drawing quite a complicated picture."

"Later."

"Now."

"No."

"Why?"

Gulli could not help laughing. "You two act like brother and sister!"

In unison, the Eagles threw fiery glares toward the Tusker. And, in unison, each one gave a different answer.

One said, "We are."

The other said, "We aren't."

Then, the Eagles locked stares on each other and once again, in unison, spoke. "What did you say?"

"I have it!" Madaliene shouted from across the room. "I think I have it!"

All four-leggers rushed to her.

"Wait! You all ran right through my drawings."

Hearing this, every creature in the room skidded to a halt. They exchanged very bewildered looks.

Gulli whispered to Mystic. "Is there anything here that we should have seen and not run through?"

Mystic sheepishly shook his head. Under his breath, he lightly whispered a response. "I don't know that answer." He looked confused.

Madaliene twisted a frown on her face that she could not hold in place. She broke into a loud smile. "I'm kidding, okay? Geesh, we are so serious today." She pulled her imaginary pen back from where she had placed it over her ear. "Everyone with me? Here we go. So, this building or dwelling as you call it here, has 48 rooms, in my opinion about three too many..." Her audience wore the blankest expressions she had ever seen. "Again, I'm...kidding? Never mind, try to keep up.

We have 48 rooms..." She continued to walk about the room, pretending to flip invisible sheets of canvas over and back again. "Now, the guard house...or dwelling, has seven rooms. That is right, isn't it Bubba?"

He nodded affirmatively.

"Good. The guest house..."

All together, her audience interjected their unanimous opinion. "Or dwelling..."

"Thank you. It has 16 rooms. The barn has five small rooms and two really big rooms. Now logical thinking would lead me to dismiss everything we just went over..."

Vincen butted in. "Please, Princess...really?"

"Yes, sir. Logical thinking would tell me to toss every idea I have had since I began this quest. However..." She turned to another drawing, "I haven't. Now, this place also has..."

She ran outside. Those left inside could see her pointing with her finger at each story and counting.

"Oh, dear ones, I do think we have lost her." Mystic hung his head.

Madaliene raced back in. "Seven different levels." She threw her hair back. "This place is really big. Anyway..."

"Vincen, if she says anyway one more time..."

"Mustanghia, a little quiet, please? Can't you see she is leading us somewhere?"

"Not really." She looked away.

Madaliene grinned. "Anyway..."

"Ah! Princess, please."

Now Madaliene was laughing at Mustanghia. "I'm sorry, ma'am...furthermore...as I was saying, my fortress also has seven levels. Well, really it has 13, but it has six above the living quarters and six below so if you count the living level as one, then you have seven either way you go and they tell me seven is a good number. Anyw...furthermore, I thought this looked very familiar, the layout that is, and the reason it looked familiar is because..." She pointed her imaginary pen at Mystic. "Because..."

"Because it...is?"

She ran to him and gave him a wonderful hug. "Yes, Mystic, it is! Everyone of these rooms corresponds with a room in my mountain. I won't bore you with the details right now...but follow me!"

She raced through the room, collecting all of her invisible drawings and tossing them into the air as she ran through the garden to the barn.

"Vincen," Mustanghia said out loud. "That girl might well be crazy."

Arlis had been quietly following Madaliene's presentation. "Tanghi, I'd say genius is more like it."

Vincen laughed as he tried his best to hold on to Gulli with his fellow sky-travelers as the Tusker thundered on behind the princess, the Wolf and the Cheetah.

30

Linnaeus played continuous memories of Rakki in his head as he flew. He wasn't sure if what he saw below was destiny or fate, still he decided to investigate. The cart he spied was not completely out of the ordinary given the current status of Nuorg, but the team hitched to it was.

"I must be seeing things." He flew lower and lower until he was directly over the draft team. "Stewig, what…? And Donkhorse?"

He landed on the severely sloping yoke tying the two leggers together.

"Hello there Linnaeus, what have you to do besides spy on us?"

"Stewig, what is this all about?"

"We are transporting the King and his stick throughout all of Nuorg and returning to the evil yellow ball all those who rightly belong to it. We have had the best of times."

"And I tell you, Stewig, I have had the worst of times."

Jahnise stuck his head from behind the wooden barriers. "What have you to say, Golden Eagle, that is worse than what we have faced?"

"Not to demean your cause here, your highness, but I have lost two great friends today to their destiny."

Donkhorse stopped immediately in his tracks. Stewig kept pulling, very nearly pulling the wagon over his partner. "Hold on a minute, Stewig! Linnaeus, who have you lost?"

"Today, Nuorg gave up the ancient Eagle, Mystic, and my dear friend, Rakki."

"Wait a minute. They both passed over today? What was the cause for that?" Donkhorse closed his eyes.

"Eekay was not dead. She returned with a band of invaders. She caught the cart-tenders near the rendezvous point and tortured them mercilessly. Mystic and Rakki found them. Subsequently, they rescued them as well. Mystic passed on when he put Eekay down. Rakki was wounded by an arrow whilst he caused a diversion which allowed the tenders to escape. It was a joyous yet poignant moment when I let him go."

"I am sorry to hear of your loss, friends. Was the water not available to them?" Jahnise asked the question with an equal amount of concern and curiosity

"It was the first two times they needed it, King. It cannot do anything for you the third time."

"Then this was the third time for them both?"

"Yes, King."

"How about you Eagle, how many times has it been for you?"

"Two, your highness."

Jahnise slapped Stewig's hind quarters. "How about you Rhinoceros?

"Only one for me, King."

"So you have one saving left?"

"That is one way to say it."

Jahnise banged his stick on a section of Donkhorse's wooden armor. "How about you?"

"Two for me also, King. But speaking honestly..."

"Why of course, friend."

"I am ready to pass over. You may be leading me to my last battle. If so, then I am proud to do so with old and new friends alike."

"Let us hope it does not come to that. Golden Eagle, please take us to the rendezvous point. I have a surprise in store for our newest arrivals."

Linnaeus nodded. "Donkhorse, Stewig, will that be a fine thing to do for both of you?"

Stewig grunted his reply. "I'd be telling a lie if I said it was and I'd be telling a lie if I said it was not. What about you, Donkhorse?"

"I have been preceded in passing by those stronger than I. I say let's get this taken care of."

Linnaeus took a deep breath and blew it out. "Follow me. I will fly as slow as I can. Try to keep up. You two might need to hoof it!"

Donkhorse laughed. "Brilliant deduction, winger! Hold tightly to something, King!"

They pulled Jahnise at a dizzying pace. He tried to hold on to everything in the wagon. Still, he was tossed to and fro like a feather in the wind. He gave up trying to hold on. He scooted close to the front, bowed his head and prayed for strength and guidance.

With Linnaeus leading them "as the crow flies", the normal paths were not taken. They crossed many places where carts or wagons were not mean to be. However, when one of the draft pair is a 7,000 pound Rhinoceros, those types of obstacles become non-issues. Donkhorse did not utter a whimper or complaint. He pulled his weight as well as Stewig. Losing two longtime friends in a single day gave them both resolves even an invading army of thousands would not weaken. They had each been in on the vote to keep Eekay; Donkhorse voted aye, and Stewig, the sole dissenting vote, voted nay.

Linnaeus flew down. "We are approaching the spot. Are you two ready? What should I expect?"

"Are our visitors still there?"

"From what I can tell, Stewig, none of them appear to have drifted off. They look…I don't know…rudderless."

"One would expect that after losing one's leader as they did. I have seen it before in my homeland." Jahnise steadied himself to Stewig's side of the wagon. "They are, as they say…ripe for picking. Shall we barge upon them at full speed? If so, you will need to let me off now, for I cannot see myself jumping from this wagon with the speed you to can reach."

"King, that is a huge risk. Are you sure you want to take it? You have no shield."

"Do not you worry yourself, Eagle, I have a great shield. I carry it inside me, not outside. If the creator has me here for his reasons, I can only trust that he has me in mind. If it is not for a reason of his choosing, then I am on my own and whatever happens will be the result of me exercising my free will for any outcome. It would be unfair to ask more than that. No?"

"Well said, King. It is good to know you understand these things. It makes me wonder why you were brought here. We could use more like you where you came from." Donkhorse was a wise animal.

"If that is your choice, King, step out now. Linnaeus will lead you in," Stewig added. "He will also signal us with the oldest signal we know. Linnaeus, you know what to do. When you are ready for us, tilt your wings. We will come in at full speed. I feel a slight bit of remorse for those we are about to trample under foot. The carnage will be plenty and the deaths, unfortunately, will be so as well. I will not stop. If we have time, we will mount a second stampede. Donkhorse, do you have anything to offer?"

"Just this – we may be getting ahead of ourselves. If Jahnise's staff works as it has so far, will there be a need to stampede their camp?"

Stewig caught Linnaeus' eye. "What do you think? The Mule has a point."

"Very astute observation, Donkhorse. King, can you get in there and stick them before they know you are in their midst?"

"If the question was not so serious, it would be very funny indeed. Look at me, all of you. What do you see? Do I look as if my entire life as a hunter has been a lie? Trust me when I say this, they will never know I am there or was there." He smiled a broad smile exposing a mouthful of perfectly white teeth. "As long as I don't smile!"

Stewig chuckled. "As long as you don't smile. Hah! After you, King. Linnaeus, watch over him. We will wait for your signal." He turned back around to watch Jahnise, but he was gone. "Wow. Donkhorse, did you see the King leave?"

"Huh? Is he gone?" Donkhorse joined his partner scanning the surroundings for Jahnise. He was nowhere to be seen. "We may be concerned about the wrong creature."

Stewig chuckled again. "Hey, Mule, watch the Eagle."

***

Jahnise felt in his element. Stalking a prey as the Cats of the plains, he made his way silently following the path the Golden Eagle laid out for him. He covered lots of ground very quickly. Soon he was standing on the outskirts of the invaders' encampment. Several small groups had taken shelter from the always present and ominous yellow ball. Studying his prey, he decided quickly they had no second in command. There was no one to take charge after Mystic removed their leader. He walked nimbly into the middle of the scattered groups.

Holding his stick tightly in front of him with both hands, he addressed the weary invaders. "Look here, all of you. We have found you. There will be no escaping."

A King of very few words, he slammed his stick on the ground three times. The familiar light appeared to begin searching the crowd. Slowly and methodically, it made its choices. One by one, leggers were brought against their will to the feet of Jahnise. They struggled with no chance of release. Their fate was sealed. Jahnise became a little unsettled as he watched the light weave around several individuals, leaving them alone entirely. The group grew steadily as more and more leggers were chosen. Then the light stopped moving altogether for an eerie moment. Suddenly, hundreds of shafts of light shot into the trees, grabbing hundreds of ungainly, thick wingers from the branches, pulling them in with a raucous amount of high-pitched screams, hoots and cries. Jahnise knew better than to cover his ears.

In the sky above it all, Linnaeus watched dumbfounded. How had all of those wingers escaped detection? The only solution he could fathom was another open window. It was common knowledge that wingers could not come through the cracks.

Stewig and Donkhorse crept closer. They were not sure of what they were hearing.

Jahnise watched as the wingers were jerked from the trees. Soon, the selection process was over. The stick had done the dirty work. Jahnise pointed it toward the yellow ball and expelled the contents back to where they belonged. He fell to the ground, breathing much harder that ever before.

Linnaeus watched as the entire chain of events came to an end. Jahnise was on his knees, his long wiry body lay draped over them. His long arms splayed to his sides, one holding a still, firm grip on his stick. His breathing was heavy but steady. This experience had taken more from him than all of the previous ones put together. Those invaders, spared by the pool of light, cowered beneath the trees, afraid to move. Jahnise attempted to lift his head, barely raising it from the ground before it fell back. His free arm clumsily searched for something he missed.

“My hat,” he said into the ground. “Where is my hat?”

Linnaeus circled lower. When he passed by the creeping pair hitched to the wagon, he told them to approach slowly. He added there was no need for any trampling to occur. When he landed near Jahnise, he was relieved to see his breathing becoming normal again.

“King? King, will you be alright?” Linnaeus took in the frightened invaders lurking in the trees. His attention returned to Jahnise. “King, did you hear me?”

A very, muffled sound of life rose from the ground.

Linnaeus sighed. “I suppose that is a relief.”

A few of the invaders began to emerge from the trees until Stewig and Donkhorse approached sending them all rushing back for cover.

“Linnaeus, is he hurt?”

"No, Stewig, he will be fine. This last ordeal took a lot out of him. He needs some water. Did we bring any?"

"I think we have some back there, Linnaeus. Can you check?"

The Golden did as was asked of him while the pair of leggers inched closer to Jahnise.

"King, can you stand?"

Jahnise lifted his head. "I am very thirsty, Stewig."

Linnaeus made a short flight from the wagon with a nearly empty bag of water. "We have more, King. See if this will get you started again."

Jahnise rolled onto his back. "Please, Eagle, pour it over my face. The light gave me a burn this time. It became so intense."

Linnaeus set the bag down. He then pulled the stopper and drained the contents all over Jahnise's face and shoulders. Jahnise relaxed as the healing water followed its own course, finding the worse spots first and working backwards. Enough water made its way into his mouth to allow a normal speaking voice.

"Is that better?" Linnaeus held up the empty bag.

"Much better, my friend, much better." Jahnise slowly sat up. "I have no idea why that was so powerful. Did any of you three see anything different?"

"We were too far away to see anything but the light, King."

Donkhorse agreed, "I'm afraid he is correct. We saw nothing but a powerful glow."

Jahnise rubbed water into his eyes. "I was blind. The second wave, the one shooting through the trees, it took my sight from me. Intense...very intense."

Stewig moved in even closer. "King, let me help you to your feet. You don't want to appear weak in front of our audience.

"Audience, what audience?"

"Look around us, among the trees."

As his vision returned, Jahnise clearly saw the remnants of the invading army. He wrapped one arm around Stewig's horn and let the Rhinoceros lift him to his feet while he steadied himself with his stick.

"Why do you suppose they are remaining?"

"Your highness, I have been pondering a few details Rakki shared with me. He dropped the pail into a crowd below him. It broke apart on impact. It's the water. There was still water in the pail. When it blew apart, well…take a look…each one of these leggers left here must have been exposed to it. Donkhorse?"

"You must be correct. That would be the only explanation."

"That is all well and good and I hate to change the subject…but, King, can you please unfasten this yoke? It's not that I don't love my friend here, but I need my space."

"I can surely do that for you."

As Jahnise began to unhook the various ropes and hasps, the invaders began to gather about, one by one mustering enough courage to venture near enough to hear Jahnise speak. Stewig's harness was the first to fall.

"I feel like a new creature." He energetically ran a few circles which frightened even the bravest invaders. He slowed and walked back to Jahnise's side as he dropped the final hook of Donkhorse's harness.

"Donkhorse, what will we do with the wagon?"

"King, after this is over, someone will retrieve it. We have more important concerns at the moment."

A timid voice came from one of the invaders. "Sire, are you conversing with the animals?"

Jahnise looked for the man who spoke. "Which one of you asked that question?"

A good-sized man stepped up, "I did, sire. I would have never thought is possible. Of course, I had heard it was, but I was a hard skeptic and never believed it. So it's true, there really are Talkers?"

A smile appeared across Jahnise's face. "Yes, we are few…but we do exist for the time being. One day we will be gone for good, but for now we remain. Who are you, sir?"

"Please call me Rawg. My last name is Sleinton."

"I think it is a pleasure to meet you, Rawg Sleinton. We must talk. These are my friends, Stewig, Donkhorse and Linnaeus. They are Nuorgians, while I am only a visitor as yourself. However, I was brought here with good intentions. My friends here and I have to think you were not."

"I must tell you, sire, we were not. What happened to us? Where did the rest of my command go?"

"You will get the answers to your questions after we get the answers to mine. You must follow us now, we haven't time to waste."

"After the little light show you gave us, choosing not to follow you would be foolish. We will follow wherever you lead, sire."

Jahnise glanced at the man's feet. "Mister Rawg, why do you call me sire?"

"I'm sorry your highness, is it wrong to do so?"

"No, I wouldn't think so. I should have asked this question, who do you know me to be?"

"Only from paintings I saw as a child." He swept his hand over his men. "As all of us saw it as children. You are the Great King Equakembo from the South, ruler of all central plains that lie between the two oceans and north to south. Your highness, even your enemies know you well, as we were before the incident."

"Ah, you are speaking of the light."

"No, I am not, sire. I am speaking of when the pail fell from the sky and exploded after hitting my head. The strangest things happened to those of us hit by the shrapnel. It's as if we had an abrupt change of heart. Our wrongs were rights and our rights were wrong. There was much arguing that ensued. Our ranks were falling apart. My next in command accused me of neglecting of my duties. I had no answer for him. Several of my men felt as I did and they now stand around us. Those that did not suffer puncture wounds...I believe you cast them into that yellow ball up there." He pointed to the sky.

"That indeed did happen as you say, mister Rawg. Come, we are talking when we need to be walking. We can chat along the way if you like."

"I would like to very much. We are so different now. Very odd. We were sent here to ruin this place."

Rawg stepped beside Jahnise as he fell in line behind Donkhorse. Stewig trailed the line with Linnaeus on his shoulder, occasionally nudging the last reformed invader for good measure.

***

There were no more than 12 invaders remaining in Rawg's squadron out of a few hundred. They talked among themselves during the long walk to Burg Seven. Most of the conversations revolved around their drastically changed points of view and the mixed feelings of losing their friends and acquaintances in such a strange fashion. The only consistant sentiment among them was that they felt no regret for losing the Owls. Those birds did nothing but stare condescendingly at the men all day long, every day since they arrived with Commander Sleinton's orders. They were in total agreement about that subject. Good riddance!

"Mister Rawg, you surely know we will be expecting to hear about the details of your invasion. How do you feel about that?"

"Your highness, at one time I would have been interrogating you. Whatever happened to me...I can't describe it, I will gladly tell you everything I know, down to the very last detail. How much do you know of the attacks up there?" Like most visitors to Nuorg, he pointed up.

"Very interesting, mister Rawg. I believe you mean down there." Jahnise bounced the end of his stick on the ground.

Rawg smiled. "I guess you are correct. I have no earthly idea where we are anyway. We were led into a cave, then through a crack in the wall. We had to move fast because it kept moving on us. It closed on several of my men. The aftermath was sickening. I have no idea how the Owls got here. They did not come with us."

Jahnise scrunched his face, "I am sorry, mister Rawg, I am afraid I do not understand. What are you saying?"

"Your highness, the crack closed without notice. Several of my men were trapped in it. It was horrible for them and not a lot better for those of us who witnessed it. I have seen and done terrible things in my life...I can't find words yet to describe what happened...yet."

"You plan to find those words in the future?"

Rawg appeared shaken. "I think so."

***

In Burg Seven, every creature knew their job. The sentinels in the trees found the approaching soldiers discomforting. Combined with Donkhorse leading and Stewig trailing, they could not get a good read on what was happening.

Linnaeus felt the apprehension. Instead of waiting, he flew ahead to prepare for the arrival. He flew over the entrance, answering questions mandated by the defense plans. After briefing his escorts, he proceeded to the Keeper's dwelling where he would find an uncharacteristically unkempt Bongi engaged in a deep conversation with a pair of unfamiliar two-leggers.

"I'm telling you, Kirch, it will work."

The taller, thinner, sandy-haired two-legger disagreed. "I don't see it. You are always telling folk how wonderful your methods are, but honestly, I don't see it."

The shorter, stockier legger patted his hands together. "What is there not to see?"

"A plan?" Kirch put his hands in the air. "A plan, Stephane, a plan!"

He walked a few steps away. He returned to emphatically address the group. "If that is the best we have come up with...well, we are all in serious trouble."

Stephane kicked at the ground. "Free thinkers."

Kirch jerked around. "And what does that mean?"

Bongi heard enough. He bumped Kirch with his nose. "Sir, it's time for the bickering to stop. Do you or do you not have a plan?"

Kirch rubbed his rib-cage. "That was quite a jolt there, Bongi."

"If I have to be more persuasive, I certainly can be. Answer please, do you or do you not have a plan?"

"Yes, we have a plan. I have one and so does he and they will not work in tandem."

"Well that is great news!"

Linnaeus arrived just in time. "Is there a problem here, Bongi?"

"Yes, I say there is. I had to leave in a rush earlier with Hugoth, Livvy, Cirrus and the others. These two were given the task of formulating a plan to counter the offensive being thrown at us by our invaders. I made haste getting back only to find these empty headers have both made plans that cannot work together and neither will work alone!"

Linnaeus glared at all three of them. "Then fortunately for us, Jahnise is leading in a band of invaders this very instant who are more than willing to talk. Do you suppose you can persuade these two-leggers to question a group of them? We need answers to every imaginable question. Seeing that these two are from different sides of the road will give us a broader base of questioning." He tilted his head to Kirch. "Are you both Talkers?"

Kirch's head twitched. "I am, he is not. We will do whatever you ask. When will they be arriving?"

"Thank you. They should be at the gate shortly. Bongi, get prepared for our guests." Linnaeus flew back to the gate to escort Jahnise and his group.

31

Frederick froze. What did Hemoth mean? He took one last look at the pictures appearing on the wall before he ran after Hemoth.

"Wait a second…" He moved closer. "This was not here before." He ran to the doorway to call after Hemoth. "Hemoth!" His voice carried superbly down the rock corridors.

Hemoth pulled to a stop. "Frederick, you are supposed to be right behind me!"

"You need to come back here quickly! There is something else in the picture."

"What is it?"

"I don't know. You will have to tell me."

"Fine! I'm coming back, but this delay might have disastrous consequences."

"I will take that risk. You need to see this!"

Frederick ran back to the wall. He lightly traced the changing areas with his fingers. He climbed the ladder. All four corners were showing more details. Hemoth rumbled across the floor.

"This better be worth the effort, sir."

Frederick jumped down the ladder. He pointed to the lower left side. "Look at this. What does it mean?"

Hemoth nosed to the wall as much as he could. While he stared at the picture, several razor-sharp yellow lines materialized all over the wall. Startled, he jumped back to see them all. "Oh my."

"What? What is it, Hemoth?"

"Our work, Frederick! The guild's work! It's working. Look here." Hemoth was more excited than he looked. "Sig, old friend, I hope you are seeing this!"

They both stepped back from the picture. In each corner, the yellow lines were connecting various bits and pieces of the emerging puzzle.

"Hemoth, what are we seeing?"

"What is happening in front of us right now is happening outside of this mountain. See the group in the bottom corner? See the line that is now connecting that group with the directly above it? That was crucial. Evaliene is now, finally, in her fortress, but nothing is happening now. That was a huge accomplishment and I have no idea how it happened. Madaliene now needs to return to her fortress. Nuorg needs to make some headway, but we are losing help down there. See the yellow dot halfway up the other side? That is Nuorg. The line connecting it to the bottom corner shows the Staff of Equakembo is there, but it must get out. The line at the top is finally showing the path of the staff of Polinetti. We haven't heard much from that side of the world, except it is there. It is now fully forged. The picture will be clearer soon. The random yellow circles are befuddling…" He continued to study.

Frederick carefully listened as Hemoth explained. Occasionally, he would move closer in or farther out depending on what he wanted to see. "Hemoth, all of this action is taking place on the borders and corners of this map." He twisted his head to Hemoth. "What is going to happen in the middle?"

***

Belle stood over the still unconscious Barth and Ligon without making a sound. Closely following the Falcons, she located the two-leggers and sent the cast back to Tofur. With the condition the men were in, the Rottweiler knew she could handle them alone. She separated them from the many weapons they had been carrying, burying one she thought had to be the one used on her own pups. Her insides boiled knowing they had taken her sons the way they did. She wanted to rip their innate bodies apart and scatter them across the hottest barren landscape she could find. The collectors would take it from there.

***

Leiram steered Jak on a path directly to Belle, chatting with their prisoner securely lashed at his side. Bulos, defiant to the core, uttered not a single sound.

Tofur rode Porcene as a general leading his troops to battle. Surprised with their quick return, he debated with Taytay and Whistler the merits of sending them forward to protect Belle's flanks.

"Leiram, you are wasting your time questioning that Owl. Obviously, they believe themselves far too intelligent to spend any time conversing with a two-legger. Should I, once again, send the Falcons ahead?"

"Lad, you are correct. Although, I feel I must correct your statement. Too much intelligence is a not terrible thing. Assuming you have or being raised to think you have more than the next creature is a bad thing. As you will see very shortly, the latter is a very bad thing. You see, these Owls for so long have been looked to as the wisest creatures. Everywhere they have relied on their own and only their own for guidance, discrediting every other living creature on this earth. The times are catching up to them. They have created their own universe apart from this world in this world. It was doomed, but they were too stubborn to accept it. Now...well, let us allow their fate and destiny to meet, shall we?" Leiram looked out to the middle distance ahead. "And no, now that they are back, you will definitely not send your cast out. Not until it is safe once more. Look at your staff."

The last thing Leiram said received more attention that the first things. "My what?"

"Laddie, your staff. What was earlier called a sword."

"Oh yes, I forgot. What should I look for?"

"Tell me, is it casting any light of its own?"

Tofur pulled it from his belt. He turned it over. "No...wait...what is it doing, sir?"

Without prodding, Porcene swiftly moved to Leiram's side.

"Look, sir. It is glowing a little."

Leiram glanced at it. "So it is. Listen to me, lad. Lesson one; do not take your hand from the staff while it glows."

Tofur's eyebrows raised. "Why not?"

"Lesson two; just don't."

Tofur longed for some other creature to share his trepidation.

"You can look around all you want, lad, but we are it."

"How did you know I was looking anywhere?"

"I told you I am now an ainjil. I can see more than you imagine. I can also hear what our caged friend here is thinking and I am so disappointed for him. His wishes will not come true."

Tofur casually pointed the staff at the cage. "Poor, stupid creature."

Bang! A jagged light beam shot from the sword's tip. Bulos was obliterated, feathers and all. The light passed through several layers of sacks and packs, burning a tiny hole as it went.

Jak jumped. "Gosh a mighty! What just happened? My side is burning!" The Mule was upset.

"Now, Jak, settle down. The blast did you no harm. It might have ruined a few of your bags. It might have singed your hairy hind quarters, but it did not burn you. Calm down, try to be a grown-up, shall we?"

Porcene tried not to laugh. She failed. Jak did not appreciate the moment. Tofur's chin nearly hit his chest after the jaw-dropping display. He could not take his eyes off where Bulos was.

"Leiram! What just happened?"

"Couldn't tell you, lad. From what it sounded like, your staff there didn't take too kindly to your prisoner. I suggest you be more careful with it from now on."

"But, I…I didn't…"

"It's gonna be alright there. Our dear departed prisoner already told me all I needed to know."

"And that is?"

"We are about to be up to our ears in trouble. But, you shouldn't worry too much. They can't hurt me."

Porcene stared with big, beautiful eyes at Jak. Jak stared back. Tofur stared at Leiram. Taytay and Whistler stared at each other. Their voices combined in unison, sending one crystal clear question back to Leiram.

"What?"

***

Evaliene's hand held tight to those holding hers. Patrick, Emiliia and Sean lay at her side, motionless. The Horses were motionless heaps off to the side. Nothing in the cave, if that is what it was, stirred. Nothing that once breathed felt any pain of any kind.

***

Pandion and Corvus flew fast. The scenery far beneath their wings blurred as the two wingers passed over. Knowing the messenger was being cared for was a good thing to report. Her miraculous over-night recovery was more than they could hope for. They needed to push through even though their bodies thirsted for sleep.

At the coast, Pandion's army of fixers awaited their final orders. The captured Owl had not spoken in days, nor had she eaten. As her condition deteriorated, so did the hopes of discovering her secrets. Pandion's last words allowed for no torture. They were told to treat her with as much respect as she thought she deserved. They were also ordered to stay put until either he or his instructions returned. The time was passing too quickly.

***

Madaliene led the way into the barn. The door latch, much to her satisfaction, worked perfectly. She knew where she was going. They passed through the first arena and into the second. At the back were the two smaller rooms. She again was relieved as the door latch opened with her slightest touch. Inside the room was a large, heavy wooden table surrounded by 12 chairs.

"This is it, Mustanghia. This is the room. It matches the room in my mountain to a tee. Now what?"

Mustanghia took in the room. "You are correct, princess. This is the room. Everyone gather round. Madaliene, please close the door."

Madaliene went out of her way to give each individual a hearty hug as she circled the table after closing the door. She swept her fingers over seams in the wall. "If it is here, Mustanghia, I will find it." She paused to collect her thoughts and closed the inside shutters of the only window in the room. In total darkness, she knew her way around. Near the door, she found what she was searching for. She pulled a key out that was wedged behind a sliver of wood near the wall's base. The key was slipped into a slot beneath the latch. She turned it a quarter of a turn. After taking a deep breath, she spoke to those in the room. "Wish me good fortune." She pulled up on the latch, opened the door and stepped from the room. The door shut behind her. The room became slightly smaller as each creature remaining took a deep breath. None of them had any idea of any question to ask.

***

Paddy arrived near the holding cellar around mid-morning. He greeted his fellow Protectors warmly. “So, how is our prisoner?”

“I was coming to tell you earlier, brother, that the Rider was fading. He didn’t make it. We hardly recovered any information. What little he divulged was recorded.”

The scribe sat finishing his notes from the interrogation. “I’m sorry, Paddy, you know what our orders were. Get the answers and don’t worry about...well you know.”

“I understand. Don’t bother burying him. I don’t want him seen again in public. Sean may not he happy with this outcome. Did he say who sent him?”

The scribe spoke softly, “We asked him that question and all he said was ‘the intelligents’.”

“The what?” Oh well. This man was a waste of good human flesh and bones. He deserved what he got. Pack it up and light this place as a pyre. See what you can get from the other prisoners.”

Paddy walked back to his house, disgruntled but hopeful.

A small Numbat followed closely at his heels.

***

Hugoth arrived in front of the Keeper’s dwelling just as Linnaeus flew off.

“Why did he not wait for me? Did he not see me coming?”

“It’s a pleasure to see you too, Hugoth.”

“Bongi, please? I’m afraid my manners might be taking a back seat to other things at the moment. Where is he going?”

“To the gate to meet Jahnise.”

“To the gate? Jahnise was not...I said no one was to leave!”

“I guess if you are a king, you can do about anything you want.”

“Wonderful. Anything else?”

“He had a lot to say. Unfortunately he left before he shared any of it. When can we venture outside of the gate? I need to take a swim. I am filthy.”

Hugoth ignored the last comment and the two-leggers. “I guess I’d better meet Jahnise at the gate also.” The Grizzly again showed his speed and agility as he trotted past group after group of Nuorgians working diligently, readying the Burg for impending breaches.

***

Lightning was walking too slowly for his taste. Oliviia was hurrying, but there was no way she could walk as fast as Lightning.

"Oliviia, would you like a ride back?"

"No thank you, Lightning, I'm thinking."

"Okay."

Perrie and Karri were exhausted. They were already on Lightning's back enjoying the ride.

"Has anyone spotted my brother or Mystic lately?"

"Mystic?" Lightning asked. "Which one?"

"The Eagle. Rakki was with him the last I heard."

"I'm sorry, Karri. I haven't seen much of anything to tell the truth."

"I was just wondering."

Oliviia stopped abruptly. "Lightning, remember when I was asking about that axey thing of yours?"

"Yes."

"Did I hear correctly? It takes you where you need to be or where you want to be?"

"It takes you where you need to be. Sometimes, exactly where you don't want to be, trust me." He held it out for her to see. "Not much to look at really."

"Will it take me where I need to be?"

"Hold on there, Livvy." Karri used her mother voice. "You, my dear are not going anywhere."

"Oh no, Karri, you're right. It's not just me. All four of us are going!"

Perrie had to say something. She tried, but nothing intelligible came out.

"I don't think this is a good idea, Oliviia." Lightning was never before as sure in his life of being unsure.

"Lightning, I'm out of ideas. I need someone or something to tell me where I need to be and that axey thing may be the only thing that knows...where I need...where we need to be."

Lightning held it in between himself and Oliviia. "I am going to be in so much trouble. Come on, Oliviia, get closer. We don't want to leave you behind. Ready? Here we go. Ax-pike, where do we need to be?"

Lightning was growing very comfortable traveling this way. Once again, with no fanfare, the small group of four disappeared. No one witnessed them leaving.

***

"Cirrus, once we drown these two, what then?"

"We will return to Burg Seven, unless told otherwise."

Aromatic wisps of Sweet Gulley floated in the air. The Tigers' feet were cooled by the moist soil surrounding the gulley.

"Can we take a break, Cirrus? That delicious mud would do my insides good right about now."

"Why not? Follow me."

Cirrus gracefully leaped off the gulley's edge landing softly beside a large puddle of mud. She stuck the Stork beak first into the thick goo. Duister grinned and did the same with his Stork. The wingers could do nothing. Instead, they timidly sat where stuck. The Tigers ate their fill of the sweet goo. Soon, with hunger pleasantly satisfied, they pulled the Storks free, taking a few muscular leaps up the steep bank and splashed into the river. The Storks had no warning. The Tigers frolicked in and out of the water, dragging the helpless storks along.

Interestingly enough, the Storks did not drown. Cirrus dropped hers at the river's edge. Duister laid his down, as well, after giving it an extra dip or two. The birds rested serenely as Cirrus returned to the water. Duister stayed behind to make sure the dunking took effect.

"Tiger, what just took place?"

Duister laughed. "I thought you might be asking that question."

He pounced over both them and landed at Cirrus' side, shoulder deep in the crystal clear water of the Hopen River, known far and wide for its mysterious side effects.

***

Other than the one bolt of light that reclaimed Eekay, the yellow ball had stayed relatively calm with all of the preparations against it going on in Nuorg. Maybe it had been saving its energy. That was about to change.

Donkhorse felt it first, a tiny vibration down the ridge of his back, a tingling sensation very similar to goose bumps on a two-legger which made the very sensitive hairs along his withers stand on end. Stewig felt the same sensation vibrating in his ears. In a desperate attempt to avert the dangerous onslaught, Donkhorse calmly allowed Jahnise to pass him.

"What slows you down, friend?"

"King, we have a problem."

Soon, Stewig was on the other side of Jahnise. "Did you feel it to, Donkhorse?"

"Yes, Stewig, I did. We are out in the open. There is not a shred of protection until we make the gate. You can see how hard it will be to get there in time."

"We will never make that with all of these two-leggers. Our main concern is the king. He must be protected at all costs."

"I understand."

"Friends, I am right here. You speak as if I was miles away. What is the problem?"

Rawg could not understand the four-leggers, but he did read Jahnise's body language. "Your highness, is there a problem?"

"There seems to be one, if I am hearing my friends correctly."

"What can we do to help?"

"I am not sure. Donkhorse, please explain your concern."

"Jahnise, bad things are about to happen and we have no way of protecting ourselves."

"King," Stewig warned. "You must find cover. Do you see anywhere you can hide yourself?"

"From what?"

"The yellow ball in the sky is getting angry."

"Should that concern us?"

"Yes. It should concern us very much. Normally we are not such easy targets."

"You mean, even in Nuorg, we are not protected from evils?"
"King, good is never fully protected from evil. No matter where it goes, evil wants to destroy it. That ball is a collection of years and years of evil. It has grown wise. It does not waste its energy. We are vulnerable in the open like this."

"Shall we run?"

"No, no, no, no. Absolutely not." Donkhorse shook his head so hard his ears couldn't stop. "Jahnise, we will not all make it to the gate. There is no reason to think we will. I know we have twelve extra leggers here, but you…you cannot be injured."

"Is this my fault for bringing you out here?"

"King, we brought you. Remember?"

"No, Stewig, we brought each other."

"Your highness, what is going on here? My men are getting nervous?"

"Mister Rawg, slowly gather your men close to me. Donkhorse, how much of the Nuorg water does it take to…well…to do its deed?"

"Just a few drops can do it, Jahnise."

"Very well then. Will this coming event take you, Donkhorse?"

"More than likely…yes. If I save your life, my work here will be done. I will pass over."

"And you, Stewig?"

"It will only be two for me, King. I will be fine."

Tears began to well up in Jahnise's eyes as he looked at Donkhorse. "You are giving your life for me, friend."

"If it comes to that."

"We will not go easily then, Donkhorse."

A thunderous explosion burst some of the invaders' eardrums. Before they could regroup, another explosion blew some to the ground. All around Jahnise, panic ensued. Stewig forced his way between those who remained standing and the row of strikes heading directly for them. The yellow ball was learning. It continuously refined its aim with blast after blast.

"King, climb on Donkhorse's back. He will take you to the gate. I will protect these that I can. Tell our invader friends to huddle behind me and leave the leader any water you have. You won't need it. As soon as the attack stops, tell him to pour whatever water is left on my head."

Jahnise handed his water sack to Rawg along with explicit instructions, just as Stewig instructed. He grabbed for Donkhorse's mane. He pulled himself onto the Mule's back as he galloped away. One last bolt hit too close to Stewig. The Rhinoceros' tough hide did little to lessen the impact. It did, however, save the lives of Rawg and four of his men. The lives of the rest were taken, but not stolen. Their bodies lay where they fell.

Donkhorse ran for all he was worth. As he dodged shot after shot, Jahnise clung to his flowing, black mane with one hand and swung his stick above his head with the other, deflecting any shot that came too close.

The gate was lowered as Hugoth saw the strikes coming from the sky. "Hurry!" He exclaimed.

At the bottom of the ramp, Donkhorse was hit squarely in the side. As he passed over, he kept running. Jahnise cried huge tears as the brave Mule's body became translucent beneath him. The gate never fully opened, but Donkhorse delivered Jahnise safely inside. As his body lost more color, he ran through the solid gate, willing Jahnise to come with him. The yellow ball ceased its attack.

The gate was soon lowered fully, awaiting Stewig and Rawg's men.

Donkhorse stood transparent before all eyes as Jahnise dismounted his transparent steed. With a low bow to one knee, Donkhorse passed over. Jahnise was left wondering if his tears would ever stop.

Linnaeus softly lit on Jahnise's wide shoulder. Hugoth placed an extremely large paw on his back while the two-legger from the world above bent over in sadness.

Around Jahnise, the onlookers, tearless, returned to their tasks. This was just one attack. Many more were expected.

Through his tears, Jahnise struggled with what happened. He looked into Hugoth's caring eyes. "Hugoth, you lose a friend such as this one, yet you shed no tears? How is that? What is this place?"

"King, this is a temporary home while we are crossing over."

"You must explain this to me one day, no?"

"I will, Jahnise. Go rest now. I will come for you soon enough."

Bongi was late to the gate, but after overhearing Hugoth, led Jahnise to the nearest dwelling to rest. Whatever was coming was about to start.

"Linnaeus! What can you tell me of your day?" Hugoth asked.

"Donkhorse makes three today, Hugoth."

"Three?"

"Donkhorse, Rakki and Mystic."

"I had not heard that until now. Those more fortunate than you and I, Linnaeus. One day our time to pass over will arrive."

"Was it not magnificent to see, Hugoth?"

"I never before saw that old Mule in a more handsome fashion. You know he was quite the looker in his day, or so his mother used to say."

They walked to the end of the gate.

"Linnaeus, what do we have coming our way, riding on our Rhinoceros friend?"

"That, Hugoth along with the Storks, may be the largest collection of information Nuorg has ever hoped for."

"I hope so, Linnaeus. I hope so."

At the bottom of the ramp, Stewig let the two-leggers slide from his back. He then bounded up the ramp like a Rhinoceros 200 years younger.

***

Cirrus saw the yellow ball's fury. She and Duister stayed out-of-sight as they meandered their way back to Burg Seven with the storks clinging to their backs as if their lives depended on it. Once the attack was over, they ran full speed for the gate.

***

Lightning had no idea where they were. Oliviia still felt weak and slightly nauseous. Perrie adjusted her eyes to the dim light. Karri wondered why she had agreed to come along in the first place.

"Lightning," Perry mused. "I can't believe where we are."

"Is that good or bad?"

"Oh, it's good. It's very good."

Oliviia stumbled around on weak knees. "I think I'm going to be sick."

Karri shook her head. "Get that out of your mind, Livvy!"

Lightning suddenly realized where they were. "Which way, Perrie?"

"I say we get to the library level. If they are still here, that is where they will be."

Lightning twirled his large body around. “Livvy, Karri, follow us please. Wait, Livvy climb on my back. We must hurry.”

“I don’t know if I can.”

“Oliviia, climb on my back now!” Lightning could be forceful if needed.

Oliviia got on to his back and held on as tight as she could under the circumstances.

“Lead on, Perrie.”

She took off down the corridor, made a sharp turn and headed for the library level. Lightning was only slightly behind her. Perrie flitted from room to room until she heard two familiar voices tossing ideas back and forth.

She darted into the room behind the voices. Lightning came barreling in soon after with Oliviia on his back and Karri at this ear.

Their entrance to the room was not loud, but it was far from stealthy. The voices became quiet, the eyes opened wide.

“Lightning?”

“Hemoth?”

“Perrie?”

“Frederick? Where is Sig? I have so much to tell him!”

“Rakki?”

“Hemoth?”

“Oliviia?”

“Grandfather?”

***

Madaliene stepped through the door into pitch darkness. She closed her eyes and took a few deep breaths. She spoke to herself. “You can do this. Remember the nights in the mountain? You know, the ones when you were dodging Gamma and Gann. When you found the candles you had hidden along the way?”

She slid sideways across the floor until she felt a solid wall. Bending to the floor, she found one of those candles. Underneath it she had hidden a flint. When the candle’s glow grew bright enough, she followed it to along the corridors she had memorized as a little girl. She walked for a long time before she found the exact passage she was looking for. Ahead to the right, there it was.

She held the candle closer to her feet. There it is. A wooden box loaded with the secret books Sig had told her about. He always said the box should be open when she finds it. If it is closed, the timing was not right. The box was open. She followed a trail of flour spilled out while some contents were carried away from the box. She bumped her foot against something on the floor. Again, she moved her candle to where it was needed most. As her eyes identified what she was seeing, her breath failed her. "Push on, Madaliene. It's only temporary. No matter how bad it may look, Sig said it was only temporary. The bearer must give way to the wielder. It is easier completed if one party is not breathing. What did that mean?"

She held the light steady as she examined each obstacle. She was shaking. The sight was not as easy to behold as Sig described it would be. The girl, check. The boy, check. The second girl. Red Hair. Flawless complexion. Beauty in abundance.

"Hello, Evaliene. You are prettier than I ever imagined. You look so much like Mother. Where did you hide it?" Madaliene remembered the holster she wore on her lower leg. "Of course." She pulled Evaliene's heavy riding skirt away from her boots. What she saw made her light-headed. "That is what all of this is about? That?" She slid the heirloom out of the holster and placed the hem of the riding skirt back in place. She lightly stepped past the lone man to the Horses. She admired each one of them. They were perfect creatures in every way.

Madaliene stepped back to the box to retrieve a pre-written note. She rolled it up and placed it in Emiliia's hand. She kissed Evaliene on her forehead. "I will see you soon, sister. Stay here, learn this place. You will need to know it well in the coming days."

She hurriedly retraced her steps back the way she came. The closer she got to the door, the faster she ran. Her heart was pounding. She nervously stabbed at the latch with her free hand. "Come on, open like the last time."

The latch heard her. It opened effortlessly. Madaliene stepped back into the small room. The look on each of the faces was of disbelief.

One of them asked the question they all wanted to ask. "Where did you go?"

Princess Madaliene smiled a lovely smile on her beautiful face and threw her head back, her golden mane of curls glowing in the darkened room. She held up one empty hand.

The faces in the room faded.
"Oh, I'm sorry, it's in this hand!"
She excitedly held up the staff of O'shay with her left hand.
"Is this it?"

The End

About the Author

Chris McCollum lives with his wife of 25 years, Jeanne Coffman McCollum, and their 2 children, Christopher and Madilynn, in Franklin, Tennessee. A longtime fan of J.R.R. Tolkien, C.S. Lewis, Clive Cussler, McCartney/Lennon and many more varied wordsmiths, he has spent the better part of his life crafting words into some form or another, whether it be short stories, bedtime stories, anecdotes, poems or songs. Fortunately for him, his parents allowed lots of room for creativity in his early years. Originally from West Tennessee, he has made his home in Franklin, Tennessee for the last 32 years.

Please join our fanpage "The Land of Nuorg" on Facebook or log on to our perpetually developing website: landofnuorg.com

CPSIA information can be obtained at www.ICGtesting.com
Printed in the USA
LVOW06*1624041215

464652LV00003B/10/P

9 781621 416852